FIRST SNOW, LAST LIGHT

WAYNE JOHNSTON

FIRST SNOW, LAST LIGHT

ALFRED A. KNOPF CANADA

PUBLISHED BY ALFRED A. KNOPF CANADA

Copyright © 2017 1310945 Ontario Inc.

www.penguinrandomhouse.ca

Alfred A. Knopf Canada and colophon are registered trademarks.

Library and Archives Canada Cataloguing in Publication

Johnston, Wayne
First snow, last light / Wayne Johnston.

Issued in print and electronic formats.

ISBN 978-0-7352-7256-9
eBook ISBN 978-0-7352-7258-3

I. Title.

PS8569.O3918F57 2017   C813'.54   C2016-908248-2

Book design by Terri Nimmo

Cover image © Karina Vegas / Arcangel Images

Printed and bound in the United States of America

2 4 6 8 9 7 5 3 1

Penguin
Random House
KNOPF CANADA

For my brother, who always had my back, Craig Johnston,
April 28, 1955–August 1, 2016

FIRST SNOW, LAST LIGHT

You walk home from school as you have every afternoon for years, along the same streets whose every detail you have memorized without trying to, whose every house and yard and tree you know by heart—the broken paling on the fence two houses up from yours, the rain-and-wind-bent tree that last bloomed years ago, the pattern of the line of lamps on the far side of the street, and the course of the brook that dries up in July.

It's fall, late November, nearly dark, and the lights in some of the houses have come on and fireplaces have been lit whose smoke sweetens the air. There is barely enough of a breeze to stir the leaves. You scuff through them, as you know you soon will through the first snow of the year, which, all the signs tell you, will come tonight. You have no words for what you feel in these last dregs of November. It's what you always feel on the verge of winter.

You near your house, where you expect to see what you always see—your mother at the front room window, arms crossed anxiously in front of her, hands gripping her elbows. She always looks as if she wishes you wouldn't protest if she met you somewhere on the route she knows you take each day, if you let her walk you home the way she used to instead of making her wait for you to join her in the house in which she spends the day alone.

But on this November afternoon, there is no one at the window, and no lights on in the house, not even the glow of one from deep within that would tell you that she might be in the kitchen, so preoccupied with making dinner that she has lost track of the time and somehow forgotten what you know she never would forget: the ritual arrival home of her only child.

What can explain her having done something she would never do? You look at the houses on either side of yours, which as usual are brightly lit, but no one is waiting to explain to you why yours is dark or where your mother is. She would never leave you in their hands, or leave you to ask them if she'd left a message for you.

You walk up the steps and try the latch. Locked. You rattle it loudly with your thumb. You knock on the window as you look into the vestibule, where everything is orderly as always—shoes and boots in rows beside their fellows, coats in the closet, three umbrellas in the box beneath the coat tree. You hammer on the door with both fists, but no one comes and no lights come on and there are no sounds from inside.

You go down the steps and turn into the sloping alleyway that leads to the garage whose door is closed and padlocked. There is no reason to think that the Brougham might be inside as your father is not due home for hours, but you look anyway.

You go up the back steps and find the back door locked too. This is how the house is always left when no one's home. No lights, all doors locked. You tell yourself your father will be home at six, and he'd have made arrangements for you if something had come up. She'd have made them with him. He'd have been waiting for you, for whatever inconceivable reason that she couldn't. She'd have left a note pinned to the door for you, for him, for someone. Or he'd have left one for you if, for some just as inconceivable a reason, no better idea had occurred to him.

You run back up the alleyway, grabbing a shovel that leans against the house. Using the handle, you break the window in the door, reach inside and turn the bolt.

You shout. There isn't a sound from inside. You force the storm door open with your shoulder, half convinced that Jackman, the German shepherd from next door, will soon appear. You hope he'd recognize your voice and scent and not mistake you for an intruder. All the lights are off, and the drapes, but for those in the front room, are closed, so you can see only partway down the hall.

In case of power outages, your father keeps a lantern and a flashlight on the wall, just inside the door. You grope about for the flashlight, find it and begin a search of the house, all the while shouting their names. You go from room to room, lighting lamps until the whole house is more brightly lit than you have ever seen it.

You see no sign that Edgar came home, no overshoes, or overcoat. There is no smell of food. You look out at the backyard through the kitchen window.

You go downstairs to the basement, which is empty, then upstairs to their bedroom, where the bed is made, your mother's dressing gown at the foot of it and her slippers on the floor.

It has always been a quiet house, eerily hushed except for the snapping of the logs in the fireplace and the clanging of the radiators, but now it feels like one that has been unoccupied for years, one whose residents, in the middle of an ordinary day, have left it forever, taking nothing with them.

On your way out, you see their hats in the vestibule.

You go outside and stand on the steps, surveying the yard, the fence and the trees across the road.

You shout, expecting no reply. The shout is more of an assertion to the house that it is still theirs, still yours, and that all three of you will soon be back.

Your father would have known the storm was coming. *You* know. You read the signs as he taught you to. You know it will come on slowly, but it will be a bad one. It hasn't announced itself as abruptly as others in the past, but the signs are unmistakable. The ground is cold, the rising wind northeast. The snow begins to fall and soon it snakes along the street, proof that it's dry and, despite the month, won't change to rain.

Something has made your father think it was worth the risk of venturing onto roads that in snowstorms are little used and unmaintained.

It snows harder. You run to the street and retrace your steps to school. You're really running now, running the way your coach has taught you to, trying to hold your form no matter what. You can think of no one else to run to, no one else who will agree with you that something must be done.

I

1. NED

It is a strange road that leads from London to an island in the North Atlantic and from there to the Valley of the Sun.

My parents disappeared forty years ago in the last storm of the year, the first one of the winter, though it wasn't winter by the calendar. It was late November, too soon for snow to stay. It was gone within two days.

※

Megan met Edgar in London in 1919. She was a student at the University of London, he at Oxford, the Newfoundland Rhodes Scholar for 1919. He didn't come from Rhodes Scholar stock. He grew up in a part of St. John's called the Heights, where almost everyone was a Vatcher or a Finn and where, therefore, many were both. There was a time when, such were the number of criminals who went by the name of Vatcher, the police were known as the Vatcher Catchers.

My father was plucked from Vatcherhood by Father Duggan, a Jesuit priest who coached every sport at St. Bon's, where the sons of the city's elite went to school. Duggan had heard of the boy on the Heights who was breaking records in athletics and delinquency by the age of twelve, and arranged to have him transferred to St. Bon's. Edgar joined the Newfoundland Regiment, but the war ended before he was sent overseas. The Rhodes followed soon after.

Megan, whose maiden name was Chidley, lost her father in the war and her mother, brother and sister to the flu epidemic that followed it.

Edgar went back to Newfoundland. It seemed they would not meet again, but she discovered she was pregnant. She sent him a telegram and he wrote back, "Will you marry me?"

Megan made the journey to Boston and Halifax and then St. John's on the HMS *Bruce*, a destroyer refitted for civilians that became stalled in the ice a mile from the harbour. Crew members led my mother and eleven other passengers over the ice on foot.

A baggage-laden group of men and women from England, they made their way over the jagged ice debris in street shoes, wearing clothes so thin they could barely ward off the chill back home, the women in dresses and raincoats, the men just as ill-prepared. The women's hats and the men's bowlers blew off and were carried away by the ceaseless gale that swept across the ice, which rose and fell each time a wave or tidal swell passed beneath it.

It took them four hours to reach the Narrows, so intent were they on not slipping on the ice and dodging the parts where the water spouted up like lava.

Onlookers thronged both sides of the harbour, transfixed by the apparition of these death-defying, luggage-toting ice pedestrians from London who looked as though they were coming to the city with what they had salvaged from the sinking of the *Bruce*.

Cold, exhausted and stomach-sick, Megan made it to the nearest wharf, having done what most of the population of St. John's had never done and never would. At the feel of solid wood and solid, fixed, unshifting ground beneath her feet, she fainted with relief, collapsed into the arms of the nearest Newfoundlander.

Edgar was not among those waiting on the wharf.

Conceived in the Old World, born in the New World, I was carried in the sea of my mother's body across the ocean to Newfoundland, the last frozen mile to which she walked; perhaps because of the rigours of the voyage, she had a difficult pregnancy and could not have more children.

My father called my mother and the other passengers the Frozen Dozen. He hung a framed, glass-covered newspaper photograph of them on the wall above the fireplace in the front room. If you counted me, there were thirteen in the picture, a baker's dozen.

My father was the senior civil servant of Newfoundland, appointed by Prime Minister Sir Richard Squires. We lived in a nice, old, large and drafty house on Circular Road, in one of the better parts of town. We were not rich, because we were starting from scratch.

People who had never met my father expected a Rhodes Scholar to have a slight physique and bookish look, but he was tall and wide-shouldered, had the high forehead and square jaw of the gentleman athlete—he had boxed at Oxford—and was always impeccably dressed. It was said of him that he made everything he wore look good.

"You look distinguished," Megan told him often. "Exactly how a scholar-writer should look."

Writer. One of the family fictions was that my father was writing a book. When he was at Oxford, he'd told my mother that he planned to write one. She never let him forget it. He had a thick black journal in which, occasionally, after dinner, on weekends, he seemed to jot down notes, his pen furiously scratching on the paper.

"Your father's working on his book," my mother would all but whisper by way of telling me not to disturb him.

"What's the book about?"

"A writer never speaks about his book until it's finished."

But, when I was six, he put aside the fiction of his book.

"I've decided to *collect* books," he said.

"That's easier than writing one," my mother said. "Which you'll go back to doing, mark my words."

"What kind of books will you collect?" I asked.

"Rare books," Edgar said. "Books about Newfoundland."

"Rare books," Megan said, rolling her eyes. "The only thing rare is the people who have heard of them."

Edgar loved to maintain and drive his car, an Auburn Brougham, every working part of which he knew and tried without success to explain to me. He washed it every Sunday. He meticulously cleaned the criss-crossed spokes of the narrow tires. He polished the grille and the fenders until they gleamed, as he did the four front lights, the swooping navy-blue curves of the running boards, the sky-blue roof, the steel-grey body, the tentacle-like mirrors.

We went driving on Sunday afternoons, Edgar and Megan in the front, me in the roomy rear compartment, sightseeing, Edgar said, though his main motive was not to see the sights but to be one of them, to be seen behind the wheel of his gleaming car.

We picnicked on one of the grass-topped cliffs outside the city, defying the rough and narrow gravel roads that led to them. We sat, feigning unawareness of the wind that made it necessary to weight down everything with stones.

"It *is* beautiful, sometimes," Megan said one Sunday, shading her eyes with one hand as she gazed out across the sunlit, wind-planed sea. The back of her dress flapped behind her like a wind-wagged tail.

"It always is," Edgar said.

He drank a lot of wine but left his food untouched.

"If you don't eat, you'll have a headache in the morning," Megan said.

"It will be well worth it," Edgar said.

"Where does all the snow come from?" Megan said, though it hadn't snowed in months. "How can there be so much of it? Imagine if something even remotely useful simply fell in such abundance from the sky."

"We have such bad weather," Edgar said, "for the same reasons that our waters teem with cod."

Megan sniffed. "The worst things in Pandora's box wound up in Newfoundland. After you cook *anything* that's plentiful in Newfoundland, you have to open the windows to air out the house. And the *wind*."

"You're baiting me, Megan. Don't spoil the day for Neddie."

She turned to me. "We'll be living elsewhere soon, Neddie. Newfoundland is just a way station. We'll laugh about it when we move to London."

Edgar stood and looked out to sea.

"You talk as if Whitehall has been keeping a place open for me," he said, glancing at me. "The Edgar Vatcher Niche. As if the HMS *Sinecure* has been docked in St. John's for years, awaiting our departure."

"We should go while the going is good," Megan said.

"Christ," Edgar said, sighing.

"Which way is London?" Megan said.

Edgar pointed.

My mother refused to alleviate her homesickness by visiting London. "It would break my heart to leave it again," she said. "But it would also break my heart to lose you and Neddie. I feel so trapped." She burst into tears one night at dinner, covering her face with her hands. Edgar tried to console her, rubbing her back in slow circles even as he smiled at me as if nothing was amiss.

I came home from school one day to find her sitting on the sofa in the front room, tears running down her face unchecked, dripping from her chin as she stared into the fire. Her expression was so blank, so desolate, I knew she wasn't crying about London.

"Megan?" I said, and put my hand on her shoulder. "What's wrong?"

She turned, grabbed me and hugged me harder than she ever had, flattened me against her and, with her right hand, pressed my head against her shoulder as if she wished I'd never left her body, wished it could forever shield mine from the world.

For days afterward, though she was either crying or on the verge of tears, Edgar made no more of it than usual.

But I know why Megan cried, because I heard it too—a sound like sadness seeping in as though through a crack in the house.

Megan and Edgar began to go to separate beds for their Sunday naps. There was often about the house the kind of silence that early darkness can create, winter Sunday silence when it is easy to believe there are but two kinds of people in the world—those soon to wake who have slept the afternoon away and those like me, the waiting ones who have not slept and have not yet turned on the lights.

My mother called the Vatchers "Your Father's People," which was not a term of endearment. Edgar tried to disarm her by making fun of the Heights himself, calling it the Vatcher Hatchery and Mothering Heights because his brothers and sisters and cousins had so many children that a tally of the Vatchers would not have fallen far short of a census.

At his invitation, My Father's People crammed our house on Circular Road once a year, on Boxing Day. They arrived en masse and left that way, though they stayed late into the night, walking back to the Heights like some roving mob.

My father's parents weren't part of these gatherings, my grand-father being too frail to leave the house or be left at home alone.

Most of My Father's People were fishermen. They wore their Sunday best, the men as uniformly dressed as members of some order of the clergy in black jackets, black slacks, open-necked white shirts with white undershirts, black shoes. Their hair, thick with pomade, was slicked back from their sun-and-wind-burnt foreheads. The women wore the same floral-patterned, long-sleeved dresses they'd worn to church for years, faded, frequently mended, ill-fitting.

I first met my father's brother Cyril on Boxing Day when I was seven. He and his family had—for what reason no one seemed to know—skipped the gatherings until then. Cyril was five years younger than my father, the last of seven sons, of whom Edgar was the fifth.

He and his family lived well above the cluster of cliff-clinging houses on the Heights, on the very edge of what little woods there were. Cyril's Eyrie, Edgar called it. My mother said it was a shack. We never went there.

My father took me by the hand and led me through a sea of Vatchers, grown-ups and children, to meet Cyril, who was sitting alone in the middle of the sofa in the front room, his glass of Scotch cradled in both hands in his lap. Cyril was tall and big-boned but unimposing because he was so thin and slump-shouldered. He had the thick black hair of the Vatcher men, though it was tinged with grey and faintly yellowed from cigarette smoke.

"This is Ned, Cyril," Edgar said.

"Hello, Uncle Cyril," I said.

"*Uncle* Cyril," he said. "Formal little lad, isn't he?" He winked at me.

"He was taught to be polite," Edgar said.

"Well, weren't we all," Cyril said. He sipped from his drink, smacking his lips together as if he had never sampled Scotch before. "Your father has the Vatchers over on Boxing Day to remind them he's a boxer. He could beat me up if he wanted to. He used to beat me up when we were small, but things have changed. They've changed a lot, haven't they, Edgar? For some of us, I mean."

"I suppose so," Edgar said, putting a reassuring hand on my shoulder. "But some things never change."

Cyril smiled. "That's true." He winked at me again. "See how smart your dad is. He learned that at Boxford." Cyril took one hand off his glass and poked me in the belly with his index finger. "See?" he said. "I'm smart too. Ned, what do you think of that criminal your father works for?"

"He's not a criminal, he's your Prime Minister," Edgar said.

"I don't see why he can't be both," Cyril said, winking yet again at me. "Besides, I didn't vote for him."

"You've never voted in your life," Edgar said.

"I'll vote as soon as someone worth voting for comes along. I might vote for Ned when he grows up. Did you know, Ned, that I'm the Seventh Son of a Seventh Son?"

I shook my head.

"I am. I say prayers for people who ask me to."

"Who *pay* you to," Edgar said.

"They don't pay much. Sometimes they get what they want."

"Where's Kay?" Edgar said. "I want Ned to meet her."

"It's high time they met, isn't it? The little lad we've heard so much about. I think she's in the kitchen. Hiding in the pantry, maybe. She's a bit on the shy side, Ned, as anyone will tell you."

My father led me out to the kitchen. "There she is," he said, nodding in the direction of a woman sitting by the fridge, dressed in a black peacoat buttoned to her neck, the collar turned up, as if she had dropped in for but a minute. She was slender, her straight red hair hanging down her back. She was thinner than the other women, her back and neck as straight as a ballet dancer's. She didn't have a drink, her hands in the pockets of her coat.

She looked haggard and bored, her expression blank.

Her face brightened when Edgar introduced us. She beckoned me close and put her hands on my shoulders as if to steady me so she could better size me up. "Hi, Neddie," she said. "How are you?"

I said, "Fine," and she seemed to find this laconic response hilarious. She laughed and lightly brushed my hair back from my forehead.

"He's the spitting image of you, Edgar."

"People say he looks like Megan."

Kay stared at me and shrugged. "Either way, he's a fine-looking boy," she said, her voice suddenly husky. "A very lucky boy. Not all children are so fortunate."

"Your children will do you proud, Kay," Edgar said.

She smiled at me. "Christmas always wears me down, Ned," she said.

"Why?" I asked.

She laughed as she had before and looked up at Edgar as if to see if he shared her amusement. "Why *does* Christmas wear me down, Edgar? What's your opinion?"

"It's all the visiting, I suppose. It takes its toll."

"That must be it. You feel you have to visit everyone who visits you. I'm sure the three of you will soon be dropping by to see us."

"You must be warm in that coat," Edgar said. "Let me hang it up for you."

"I'm fine," Kay said. "We're not staying long."

"So then," Edgar said.

"Yes, so then," Kay said. "Off you go, Megan's men." Her face went blank again and she turned away from us.

2.

My grandmother's house was called the Flag House because it was painted the colours of the Newfoundland Catholic flag, pink, white and green. It was located on the hill of granite that stood between the south side of the city and the sea, which is why the dense collection of houses halfway up the steep slope was called the Heights.

My grandmother was known as Nan Finn even though her husband was Reg Vatcher—not even marriage seemed like a sufficient reason to alter her name. Her hair was white, her eyebrows thick and black.

We visited the Flag House in mid-January. I was surprised that Cyril was there—having not met me until recently, here he was again, sitting in Nan's kitchen when, as was the custom of visitors on the Heights, we arrived unannounced. He occupied a wooden chair at the end of the daybed on which my grandfather, Reg, lay, awake, blinking, immobile.

"Do you want to be a priest like my boy Ambrose?" Cyril said.

I shook my head.

"Still going on about London, is she?" Nan said to Edgar, though Megan was standing beside him. She talked about people right in front of them as if she thought that, unless she addressed them directly, they couldn't hear her. "I can tell by those eyes of hers. It's a wonder dinner gets cooked what with her being so busy bawling and wishing she was there instead of here."

"You shouldn't say such things in front of Neddie, Nan," my mother said, closing her eyes as if she had to concentrate to formulate a reply.

"What do people do in London?" Nan said. "Sit around and talk to each other with their eyes closed. I better keep busy or I'll get bored and long for London."

She was the sole caretaker of her husband, Reg, who had suffered a stroke four years earlier that everyone but Nan believed had left him unable to speak or hear.

Reg had taught all his boys how to fish and everything he knew about the sea, which, on June 11, 1923, turned out not to be enough. The rogue wave came out of nowhere, out of a calm sea under a clear blue sky. Reg and his son Phonse were turned back onto the wave, which knocked Reg flat on his stomach. He said he hit his head on the floor of the boat. He might have been knocked out, he wasn't sure. He didn't know how long it took him to regain his feet. By that time, the water was calm again, but there was no sign of Phonse, no sign even of his bright red watch cap, which was meant to mark the spot where you went under. Phonse couldn't swim. Reg could, but not well, and the water was so cold he'd have been delirious within a minute, so he didn't dive in, didn't *give* in to the siren sight of a man already lost.

Nan Finn dismissed this story as a badly crafted lie.

Reg did not go on the water after his son died. He sold his boat. He took to doing what he was doing now, lying on the daybed in the kitchen, hands behind his head, his bare feet crossed.

I stared at him. He abruptly sat up on the daybed and stared back at me, expressionless. Nan put her mouth to Reg's ear. "He's never been good for anything since Phonse. Two went out and one came back. He may as well have died with Phonse for all the good he is to me. Won't work, can't work, what's the difference? All he does is lie here in the kitchen and wait for me to cook him something. Thank God the youngsters are raised and gone or they'd starve to death. He can't even say his half of the rosary. Two went out and one came back. What happened to my boy, Reg, my poor boy Phonse who was never found? He was your boy too, you know. He was your favourite. You never saw one without the other. All the more reason to take better care of him. Lost without a trace on a calm and sunny day in June, washed away by a rogue wave that missed you so completely that you came back as bone-dry as the boat. You said the sun must have dried you and the boat because you spent so much time looking for your son. A big stray wave that hit one boat but missed all the rest. No one on the other boats even saw your wave. What kind of wave is that, Reg? A magic one it must have been, a black miracle, a devil wave, hey Reg? What were you doing so far down the shore? Way down past Cape Bald? The priest came to the house and he tried to light a fire under Reg, for all the good it did. He said: 'Reg Vatcher, it is not for you to judge yourself. Leave that to God who knows the truth. If you did something wrong, don't leave it unconfessed. If you didn't, you must shape up and be the man that, by the grace of God, you used to be.' He might as well have given the stove a good talking-to. Reg sat through it all like a youngster with the sulks. So there it is. I'm short a husband and a son and no one but *him* knows why. He looks like all he ever does is think about that day."

"He's not on trial, Nan," Edgar said. "And he *can't* speak, because of his stroke. He can't even hear."

"Can't speak, can't hear, or so he lets on. He's got the doctor fooled. But he can read and write. Why don't you write down what really happened to Phonse, Reg? I'd like to know before I die, or before you do. Eight children I have left. Cyril is the Seventh Son of a Seventh Son, God help us. *Cyril.* That didn't do Phonse much good. They don't give out holy medals to the fifth daughter of a second son, which is what I am, just because five and two is seven. Too bad for me and all the souls I could have saved."

"Don't be sacrilegious, Nan," Cyril said.

"And *him*," Nan said, pointing at Cyril, "he keeps Reg company these days as if he thinks that makes up for Phonse. For years we hardly ever saw him and now he comes by every day to sit with Reg."

"I've turned over a new leaf, Nan," Cyril said. "No son should neglect his parents. I'll bet that, when he's older, young Ned here won't neglect his mom and dad, will you, Ned?"

I shook my head.

"Reg won't bite, Ned," Cyril said. "No need to be afraid of him."

"I'm not afraid."

"Go closer, then. Give him a kiss. He's your grandfather."

I ran to Reg, kissed his bristled cheek and ran back to my mother.

"There you go," Cyril said. "You have more nerve than your mother and father." He winked at my parents as if he had shared a joke about me with them.

"How are you doing, Dad?" Edgar said. Although he spoke to him, *at* him, Edgar kept his distance from Reg, never going close enough to touch him or be touched.

"You just said he can't hear," Nan said.

Reg faintly smiled, nodded his head and seemed to move his lips. Edgar and Megan looked at Reg, but Reg looked at no one but me. He stared at me as if he'd been told something about me that couldn't possibly be true.

As Nan kept ripping into him, Reg rose slowly and shuffled from the room, his thumbs hooked into the suspenders that held up his sagging trousers, his massive shoulders slumped beneath a white undershirt. "He's going to bed," Nan said. "Three-thirty in the afternoon and he's off to bed."

Cyril began to make it a habit to come by our house on Saturday afternoons. Just long enough since his last visit to make us hope that he had given up the practice, he stopped in unannounced, dressed in his best suit but without a tie, his white shirt open at the neck. By the time he arrived at Circular Road, he'd have visited several other Vatchers, an unlikely pedestrian in his gleaming black shoes and freshly ironed clothes.

Megan or I would often spot him as he was heading down the slope of the driveway to the house, smoothing back his hair, his skinny wrists extending from the sleeves of his jacket, his silver cufflinks showing. "Here comes Snack," Megan would shout, and Edgar would answer with a loud, groan-preceded "Jesus." Cyril perfunctorily offered an excuse for visiting which he knew fooled no one—he had found himself getting hungry just as our red brick gateposts came into sight.

"Why don't you let me send him away?" Megan said one Saturday.

"Oh, never mind, let him in," Edgar said.

I followed Megan, who went to the door and opened it before Cyril had a chance to ring the bell.

"Come in," Megan said, not bothering to stifle a sigh of resignation.

"How are you this lovely afternoon?" Cyril said as he came into the hall. "I'm in the middle of my walk and I was wondering if you could tide me over with a snack."

"I'll fix you a cold plate," Megan said, at which Cyril rubbed his hands together as if he had never before had the pleasure of tucking into one of her cold plates.

He tousled my hair. "There's Ned," he said. "There's Ambrose's right-hand man." He lowered his voice. "Ambrose a priest. Imagine that, hey? What about you, Ned? Megan says you're going to be a Londoner."

Edgar came up behind me and put his hands on my shoulders. "Cyril," Edgar said, and Cyril held out his hand as if it were years since they had last met. Edgar shook hands with his brother over my head.

"You know, the length of that driveway never ceases to surprise me," Cyril said. "I thought I'd starve to death before I reached the steps." He grinned at me and cocked his head as if the two of us had just shared a joke at Edgar's expense.

"Come into the kitchen, Cyril," Edgar said. "Maybe you'd like a drop to drink while Megan is making up your plate?"

"Well, I wouldn't say no to a drink, but only if you'll have one with me." Cyril grinned at me again. Edgar made no reply but turned, and Cyril and I followed him to the kitchen.

"Have a seat," Edgar said.

Cyril and I sat at the kitchen table, Cyril lightly tapping the surface with both hands as if in tribute to its sturdiness. Edgar opened one of the cupboard doors and took down from the top shelf a bottle of Royal Reserve rye whisky that was about a quarter full, and a pair of glass tumblers.

"It must be the secret stash," Cyril said, raising his eyebrows at me. "Even if it is only rye."

Cyril was sitting at the end of the table nearest the front door. Edgar, after pouring himself a small drink, put the bottle and glass in front of him and sat at the opposite end of the table. Megan made far more noise than was necessary to assemble Cyril's cold plate.

"Not going to join us, Neddie?" Cyril said, unscrewing the cap of the rye bottle. "Too early for you, I suppose. But me, I've been up since six with all the youngsters. I don't suppose one youngster makes much noise?"

I shook my head. Megan put his cold plate in front of him as he poured his drink: slices of ham, devilled eggs topped with paprika, lettuce, slices of tomato, potato salad, raisin tea buns.

"Ah, a feast fit for a king," Cyril said.

I knew that Cyril would not so much as pick up his fork and knife to make a token rearrangement of the food, let alone eat any of it. But neither would he, no matter how long he stayed, push the plate away.

"How are things at work?" Cyril said, after gulping from his glass.

"Work is the same," Edgar said. "The same as it will be on Monday morning and next Friday afternoon."

"It must be nice, though, being second to Sir Richard."

"Do you think all this just dropped into his lap?" Megan began, but Edgar stopped her with a wave of his hand. She folded her arms, leaned back against the kitchen counter and stared at the floor.

23

After a few seconds of silence he turned to me. "Ambrose will go to St. Bon's next year, thanks to your dad."

Megan gave Edgar an accusing look.

"You didn't tell her, Edgar? I guess I spilled the beans. It's a shame he can't afford to sponsor all my youngsters to St. Bon's." After the awkward silence that followed, Cyril addressed me again. "Edgar broke a lot of hearts when we were younger. He had a reputation as a lady-killer. All the girls were crazy for him. Your father was a star athlete, you know. Not just a boxer. A runner, and a jumper too. But mostly a boxer."

"I know," I said.

"Maybe, Ned, you'll break his records someday."

"I'm already on the junior team."

"Are you now? Already?"

"The other boys are older, but I'm faster than them."

"Are you Father Duggan's pet like Edgar was?"

"He likes Duggan a lot," Edgar said.

"Well isn't that great. Wouldn't it be something if Edgar Vatcher's records were broken by his son? That's just the kind of thing that would happen to Edgar—the golden-boy kind of thing. The only one of the Vatcher boys to escape the Heights surpassed by none but his only son and heir."

"Drink up, Cyril," Edgar said. "Megan has to start getting dinner ready soon."

Cyril drained his glass and poured himself another large one, his forehead shimmering with sweat. We all knew that Edgar would not ask him to leave before the bottle was empty.

"So Megan," Cyril said, "what about you?"

"What *about* me?" Megan said.

"Knock it off, Cyril," Edgar said.

Cyril shrugged and bit his lower lip as if he was mystified as to why Edgar would speak to him like that. "I thought you might just be feeling left out of the conversation, Megan. What's new with you is all I meant to say."

"You were going to say what you always say," Megan said. "You were going to ask if I had any news on 'the London front.'"

"As God is my witness—"

"Just drop it," Edgar said.

"All right, all right," Cyril said. "I don't know what I'm dropping, but consider it dropped. To tell you the truth, I'd get out of here too, Megan, if I could." There was another long silence as Cyril drank deeply from his glass. "Ahh," he said, setting his glass down. "I think I would get lost in a house like this. I consider myself fortunate not to have Edgar Vatcher's burdensome wealth."

Megan strode past Cyril to the hallway and noisily climbed the stairs.

Cyril gave me a look of mock sheepishness and filled and emptied his glass again.

Megan waited until after he left to come downstairs. "Why, why, why do you let him in your house? He's not the Seventh Son of a Seventh Son because of anything *he's* done. He's not *your* brother because of anything he's done.

"Cyril is a charlatan. He gives people false hope in return for money. Yes, yes, I know. Reg asked you all to look out for Cyril. But no one does but you because the others can't afford it. In other words, Reg made *you* promise to look out for Cyril. Reg has been oblivious to all of you for years. So when exactly did he intervene on behalf of Cyril?"

"I don't remember exactly when. It doesn't matter. The others have nothing to spare Cyril, so his and his family's upkeep falls to me."

Megan said, "He might as well know," and turned to me. "Every time Cyril is leaving, your father slips some money in his jacket pocket. I don't know how much. And now, it seems, he's sponsoring Ambrose to St. Bon's."

"I don't do anything for Cyril's sake per se. I do it for his family."

"You don't really think he spends the money you give him on his family, do you?"

"Kay told me that he gives her some of it. That's better than nothing."

"When did she tell you that?"

"I don't know, Megan. A while ago."

"You don't know when Reg told you this or when Kay told you that."

"Who remembers such things exactly?"

"I would."

3.

"You're in grade four now, nine years old," Edgar said. "Old enough to join me this Saturday. I have to host a party for Sir Richard and some friends of his."

"A party like the one on Boxing Day?" I said, not trying to conceal my disappointment.

"No, not that kind of party. A shooting party. Sir Richard likes to show me off to rich men from St. John's and the mainland. Men that we do business with. Canadians, Americans."

"Why does he like to show you off?"

"I grew up with guns. Reg taught me a lot. I'm a good shot, a good hunter. I show them how to shoot. That sort of thing. You can come along if you keep out of the way. Other boys will be there too. You can watch with them. You might learn a thing or two that will help you when I teach you how to shoot. Don't tell your mother. We'll take our fishing rods so Megan will think we're going fishing. All the guns we'll need will be there waiting for us."

We drove out to the sea cliffs at Black Point on Dead Tree Road, which wound through acres of deadwood, white, leafless skeletons of trees propped up by moss grown so high around their trunks it looked as if the trees were slowly sinking into it.

It was an early morning in May, a light drizzle falling and shrouding the cliffs, but there was not much wind.

"I don't see a single bird," I said.

"They're on the cliffs nearest to us," Edgar said.

There were many cars in the clearing beside the road when we arrived. Sir Richard and the others were waiting for us. "Edgar!" Sir Richard called as we stepped out of the Brougham. "The man of the hour." Sir Richard, whom I'd met before, was tall, spare, almost gaunt. He slicked his brown hair straight back from his forehead and wore spectacles with small round lenses.

Edgar raised his hand in a kind of salute.

Most of the men who worked for my father were there; their participation was mandatory. He didn't acknowledge them in any way, nor they him.

"It's just a short walk from here," Sir Richard said to his guests. There were about twenty men and half a dozen boys, each of the boys standing beside a man I took to be his father. There wasn't a gun to be seen. "Lewis will be set up by now," Sir Richard said.

Sir Richard turned abruptly and began to make his way along the path and into the woods. The path was narrow, so we had to go single file. My father nudged me in front of him and kept his hand on my shoulder.

We reached another clearing, this one just a few hundred yards shy of the ocean cliffs, which were lined with juniper and tuckamore. At the edge of the clearing, behind a long, flat, folding table piled high with guns and boxes of ammunition, stood the man named Lewis. He was tall, heavily muscled, completely bald, and wore a pair of spectacles that were like Sir Richard's, only smaller still.

"Follow the other boys, Neddie," Edgar said. "Over there behind those ropes. Don't come any closer than the ropes." I took my place among the boys behind the ropes that I guessed Lewis had strung between two trees, all of us standing side by side as if facing a firing squad.

The roar of the birds echoed all about us, but I still couldn't see them. Their cries swelled and faded, swelled and faded as if a restless army of them were waiting for the order to take flight.

What might have been a reconnaissance squadron appeared from the overhead mist, a scattering of small black birds.

A shot rang out. Those of us behind the ropes jumped with fright. A bird fell like a stone from the sky. When it hit the ground, the sound of the shot was still echoing from cliff to cliff.

Edgar had shot the bird. Yet to lower his rifle, he seemed to be posing for a photograph.

The other boys looked as awestruck as I felt. No one said a word.

"Magnificent, Edgar," Sir Richard said. "I couldn't make a shot like that in a thousand years."

Sir Richard's two beagles raced to the bird, picked it up in their mouths and trotted in tandem back to Lewis, at whose feet they dropped it.

"Tell them how it's done, Edgar," Sir Richard said. "He makes it look so easy, doesn't he?" There was a faint murmuring of assent. All the men and boys watched and listened to my father, who aimed his gun at the empty sky.

"No light between the sights, no light between the sights," Edgar said. "Repeat that to yourself before you shoot. Breathe out after you say it, then breathe in again. The less you do, the more success you'll have. I recommend starting with a .22 like this one because it's a good gun for beginners, compact, precise. You can bring a moose down with it if you use it right. But the first living thing you shoot should be something smaller."

"That rules out Penny," one of the men said to a burst of guffaws.

"Something smaller like a bird in flight," Edgar continued, his voice betraying his exasperation. "Don't aim straight at it. Lead it by just a bit. Let it catch up with the bullet."

Lewis, after handing out .22-calibre guns to Sir Richard and the others, flushed out another scattering of birds by shooting a shotgun into the air several times. Edgar brought down three birds, but the other men missed.

"This gun is like a peashooter," complained the beefy, red-faced man who stood nearest Edgar. "And it's soaking wet. I can't get a grip on it."

"I'll wipe it dry for you, sir," Lewis shouted.

"Edgar Vatcher who was almost in the war," the red-faced man said.

Edgar looked at me, slightly shaking his head as if to warn me not to say a word.

"Now, Mr. Penny," Sir Richard said, laughing, "try to behave yourself."

A sound like that of a continuously crashing wave rose up from below the cliffs.

"Here they come," Lewis shouted.

"Don't use the shotguns," Edgar said. "There's no sport in shooting at so many birds with a shotgun." But many of the men ignored him. They went to Lewis's table and traded their .22s for shotguns with gleaming double barrels.

A mass of birds so thick they blotted out the sky passed over, all of them intent on some earth-excluding purpose, some destination to which all else was irrelevant.

The men discharged their shotguns as fast as Lewis could load them. They even shot at the birds with pistols. They unloaded and dropped to the ground each gun that was handed to them by Lewis as fast as they could fire. Dead birds began to rain down from above, thudding on the ground, the heads and shoulders of the men who had shot them, on my father, and on me and the other boys, who, staying behind the ropes, ducked and laughed and covered their heads with their hands.

It was as though the men were shooting the sky, shooting it to pieces. I put my hands over my ears to drown out the ceaseless thunder of the shotguns, which didn't seem to fire so much as explode.

The flock flew on, the deafening cries of the surviving birds at the same pitch and volume no matter how many fell, as if the whole flock were one great bird and all that the laughing and whooping shooters on the ground had done was relieve it of some feathers.

The only thing I heard above the shrill roar of the birds and the sound of gunshots was my father's voice.

"This is disgraceful," he yelled at Sir Richard.

The beagles ran about in a frenzy, squabbling, grabbing up birds in their mouths and bounding back to Lewis with them, then bounding back to retrieve more. The other boys became caught up in the spectacle, mimicking the shooters with their hands and arms, "firing" as the shooters fired randomly into the flock.

"Stop," my father shouted. "This is nothing but a pointless slaughter."

No one paid him the least attention. He broke the breech of his gun and gave it to Lewis. I watched him wade in among the shooters. "Keep your goddamn gun pointed at the ground or at the sky," he told one of them. "Otherwise, open the breech. You'll kill someone, waving that thing around like that."

My father grabbed a gun from another of the men, cracked the breech and handed the gun back to him. He moved on and put his hand on the shoulder of the man named Penny, the one with the bright red complexion.

Penny swivelled about as if he meant to shoot my father, who ducked under Penny's gun and stood face to face with him.

"Don't forget that your gun is a *gun*," my father said.

"I'm not an idiot."

"You didn't do anything wrong. I'm just making sure you don't, that's all."

"Well then, excuse *me*, Mr. Vatcher who was almost in the war."

"Penny is just having fun," Sir Richard said, hurrying toward them. "We all are."

"He shouldn't be shooting when he's drunk," my father said. "I'm just making sure he doesn't blow someone's head off, maybe his own."

Penny, red-faced from drink and embarrassment, threw his gun to the ground.

"That could have gone off," my father shouted at him.

Penny kicked the gun toward my father's feet. Edgar took a step forward and slapped Penny hard across the face.

All the shooting stopped, the men and boys gaping. Penny, whose cheek now bore the imprint of Edgar's fingers, looked astonished for a moment, then swung a roundhouse punch at my father, who dropped into a crouch and swivelled as he drove a fist up into Penny's ribs. Penny gasped as one of his lungs emptied of air like a burst balloon. He doubled over from the waist, his hands on his knees, mouth wide open as his chest and shoulders heaved.

The other boys looked as awestruck as I felt.

Sir Richard got between the two men before anyone else. He put one hand against Edgar's chest and, with the other, kept Penny from falling, his hand gripping his armpit.

"I was defending myself, Sir Richard," Edgar said.

"He should be arrested," Penny said. "Slapping me. Punching me."

"No one's going to be arrested," Sir Richard said. "No real harm's been done."

"I'm twice your age," Penny said to my father. "Afraid of a fair fight?"

"A fight between me and any one of you would not be fair," Edgar said.

"I demand an apology from your man, Sir Richard."

There were sounds of vigorous assent from those of the other men who didn't work for my father.

"You're right, Mr. Penny," Sir Richard said. "My man, Edgar, owes you an apology. Edgar?"

"Sir Richard," Edgar said, "this—this—*man*—"

"That's enough," Sir Richard said. "Just get it over with."

Edgar abruptly thrust out his hand. "I apologize," he said.

Penny ignored it, pointed at Sir Richard and said, "You're nothing but his bagman." He shook his fist at Edgar. "You're a performing monkey, an errand boy. Everyone knows that you dirty your hands so that he can keep his clean."

Edgar stared at the man for a long moment, then turned to Sir Richard. "You'll have my resignation in the morning."

"I won't accept it," Sir Richard said.

I followed my father back to the Brougham along the narrow path. I had to run to keep up with him. We got in the car and he slammed his door so hard I thought his window would break. He was livid, his mouth twisted in a snarl of disgust and self-loathing.

"I don't like those men," I said.

He hit the dashboard with the heel of his hand over and over again. "I didn't have to slap him *or* punch him. I shouldn't have."

"Will you get fired?" I asked when he got himself under control.

"No."

"Are you sure? Mr. Penny was pretty mad, and Sir Richard made you apologize."

"Sir Richard won't fire me."

"How do you know?"

"I know. In fact, he won't even mention it again."

"Those men were all afraid of you."

"Not all of them."

"Why did Penny call you those things?"

"He was upset. He had to get back at me somehow. He'll go back to Boston and he'll never forget what happened here today. He'll never mention it to another soul, but he'll never forget it. He'll brood about it and take it out on someone else."

"Are you really going to resign?"

Edgar stared blankly at the dashboard. "No," he said at last, "I'm not going to resign."

"Will you be arrested?"

"No. Almost in the war. Almost arrested. Almost a lot of things. Don't worry. Sir Richard will sort things out. He always does."

"Good."

"Your mother hears nothing about this, understand?" my father said, sounding as if he was talking to himself, as if he wished he was alone in the car. "It would only upset Megan. It's not what she's accustomed to."

It's a measure of how tightly sealed my mother's little world was that she never did get wind of what happened at Black Point.

A few weeks after the shooting party, Edgar had to let some of his staff go due to the ever-worsening economy. Citing a consequent need to work overtime, he began to spend less time at home. Often, when he did come home, it was only to take me away with him to teach me things he said he should have taught me long ago, the knowledge and skills that, under Reg's and his older brothers' tutelage, he had acquired as a boy.

"Maybe I wasn't meant to work behind a desk," he said to

Megan. "Maybe I wasn't meant to work indoors. I've taught Ned nothing of the place where he was born that you can't learn from a book. It's time he learned about the water and the woods."

"Are you regressing to Vatcherhood, Edgar? I crossed the ocean to marry a Rhodes Scholar, not the sort of primitive you were raised to be. Why this sudden determination to return to the sort of pastimes you outgrew as a child?"

"They're not pastimes for my brothers, they're honest occupations. No matter what it comes to, the world will always need men like my brothers, though it may not always need the sort of man that I've become."

"An educated, sophisticated man," Megan said. "A civilized and cultured one."

"The civil service," my father said, "is not as civilized as you think it is."

"Perhaps not here, but in London—"

"I have heard enough about London—"

"You've been away from civilization so long—"

They went on and on in this manner.

"Have you forgotten our dreams?" my mother said. "Our plans. Your ambitions."

"I haven't forgotten anything. But you wishing I was a great writer won't make me one. You wanting to be the wife of a great writer won't make you one. It was never my ambition to write a book—great or otherwise."

One weekend, we camped in a tent, Edgar having been able to mollify Megan, who objected that she'd be lonely in the house by herself all night, by promising that we'd only camp out this one time so that I could see what it was like.

He wanted to show me how to build a moss house, something he said Reg had taught him. "If you're ever caught in the woods in a snowstorm, a thing like this could save your life. It saved mine once."

"What happened?"

"Stupid mistake. It was sunny and warm when I left the house. By the time I noticed that the wind had changed, I was too deep in the woods to get back before the snowstorm started. So I made a moss house and stayed in it all night. I walked out in the morning when the storm.let up."

We searched out a patch of moss so deep the trees in it were dead. You could pull them out by what little roots they had with one hand. The moss came up as clean as sod and I was able to get a roll started. When it got so big I couldn't budge it, he took over. He carried the moss on his shoulder as you would a rolled-up rug, only it was thicker and heavier than any rug, and its underside was nothing but soil and hanging strands of string-like roots.

"It's better if it doesn't break," he said. "Every break might mean a leak, no matter how we plug it."

I watched as he wielded his knife and axe with an expert urgency that I admired but that also faintly scared me, for it made me think of what it would be like if weather *was* coming and our very lives depended on how fast he worked. I had never seen anyone so grimly intent on getting something done.

He broke into a sweat. It seemed he'd forgotten I was there. It was as if he was not so much remembering as reliving the time a moss house saved his life. We bared a square of the forest floor, made support poles of pulled-up trees and left the knots to hang the moss on.

When he was finished, we stood beside a shed-sized mound of moss. "There you are," he said. "Forty minutes." We went inside, leaving the door flap up so we could make each other out in the darkness. We sat down side by side.

"Were you scared that night when you were caught out in the storm?" I asked.

"A little bit." He lay on his back, his hands behind his head. I did the same. "Reg once told me that Oxford made me soft, taught me things I'd be better off not knowing." He was silent for a while. "You know, you can taint your whole life by doing one thing wrong, Neddie. It doesn't matter what you did before or what you do after, because everything is spoiled."

"What did you do?"

"I just meant it can happen to anyone."

"Everything is spoiled for Reg," I said.

"Yes it is. But it might not be his fault. It might be someone else's."

"Whose?"

"I don't know."

"It might be Phonse's fault," I said. "Maybe two went out and one came back because of Phonse. Maybe he did something wrong and Reg is keeping it a secret. I think the way Reg is is Phonse's fault."

"Maybe. Or maybe no one's to blame for anything."

We got home Sunday evening. My parents stayed up long after I went to bed and I sat on the top step of the stairs and listened to them.

"You need to get out and make friends," Edgar said. "You hardly know a soul whose last name isn't Vatcher."

"I lived through the war and the Spanish flu. I made my way over that Gobi of ice after crossing the Atlantic on the *Bruce*, which was not some posh passenger ship like the ones you came back and forth on. I'm not flat on my back like your master mariner father."

"Reg was caught off guard," Edgar said.

"I don't want to live in a place where being caught off guard can *kill* you. In London, to be caught off guard by the weather means to be caught in the rain without an umbrella. And then this moss house thing. What good is it to know how to build a moss house?"

"It's something you build when you have to and know how."

"If we lived in London, you would never have to, and Ned wouldn't, and knowing how wouldn't matter."

Edgar took me out in a skiff that he borrowed from one of his brothers. He said we wouldn't go far from shore—he just wanted me to get the feel of the water.

It was a calm day, but, as Edgar said, the sea is never calm. Even though there was not a ripple on the water, there was a ceaseless, rolling swell on which the skiff bobbed so much I soon felt giddy. I looked over the side. There was nothing between us and the jet-black water but an inch of wood.

Edgar said that cod were bottom-dwelling fish that had to be dragged up from the ocean floor where they fed on whatever fell in front of them. Since Megan would refuse to let us bring them into the house, we would give away whatever we caught.

We baited the hooks with capelin, squid, sounds, the more rotten and reeking the better. Even though there was not yet a single cod-fish on it, the handline that Edgar and I lowered into the water was so heavy that I felt the burn of it straight through my gloves. Hauling the line back up was much harder.

Six hundred feet, four hundred feet. At about a hundred feet I could just make out the white underbellies of the fish, each one a touch dimmer than the one above it, as if they were all climbing a tightrope to the surface to escape the deep. I got dizzy looking down into the water.

The cod were dead by the time Edgar yanked them over the edge of the boat, their flotation bladders having burst from the ascent. Edgar filleted a fish in a knife-wielding blur, turning it about this way and that. Gulls that hovered just feet above the boat plucked the guts straight from his hands.

He beat sculpins off the line with a cricket bat. There was no other way to get rid of them. They were the ugliest things I had ever seen, bearing many spikes and horns that Edgar said could give you a good gash, wart-encrusted blowfish with wing-like fins that exploded like bombs of fish flesh when Edgar whacked them with the bat.

We were about a mile from the Narrows. "This is not really being on the water," Edgar said. "You're not on the water as long as you can smell the land."

"I can't."

"You think you can't. You don't really know what the land smells like until the smell is gone."

After hours of light rain and a faint breeze from the south, the sun briefly broke through overhead. Edgar released the oars of the skiff and pointed at the sky. "When you see the sun for a second like that, it means the wind's about to change. We'll hear it howl tonight."

I looked up at the sky as if I could read it as well as he could. "Should we head back?"

"There's a big wind coming, but it's hours away. For now, the water might get choppy, but that's about it."

"Let's go back to shore," I said.

"Seasick?" he said.

"A little bit, maybe."

He smiled, nodded and deftly turned the boat about.

We were just outside the Narrows when the wind came up, though it wasn't the wind but the waves that I paid attention to, the foam-strewn waves that, despite the clear blue sky, were suddenly and impossibly immense, each one looming over us, blotting out all else until, as if it had pardoned us, it bore us up and we safely skidded down the other side. "Whoa," my father said, laughing.

A sunny day, I thought. Waves when there should *be* no waves. Wind when there should *be* no wind. There must have been sounds, but I was unaware of them. A torrent of sea spray washed over me, but I didn't feel it.

When we pulled near enough to the headlands of the Narrows that the wind died down, I realized that I was quivering from my scalp to the soles of my feet. Salt water stung my eyes.

After we moored the skiff and climbed the ladder to the wharf, he put his hands on his hips, looked down at me and laughed. I threw my arms around him and pressed my head against his stomach. "*What*?" he said. "What's wrong? We got a good soaking, that's all."

I nodded and looked at the water that was pooling round his feet. "We got a good soaking," I said.

"That's right—like a fisherman gets every day of his life."

❦

Again I listened to them from the top of the stairs.

"Did he fall out of the boat? Did you have to drag him back into the boat? Tell me the *truth*, Edgar."

"*No.*"

"I saw the look in his eyes. I could lose you and survive, Edgar. But I would not survive losing him. I'm not saying I don't love you. I do. But I know without a doubt that he loves me."

"It's not as if I risked his life."

"One risks one's life doing *anything* here. How many times did Reg get Phonse home safe and sound before two went out and one came back?"

Edgar didn't answer.

"Rogue waves. Rogue storms. I am *sick* of it. Ned's outdoorsman days are over."

"The water—"

"Who's in charge of the water, Edgar? Should he be fired for incompetence? Has it occurred to you to wonder how I feel knowing that the two of you are out there, somewhere? You can't bring me to visit Nan Finn and have me listen to her say 'two went out and one came back' a hundred times in the company of the ghost of Reg Vatcher and expect me to relax while you and Ned are out there somewhere. I sit by the fire in the front room all day long, thinking all sorts of dreadful things."

"That's because you have no life apart from us. You've made no effort to make friends, not even with your fellow Londoners-in-exile."

"They're depressing. So grimly reconciled to never going home. Always making fun of a place they know they'll never leave. It's easy for you. You have your job. You *could* still have your book. You have Neddie. I open that front door a hundred times because I think I hear you on the steps, but it's just the wind. From now on, you can play frontiersman on your own. I'll speak to Sir Richard if I have to."

Her voice dropped to a whisper that I couldn't make out. Minutes of silence followed until I heard her start to climb the stairs to their room and I hurried back to bed.

Edgar and I never went back to the water or the woods.

II

By Sheilagh Fielding   August 12, 1931

FIELD DAY

AT HIS INVITATION, I interviewed Sir Richard, who said he wanted the Newfoundland people to know that he could not afford to have a black cloud hanging over the skeletons in his closet while waiting for the other shoe to drop.

He was referring to the fact that, at the end of his first tenure as Prime Minister, he had been arrested for fraud and embezzlement of public funds, but later released for lack of evidence. He said he had re-won the trust of the public, hence his subsequent re-election. But he had to be allowed to do his job, the swelling number of naysayers and moralizing churls notwithstanding.

I asked him to sum up his plans for improving the country. "Misery now for minimal improvement somewhere down the road," he said. "Starvation now for the possibility of caloric intake some-where down the road. Work works up an appetite. Conserve energy through idleness. Misery has met its match in the miserly. The passage of a bill concerning the conservation of calories through idleness may save the day. Torpor is a pauper's friend. Stay put. Don't move, even if you think you can. You made your bed, now die in it. Shirkers of the world unite. You have nothing to lose but your gains."

Sir Richard has nothing less in mind than the curtailment of our gluttony. He has decreed that belts must be tightened notch after notch until they go twice around the waist. Told by me that they already do, he asserted that they must be tightened until they go thrice round. Thus will soon be ushered in the era of wasp-waistedness and minimal ingestion because of which the girth rate of Newfoundlanders will be reduced.

At this point in the interview, we were joined by Sir Richard's right-hand man, Edgar Vatcher. "Pleased to meet you, Mr. Vatcher," I said.

He said that his friends called him Vatch.

I told him I was sure they would stop if he asked them to. "People also call you Vatcher the Vulture, Vatcher the Butcher and Vatcher the Snatcher," I said.

"They do?"

"Sorry, I assumed you knew. These people are merely lovers of language, drunk on words. They mean no disrespect. I couldn't swear they know the difference between a plaudit and an audit."

I asked what was involved in being Sir Richard's right-hand man as opposed, for instance, to being his underhanded man. The three of us chuckled.

"Some leaders have personal physicians," he said. "I am Sir Richard's personal magician."

"How so?"

"I make Sir Richard's problems disappear. *Presto* and Sir Richard is out on bail. *Presto* and the charges against him are withdrawn. *Presto* and Sir Richard is Prime Minister again. *Presto* and Sir Richard is rich again."

"One might say that you are his sleight-of-hand man."

"One might."

"He kept you on as his man after he was voted out of power."

"He did. Generous to a fault."

"He paid you from his own pocket?"

"He paid me from what was in his pocket."

"A fine distinction."

"Precisely."

NED

I was ten when Edgar brought me to the *Telegram* to meet a woman named Sheilagh Fielding, known to almost everyone as Fielding.

"Why do you want *me* to meet her?" I said as we drove across town in the Brougham to the *Telegram* building.

"We worked together long ago when I was a cub reporter before I went off to Oxford," he said. "She's very nice. I'm going to invite her to dinner at our house."

"Why can't I just meet her then?"

"Because it wouldn't look right if I came to see her by myself. Those reporters would think I was upset with her because of what she writes about me."

"Megan thinks what she writes about you is funny."

"Megan thinks highly of anyone who doesn't think highly of me. That's a joke." He threw a cigarette butt out the window and was silent for a while. "Fielding usually works at home," he said at last, "but she's been using an office the past few days. No one from the *Telegram* has ever seen the room she lives in. She's a bit unusual, but I think you'll like her."

When we got there, I looked around the newsroom in which there hung at eye level a blue haze of smoke from cigarettes, cigars and pipes. "Edgar Vatcher in the flesh," all the faces seemed to say.

Fielding's office was at the end of a dim corridor at the back of the building.

"Why is she all the way back here?" I said.

"She likes quiet. She's a very private person. She lives in the Cochrane Street Hotel."

"But that's—"

"She's the only woman there who isn't a prostitute," Edgar said.

"Why does she live there?"

"I think it's all she can afford."

There was no name on the frosted window of her office. When Edgar rapped, the door fell slightly open. Cigarette smoke billowed out into the corridor. "Leave it on the floor outside. Herder will pay you for it." The voice was loud but also faintly hoarse.

"It's Edgar," Edgar said. "Edgar Vatcher."

"The only Edgar I know," the voice said.

Edgar pushed the door open and led me inside. The walls were bare, the room lit by a single banker's lamp on the desk, which was an old rolltop, scarred, nicked, battered and bearing the scorch marks of cigarettes. A cigarette dangled limply between her fingers. She stared at a piece of paper, elbows on either side of it, and didn't look up as we came in.

"What can I do for you, Edgar?" she said.

She wore a long pleated brown dress, had thick grey hair that hung in ropelike strands down her back almost to her waist.

"I've brought someone to meet you. My son, Ned."

She looked up from the piece of paper. "Your little boy," she said, the tone of her voice softening. She gave me a wide, welcoming, generous, face-transforming smile—it transformed hers *and* mine. She seemed even more pleased to meet me than Aunt Kay had. "I think he likes the look of me," she said, putting both her hands on her left leg, which was extended straight outward as if it bore a cast. I saw the high heel on the left black boot, around the bottom of which a metal strap was fastened.

She held her hand out to me. "Pleased to meet you, Ned," she said.

"Say hello to Miss Fielding," Edgar said.

I took her hand and she gave mine a tight squeeze. She patted her leg. "I'd get up if not for this. You can call me Sheilagh, Ned. But I have a feeling you won't call me anything." She smiled at me again.

I looked up at Edgar. His eyes were fixed on Fielding as if he hadn't heard a word.

"I'm expecting a delivery of spiked spruce beer," she said, scrutinizing him. "Spiked with moonshine made somewhere in the woods behind where you were born, Edgar. Probably by a relative of yours."

My father laughed at last.

"Why do you live at the Cochrane?" I blurted out.

"Ned," Edgar protested.

"That's all right," she said. "It's a perfectly reasonable question."

I noticed, as she considered me, the sunken look of her eyes, the dark shadows beneath them, the sharp angle of her chin, the thin shapes of her arms and legs beneath the threadbare garment of her dress.

"I'm not sure why," she said. "It's like a convent but noisier and with smaller rooms. The room beside mine is being—well, I've been told renovated, but I'm sure they mean repaired. That's why I'm in here. That's why I'm awake. I usually work through the night and sleep all day. I haven't slept in a while, but I'm hoping my delivery, if it ever turns up, will help with that. Where do you go to school, Ned?"

"St. Bon's," I said.

She nodded and smiled. "I went to Bishop Spencer." She made it sound as if she was not much older than me. "You're going to break some hearts when you grow up."

"Well, we don't want to keep you from your work, so we'll be going," Edgar said. "Ned just wanted to meet you. I've told him a lot about you."

"I'm sure you think you have," she said, and Edgar blushed.

"I'd also like to invite you to dinner," he said. "At our house, I mean. You can meet my wife, Megan."

"Dinner?"

"Yes."

"I don't often receive invitations of the kind that can be made in front of children."

"Will you come?"

She looked as puzzled as I felt. "All right," she said, glancing at me as if hoping for an explanation. He named a day and told her he would pick her up at the Cochrane in his car. She raised her eyebrows. "Let's meet up the street from the Cochrane unless you want all of St. John's to think Edgar Vatcher is patronizing a bawdy house. I don't suppose Sir Richard put you up to this?"

My father smiled and shook his head. "No, my wife did."

"Your wife put you up to inviting Sheilagh Fielding to dinner?"

"You'll understand when you come to dinner."

FIELDING

Edgar had put me on the spot, what with his boy being there. Edgar Vatcher, Sir Richard's man. He'd never have come to see me without his boy in tow to make it look shipshape. And he'd acted as if he didn't know I'd done a number on him in my column more than once.

I was far from the woman I was when we'd first met. He'd avoided looking at my leg.

When he worked there, years ago, I used to visit the *Telegram* office, though my appearances were still relatively rare. The least faint-of-heart in the newsroom would sacrifice himself by provoking me. "Well, look who it is—Fielding, her sodden self. To what do we owe the honour?"

"I've come to resign, Mr. Trask, which means that soon this paper will be a sinking ship and you will be among the rats deserting it."

"I make more money than you."

"No, Mr. Trask. You and your colleagues are *paid* more than me because you are all thought by Herder to be men."

Edgar always told the others to leave me alone and, aware of his prowess as a boxer, they listened. None of us saw any reason to think he'd be so successful. The other men thought that to think Sheilagh Fielding worthy of chivalry was the mark of a chump.

I never thanked him for speaking up on my behalf, in part because it was obvious that he had a crush on me, which I didn't want to encourage. He may even have been in love with me. I wasn't sure.

He went off to Oxford and wound up married to an Englishwoman he'd made pregnant. An open secret, as open a secret as her home-sickness and dislike of Newfoundland. I wondered if he, because of her unhappiness, was unhappy too, so unhappy that he was casting back into his past, reviewing all his might-have-beens.

But what a beautiful little boy Edgar had. Not that much younger than my lost son, David. A closed secret.

NED

That night, my father reported the success of our mission.

"She does have a way with words, doesn't she?" Megan said, as if she might be having second thoughts about the dinner invitation.

"A way with words?" Edgar said. "That's an understatement, don't you think?"

"Maybe she'll be seen coming to our house and Sir Richard will fire you and we'll have no choice but to go to London."

"He won't fire me," Edgar said, sounding as blandly certain of it as he had after the incident with Penny at Black Point. "He's not afraid of her, even though she writes a column a day and everything she writes is very good."

"I've agreed to have her to dinner. You don't need to sing her praises anymore." She looked at me. "The agreement, Neddie, is that, in exchange for your father not drowning you or otherwise doing away with you while trying to complete your education, I will be more social and have people in who will enrich his life, your life and mine in non-lethal ways."

FIELDING

"I'm a big fan of your writing," Edgar said after I got in his car.

"Most people are until I write about them."

"I don't mind you writing about me. They say you're no one in this town until Fielding writes about you."

"I wish people said that you're no one in this town *after* Fielding writes about you. But things stay the same no matter what I write."

"I've been reading your columns ever since we met at the *Telegram*. I think we're much alike. Having next to nothing is like having next to everything. It makes you beholden to no one, dependent on no one."

"There are far more conscripts than volunteers in the army of the poor. I'd love to see you tell a person who's poor and not taking it very well that, unbeknownst to them, they have all the advantages of being rich."

"You're a loner, is what I mean. You never have to be a part of anything."

"I once considered joining a choir, but all the singers looked as bored as if the song they were singing was the only one they knew."

He laughed. "You'd make a good debater."

"I've never been fond of debating. It's too polite, too civilized, founded on the premise that two people arguing while being moderated by a third is a fascinating form of entertainment. That's why it's so much easier to get a seat at a debate than it was to get one at the Roman Colosseum."

"What do you think of my car?" he said. "I love to drive."

"I don't mind being driven, but I don't know how to drive. It would be difficult if not impossible for me to learn with this leg of mine."

"Oh—yes, of course, I'm sorry."

"Don't be. I get along."

There was much grinding and clanking when the car went up a hill. When we were going downhill, I thought we would plummet to the bottom. That we didn't seemed to have something to do with him stamping on the floor. He ripped what he called the clutch around as if he were trying to dislodge it so he could throw it out the window.

Debating. He had flirted with me, but I, in my way, had reciprocated. I had so rarely been openly flattered by anyone, I couldn't resist.

"What should I call you?" he said.

"Fielding."

"I can't call a woman by her last name."

"Then go on calling me Miss Fielding."

"Miss Fielding it will be."

He was still something like in love with me. Trying to convince himself that he was in love with me?

NED

My mother had asked Edgar to invite a Mr. Prowse, a young man who worked for him and made no secret of his low opinion of Fielding. "We'll pit him against her," my mother said. Edgar had assured her that she'd make short work of him.

"Good evening, Mrs. Vatcher," Fielding said as my mother greeted her and my father at the front door. "It's nice to meet you." Before my mother could respond to Fielding, Prowse strode into the vestibule from the living room. He looked alarmed but less so than Fielding, who turned about and made to leave.

"Running away again?" Prowse said.

Fielding stopped, but stood with her back to all of us for a few moments as if trying to compose herself.

"I'll spare you the trouble," Prowse said. "You stay and I'll leave."

"You're not going anywhere, Prowse," Edgar said, laughing and patting him on the back. Prowse performed a quick about-face and, head down, strode back into the living room. "Miss Fielding?" my father said. "*Are* you running away? Have you two met before?"

Fielding turned around and looked at him. "I'll stay," she said. "And yes, we've met before."

"We're having roast chicken if that's all right with you," Megan said to Fielding.

"It's all right with me that *you're* having it," she said. "But I eat only once a day, just before I go to bed, which is roughly an hour before the sun comes up. It's a habit I got into"—she looked at me and then back at my mother—"when I acquired a certain other habit. But I'll sit with the four of you while you eat."

"You should have told me, Miss Fielding," Edgar said. "I could have come to get you later. There was no need to inconvenience yourself."

"I wanted to meet everyone," she said, looking at Megan and me. "I wanted to get here before Ned started his homework or went to bed."

We took our places at the table, Fielding at one end, Prowse at the other.

"You can't *write* about me," Prowse said. "You can't write about having dinner at the Vatchers'."

"I write for the public about things that happen publicly," Fielding said, her face flushed as if from drinking.

Prowse cut and chewed his food the same way he went at Fielding. He made eating look like a form of vigorous exercise which, though not enjoyable, was said to be good for you.

Fielding's eyes softened only when she looked at me, which she did a lot—and I couldn't help staring at her. She was like no woman I had ever seen. Her hair, parted down the middle but otherwise untended, bore a natural wave that continued far below her shoulders, flanking her face and her chest. She smoked cigarettes the way my father did, between her index and middle fingers. She lit one cigarette off the other, extracting the next one from some seemingly unlimited supply in the inner pocket of the jacket that she wore about her shoulders like a cape. When she caught me looking at her, she treated me to that ear-to-ear smile of hers. I grinned back, but when she wasn't looking I thought something like: what is this woman doing sitting at our table, smoking and drinking while the rest of us have dinner, smiling at me as if I am the only child she has ever met, provoking my father to laughter as no one else has ever done, in my presence at least, while my mother looks on and, in the bantering, takes the side of this woman whom my father, it must be plain to all, is flirting with? So. Fielding had that much of his heart, but he, I felt certain, had none of hers. He must have known it. I wondered if even Mr. Prowse saw what I did.

FIELDING

Prowse. Of all the people Edgar might have invited. I thought at first that my secrets had somehow become common knowledge, but then realized that, if they had, Prowse would not be there. It was also clear that he hadn't known *I'd* be there.

He *spoke* as if I wasn't.

"Mr. Vatcher," he said, "there aren't many you feel sorry for, so why start with her? I've seen her walking like there's a ball and chain around her ankle. Has it ever occurred to you that it might all be for show?"

"It's not."

"She plays it up for sympathy, is what I mean. She gets away with saying God knows what about God knows who because of her leg. And if Sir Richard ever finds out that I had dinner with her, he'll keep you on and I'll be fired."

"You won't be fired. You have my word."

"She humiliates you in public when she criticizes Sir Richard and his policies, don't you realize that? When she writes about him, she writes about you, and vice versa. She does nothing but tear things down. She has never made a single constructive suggestion."

Edgar smiled at me. "I don't mind what she writes about me. I'm not offended. It's not as if you dig up dirt on people, Miss

Fielding. You merely comment on what others dig up. Nothing that isn't common knowledge appears in your column. You're a critic who has an entertaining way with words. But nothing changes because of what you write. You said so yourself on the way over here."

"What results from telling the truth is not the point," I said, looking at Prowse. "The truth is the point."

"So we agree to disagree?"

"I agree that we disagree."

"She's disgraceful," Prowse said. "Everybody knows that. She drinks like a fish. She lives in a *whorehouse*."

"But *she's* not a whore," Ned said.

"*Ned*," Megan said as she glared at Prowse.

I smiled at Ned, who blushed and looked away.

"I'm sorry, Mrs. Vatcher," Prowse said. "But it's not as if she grew up disadvantaged. She's the daughter of a doctor."

"A lot of people read her column. Proper people. Educated people," Megan said. "As many of such people as there are in this place."

"I don't understand why *you're* taking her side. She's a woman. She should act like one, not like a man."

I thought about not engaging Prowse, but I couldn't resist. "When Mr. Prowse was at Bishop Feild, I was at Bishop Spencer," I said. "Two schools side by side. I wanted to be one of the boys and Prowse wanted to bed one of the girls. I can't begin to tell you what a difference a single letter can make."

"That is a disgusting lie," Prowse said.

"You *are* being rather forward, Miss Fielding, especially in front of Ned," Edgar said.

I looked at Megan, who abruptly looked away. "I'm sorry, Edgar," I said, "but it was you who played matchmaker with Mr. Prowse and me."

Edgar darted a glance at Megan, whose eyes were now downcast. "Perhaps we should speak of something else," Megan said.

"I've a mind to make a full report," Prowse said.

"And I have half a mind to make three-quarters of one," I said.

"I must leave, Edgar," Prowse said. "I *must*."

"Calm down, Prowse," Edgar said, putting a hand on his shoulder. "You're not going anywhere."

Megan folded her arms and gave me an appraising look. "Will you ever marry and have children, Miss Fielding?"

"I'm not able to have children."

"That's right," Prowse began, but Megan cut him off.

"Miss Fielding is our dinner guest, Mr. Prowse."

"About whom I have said nothing that isn't true. Isn't that right, *Miss* Fielding?"

"Your account is factual, but you don't have all the facts."

"What have I left out?"

"My private life."

"Which I've no doubt is worse than your public one."

"Mr. Prowse," Edgar said, "if you insist on further insulting Miss Fielding, you will have to make good on your threat to leave and I will not be pleased."

"Can you not see, Edgar, that it is she who has insulted you? It's not polite for a guest to turn up her nose at dinner. To sit with people who invited you to their house and not eat while they're eating is not how I was raised."

"Nor how I was raised," I said. "You're quite right, Mr. Prowse. Mrs. Vatcher, this is very rude of me. I should go—"

"No, don't go, please," Ned all but shouted. He sounded desperate, as if my visit was a respite from some dinnertime atmosphere that he had come to dread.

And so I stayed. To my relief, Prowse left not long after we retired to the living room, bidding everyone but me good night. He was clearly as much Edgar's puppet as Edgar was Sir Richard's.

Prowse. The father of my twins, though he didn't know it. No one did but for me, my father, my mother and her second husband. My children were in New York, living with my mother, whom they thought was *their* mother. I had given birth to them in my mother's house in New York, where, after I went back to St. John's, they were passed off to the world as hers.

"I'm going to take Ned up to bed," Megan said. "I'll come down and do the dishes later." She looked at me, smiled and said, "Good night, Miss Fielding."

"Good night, Mrs. Vatcher," I said. "I should be going." I planted my cane on the floor and began to get up.

"Please, don't leave on my account," Megan said. "We shouldn't have let Mr. Prowse loose on you. It was mean of us, but we didn't know you had . . . a history."

"It was merely a school-age crush. But such things sometimes linger. Good night, Ned."

"Good night," he said, and dashed upstairs, his mother following.

"Will you join me for a Scotch, Miss Fielding?" Edgar said.

"Thank you," I said, "but I always drink alone."

Before I could get out the door, Ned came downstairs in his pyjamas, accompanied by his mother. "He never sleeps," Edgar said. "He wouldn't if we strapped him into his bed."

Ned was almost eleven but they treated him as if he were five.

"You're sure you won't have a drink?"

"You're surprised that Sheilagh Fielding would decline a drink. I take no pride in saying this, Edgar, but I could drink you under the table without getting tipsy."

"Newfoundlanders drink too much," Megan said. She looked at Ned. "Last chance to be tucked in?" He shook his head and grinned at her. Megan, not smiling this time, said good night to me again and went upstairs.

"It's nice to have a conversation," Edgar said. "Megan and I used to go on for hours when we were students. I hope that you'll come see us again. I promise not to pair you with Prowse."

"I'd like to. I will, but only if Mrs. Vatcher and Ned want me to as well."

"I want you to," Ned said. He gave me an eager, entreating look.

"All right," I said, forgetting my pledge to come back only if he *and* Megan wanted me to.

Week after week, Edgar invited me to dinner. He picked me up in his car, Ned often in the back seat, over which he leaned to listen while we spoke.

I wore my best, least awful, dress, and my cape, sixteenth-birthday presents from my mother, who may have fancied they would mollify me for the loss of my children. I supported myself with a cane that she had sent to me from New York when I was even younger. Battered and nicked though it was, its handle was like a gleaming glass doorknob. The heel of one of my boots was three times as high as the other, the legacy of the tuberculosis I'd come down with when I was twenty-five.

Everything seemed just out of kilter in that house. There were awkward pauses in conversation that didn't just have to do with my being there. The Vatchers made eye contact with each other only briefly.

I'd never befriended a woman. I'd never stopped to wonder why.

One evening, when Edgar was the one to attempt to put Ned to bed, Megan asked me if there was a man in my life. I told her, too frankly, that I had once been in love with someone who was not in love with me, someone who was not yet married but was soon to be, having recently become engaged. "I'm not speaking of Prowse," I said.

She nodded slowly but said nothing.

She went upstairs when Edgar and Ned came back down. Edgar and I conversed at length in the front room, Ned dozing in his pyjamas in a chair opposite his father like some bored chaperone.

"Did you know that I collect books that contain any mention whatsoever of Newfoundland?" Edgar said one night. I shook my head and he looked miffed. "I'm surprised you haven't heard of it. A chapter, a page, a paragraph, a single sentence, an allusion in a footnote, a mention in a bibliography. I've been running a small advertisement for years in New York, Boston, London, Halifax and St. John's, offering to buy any book that has in it a mention of Newfoundland."

"Your collection sounds impressive," I said.

"You must come upstairs to see it," he said. "I don't think I've shown the stacks to more than a dozen people."

Megan's voice startled me. "Edgar would be deeply offended if you declined. I often lie in bed and listen to him moving around among his books. They're in the room above ours." I hadn't heard her come down the stairs. I wondered if she'd gone up partway and had all along been listening.

"This house would be far too big for us if not for my collection," Edgar said. "Megan, Miss Fielding, let's go upstairs and take a look at it."

"I've seen your collection, Edgar," Megan said, casting a glance at me as if I was part of the collection too. "Be quiet up there. Ned's finally asleep."

Climbing as best I could, I followed him up the stairs, past the storey that contained their bedroom, until we reached the top-most part of the house. There was now one large room where five had been, and one door that led to it.

A large wooden sign affixed to the door read *The Newfoundland Book Room*. Hung on a nail on the wall beside the door was a flash-light, which he had me hold while he unlocked the door with a key that was attached to the inside pocket of his vest by a silver chain. He opened the door outward and took the flashlight from me.

"Stay close behind me," he said. "Otherwise you may disturb the books. If one stack falls, it will take a lot more with it."

Once we were both inside, he closed the door behind us.

"The roof of the attic and the ceiling just above us were water-proofed by the best carpenters I could find. There has never been a leak since I began the collection."

I was able to see down the length of the two shelves we stood between. I tried to read the spines of the books on either side of me but was unable to make out much more than the publishers' colophons, a paddling canoeist, a trapper dressed in furs and wear-ing snowshoes.

A moth fluttered into the halo of the flashlight. "It's impossible to keep everything out," Edgar said. "Eventually, because of the moths, there will be nothing left of these books but dust."

"Do you have occasion to consult the books?" I said. "Or allow others to consult them? You must have requests . . ."

Without turning to look at me, he shook his head. "Half of these books would fall to pieces if someone were to touch them. The rest would be damaged soon enough if I gave people access to them.

"You're probably wondering what the point is of collecting books that no one ever reads or even sees. All I can tell you is that there are those who understand and those who cannot be made to understand. I never bother to explain myself."

I followed him as he turned left down another passageway of books. He stamped the floor lightly with his foot.

"Another of my obsessions," he said. "That, beneath the weight of the books, this floor will give way some night and Megan and I will be buried alive in bed."

"I'm sure you needn't worry," I said, at the same time picturing books falling through the ruptured ceiling, entombing the Vatchers while they slept.

"It's not finished, of course," he said. "New books will be published, old ones may come to light." He shrugged.

The room reeked of books, of the dust and ink and old paper that I loved in moderation but which here made it difficult to breathe. It felt as if all of Newfoundland was contained by that crypt-like room.

I followed him throughout the stacks until he stopped and, holding the flashlight close to a row of books, pointed at a massive leather-bound volume.

"Judge Prowse's *History of Newfoundland*. The first book of my collection. Not exactly a page-turner. The books on either side of it were the next ones I collected. These forty or fifty I think of as the cornerstone of my collection."

I thought: *books that will literally never see the light of day*.

He raised the flashlight. I thought a moth had fluttered past my face but realized that, with his free hand, he had caressed my cheek and gently passed his fingers through my hair.

"Excuse me," he said. "I was only reaching for a book behind you."

"That's all right," I stammered, and took a step back as if to allow him access to the book. He momentarily shone the flashlight at me, then tilted it upwards at the ceiling. What had he thought—that we would share a kiss one floor above the room in which his wife was preparing for bed? He seemed not the least bit embarrassed. Perhaps he *had* been merely reaching for a book.

"So what do you think of it, this collection of mine? A bit eccentric, I suppose."

"It defies comparison to anything I have ever heard of," I said.

"You're being ironic."

I shook my head, taking care not to look him in the eye.

"I have nightmares of the whole thing burning down."

"It would be like the burning of the library at Alexandria," I said.

"Now I'm *certain* you're mocking me."

We left the room and went downstairs, where he fished for compliments on his collection and I continued to withhold them. Eventually, he fell into a brooding silence, in the midst of which Megan came downstairs. She looked back and forth between us. "Tour over already?" she said.

"Yes," I said. "And I must go."

I doubted that he had given much thought to the purpose or effect of having an affair with me. Perhaps he thought the time had come for him to *do* something, for he and Megan to *do* something, to throw a wrench into the works of their unhappiness, if for no other reason than to see if, by sheer chance, something good for all of them might come out of recklessness.

III

NED

When the effects of the American stock market crash took full hold in Newfoundland, Sir Richard announced that the civil service had to be trimmed and appointed Edgar, whose salary he halved, to decide who and what constituted the fat. My father became known as the Grim Trimmer after Fielding used the term in *Field Day*.

He came home late night after night, denouncing Sir Richard, who, he said, had secretly topped up his salary with money that had been set aside for the pensions of war veterans.

"I am the mouthpiece of a man I know to be corrupt. Everyone knows that every word that comes out of my mouth about him is a lie."

My father was at home with a bad cold on the day of the Colonial Building Riot, when a mob ten thousand strong staged an ad hoc revolution that petered out into a bid to get hold of Sir Richard, who wound up running from the mob through the streets of St. John's, barely escaping with his life. He resigned shortly afterward. An election followed in which Sir Richard's party was defeated and Sir Richard lost his own seat in the House. The new Prime Minister kept my father on as his interim second-in-command.

"What will Sir Richard do?" my mother asked one night when we were having dinner.

"He has a law practice, which is not much good at a time when no one can afford a lawyer. But he's *Sir* Richard, so they'll let him have his pension."

"And what happens to you after the interim?" my mother asked.

"Let's hope for a very long interim."

"Why did we not get out of here before there was nothing but hope left in the larder?"

My father's tenure as interim second-in-command was very brief. With the country on the brink of bankruptcy in February of 1934, the parliament was dissolved and a British Commission was put in charge of everything indefinitely.

"Not even Whitehall can fix this place," my mother said when my father came home one evening. We were in the living room, Megan and me sitting in chairs in front of the fire.

"It was Britain that knighted Sir Richard Squires," my father said.

"London is just a pipe dream now," Megan said. She got up and went to him. I turned about in my chair.

"That's all it ever was," my father said, looking down at her. "No wonder, my dear Megan, that you feel so out of place in Newfoundland. Your only inner organ is your spleen."

"Edgar, are you drunk?"

He said something I couldn't make out.

"You're joking just to scare me, Edgar, now stop it, please."

"No, Megan, I am not joking. I was sacked this afternoon. No pension and one week severance, for which I'm told I should be grateful, for it is more than most of us are getting or deserve."

"My God. Can Sir Richard help us?"

"He helped himself to everything he could. It's all gone."

The next day's headlines read:

SQUIRES FRONT MAN SHOWN BACK DOOR;
VATCHER DISPATCHED BY COMMISSION; GRIM TRIMMER TRIMMED.

The British Commission's audit found no evidence of criminal wrongdoing, saying that Sir Richard and his government seemed to have broken no laws but those of common sense.

"*Seemed*," my father said. "I think they've guessed why it *seems* that way."

He spent the evenings reading the New York papers, telling my mother that New York might be our best bet.

"New York?" my mother said one night when the wind whistled in the chimneys. "That's where this Depression started." I sat on the floor with my back to the fire, smiling at her when she warned me that my shirt would soon catch fire.

"Megan," Edgar said, "there's a story here about some fellow from Poland who arrived in New York in the Twenties with little more than the clothes on his back and in three years made a million dollars in the button business."

"No one's getting rich overnight in New York these days."

Edgar leaned forward in his chair as if the better to make out the remnants of something in the fire. "America's recovering, slowly but surely," he said. "A person's past doesn't matter in New York."

"Never mind the past," she said.

"I know what I am, Megan."

"It's not just *you*, Edgar. Concern yourself with *us*."

"Even the British couldn't pin anything on Sir Richard. That's how well I did my job. Sir Richard once said there was no point in being clever unless there was at least one person to appreciate your cleverness. I was that person. His witness. His audience, I regret to say."

"More regrets. I've never met a more regretful man in all my life. You seem to want to be anything but what you are. Whatever that is."

Every morning, my father dressed as he always had for work and then went out to *look* for a job. Each evening, when he came through the door, my mother would look entreatingly at him and he'd shake his head. We'd have dinner in silence, my father pretending to eat, drinking glass after glass of red wine. Then it was back to the front room, where he started on the Scotch. We no longer turned on the radio.

"Newfoundland is no place to begin again," he said one night.

My mother sighed. "Where did you go today, Edgar? Whom did you speak to about a position?"

"Did you know that the police shared with Sir Richard the rum they confiscated from smugglers?"

"It doesn't surprise me."

My father turned to me. "This is still a new land, Neddie. A place where a man can free himself of many things."

"Such as what? His wife?" my mother said.

"I have Reg's hands, a fisherman's hands. A boxer's hands."

"Edgar—"

"There is much that I don't understand about myself and which therefore you will never understand, Megan," he said.

"I understand that we're in trouble. So does Ned. Please don't forget that he's in the room. And in your *life*."

He vigorously shook his head and rose as if about to protest his innocence or flee the room.

"What are you doing?" my mother said, casting a glance at me.

He consulted his watch as if he hoped it held the answer to the question.

I spoke loudly so my voice wouldn't break or quaver. "What's wrong, Dad?"

Just as abruptly, he sat down again.

"I didn't lose my job on purpose," he said. "I didn't lose it to teach Ned some sort of lesson in self-reliance or moral complexity."

"I didn't say you did."

"Ned is well-suited to achieve in our names what we have come to think of as success. When you're older, Ned, you can make your way in any part of the world in any way you choose."

I tried to smile.

"I hope he can think of a higher calling for himself than penury."

Edgar nodded.

"At least tell me what you *think*, Edgar. What's going to happen to us?"

"I don't know what to think."

Megan got up and walked to his chair. She brought her face to within inches of his, staring through his glasses at his pale blue eyes. "Was there ever a man who might have done so much, yet did so little?"

"Fielding has taken to calling her correspondents 'my poor despondents.'"

"So what?"

"You should pay less attention to surfaces and more to trying to discern what lies beneath them, Megan. You think that goodness looks good and truth looks truthful. They almost never do."

FIELDING

I thought that Edgar would surely find some way to ride out this downturn in his fortunes.

He was caught up in a life that, even when he'd prospered, he couldn't stand. I hoped for Ned's sake that he would not leave Megan. Ned reminded me of my own son—that is, he reminded me that I had a son and a daughter whom I wouldn't have recognized if they passed me on the street.

In spite of everything, Edgar continued to invite me to dinner about once a month and I continued to accept. My father had recently died and it had hit me hard, though I'd been estranged from him since I'd left the tuberculosis sanitarium. I was drinking more than usual, and brooding more than usual about my lost children. Except for the Vatchers, I had no one whose life I could even pretend to be part of.

Perhaps I should never have gone back there after I found myself seated just feet away from Prowse. But it's hard not to be intrigued and flattered when someone is in love with you, however little you feel for them. And there was Ned. I suppose I was vicariously loving my lost children through him.

I would have told him the truth if I had been certain he would keep it to himself. I might even, with the same caveat, have told Edgar, even Megan. I would have been happy to have the whole world keep my secret to themselves, speak of it to no one but me, each person thinking himself to be my sole confidant. To be able to speak openly about my children to others would have given me such relief:

"I have two children who live in New York. They believe that my mother is their mother and that her second husband is their father. They know of me as their half-sister who lives in Newfoundland. I have never touched them since they left my body. I first set eyes on them three years after they were born when, feverish from consumption, I watched them from a distance, hiding lest their parents see me. They have grown to near adulthood now, which seems especially strange as it isn't long since I was myself a child."

How I wished I could say those words even once to another living soul. When I looked at Ned, it was as if no time had passed, no *thing* had been lost since I left New York. Prowse. I would have cleansed my mind of him forever if I could, father of my children though he was. He would still live on in them if he vanished from the earth. Perhaps I was not much better. We had renounced them, each in our own way.

These and other things were on my mind when, months after Edgar's dismissal from the service, I visited the Vatchers one evening. Ned wasn't there. He was attending practice for some sport at school. As always, I ate nothing.

"I believe," Megan said, "that Miss Fielding foresaw the day that food would be scarce for us. That's the real reason she declined everything we offered her. She knew someday we wouldn't have enough to feed ourselves, let alone guests."

"Things are not as grave as Megan thinks," Edgar muttered.

"Eating once a day by yourself in your single room at sunrise," Megan said to me. "It's a strange, unhealthy way to live. Morbid. You build your entire day around your drinking, which food gets in the way of. Food sobers you up, doesn't it? Makes you too full to drink. Spoils it."

"I think perhaps I should leave."

"Don't worry," Megan said. "You're among friends. You don't like to talk about yourself, do you, Miss Fielding?" She stared at me for a long time without blinking.

After dinner, Edgar went upstairs, having said that he wasn't feeling tip-top. He had the preoccupied look of someone who wasn't as drunk as he'd like to be.

"I'll be leaving," I said to Megan.

"For once *I* get you to myself and you want to leave?"

And so I sat in the front room with her, each of us in an armchair at an angle to the fire.

"I don't see the point of writing if no one gets your meaning," Megan said at last. "Perhaps you're writing for people who mistake impenetrability for cleverness." I stood up and she all but jumped out of her chair. "I'm sorry, Miss Fielding, please, don't go. I don't know what I'm saying half the time these days. I can't stand it when this house is silent."

"I'm sorry, but I do have to go."

Still seated, she looked up at me. "Why *do* you drink so much? I look at you and I see a woman committing a protracted suicide. You're young and so very clever. I've heard that you were once quite beautiful."

"I must leave—"

"Have you never wanted to be more than what you are?"

"Whenever I told my father that I wanted to be famous for something, anything, he always said, 'The Sirens of Paris. You'll come to grief on the reef of hope because you will forever long for what you cannot have. Don't listen, my dear, to the Sirens of Paris.'"

"So you blame your father."

"No—"

"I had a difficult time when I was pregnant with Ned. That's why we only have one child. Did you know that?"

"I didn't know," I said, "but I'm very sorry to hear it."

"Edgar didn't tell you?"

"Of course not."

"Why say you're sorry when you have no idea how I feel? You've never carried a child and never will. To want to have another child and not be able to—the guilt, the feeling of failure—"

"However far I might be from knowing how you feel, I am not altogether unacquainted with sorrow and with guilt, earned and unearned."

"In what you call your private life."

"In my heart."

"My boy, my precious Ned, is my greatest consolation. I don't know what I'd do if not for him. Please don't pretend to know what I mean."

"No, I won't pretend."

"I'm sorry," Megan said, her tone again changing abruptly. "It's just that I'm upset by—recent developments. Edgar did right by me, but he wishes he hadn't."

"I'm sure he doesn't."

"You're sure? How can you be?"

"I—I suppose I can't."

"Have you and he spoken about it?"

"Of course not, Megan."

"*Now* you call me Megan. It's always been Mrs. Vatcher. Let's drop the pretence, shall we? It's common knowledge in St. John's. You may as well own up to it."

"I don't know what you mean."

"I saw that look you gave him when he said he wasn't feeling well and went upstairs. You couldn't believe that he was leaving you with me."

"I'm not sure what you mean—" I said.

"As I said, it's common knowledge in St. John's."

"Mrs. Vatcher—"

She looked at me with the hint of a knowing smile. "Yes," she said, "I *am* Mrs. Vatcher. But what does Edgar call me when you speak about me? 'Poor Megan'? Or does he never use my name?"

"We never speak of you behind your back."

"Not even after dinner when I'm upstairs and the two of you are down here all alone?"

"Your name comes up from time to time, of course, but Edgar talks about almost nothing but my writing and how I should be reading 'Field Day' on the radio."

She laughed. "Your writing?" She glanced upstairs. "He has never cared in the least about your writing. Is it your writing that he talks about when you meet in that hotel of yours? Did you know that every letter in *hotel* appears in the word *brothel*? You merely have to put the *h* before the *o*."

"Edgar has never, to my knowledge, been inside the Cochrane," I said. "When he invites me to dinner at your house, I wait outside until he arrives in his car, often with Ned. I would walk here if my leg was fully mended, but the hill is too steep. If there are rumours—people talk just for the sake of talking."

"Just because you're the kind of woman who inspires rumours doesn't mean they are unfounded. You have all but supplanted me, to the point of spending more time with my child than I do. All that time that Ned and Edgar are away when they go to get you at the Cochrane. He admitted that, on the way back, he drives around the city before he brings you here."

"He never does that."

"People have seen you. It is because of you that Edgar can't find a new position. They all despise him because of what you've written about him, all those lies tied up in clever riddles. What did you think I would do when I discovered that Edgar was consorting with you? Do you ever really think, Miss Fielding? Are you ever sober long enough to think?"

She shouted the last word, then covered her face with her hands and began to sob.

I left the house as quickly as I could, hoping that Edgar was on his way downstairs.

NED

What do I remember of the Fielding of my childhood? That the look of her delighted me. She was like a great house that, though not old, had been ill-maintained and for which, though it held some of its early glory, no new owner could be found.

I loved her height, her hair-mantled shoulders, her eyes that were as lively as a child's, though the rest of her face looked older than my mother's. The crystal-knobbed cane that she leaned on with her left hand, the layers of her clothes, her cape and coat and dress, the fringe of a camisole that might have been silk at the base of her throat, all faded to the same degree, as if she'd bought nothing new in years. Her man's boot-like mismatched shoes, one with a heel so much higher than the other. All of this had come, at Edgar's invitation, through the doorway, as had the sound of her laboured breathing and the faint but certain smell of Scotch.

And then, just as suddenly, it was gone.

IV

Dear Miss Fielding:

A letter from me must come as a great surprise to you after more than a year. I have begun letters and abandoned them, destroyed them so that Megan, who frequently ransacks the house, wouldn't find them. I suppose this is the very sort of letter that she hopes or dreads she *will* find. She is ill, I think, though the doctors tell me she suffers from nothing but excitability.

I have tried for more than two years to find employment, but those very few who are hiring don't want the embarrassment and awkwardness of having such a conspicuous reminder as I am of the Colony's "self-caused destruction." I might be employable, in other words, if I was less accomplished and more obscure.

I can't bring myself to say that not having seen you for so long doesn't matter, as I know you guessed my secret long ago. Every night feels like the night I came home drunk and told Megan I had been let go. "This may all be short-lived," I told her, contradicting every paper that has ever quoted me. "We have some money put away. If we need to, we can borrow more against the house." But she knows that the bank owns the house. I've so far managed to defer the final insult of eviction. I can't bear to tell her that we can't sell the contents of the house because I have borrowed against them too. We can't sell the car for the same reason.

The truth is that I'd welcome charity from the evil one himself.

I don't know why I'm writing to you. I don't know what effect on you my words may have. Maybe I'm writing for Ned's sake. He greatly enjoyed your company, always looked forward to your visits. No sooner had you left than he asked when you'd be back.

I must tell you that I don't know how much longer I can stand to live as I've been living. I don't want to blackmail you into feeling sorry for me. But I must do *something* soon or else go mad.

It's a terrifying thing, Miss Fielding, to know you made no mark at all. And to have no hope, not even the slightest, of an afterlife. One is alive and then, as suddenly as if one had been beheaded, there is nothing. Not even darkness.

Megan almost never leaves the house now. When she does, she is gawked at as if it is a funny sight, Mad Megan doing something as mundane as shopping.

"We should go back to England, Edgar," she says, "to London. Things are not as bad in London as they are here. They aren't as bad anywhere as they are here. We should go, the three of us, right away." She puts her hands over her ears and closes her eyes when I tell her it's not as simple as that. The truth, or part of it, Miss Fielding, is that our money woes began long before I lost my job. I suffered losses, setbacks that are best left unexplained.

But Megan has convinced herself that I have options. In her state she can imagine nothing worse than a short interval of having to make do. She doesn't know that, soon, I will discontinue my charade of looking for a new position and start doing what most of the Vatchers have been doing for centuries, provided that I can persuade one of my brothers to let me share his boat, which will be difficult, for there is almost no market now for fish and my brothers have been catching only what they and their families can eat.

Can you imagine Megan reduced to living on the Heights, Miss
Fielding? Keeping house for a fisherman who, when he isn't fishing,
is setting snares for rabbits and traipsing the woods with a gun?

I envy you. You have no less than you are accustomed to having.
To have more would have come at the price of obligations, duties,
collaboration, others depending on you and you on them.

Simply writing to you has lifted my spirits, though I don't want you
to reply. There is so much more I could say that is better left unsaid.

Yours truly,
Edgar Vatcher.

FIELDING

Edgar sounded in his letter almost as close to a breakdown as he
believed his wife to be.

I saw them around town, always the three of them together, the
only one of them looking different than he used to being Ned, who,
every time I set eyes on him, seemed to be taller. I might have
noticed signs of their decline if I hadn't been so careful to keep my
distance lest Ned notice me and wave or, worse, not wave, lest he
look away and pretend not to have seen me, or approach me and
start up a conversation that his parents would have had no choice
but to join. Edgar mortified, Megan scandalized.

The *Telegram* was pared down to the bone. Herder told me that,
barring insolvency and the shutting down of the paper, he would
keep me on. It may have been mere bravado, but I told him that, if
I had to, I would peddle my columns in the streets, one broadsheet
at a time.

The women of the Cochrane seemed to like me more now that

the times were worse. They called me Sheilagh and asked me unselfconsciously about my leg. "How's your leg, my love? Does it get worse when a storm is on the way?" That was Daphne. Unless she was entertaining, she always opened her door to chat when she heard me clumping down the hallway.

They knew I'd had TB. They knew the widely accepted version of my story, knew I'd spent time in New York, and often asked me what it was like. I told them what they wanted to hear, which was that I caught TB in New York and, for reasons I had to keep secret, could no longer stand to think about the place. I told them all the women dressed in furs and went about in limousines in which they drank champagne with gentlemen of honourable intentions who paid for dinner every night at fancy places to which they went after they enjoyed a Broadway play.

NED

The last night of the Vatchers.

The three of us were in the front room, my mother reading a magazine, turning the pages so slowly it was as if she thought we were asleep and was trying not to wake us. I lay on my stomach on the floor, my face cupped in my hands as I stared into the fire. My father sat in an armchair behind me.

"Don't spend your life as I spent mine, Neddie," he said. "Get away from here as soon as you can. There is more to life than this elsewhere, anywhere.

"If I were your age, I would go where no one knew me. It doesn't matter where you go as long as you're a stranger there. Erase the record. *Tabula rasa*. Wipe clean the slate. Learn how to forget. A man unfettered by memory is free."

"Edgar, *please*," my mother said.

My father fell so silent, became so motionless, I thought he might *be* asleep and turned my head only to find that he was mesmerized by the fire, which reflected in his glasses, flickered as if keeping time with the working of his mind.

"Time for bed, Neddie," my mother said. I got up and went to Edgar, who held out his arms to me. I hugged him as he sat there, my cheek brushing the stubble of his. He patted my back a few times with both hands. "Pleasant dreams," he said, his voice quavering ever so slightly. Since I blocked his view of the fire, I was able to see his eyes behind his glasses. They were faintly blurred with tears, but he managed to smile. "Anon," he said.

I smiled back and said, "Anon."

My father had left the house by the time my mother came to wake me in the morning. At the breakfast table, she said: "A lot of things have changed, Ned. We have to get used to that."

"Where's Edgar?" I said.

"He's meeting with a man who might give him a job."

"He doesn't do that anymore," I said.

"Sometimes he does. It's very hard for a man like your father to swallow his pride and go cap in hand to lesser men. I hate what I see in his eyes every morning, and every night when he comes home. It's very hard for both of us, but it doesn't mean we hate each other. People raise their voices even when they love each other. But we're about to turn a corner, I think. There won't be so much shouting from now on."

As I was heading out the door to walk to school, my mother

hugged me as she always did, but as we broke our embrace, she clutched my shoulder and drew me back to her with such force that my head knocked against hers. I returned her hug with equal fervour. She tilted her head back, looked up at me and smiled. There were no tears in her eyes, but she stared into mine as if she was committing them to memory.

As I walked home from school that day, I could tell that snow was on the way, a storm that I would watch from the window of my room.

My mother wasn't at the front window, waiting for me as she always did. Though it was dark, there were no lights on in the house. The driveway was empty. The front door was locked. She would not have left the house unless she was certain she'd be back in time to meet me at the door. If she wasn't certain, she'd have made allowances for being late. I checked the mailbox for a note, but there wasn't one. I knocked on the door, but no one came. I looked at the houses on either side of ours, but I knew that my mother would never have trusted the neighbours to keep an eye out for me.

Using a shovel, I broke the window in the back door. I reached inside, turned the deadbolt and reversed the latch.

I searched the house from top to bottom. No one.

Snow began to fall and the wind came up. I left the house and ran back to St. Bon's in search of Duggan.

I was crying as I never had before by the time I reached the school, which may have been why the priest I encountered while crossing the playing field agreed, without asking for an explanation, to go inside and tell Father Duggan that Ned Vatcher said something bad had happened.

Duggan came hurrying out to me. As we jogged back to the house, he told me not to worry, that my parents were only an hour late. There was sure to be a simple explanation such as that my mother had meant to tell me something but forgot. Or she and my father had got their signals crossed, each of them thinking the other had told me of some change in plans. But the only thing my mother was less likely to do than forget to tell me of a change in plans was trust my father to tell me.

We went from door to door on Circular Road, trudging through the snow that was collecting in the driveways, Duggan wearing only a light black jacket and no hat or gloves. Some of the neighbours said they had seen Edgar come home in his car at two o'clock. Nothing about how he looked led them to think that he was more care-ridden or upset than they had lately come to think of as usual. They said that Megan conveyed the same impression when, minutes later, she left the house and got into the Brougham with Edgar.

I told Duggan that she'd never been alone in the car with Edgar. It was either the three of us or only Edgar.

Duggan called Nan Finn from our house. After he hung up, he said she seemed unconcerned—she was sure that her son and his wife were merely late. She suggested that perhaps I'd forgotten what their plans were for the evening, or maybe they had meant to leave a note but it had slipped their minds. When Duggan explained to her why I was convinced that none of this made sense, she simply went on talking, assuring him that she knew her son and that he'd soon be home.

Duggan called the police next, who said that, because of the worsening storm, they had pulled all their cars off the roads.

We waited, Duggan pacing while I kept watch at the window, my heart pounding.

Nan Finn called at midnight, and when Duggan told her my parents had still not come home, she asked to speak to me. She told me that they'd be fine and I'd be fine, and then suddenly began to cry. "Another son gone. This time, two went out and *none* came back. I never knew Edgar, not like I knew Phonse. This is what he gets for being too big for his boots."

"It's only been a few hours, Nan," I said, though that they might be truly gone had occurred to me.

"First Phonse, and now Edgar. Nothing left of both of them but empty graves. Headstones to mark the spots where no one lies. Purgatory is the best we can hope for. It might be more than Edgar and Miss Fancy Pants deserve. Who knows what they were up to when no one but God could see them? I know more secrets than any priest I've ever met." Duggan took the phone from me, shouted "Goodbye" into the mouthpiece and hung up.

"Five hours, Duggan," I said. "They'd have called if they could, which means they've been out there for eight hours in a snowstorm. Even if they're in the Brougham—"

"We have to wait," Duggan said. "Sometimes the strangest-seeming things have the simplest explanations." He told me to go to bed and said that he'd stay up.

I reluctantly climbed the stairs and lay on my bed fully dressed. I didn't sleep. I thought of Reg and Phonse having been fooled by the rogue wave. I had an absurd image of my parents lying side by side in a moss house that my father had fashioned, sheltered from the cold and the wind and the driving snow. Edgar had once told me that, when we were indoors, the wind couldn't hurt us, so never mind how loud it was. The wind was just a blowhard if you were safe inside.

The wind slammed against the walls and the whole house gave a bit, though there should have been no give left in it, the wooden beams of the attic snapping like the logs did in the fireplace.

I listened to it roar and then roar louder and louder still in the highest branches of the trees behind the house. It seemed to me that time had stopped, that it would be just as dark when the sun came up.

I heard what sounded like the slamming of a car door. I got up and went downstairs, ran past Duggan, who was sleeping on the sofa, and opened the front door, which, had I not let it go, would have tossed me over the railing of the steps. The snow went by like torrents of white water. The only colour was white, the only sound that of the wind.

The snow stung my face like flecks of glass. I was as suddenly cold as if I had been dropped into a bathtub filled with ice.

Duggan came running and the two of us barely managed to get the door closed again, pushing it as one would a broken-down car, then scrambling around it to pull it the rest of the way. And then, suddenly, the door was closed, the sounds of the storm muted. We were inside and warm again, shivering but warm, and for some reason I pictured Megan laughing, doubled over and holding her stomach in hilarity at the lengths to which one had to go in Newfoundland to save a door.

The storm got worse, but I somehow slept and woke to what for a few seconds I thought was life as usual. But then I remembered and felt as I had when I first saw that the house was dark.

I could barely hear the wind. That the sun was up I knew because of the light coming through the creases of the curtains. The night's darkness had given way to a dim gloom.

"EDGAR," I shouted. "MEGAN."

After knocking at my door, Duggan barged in and, failing to coax me from the bed, dragged me from it by my feet onto the floor, telling me to come downstairs before he fed my breakfast to the dog next door.

"No word yet," Duggan said as we went downstairs. "The storm is over. It blew itself out. We might know something soon." I could tell by his voice what he thought that "something" was.

Later that morning, he told me that he had been granted leave from St. Bon's and that he would stay in the house with me for as long as his superiors allowed.

My parents had done what parents were never known to do. They had vanished as unremarkably as if they had done so a thousand times before, locking and leaving the house and going off to nowhere in the Brougham.

Word that my father and his wife were missing quickly spread. I gave a statement to a Constabulary officer who came by, a stolid, wheezing fellow named Breene who did not inspire confidence. "We're most likely looking at a car accident," he said. "It wouldn't be the first time a car went off the road in a snowstorm. The wreck will turn up."

"They didn't have an accident," Duggan said. "Ned is certain that his mother would never have let him come home to an empty house."

"Well," the officer said, "he did come home to an empty house and his mother *was* seen getting in the car."

"A wreck would have been reported by now."

"Not if it's underwater."

"Well, someone would have noticed if they drove into the harbour in broad daylight, don't you think? And you can't get to any other body of water by car, not even the sea, from any road that begins or ends in this city. The coastal terrain is too rough—rocks, trees, bogs."

"And yet the car exists, so it must be somewhere."

"Something's not right," Duggan insisted. "Mrs. Vatcher shouldn't have been in that car."

"But she was. She wasn't forced. The neighbours say that both of them looked very calm."

The only thing I said that seemed to interest him was that my parents argued a lot.

"About what?" he said.

"About moving to London," I said. I couldn't bring myself to say that they had been arguing about almost everything for years. I admitted that lately they had argued about money, about not having enough because Edgar didn't have a job, about what to do if it ran out.

People came on foot from nearby streets, slowed or stopped in front of the house to stare. Duggan answered the door and the phone. Nan Finn, some of my aunts and uncles, Edgar's former colleagues and newspapermen came by for their various reasons, only to have Duggan tell them he knew no more than the Constabulary did, which was nothing, and that I was too upset for visitors. "I want to see my grandson," I heard Nan Finn say when I was upstairs.

"You will when he wants to see you," Duggan said.

I don't know what they made of the sight of Duggan there in front of them when the door opened. Perhaps they assumed that my being minded by a priest meant that the worst had been confirmed.

FIELDING

The papers reported that, in two weeks, Edgar would have had to leave his house and his beloved car, for his mortgage had been foreclosed upon, his debts far exceeding the assets of his never-more-than-modest fortune.

He and Megan and Ned would have had to move in with Nan and Reg. Megan would have had to find a way to live down their ruination. She would have had to find a way to gulp that down and keep it down and move on as an object of scorn, the main player in a cautionary tale.

Ned spent the first night of their disappearance at his house with a priest. Two days, two nights. Three days, three nights. The snow from the storm which it seemed had swallowed up the Vatchers melted and November returned, bare trees and blowing leaves and brittle, frost-coated grass in the mornings.

Where were Edgar and Megan Vatcher? Where was their car? The search turned up nothing. The *Telegram* quoted the police as saying they were considering all possibilities, but also as refusing to name a single one of them.

What *were* the possibilities? The most obvious was that the Vatchers had had an accident in the snowstorm, but this seemed less and less likely as time went by and the wreck was not discovered. At first, everyone agreed on one thing: it was very unlikely that the Vatchers were both unharmed. Sir Richard, who was now Worshipful Grand Master of the Grand Orange Lodge of British North America, expressed his grave concern, as did the six Commissioners of the British Commission of Government and scores of Edgar's former colleagues.

By way of ruling out what could not be spelled out in public, many said the Vatchers were not the kind of people to simply forget about their only child. Photos of Ned taken before his parents' disappearance filled the papers—Ned in his track and field uniform, posing with trophies. He was fourteen, not yet filled out, but already as tall as his father and grandfather.

One week went by, during which the city was searched over and over, every street, backyard, enclosed parking area, park and thicket of woods. Police officers with scent hounds pored over St. John's. Because the Vatchers might no longer be anywhere near their car, all known footpaths within the city were searched, as were outbuildings, deserted or not, that could not be reached by vehicle. The general mystification was such that places the car couldn't possibly be were searched and searched again.

Despite the scores who publicly vouched that Ned was paramount in their lives, a rumour began that the Vatchers had abandoned him and gone to the mainland to start over, perhaps in disguise and using phony documents, to escape the consequences of their spendthrift ways without the encumbrance of a son. They might, people said, be somewhere in Canada, or the States, or on their way to England.

Or Edgar Vatcher had devised a plan that included neither his wife nor his son, but required him to dispose of the former and abandon the latter. Another woman was involved. Or it might simply be that the Vatchers had been robbed and murdered, their car stolen and, by some inscrutable means, disposed of. Nothing was missing from the house, but neither had there been any money or much in the way of small valuables such as jewellery, silverware, antique coins or keepsakes, because the Vatchers had parted with most such things bit by bit. How much money they might have had on them was impossible to say, though it was not likely to have been a significant amount. But the police were said to know of villains who had murdered couples for their wedding rings.

There was a tribute to Edgar in one of the Liberal papers that all but said he had done away with himself and his wife. "Certain circumstances can for certain people be simply overwhelming. Edgar Vatcher had the kind of quiet confidence that accompanies success. It is not for us to speculate what the effect on him of failure might have been."

Various searches were conducted by sea. All of the Vatchers who owned boats took part. The island's few float planes patrolled the coast and headlands of those areas that could be reached by road. Fishermen scanned the shoreline from dories, hoping to find what, after a long fall down a ragged face of granite, would have been left of the Brougham. "We're doing it for the boy," the fishermen said, as if the Vatchers were guilty of something, as if to have their bodies searched for was more than they deserved.

I tried to imagine how he must be feeling, what he must be thinking, pictured him sitting on a couch, a kitchen chair, or lying awake at night bereft of his parents, near certain he would never again have them in his life, a fourteen-year-old boy suddenly confronted with the prospect of being the last living soul of his family, of facing a future that bore almost no resemblance to the one he had been facing, a future that would nevertheless continue to play itself out in his mind, the might-have-been future that would always be there. Was it vanity to think that a visit from me would lift his spirits?

I went past the Vatcher house several times each night. It was under twenty-four-hour guard, a police car idling across the street, two constables inside. Knowing they'd recognize me, I kept my distance. It had been a year and a half since my last visit, the one during which Megan made her accusation. I assumed she had accused Edgar too, but doubted that she had done so in front of Ned. It seemed to me that Megan, no matter what her state of mind, would have shielded Ned from the supposed truth.

As I was going past the house, I saw Ned sometimes, sitting in the front room amidst aunts and uncles and others who were keeping vigil with him. Each time, after pausing to look in from the far side of the street, I moved on, wishing I could muffle the clacking of my cane, the scuffing of my boots.

I thought often of the Brougham, somewhere out there in the falling snow. I imagined the car parked, idling, the Vatchers talking, the two of them staring straight ahead. I tried without success to imagine what came next.

NED

Nan Finn said I could stay with her until my parents came back, but Duggan said that he would stay with me in my parents' house until everything had panned out. "He's much closer to school here," Duggan said, "and it would be a shame if he wasn't home when they came back."

"Well," Nan Finn said, "it won't be a Vatcher house much longer."

I hated to see it getting dark or getting light. In the early evening, just before the lights came on, there were hardly any visitors and, because of the quiet, anyone who was there spoke in whispers and all but tiptoed from room to room. It was then, at the change of day, the sunlight fading, that I was reminded of the purpose for which we were gathered, everyone waiting and wishing the dark would hurry up.

But I also knew that, when the sun went down, the search would be suspended until morning and ahead of me lay a stretch of hours when there would be no news, not the confirmation of the worst or the coming true of my far-fetched hopes.

Worse than early evening was early morning. If I fell asleep at all, I woke before the sun came up and watched the dark give way to day, the window turning blue above my bed.

The bank would already have taken possession of the house if not for how it would have looked, ousting the likely orphaned Vatcher boy and a priest from the Vatcher home a month before Christmas.

The neighbours brought us far more food than we needed, but I'd have eaten almost nothing if Duggan hadn't urged me to. "When you go back to school," he tried to joke, "don't say a word about how much we had to eat. There's enough on my plate every night to feed a dozen Jesuits."

Sometimes I was certain that my parents' remains would be found soon and with them the answers to the questions that no one, not even Duggan, asked in front of me.

At other times, I was absolutely certain they were coming back. I couldn't help but try to contrive scenarios that ended with them coming home unharmed. I couldn't help hoping that there was an explanation that no one had yet thought of, that no one *could* think of without having read their minds the day they left the house.

Duggan and I spent hours sitting side by side on the front room sofa, leaning forward, our forearms on our thighs. Every now and then Duggan would lift a hand to reassuringly squeeze my shoulder, or the back of my neck. In the evenings, he turned on all the lights on the ground floor and lit a roaring blaze in the fireplace. He offered no empty encouragement or condescending reassurance that things would be all right. He gave no sign that he was inwardly speculating about what might have happened. He looked as if he had made up his mind and was merely waiting for the evidence to bear him out.

We went out walking at night, usually late when it was unlikely we would encounter anyone or be gawked at from the windows of the houses that we passed. The Vatcher boy and Father Duggan. Once, we stopped on a height of land at twilight and surveyed the city, the hundreds of columns of blue smoke rising straight up from the chimneys now that the wind of day had died down, a lull before the gale that would blow all night began. We stared at the ice-jammed harbour and the cruciform masts of the fishing fleet, and the Brow that for centuries had sheltered the city from the sea, and above the Brow the sky that, even though it wasn't cloudy, had a snow-grey look about it.

When we got home, Duggan made me drink a double Scotch from Edgar's dwindling supply, as he did each night at bedtime. "Go on, get it into you," he said. I gulped it down as fast as I could, though never fast enough for Duggan, who, as I drank, tipped the bottom of the glass upwards with his fingertips. The Scotch knocked me out, but I stayed asleep for only a few hours and then woke with a jolt as if at the sound of someone banging on my bedroom door.

I heard the Constabulary car start up from time to time, heard its doors being opened and closed when the officers were changing shifts or stretching their legs, heard the subdued tone of their voices, felt certain they were looking at the house, perhaps even at my window. The officers going off shift sometimes lingered for a while, the four men regarding the house in a way that made it clear they knew their assignment to be pointless, purely for show, a stakeout staged by the British Commissioners who had fired Edgar, a token and likely posthumous acknowledgement of his former standing in the world.

FIELDING

I ruled out a suicide pact in part because I thought that two people who agreed on almost nothing would not agree about the pointlessness of everything.

I thought of phoning the house to more or less make an appointment to come by and see Ned. But if the priest answered, how would I explain my interest in a teenager whom I hadn't spoken to in years? It seemed that there was nothing for me to do but stay away or drop by unannounced.

I decided on the latter.

As I walked slowly down the street toward the house, I was all too aware of how conspicuous I was. What if, at the sight of me, Ned repeated his mother's accusation?

He had been twelve when we last spoke. He was no longer a little boy. Close to two years with no one but Edgar to object to what Megan might have said to him about me, plenty of time for her to fill his ears with who knows what when Edgar wasn't there. He might have come to see me as having somehow aggravated his parents' unhappiness.

I approached the Constabulary car from behind, stopping just short of it. The driver's door opened and an officer stepped out, leaving the door open, I assumed, so that the man still in the car could hear what we were saying.

"Fielding," he said. I didn't know him but was not surprised that he knew me. "Constable," I said.

"You should be moving along now."

"What if I said I have Father Duggan's permission to come and visit?"

"I wouldn't believe you. Move along. No press allowed. Those are the orders."

"I am not here as a member of the press, but as a family friend."

"*You* were a friend of the Vatchers?"

"I *am*, yes."

The other door of the car opened and an older constable whose name I didn't know but whose face I recognized joined us. I nodded to him.

"What are you up to, Fielding?" he said.

"I'm here to visit Ned."

"She says she's a friend of the Vatchers," the younger constable said.

The older one sniffed. "Well," he said, "I guess I'd better go and check with Father Duggan, or we'll be reading lies about ourselves in tomorrow's *Telegram*."

He walked slowly across the road, down the tree-lined laneway and up the steps and rapped on the door. It opened quickly, as if Ned or the priest had seen him coming. He stood so squarely in the doorway I couldn't see who had answered. I barely heard the murmuring of voices. My heart thumped. The constable turned around. The door slammed shut. The constable ambled back.

"Father Duggan says to come inside," he told me. He got back in the car, loudly shutting the door. I guessed that he and Duggan had argued, hence all the slamming of doors. The younger constable walked hurriedly around the car and got in on the driver's side.

I made my way across the street. I knew that the priest was Ned's coach and his sole minder since the Vatchers had disappeared, but I had never, to my knowledge, set eyes on him. As I approached the house, the door opened to reveal a trim man of middle height with short but thick grey hair, dressed in black, though not wearing a jacket or a clerical collar—only a button-down shirt open at the throat, rumpled slacks and black shoes. He came briskly down the steps.

"Let me help you, Miss Fielding," he said, taking my free arm in both his hands.

"You're Father Duggan," I managed to say.

"Just Duggan will do," he said. "You're out of breath. Ned is up to his elbows in dishwater or else he'd be helping me help you."

I almost blurted out that I didn't need a man, let alone two, to help me up a set of steps. As if he had read my mind, or deduced its contents from the tension in my arm, Duggan said, "I'm sure you could do this yourself, but I might as well finish what I started."

Still, I was about to protest when I looked up and saw Ned, all six feet three of him, long, skinny arms and legs, a throat that looked like one large bobbing Adam's apple. Even his face was long and thin, his hair as jet black as his father's.

"Hello, Ned," I said. "I'm so sorry about your parents."

He seemed about to speak, perhaps even tried to. He pressed his lips tightly together and knit his brow. Seeing him fight the urge to cry, I removed my arm from Duggan's grip, climbed the last step and pulled Ned into my arms. He cried without making a sound, his whole body convulsing, his fingers digging into my back as if he was afraid he would fall if he let go.

NED

I felt such a surge of hope when Duggan told me that Fielding had come to see me. Hope for what, I didn't know. At the mere sight of her I almost fainted with relief, as if the one person who could set things right had shown herself at last, as if it had been Fielding, not my parents, for whom Duggan and I had been keeping vigil. I hugged her as I would have hugged my mother if she had turned up on the doorstep. I don't know what she thought when I held on so hard and hid my face inside her cape.

After I had calmed a little, the three of us went inside. We sat down, Duggan and I on the sofa, Fielding in an armchair at right angles to us, the same chair she used to sit in when she and Edgar had their after-dinner conversations. There was a long silence interrupted only by the snapping of white birch in the fireplace.

Duggan spoke at last. "I read your columns. They're very sharp, very clever. I'd hate to be on the wrong end of one."

Fielding smiled. "Some take it better than others," she said, looking at me as if to say: "Remember how well your father took it when I wrote about him or Sir Richard?"

I smiled back at her. The leaden sensation in my stomach that I had been feeling for weeks went away.

Fielding turned to Duggan. "You've been very kind to Ned, very generous with your time."

Duggan shrugged. "I live in a room the size of a prison cell," he said. "This makes for a nice change."

Fielding nodded. "It sounds like your room is much like mine," she said. "This house is more like the one that I grew up in. My father lived there, alone, for years."

"I'm sure he liked it when you came to visit," Duggan said. I had told him that Fielding and her father had been estranged before he died.

"He did," Fielding said. "I should have gone more often."

"Water under the bridge," Duggan said. "If we had world enough and time, brooding on the past would be no crime."

Fielding smiled. She looked at me. "So—"

I told her that I was waiting for them to come back. That they would come back seemed far more likely than not, I said. No scenario of their return seemed more absurd than their never coming back. Three weeks after they unaccountably disappear, they turn up at the house in the middle of the night with a story that perfectly explains everything. What the story might be, I couldn't imagine, but it trumped oblivion. The graveyards were full of the dead, those who had died and never since been seen, but I hadn't known them. In my experience, something always came next— always. I knew that lives ended, but I couldn't credit it. No one I knew had ever died.

So Fielding and Duggan sat with me. We talked ourselves back into silence.

FIELDING

I didn't realize until that night how much I disliked that house and had done since I first set foot inside it. I had the absurd feeling that the house itself brought down the Vatchers. Ned was dreading life at Nan Finn's, but I felt like telling him that, if no other good came of all of it, he'd be well rid of the house where he was born. But to see him experience the sudden intervention of inexplicable misfortune broke my heart. Unlike me, Ned had done nothing to bring such a twist of fate upon himself. There had been no Prowses in his life.

Duggan seemed to me a good and decent man who expected no compensation in this life or the next for being good and decent. Throughout the evening, he regarded me appraisingly. I felt useless, helpless. I had no money, no influence.

Ned seemed unable to look at anything but me. I hoped I reminded him of his less unhappy days, of the times he sat in the back seat of the Brougham as his father drove us from the Cochrane to their house, Edgar and I talking, Ned interjecting now and then, asking for the definition of some word that one of us had used, trying to follow the gist of our conversations.

There were many silences but no awkward ones.

Later, Ned fixed stiff drinks for Duggan and me and one for himself, sipping from it unselfconsciously. I could tell it wasn't the first time he'd had a drink. He downed a second one.

"Go up to bed," Duggan told him. "I don't like my chances of making it up those stairs with you slung over my shoulder."

I hugged Ned good night and told him I hoped I would see him soon. He pulled away from me and all but ran up to his room, taking the steps three at a time.

Duggan said he wanted to start a fund in Ned's name. He asked me if I could mention it in my column and I told him I would. I suggested that the donations be sent to the *Telegram* and I would forward them to him. He agreed.

When he walked me to the door, he said, "He's very fond of you. If you want to spend time with him, even after he moves, I'll set it up. I'll make sure that Nan Finn doesn't get in your way, but you have to do your part. I don't believe all the rumours about you, but I do believe what my own eyes tell me. I can tell that you're a heavy drinker just by the way you hold your glass. I don't mean to give offence, but for Ned, if for no one else, you have to be reliable or I will cut you off from him for good."

"I won't let him down," I said, wishing my voice could muster more conviction. I saw the doubt in Duggan's eyes, but he nodded and bade me good night.

NED

The snow, the snow, that's all people talked about, as if the snow itself had made off with the Vatchers. It was as if the snow somehow explained why my mother left the house when she did and what brought my father home in the middle of the day.

As Nan Finn said of people who went missing in the woods at twilight, they had been led astray, not by fairies but by snow when there should have been no snow, a rogue blizzard when winter was a month away, led astray by the pale, bewitching light of late November, the lulling light of sunset in the fall.

Nan Finn believed the Vatchers had been made off with by something that she thought it better not to speculate about.

"It's not like Phonse," she said when she came by one night. "Phonse wasn't meant to go, but I think your parents were."

Duggan winked at me and I grinned.

"I saw you smile at the priest," she said. "Priests think they know everything. They think God looks out for them no matter what. They find out the truth the hard way. It's the Church that looks out for them no matter what. There's a big difference. God doesn't shed a tear when a priest is lost. This one here is lost, you mark my words."

Duggan looked perturbed but didn't answer her.

Cyril, from whom I'd heard nothing since my parents vanished, at last stopped in with Ambrose. He took a seat. Ambrose stood, shoulder against the jamb of the door of the front room.

"It's an awful thing," Cyril said, appraising me, as if it was my dishevelment that he was referring to. "It's an awful thing that's happened to my brother and his wife. Now here you are, young Ned. You once had everything that a boy could hope for, and now you have no more than Ambrose here. Less, you might say, because you have no parents."

"You don't know anything for certain," Duggan said, sounding as if, had I not been there, he would have spoken more harshly.

"Oh no, no, Father, I wasn't saying that. I understand. There's no telling with this sort of thing. I said the very same to Kay this afternoon, didn't I, Ambrose? I just meant that, for *now*, young Ned has nothing. But if it's God's will, his mom and dad will soon come back and explain themselves and sort out all their problems, and the three of them will be riding just as high as they were years ago when you might say all of this began. Still, it's an awful ordeal you're going through, young Ned. I doubt that Ambrose here, no word against him, could hold up the way that you are, even with the help of Father Duggan. It's a credit to you both."

Duggan nodded slightly.

"I was older than young Ned when Phonse was lost at sea, but it was hard. Phonse always looked out for me. There were some who didn't think too much of me because I never joined my father on the boat. I was never one for fishing. Too delicate, too soft, I suppose. Everyone else says it, so I might as well. There's none of us can help how we were born, is there, Father? Phonse was always there when someone tried to pick on me. He stood up for me and the word spread pretty fast: *Don't lay a finger on Cyril Vatcher.* And let me tell you, no one did. I think I was meant to have a job like Edgar had. Nothing as grand, of course, but still. Now I may have lost another brother, Father. Two brothers. It's an awful thing when people disappear at sea, but you almost expect it, don't you? What with everything they're up against, I mean. But with Edgar, well, who expects a man who makes his living in an office to up and disappear?" Cyril lowered his eyes and shook his head. "And Megan, well, I know she never liked me, but you can't always help who likes you and who doesn't, can you? In times like this we turn to God, don't we, Father? Young Ned is lucky to have the company of a priest."

"His name is Ned, not Young Ned," Duggan said.

"I don't mean anything by it. I call a lot of boys and girls young this and young that."

"I don't want anyone calling him Young Ned," Duggan said.

Cyril sat forward, on the very edge of the sofa. "I see the problem, I do. Once a nickname catches on, there's no getting rid of it, is there, Father? Ambrose tells me at school he's known as Utmost because you told him that, although he did his utmost to make the team, you had to cut him from it."

"I'll tell the boys not to call him that," Duggan said.

"That's not what I meant at all, Father. Pigs will fly the day that Cyril Vatcher talks back to a priest. Sure I wouldn't say boo to a ghost, let alone a priest." Cyril winked at me as if I was the person in the room who knew best how harmless he was. "I was just citing an example to help you prove your point, Father. Sure it's only the boys on the track and field team that calls him Utmost anyway. Ambrose tells me they all have nicknames for each other. Why shouldn't the equipment manager have a nickname too? It helps to build team spirit, I expect, but correct me if I'm wrong, Father. They call Ned Mad Ned because he goes all out, and another boy— Oh, what is it they call him, Ambrose?"

Ambrose pursed his lips and shrugged.

"Walter the Vaulter, that's it. They're not quite the same kind of names as Utmost, are they?"

Duggan said nothing.

"When I was a boy, they called me Cyril the Squirrel. That's what I mean. Boys don't know any better, but *we* do, don't we, Father?"

Duggan cast a glance at Ambrose, who was still leaning against the door jamb.

"Megan always made me a cold plate when I came to visit," Cyril said. "She was a great one to cook."

"Well, I'm not—" Duggan began, but I interrupted him.

"Would you like a drink, Cyril?" I said.

"Well, Edgar may be gone, but you're still your father's son. He wouldn't let me leave until I'd had a drink. He used to put money in my jacket pocket, too, but I'm not expecting that. So I will have a drink. And I hope you'll have one with me, Father, in memory of my brother Edgar, and Megan, though who knows but they might turn up any minute safe and sound."

"I'll have *one* with you," Duggan said.

I went to the liquor cabinet and poured a double Scotch for Cyril and a single for Duggan and handed them their glasses.

"To Edgar," Cyril said, raising his glass.

Duggan, leaving the toast unacknowledged, drained his own and brought it down with a loud thump on the sideboard. "Your turn," Duggan said. "It's getting late, so down the hatch."

"Well, I never saw a drink disappear so fast," Cyril said, winking at me.

"Down the hatch," Duggan said again.

Cyril brought his glass to his mouth and drank the Scotch slowly but without a pause, his Adam's apple going up and down, his eyes closed. When he was done, he gave a small sigh of satisfaction. Duggan held out his hand for the glass and Cyril gave it to him.

"Well, we'll be going now, Ambrose," said Cyril, rising to his feet. "We have a long walk home ahead of us and it's cold outside."

But before they could leave, Fielding arrived.

FIELDING

He bore a marked resemblance to Edgar but, though younger, looked older, his face unnaturally pale.

"So this is Cyril," I said.

"So what?"

"I know you by your reputation."

"And I know you by yours."

"Long ago you suffered an impossible-to-pinpoint injury because of which you don't work."

"I can't work. I'm not some broken-down machine—"

"Or a horse that should be taken out and shot."

"What are you doing here, anyway?"

"She's a friend of the family," Duggan said.

"First I heard of it," Cyril said.

"She's welcome as long as Ned says she is," Duggan said.

"Well, then," Cyril said, "a friend of the family." He nodded as he stared appraisingly at me. "How did that come about?"

"Oh, you know how it is. Their usual table at the most expensive restaurant in town was next to my usual table at the most expensive restaurant in town. We hit it off and here I am."

"She befriended them—they befriended her," Duggan said.

Cyril said, "There's not much talk about you having friends, especially ones who live like this. There's a word for you that I wouldn't want to say out loud in front of Father Duggan and the boys."

"If we cozied up on the couch, you could whisper it to me."

"You're a drunken whore."

"Cyril!" Duggan shouted.

"Edgar told me you were not uneducated," I said.

"Did he now? 'Not uneducated.' Yes, it sounds like him. He got to go to Oxford and I got to stay right here."

"He said that, at one time, the smart money was on you to be the star of the family. What a falling off was there."

"The family friend," Cyril sneered. "Also not uneducated, in spite of being expelled from school. And a woman to boot, a young woman from a family better than the one Edgar came from, but not the catch she would have been if not for certain circumstances— on the other hand, I imagine, a welcome break from the woman he was saddled with, the woman he married because he knocked her up, meaning that he could have done much better than either you or her."

I was so taken aback at being accused, in front of Ned, of having had an affair with Edgar that no words came to mind.

"Get out of this house," Duggan roared, advancing on Cyril with his right fist raised.

Cyril, grabbing Ambrose by the arm, fled from the house, Duggan chasing them out the door.

NED

I went to bed after Cyril had fled, but I couldn't sleep. I heard voices in the kitchen. I came partway downstairs and saw Duggan standing slumped at the sink in the kitchen, his hands spread wide on the counter, Fielding beside him. They didn't notice me.

"Men don't often stand up for me. I don't often need them to."

"Cyril will tell Nan Finn and she'll tell my superiors, who might recall me to St. Bon's."

"I hope not." Fielding raised her hand as if to place it on his shoulder but then slowly let it drop.

Duggan turned from the sink. I saw that his eyes were filled with tears. "Where in the name of Christ could those people be? I don't know how to tell him that they're gone, but they are. You think so, don't you?"

Fielding said nothing. Duggan shook his head, rubbed his hands over his face, let them fall as if to say that he had done his best but it was clear that there was no helping someone as deluded as me.

"Don't you think the strangest thing is that they haven't found the car?" Duggan asked her. "I lie awake at night knowing it must be out there somewhere, in the woods, the water, *somewhere*. *They* must be. I go out sometimes and look for them in places that I've looked for them before, knowing I won't find them, but I can't help myself. I was Edgar's coach. I knew him for years."

"I'm sorry," Fielding said.

He turned back to the sink. Fielding raised her hand again and this time placed it on his shoulder. He patted her hand.

I went back upstairs, but I didn't lie down.

I thought of the tender way Fielding had looked at Duggan as he stood there with his back to her. I wondered if she ever looked at me like that when I was unaware. Her hand on Duggan's shoulder. How nice that must have felt.

I went into my parents' bedroom. It was spacious, its ceiling so high that their bed looked as if it had no purpose but to decorate the room. I remembered cuddling up with them on Sunday mornings.

"It's like a puppy's name, isn't it?" my mother used to say. "*Neddie*. Let's squeeze his belly until it squeaks." And they would tickle me until long after I began to scream for them to stop.

Megan had once said to Edgar: "It's just your childhood that you miss, your childhood when everyone was nice to you, when you had no enemies, no one who was out to bring you down."

FIELDING

The nights I didn't go to Ned's, I worked in my room at the Cochrane until the sun came up.

Nighttime was my time. The time of reading, writing, remembering, reflecting, which began with the dying down of the busy, noisy, mind-erasing tumult of the day.

Pacts were made and broken, secrets confided and repeated in the night. Love was made, children were made, betrayed, discovered and renounced. Poetry was read and written. Even war died down. The wounded were attended to, and the ones beyond attending to slipped away, their light-linked souls guttering like candles.

Time stopped at night except for astronomers, who tracked the moon and stars across the sky.

But not enough was hidden by the darkness, not enough erased or made to seem less worrisome than it was by day.

And so I needed my supplement to convince me that night would never end, day would never come. A drink, two drinks, as many as it took. Some nights many, others just a few.

And then, in the "morning," though the clock was long past noon, I thought of Ned and I thought of Duggan and the way he'd patted my hand when I put it on his shoulder, and I told myself, "You must get up, you must, and start again."

I decided to quit drinking for a while. I'd done it before. But I didn't rid the place of booze. I needed to know that it was there, that it would be there should the time come when I couldn't stand another second.

Knowing I *could* have a drink kept me from panicking, running out into the streets when the stores and bars and all the doors where I might have begged a drink were closed. "I'm not stranded on a melting pan of ice," I thought. "I'm not."

NED

Two weeks before Christmas, in the afternoon, the city sheriff came to the door accompanied by a constable and two men in bowler hats and overcoats. The sheriff said that, in the last few months before he disappeared, Edgar had borrowed frequently from the bank. He borrowed against the house, the car. Big loans at first, then smaller and smaller ones. He'd cashed in his life insurance policy in mid-July. It was only a couple of years old, so it wasn't worth much. He left a will, but his entire estate was under lien. The bank was seizing the house and all its contents except for my clothing and whatever items of memorabilia that, subject to the bank's approval, I wished to take with me.

Fielding was there, having come by earlier than usual.

We could, the sheriff said, absent ourselves while the two bank officials, overseen by him and the constable, took inventory of the house to ensure that we took nothing from it between now and the day I moved out.

"We'll stay," Duggan said. "It's very big of you to distrust us but to give *us* the choice of trusting you or not. We'll stay. We'll keep our eyes on *you*. We might, by watching you, revive your long-dead sense of shame."

"We're only doing our jobs, Father," one of the bank's men said.

"We don't want any trouble, Father," the sheriff said.

"Do you always expect trouble from priests? Or perhaps it's Ned you're worried about. You have my word that all he'll do is watch while you rummage through his mother's underwear."

Fielding touched his sleeve and, for the time being, he said no more.

They stayed for three hours. The constable, the sheriff, Duggan, Fielding and I followed the bankers about as they made the rounds of every floor with their clipboards and their pens, one man taking photographs from time to time. I didn't really watch them. I looked out the nearest window and tried, by concentrating on Duggan's voice, not to hear what they were doing or guess what they were touching.

"By any chance are any of you Catholics?" Duggan asked.

None of them answered. All four of them were scarlet-faced and sweating.

"It galls me that Ned's parents didn't leave their wedding rings behind. The thought of a bank being out of pocket for want of two rings that, if the Vatchers were still here, could be pried from their fingers, will keep me up all night."

As if Duggan had handed her the ball, Fielding said, "I understand that you don't want the contents of this house to follow the example of its owners and disappear without a trace. I think you'll be making a mistake if you sell the contents with only the usual fanfare. Why not put an ad in the paper saying, 'Now available, in whole or in part, the Vanished Vatcher collection? Be the first person on your street to own an authentic Vanished Vatcher piece.' You could discreetly emboss each item *VV*. Don't you think that a soup tureen bearing those initials would make a lovely conversation piece?"

She raised her cane and deftly tapped the brim of the sheriff's bowler, sending it toppling off his head onto the floor.

As he bent to pick it up, she said, "I was worried he'd slip out of the house with a piece of silverware cleverly concealed beneath his hat."

"The two of you are trying to start something," the sheriff grumbled, holding his bowler in front of him. "It seems you want a fight of some kind."

Duggan moved to stand directly in front of him. "All I ever do with fights is finish them," he said.

"Back away now."

"Of course. If I know what's good for you, I'll keep my distance."

The sheriff dismissed him with a wave of his hand. "We're done for today."

Duggan said, "I believe I've never met such a conscientious group of men—the bankers especially. Two weeks before Christmas. Examined the house, made sure the lights worked, noted light bulbs missing and burnt out, made sure the radiators and the furnace worked, looked for pests or evidence of same, checked out all the windows for cracks and the ceilings for leaks. The word *thorough* doesn't come close to doing you justice."

"We could have moved the boy out long ago," the sheriff said.

"True," said Fielding. "Someone must have imagined how that would look."

"A month at the bank's expense is what he's getting."

"And what an expense it is. A month's interest on the mortgage, which you'll add to the price of the house."

Duggan followed them all to the vestibule. "I'll say a prayer for you," he said, "if you can tell me who the patron saint of heartless bastards is."

He slammed the door so hard behind the men that two pictures in the front room fell from the wall onto the sofa.

The four of them came back the next day with another man the sheriff introduced as Mr. Kitchen. "He's an antiquarian," the sheriff said.

"Yes, now that you say it, I can see that he is," Duggan said.

"He's here to examine Mr. Vatcher's book collection."

Fielding was with us again. "A man who knows the value of a book he's never read," she said, "is a good man to have around."

"Mr. Vatcher acquired many of his books through me," the antiquarian said.

"Well, he'd be happy to know his books are back in your good hands," Duggan said.

"I don't want a repeat of yesterday." The sheriff pointed at Fielding. "You keep that cane of yours to yourself."

"What are you going to do, Sheriff, arrest a Jesuit priest, a crippled woman and a newly orphaned child?"

Duggan and Fielding followed them upstairs to Edgar's book room, but I stayed behind. I listened to their footsteps two storeys up, the floorboards creaking, their voices so muffled I couldn't even make out what Duggan was saying.

I decided that day that I would never want for money if I could help it, no matter what I had to do to get it. I decided that, one day, no one that I cared about would want for money.

The Vanishing Vatchers. I was left with nothing but the setting of their lives, the stage, the props and costumes, the performance that only I had fallen for and which had moved on to somewhere else. That its run was done, everyone but I believed.

※

Duggan tells you one night he thinks a storm is on the way. "Wind for sure. I can feel it in my bones." He says he burnt the last of the birch, so there's nothing left but coal in case the lights go out. You tell him you're going upstairs to get what sleep you can before the wind makes sleep impossible. Passing the liquor cabinet, you see that there is one bottle left of Edgar's Scotch. You grab it and tuck it beneath your right arm, which, as you climb the stairs, is hidden from Duggan.

You close the door of your room, sit on the edge of the bed and open the bottle, which you hold up in front of you. "The last of Edgar's Scotch," you say, as if the words are written on the label. A forty-ounce bottle of very good Scotch. You look around the room for a glass, but there isn't one. You tip the bottle back and take a sip, which goes down the wrong way and makes you gag. You grab a pillow and cough into it so that Duggan doesn't hear you. You clear your throat, toss aside the pillow and appraise the bottle again.

You decide that, if you can't drink it all, you will pour what is left down the bathroom sink. And then you will climb into bed and sleep through the storm.

You drink a third of the bottle in an hour, pausing between sips to listen for Duggan's footsteps on the stairs.

You wish you were somewhere, anywhere, that you have never been before, among people who have never heard of you or the missing Vatchers.

You put the cap back on the bottle, tuck the bottle into the back of your slacks and tighten your belt.

Your coat, hat, gloves and boots are downstairs. You consider going outdoors as you are, in your shirt and slacks and shoes.

Instead, you choose the heaviest two sweaters in your closet and put them on.

You decide to do what you often did when you were younger—
sneak out by climbing down the tree outside the bathroom window. You open the bedroom door and walk across the landing at
what you fancy is the pace least likely to make Duggan think something is amiss.

The bathroom window slides open as easily and quietly as you
remember, but cold air rushes in and the door rattles in its frame.
You go out sideways, step onto the nearest branch and, when
you get your balance, slide the window closed and climb down
the tree.

You make your way to the backyard gate and, skidding and slipping on shoes not meant for snow, follow the laneway to the street
behind your house. You take the bottle from behind your back and
unscrew the top, which you put in your pocket.

You stop when you see an old man at the end of a driveway, his
hands in the pockets of his coat as he looks up at the moon, which
comes and goes depending on the clouds. He is looking for a sign as
to when the snow will start and how bad the wind will be. You
don't know him, but he might know you from your picture in the
papers. But he turns before he sees you, trudges up his driveway
and goes inside.

You make your way against the wind that, though not a gale, will
be one soon. A flurry of snow sifts along the frozen crust beneath
the trees.

Now there is nothing but darkness when you look up at the sky.

You blow on your hands and cover your ears to keep them warm,
the Scotch sloshing about in the bottle.

It seems to you that your parents might be in any of the houses
that you pass, bound and gagged, hidden in some attic or some

basement for some impossible-to-fathom purpose, the whole city having conspired in their abduction and in keeping secret the place of their confinement. You are convinced that everyone but you knows where your parents are. It seems that every face you've looked at since they disappeared, every pair of eyes that have met yours, has confirmed it. It seems an affront that everything should look so unremarkable, houses and trees still standing, street lamps lit, people driving cars, undeterred by the vanishing of the Brougham.

But there is word of a storm, so there are no cars on the streets tonight, no one out walking.

There sweeps over you the certainty that, like your parents, you are but a fleeting incongruity that will leave no sign on this place of ever having been here, that you will one day vanish from it as surely as they have.

You crest a hill and all but ski down the other side, waving your free arm for balance, the soles of your shoes encased in ice. You fall many times, clutching the bottle to your chest, rolling when you hit the ground the way Duggan taught you to.

You get to Duckworth Street with the bottle still intact where you hold it high in celebration of victory, imagining the street lined with cheering crowds.

You turn right, into an alleyway, descend several flights of stairs until you reach a landing, a door, a huge, oaken, windowless thing that you knock on but get no answer. You try to open it with one hand, tugging on an iron handle. It is locked, perhaps nailed shut. What you'd have done had it opened, what you'd have said if someone had answered, you have no idea.

You look about. The alley is lit to a smoky gloom by overhead lanterns.

You go down to the next landing and try another door. It too is locked. You feel as if you've wandered into some long-deserted part of town.

You follow a narrow alleyway and see, by the light of an open door, a woman wearing nothing but a man's undershirt that extends to her knees; from her corpulence, steam rises in the winter air as it would from a tub of water.

"I'm Edgar Vatcher," you shout. "I mean I'm Ned. *Ned* Vatcher. Edgar Vatcher's son."

"Mr. Vatcher, you should take me with you," the woman says to snorts of laughter from what might be her twin sister, who appears beside her and leans an arm on her shoulder. "Looks like you're having quite a night."

"Nothing you'd like in there, Mr. Vatcher," a man says as he walks by. You look at the red cast of lantern light that falls across the snow. "Just women. No men or boys or little girls. Mind yourself now. Don't wind up like your parents." He blocks your way, stepping to his right when you go to your left and left when you go right.

"Excuse me, sorry, excuse me," you keep saying. He laughs.

He wears a heavy black overcoat but has no hat. Long strands of what hair he still has blow flat against his freckled scalp. His broad nose is red, marbled with purple blood vessels.

"Do you know something?" you shout at him. "Do you know where my parents are?"

"I might know something if ya made it worth my while."

You pat your pockets to indicate that they are empty.

He sniffs. "By the look of you, I need that bottle more than you do. Hand it over."

"It's Edgar's," you say, putting the bottle behind your back.

"We'll share it," he says. "Pass it back and forth. We'll get to know each other, drink a toast to your father and your mother too."

You hold the bottle out to him, but as he reaches for it, you drop it. It breaks and the Scotch spills out into the snow.

"Prick. Worse than your father."

"Do you know what happened to him?"

"Out here all alone you are," he says. "Out here in the snow with nothing to your name but the clothes on your back. Not too smart. What happened once can happen twice. That's a message."

"From who?"

"It's yours now. Ya won't tell no one where ya got it if ya knows what's good for ya."

"What?"

The next you know, you are on your hands and knees, clutching your stomach after having been punched so hard you feel you might die before your body relearns the knack of breathing.

Not thinking to shield yourself from another blow, you rise to your knees and lift your sweaters and shirt to inspect the spot where you were hit. There is a great purple welt on your stomach. You try to hide from the man who hit you how much it hurts. You try to make every wince seem like a smile. You begin to stand but slip in the snow. You think of Penny doubled over in front of Edgar, both hands pressed against his ribs.

"Stan, Stan, get over here now," the woman who called you Mr. Vatcher shouts. "Len Morry is at it again."

Soon, a man who, by the drab-but-formal way that he is dressed, could be one of your uncles stands over you.

"How'd ya get so drunk without money?" Morry says to you. The man called Stan pushes him away. "I know all about your parents," Morry says.

"Don't listen to him," Stan says. "He's been telling lies since he was born."

Morry shrugs, turns away and, head down, hands in his coat pockets, begins to shuffle off through the snow.

"Lousy bastard," Stan yells at his back. "Don't show your face back here tonight."

Morry raises his right hand, waves it back and forth in mock farewell.

"Let me look at ya," Stan says, pulling up your shirt. "He got you pretty good, but I think you'll be all right."

"He knows about my parents."

"He's drunk. So are you. Go home now, okay?"

You nod. You want to go straight home so you can tell Duggan and the constables what Morry said.

"Do you know your way?" You nod again. He helps you to your feet. "Get home before you freeze to death."

You climb the nearest set of steps, one hand in your pocket, the other pressed to your stomach.

You wake up in a different alleyway, alone, lying on your back on a set of steps, covered in snow, though it is raining now. You realize that you passed out and that, while you lay there on the steps, the wind changed just enough to save your life by warming the air by one or two degrees. A snowstorm on the scale of the one your parents were lured into is now a storm of rain driven slantwise by the wind. If the snow hadn't changed to rain, you'd likely have been found on those steps, a young drunk caught outdoors who mistook death for sleep. There would have been some symmetry to it, the son who ventured out of his house with a snowstorm on the way, just like his parents. But at least you'd have been found.

You remember Morry. You get up. In spite of the rain, your sweaters are encrusted with ice. Your fingers and toes sting from the cold. You blow on your hands.

You hear nothing. The lanterns that dimly lit the alleyways have been extinguished.

Queasy, dizzy, you manage to climb the steps to a street which, except for a single parked car, is deserted. You hurry to the car as if it is the Brougham. You look inside and find it empty.

You shout: "MEGAN VATCHER."

No longer sheltered by the alleyway, you feel the full force of the gale in your face and wonder if it is because of the storm that the streets are so deserted. You have no idea what time it is.

You shout: "EDGAR VATCHER."

Rain drums on the roofs of nearby houses and gushes from their drainage pipes. There is not a light burning, no smell of smoke from lamps or chimneys, no sounds, not even the barking of dogs that might have been awakened by your voice. It's as if every soul has vanished as abruptly and completely as your parents.

What you think is melting snow trickles through your hair onto your forehead. When you wipe it off, you see that your hand is smeared with blood. A wave of dizziness hits you and you almost fall.

You climb the hill, as often on your hands and knees as on your feet.

You begin to cry and can't stop. You're still crying when you turn onto your street. Duggan is standing on the steps with the constables, one of whom sees you and shouts, "A lot of people are out looking for you."

Duggan runs to you and pulls you against him. "I thought you were gone for good," he says. "I thought you had done yourself in. I'd never have forgiven myself."

You realize that the pounding heartbeat you can feel is not yours but his.

"Len Morry," you say. "A man I met. He knows about my parents. He told me."

The constables burst out laughing. The older one says, "Len Morry has been going around town telling everyone he knows about the Vatchers. He only does it when he's drunk. We've spoken with him. Drunk or sober, he doesn't even know the colour of their car. He told us it was black."

Duggan puts his arm around your shoulder.

The older constable says, "What in the name of God were you doing outdoors dressed like that?"

"I drank the last of Edgar's Scotch," you say. "Most of it, anyway, before I broke the bottle. I wouldn't let Morry have it."

"Christ, he's drunk."

He shakes his head and he and the other constable walk back to their car, brushing rain from their shoulders.

Duggan gets you inside and sits you at the kitchen table. He improvises a bandage for what he says is a small cut just above your hairline. The bruise on your stomach he dismisses as nothing.

"I should have defied your mother and taught you how to box."

You grin and nod.

"You *are* drunk," he says. "You smell like you took a bath in Scotch."

"Morry," you say. You repeat Morry's words.

"I'll tell them to speak to him again."

The next morning, when you are hungover for the first time in your life, the constables show up on the doorstep with Len Morry. Duggan goes to the door and invites them in, but you hear the older constable say, "This won't take long. Right here on the steps will be fine."

You go out and see Morry, flanked by the two constables, who seem to be propping him up. His left eye is bruised and closed.

"That's the Vatcher boy," Morry says. "I've seen his picture in the paper."

"You hit me," you say, "because I wouldn't let you have my father's Scotch."

"I might have," Morry says. "I don't remember last night."

"There were witnesses. A man named Stan, and two women."

The younger constable laughs. "They'll never testify."

You jab Morry's chest with your finger. "You said, 'Mind out you don't wind up like your parents. What happened once can happen twice. That's a message.'"

Morry says, "I might have. I've said stranger things."

"The day your parents disappeared," the older constable says, "Morry was in jail. He went in a week before that. He only got out a week ago."

"I'm sorry if I hit you," Morry says, "but you can't prove I did. For all I know, you gave me this black eye."

"Morry the mastermind," Duggan says. "In jail. You can't get a better alibi than that."

I was evicted a week before Christmas. I took little more than my clothes, a stack of photo albums and some books. My mother had a locket inside which were two small photographs—one of me not long after I was born and one of her. The bankers pried out the photos with a pen and gave them to me but said they had to seize the locket.

I took Edgar's list of the books in his collection from the top of the desk in his study. It ran to over fifty pages.

"I'll walk to Nan Finn's with you," Duggan said.

FIELDING

The contents sale began not long after Ned and Duggan set out for Nan Finn's.

I walked up Circular Road, both sides of which were lined with unoccupied Constabulary cars. At the outer edge of the crowd, a young woman who recognized me said, "People have been coming out with as much as they can carry."

I surveyed the crowd. I saw that most of them hadn't come in the hopes of buying something but to witness the closest thing to an official end of the Vatcher case as there was ever likely to be. I felt sick to my stomach.

Men who looked solemn, defiant, even sanctimonious, helped customers out the door with their purchases. Some of the people in the crowd wiped tears away. Others shook their heads as if trying to puzzle out the moral of this final spectacle. I felt as if we were all standing by while a legalized looting took place.

As I turned and walked away, I thought of the nights I had spent in the front room, drinking Edgar's Scotch with Ned and Father

Duggan. It had never been a happy house, but it was being emptied now of things the Vatchers had treasured and used and lived
among for the whole of Ned's life.

Duggan and I lived in single rooms because we chose to. However
wrong-minded our choices may or may not have been, we had had
the freedom to make them. What if Edgar and Megan had made
a choice that left Ned with none? I decided that I would rather they
had been murdered. I wondered if Ned blamed them. They were
not blameless, no matter what the truth turned out to be. Nor
was I. I wondered if my children would blame me if they knew
what I had done.

His heart won't heal any faster than it can, no matter what he does.

V

NED

It was a Saturday. Duggan and I, each toting a duffle bag, climbed the hill, children gaping at us from snow-covered front yards, their parents doing likewise from windows.

"There it is," I said when we came within view of the Flag House.

Because it was so narrow and its basement so high, it was tower-like, as if the house had been raised to that height to protect it from burglars, Brow-bred rock slides, torrents, avalanches. On the front it was one-third house and two-thirds foundation. Before his stroke, Reg had painted the foundation pink. The house itself was two-toned, the first floor white, the second green. Pink, white and green, the colours of Newfoundland's unofficial flag, the renegade flag of token insurrection.

Nan was waiting for us outside on the steps, clad only in a dress and a sweater, her arms folded against the cold.

"Hurry up and get indoors before I freeze," she said.

As we climbed the stairs, she held the door open for us.

The three of us went into the kitchen, where Duggan and I leaned our duffle bags against the wall.

"I didn't know the priest was coming," Nan said. "Not that I'd have put on a big spread or something if I had."

Duggan smiled at her.

Nan looked at Reg, who was lying on the daybed, eyes open, staring at the ceiling. "That's Reg," Nan said to Duggan.

Duggan looked at him and nodded. "I knew him in better days."

"He doesn't deserve pity," she said. "He made the bed he lies on all day long." She turned to me. "You'll have your own room," she said. "Smaller than the one you're used to."

As if he saw in my eyes my dread of sharing a house with Nan and Reg, Duggan said, "You can leave as soon as you're old enough to support yourself, which, given the size of you, won't be long."

He told Nan I would continue to attend St. Bon's. Nan said that St. John Bosco was closer and was good enough for all the other children on the Heights, and had been for Edgar until Duggan came along. She asked him had it been his practice to tell my parents how to raise me, and he asked if it was her practice to contradict a priest. Nan, not looking at him, said, "You are not my priest," and Duggan said that any priest was her priest and she ought not to speak of a priest as if she owned him, but speaking of the man who *was* her priest, he knew him very well and he would be glad to have a word with him about her and the best way of dealing with her recalcitrance.

"Well, it's a long way from my house to St. Bon's," Nan Finn said, "especially now that it's getting colder and the snow is here to stay."

"It's all downhill," Duggan said. "Ned can run it in ten minutes, so there's one less thing for you to be concerned about."

"Very well for now, then," Nan Finn said.

"It's as well as it will ever be," Duggan said. "Ned will have no trouble for the short time that he's here, not even from your sons, who are all grown men. I went to school with some of them when I was at Bosco—not a troublemaker in the lot. Tell them Father Duggan, Edgar's first boxing coach, says hello."

When I was next alone with Duggan, I asked him if he thought Reg had faked his stroke. Duggan said he doubted that anyone who could speak could forgo doing so while living with Nan Finn.

FIELDING

I arrived at the Flag House not long after Ned and Duggan did. "Mrs. Vatcher," Duggan said, as if he didn't know she went by Nan Finn, "this is Miss Fielding, the woman I told you about who's helping me manage Ned's trust fund, a friend of Edgar and Megan and Ned."

Nan Finn looked me up and down. "Well," she said, "you must have stolen someone else's food when you were growing up. You could rest your chin on my husband's head, not that he'd notice."

I laughed. My first thought was that she wasn't what Duggan had led me to expect. "I'm an only child," I said.

"Like Ned," she said. Her face went blank. "An only child who is still only a child. What would an overgrown woman like you want with Ned?"

"To go on being his friend," I said.

"Father Duggan said you were a family friend, but I'm Ned's family now, and you're not my friend."

"You don't know me yet."

"I know you well enough. Edgar couldn't shut up about Miss Fielding. Miss Fielding this, Miss Fielding that. Megan didn't like it, I can tell you. And don't tell me that you were friends with *her*."

"No," I said, "we weren't friends, but I wish we had been."

"Why?" Nan said. "I never liked her. I never heard of anyone who did. I can look after Ned's trust fund from now on."

"It's safe in Miss Fielding's hands," Duggan said. "She puts it in the bank and that's where it's staying."

Nan Finn was offended, telling Duggan it was clear he didn't trust her, to which Duggan replied that he was sparing her the extra nuisance of managing the fund, to which money would keep coming in for who knew how long. Nan Finn said she didn't consider her orphan grandson to be a nuisance. If she could look after a man who might or might not be deaf and mute, and never left the house except to go to confession and Mass, if she had nine children and no help from Duggan in raising them, she was sure she could take care of a few extra dollars and not do something stupid like give them to the Church, which would only use them to keep Jesuits in pocket money. But Duggan prevailed.

She looked me up and down again and shook her head. "Well, it's out of my hands," she said, "now that you have Father Duggan vouching for you."

1. NED

When Duggan and Fielding left, Nan led me to the daybed on which Reg was now sitting, his hands on his thighs.

"I can tell by the look of him that he could talk if he wanted to. I bet he'd say 'help' pretty fast if he was stuck inside a sinking ship. He sleeps in the attic where the girls used to sleep and he keeps the hatch closed and locked. If he has nothing to hide, why does he lock the hatch? Why won't he sleep in the same bed as his wife? The doctor says that, with a certain kind of stroke, you can read and write but you can't hear and speak. A certain kind. The imaginary kind."

She bent over and put her mouth close to his ear. "Reg," she shouted, looking at me as if to gauge my reaction, "Ned has come to live with us. He got nowhere else to go. Edgar and Miss Fancy Pants took off and left him all alone with nothing but his clothes." Reg seemed to nod. "Shake hands with Ned, now," she said. She lifted his arm and extended his hand to me. I took it, but it lay limp in mine. Nan dropped his arm and Reg lay back on the bed.

"He can read and write," Nan said. "He never does in front of me, but he can. He goes to confession with his sins written out for Father Clarke. He reads the penance Father Clarke gives him. Puts on quite a show. He goes to confession every week. What does he need to go that often for? He never does anything but lie around the house. He must think some evil things while he's staring at the ceiling."

Nan led me up a set of stairs then down a dim hallway, all the doors of which were closed. She stopped at the second-last one on the left and opened it.

"No one ever died in this bed, so don't worry about ghosts or anything."

"All right," I said.

"This is the best room, the biggest. It was Reg's before he went up in the attic. Before that, it was your father's and Phonse's and Cyril's, all at the same time. Three men more unalike you couldn't find. But they were only boys back then, so I suppose it didn't matter."

No one had died in the bed, but it had once been the bed of one man who was dead, another—my father—who might be, and of Cyril.

"Reg has the whole attic to himself. Two floors away from the kitchen. I hear him talking, but I can't make out the words. You might have better luck. He can't talk, the doctor says, but I've heard him." She folded her arms and gave me a long look. "You can count your blessings if, at the end of your life, your biggest complaint is that you had to live with Nan Finn for a while. I'll take good care of you, don't you worry. You won't starve or be too cold. You can always talk to me, even if God only knows what I'll say back to you."

The whole room was smaller than my bed at home. The bed took up most of the floor space, the only other piece of furniture being a small chest of drawers with an oval mirror on a pivot.

I couldn't imagine Edgar crammed into this bed, at my age, with two of his brothers, huddled together not for warmth but due to scarcity of space. How glad he must have been when he realized he would never have to live that way again. Now here was I, reversing the order, sleeping in the Flag House after years of living on the good side of the harbour.

At night, Nan Finn heated bricks in the fireplace, wrapped them in cloth and put them beneath the mattresses of the three beds in the house that were occupied. My back too warm because of the heat radiating from the bricks, I lay awake and listened in vain for the sound of Reg talking in his sleep.

Every morning, I felt as if I had gone to sleep in one room and woken up in another, far more narrow one whose ceiling looked close enough for me to reach it with my hand. I felt hemmed in by the walls, by the door that Nan Finn insisted on closing to keep the heat in, the low ceiling, the knowledge of how near Reg and Nan were, Reg in the attic above me, Nan next door, able to hear every sound I made as I was likewise able to hear them, the squeaking of my bedsprings every time I moved, the creaking of the floorboards as I paced the room in the vain hope of relieving my claustrophobia-induced insomnia. It seemed to me there could not possibly be sufficient air to breathe in a room of such dimensions. I longed for my room back home.

Christmas. Nan all but ignored it. "There'll be no Christmas tree and no presents in this house as long as Phonse and Edgar are missing. I told your aunts and uncles years ago when Phonse was lost. I'm sorry, but that's the way it is."

On Christmas Eve, Reg turned in for the night, climbing the ladder that led from the second floor to the attic and drawing up the hatch behind him with a piece of rope. Nan went on about him as if he were still in the kitchen.

"A fake stroke is what you had, isn't it, Reg?" she shouted at the ceiling.

We were sitting at the table, each with a glass of blueberry wine in front of us.

"So," she said, sighing. "You're the most excitement we've had in a while."

I sipped my wine and cleared my throat to dispel the melancholy hush of the house.

"Reg and Phonse," Nan said. "They were like that." She put her index finger and middle finger together. "You couldn't fit a sheet of paper between them. They doted on each other. Edgar went his own way. Cyril went his own way, whatever way that is. But Phonse stayed with Reg. Phonse and Edgar are in Purgatory together. Reg, now, he's probably like you, Ned, and thinks poor Edgar is still alive. It's hard to lose one son and then, years later, another one. No one knows that better than me, but you don't see me having a stroke, do you?"

I shook my head.

"Lots of things cast spells," she said. "Death does, birth does—things that no one understands. You've been spellbound since your parents went away. I've been spellbound since Reg came home without our son. So has he. Megan lived under the spell of London. Edgar lived under the spell of something, but I don't know what it was. It wasn't Megan, it wasn't you. Despite the way he carried on, it wasn't Newfoundland.

"Guilt casts a spell like the one cast by despair. The spells of love and hope don't linger like the others."

She was in a kind of trance of eloquence and spoke as she never had before and might never do again. She spoke of the spells of lust and vengefulness, the spells of pity and compassion. She said that if you could balance your spells, you wouldn't do any harm, not even to yourself. You might be happy.

She spoke of the spells of greed and self-denial, ambition and contentment, the spells of pride and modesty.

She raised the glass of wine to her lips, drained it dry and brought the glass down hard on the table.

"Pour me another one," she said. "This is the only night of the year I have a drink."

Cyril came by the Flag House often with Ambrose.

Like all who came to visit, they simply walked in without knocking. One day, when they arrived, Nan Finn was kneading bread, and I was at home because practice had been postponed due to the death of one of the elderly Brothers.

"Cyril and Ambrose," Nan Finn said, not sounding very glad to see them. "You're just in time for a feed of toutons and a cup of tea."

"Oh, that's lovely, Nan," Cyril said.

I was at the kitchen table, reading a copy of the *Telegram* that Fielding had left behind the day before.

Ambrose sat at the middle of the table. "Hi, Ned," he said.

"Hi, Ambrose."

Cyril drew up a chair beside the daybed. "How are you today, Skipper?" he asked, shaking Reg's shoulder as if trying to rouse him from sleep, though Reg's eyes were open. Cyril shook Reg's shoulder again. "You're not looking too bad, Skipper. Better than last week."

Nan raised the fry pan from the damper with both hands as if she meant to hurl the sizzling balls of dough at Cyril. She put the pan on a cutting board beside the stove. Cyril, hoisting his chair with one hand, carried it to the table, where he sat opposite me.

"It's too bad about old Brother Stamp," Cyril said, looking at me, "but he never taught you, I suppose. Before your time."

I nodded.

Nan said nothing and, looking at her face, I saw that Cyril was not the pet to her that he was to the other Vatchers. I glanced at Reg, who lay on the daybed, eyes now closed, hands folded on his belly.

"So how are you?" Cyril said to me. "Still hoping, I suppose?"

"You never know," Nan Finn said in a tone of grave finality, as if deeming "you never know" to be the official, not-to-be-challenged status of Edgar and Phonse.

Cyril looked around the kitchen. "Not Circular Road, is it?" he said, winking. "It's hard to believe I'll never be a guest in Edgar's house again. He always gave me money when he could. Not that he went bankrupt because of me." He smiled at me, shaking his head as if he hoped I'd shake mine in agreement.

He leaned on the table and brought his face close to mine. He all but whispered. "There are boys worse off than you and no one is raising funds for them. They're looking out for you because your father was a big shot and your name was in the papers. People never feel sorry for the ones they should feel sorry for. They always fall for a sob story. A snob story. So what if a rich boy loses everything. It only makes him like the rest of us. If people bawled for every boy as poor as you, they'd be bawling all the time."

"What are you mumbling about, Cyril?" Nan said.

"Just pulling his leg," Cyril said.

Nan sniffed, tossing her head.

"You don't know how it is between brothers, Nan," he said. "There are things that go on that no one knows about but them. Look how close Phonse and Edgar were at one time. Sure I wouldn't be surprised if they had their little secrets."

I scrutinized Nan Finn's face, looking for any sign that she knew what Cyril was getting at, but her expression was blank.

"Well, they wouldn't be secrets if everyone knew about them, would they?" Cyril said.

"I know my children," Nan said, "you included. Ambrose is going to eat your toutons while you have the drink of Scotch you've come here to bum from me and then you're going to leave and go somewhere else where you can bum another one. You see, that's how well I know you."

"Well, you're bang on," Cyril said, smiling and cocking his head at me. He drank his glass of Scotch, eyes closed as he eased it down.

"A stranger character than him you'd be hard pressed to find this side of the River Styx," Nan said after Cyril and Ambrose left.

2.

Reg never made eye contact with me or, as far as I could tell, with anyone. If he was faking the effects of a stroke, he was very good at it. It seemed to me that no man whose faculties were even partway intact could sit immobile for so long. He seemed to be animated only by basic needs.

He knew when dinner was ready, had no trouble getting himself to the table, and he ate rapidly and seemingly with relish. But no sooner was he done eating than he'd go back and lie down on the daybed opposite the stove. He went to bed early. He dressed and undressed himself. Nan prepared the tub for him, but he had no need of her after that, though for all I knew he merely sat in the water until she came back with towels and fresh clothes.

He was still a massive man, always slightly wheezing even when he was lying down. At meals he would sit across from me, his hands flat on the kitchen table as he moved them slowly, forward and backward. There was always that sound, his hands smoothing the table, never slowing down or speeding up no matter what Nan said.

The daybed was too short for him. To lie on it, he had to draw his knees up until his feet were flat on the coverlet.

Wearing nothing on his feet but socks, shoulders forever slouched, Reg was still taller than me. I imagined his frame when it was upright and muscled. He would have been an intimidating figure even if he had been as mild-mannered as he looked now. But add to that stature a short temper that at any moment might boil over into rage and you had, as Edgar had said, someone it would be folly to look sideways at. Now here he was, suffering Nan Finn from one day to the next without so much as the raising of an eyebrow.

"He dreams when he's asleep," Nan said one night, staring at the daybed from her chair at the table. "And he dreams when he's awake, and there's a lot that he could tell us if he wanted to. Isn't there, Reg?"

"I don't think he can hear you, Nan," I said.

"Well," Nan said, "if he can't, then there's no harm in talking to him no matter what I say."

"Maybe he can read lips," I said.

"He doesn't look at my lips and he won't look me in the eye. If I wasn't sure that he'd notice it, I'd put a tape recorder in his room.

That's where his real life is—up in that attic. He even keeps his window closed on hot nights in the summer. He'd rather sweat to death than take the risk that I might go outside and listen below the window. And those confessions of his—I clean his room every day and I've never been able to find one."

At night, I heard Reg pacing the floor above me, the floor of his room serving as the ceiling for all the other rooms. Though there were parts of the attic that were too low to stand or even kneel on, the floorboards squeaked even at the perimeter, as if Reg were for some reason lying flat on his stomach, wedged into the most cramped space between the attic's floor and ceiling. I imagined him lying with his ear to the floor, trying to detect vibrations from below.

Aside from coming by to take him to confession and Mass, people—not his relatives, as none of them had cars—came by once every few weeks to take Reg for a drive.

"They've been doing it for years," Nan said. "They say they hate to see him housebound. They take him out to see the sights, don't they, Reg? They buy you a custard cone or a plate of fish and chips. They treat you like you're ten years old. Poor Mr. Vatcher, stuck with Nan Finn all day, his wife who won't leave him be about their son, picking at him all the time. Poor Mr. Vatcher. But it wasn't *their* son you came back without, was it? Your rogue wave made off with *my* son, not theirs. Cyril goes along for the drives around the bay sometimes. He comes in to fetch Reg and off they go with God knows who in some car or truck. Cyril is always half drunk when he comes back with Reg. I think they all are, except for Reg. Reg could drink a tub of rum and not get drunk. I suppose

Reg is their excuse when they get back home. 'Nan Finn won't let him have a drink, so we stopped in at such-and-such along the way.'"

Many people came to the house to take Reg to the Bosco church whenever he wanted to go, which was often. "I don't interfere," Nan said. "It's easier for me to let others take care of him for a while. I sit by myself in church on Sundays, but I keep an eye on him."

I'd made up my mind that I'd never see Reg in church because I went to the Basilica, which was near St. Bon's, and spent time with Duggan after Mass.

But one evening, I pretended to be sick, snuck out of the house when Nan lay down for her after-dinner nap and followed Reg to vespers at the church, keeping my distance so that he and those whom Nan called his worshippers wouldn't see me.

On the way to church, Reg's retinue grew gradually larger, men and women coming out of their little houses to join what might have been a peaceful march that Reg was leading through the dark upon the church. Old men and women I'd never seen shook hands with him, and Reg nodded as they wished him well. A couple of the women took him by the arms and led him up the church steps, which he climbed gingerly, head down.

They sat on either side of him in one of the middle pews and turned the pages of his prayer book to the page the priest was on. If he was playing a part, he was playing it for all it was worth. I thought of him going to prayers like this every evening at the Bosco church with people summoned by the bell he couldn't hear. He knelt there in the pew, telling the beads of his rosary in silence, the beads that, at home, he left untouched, watching the priest and the altar boys as they went round the church making the Stations of the Cross.

After Stations came confession. When it was Reg's turn, the two women helped him to the confessional, opening the door for him and closing it behind him. In the hushed, hollow church, where the only sound was the echoing of footsteps and the opening and closing of the doors of the closet-like confessionals, the old men and women blessed themselves as they waited for Reg to emerge, shaking their heads as if in wonder at his humility and patience, his ability to hold up in spite of all that he had lost.

The two women waited outside the door until it opened, then escorted Reg to the altar rail. He held a scroll of paper in his hand like a child going to the grocer's with a list from his mother. With the help of the women who stood on either side of him, he knelt down and appeared to read whatever the priest had written, his lips moving.

After saying his penance, head bowed at the altar rail for ten minutes, he got up and, with the women's help, unsteadily genuflected in front of the tabernacle, then turned and began to make his way down the middle aisle, the women attending to him as if he were a bishop.

I left and ran back to the Flag House.

When I got there, I was startled to see Reg in the porch, clearly waiting for me. He had removed his glasses and was polishing the lenses with the hem of his jacket. He looked straight at me as if waiting for me to say something, but his milky blue eyes were as expressionless as if he were not only deaf but blind.

"I'm sorry," I said. "I shouldn't have—"

He grabbed me by the throat and shirt with one hand and pushed me back against the wall. I took hold of his wrist, first with one hand, then with both, trying in vain to free myself from his grip.

He pressed his fist against my Adam's apple, making it impossible for me to swallow.

He was livid, his mouth tightly closed, his eyes bulging like those of someone who, in spite of being in great pain, is determined not to make a sound. His eyes met mine and opened slightly wider as if he was about to speak. His face took on a look of revulsion, as if he had detected some awful smell that eluded me. Then his face went blank again. Exhaling loudly, he shook my hands free of his arm with a quick twist of his wrist and went inside. I coughed and felt like retching.

I waited for a few minutes in the porch before making my entrance.

There he was, sitting in a chair beside the stove with Nan standing in front of him.

"Reg is just back from church," Nan said, with a knowing look at me. "Someone brought him home in their car. All shriven of sin he is, soul scrubbed as clean as the kitchen floor. Like he just took a bath. What does a man who never leaves the house except to go to church have to confess?"

He furrowed his brow, began to shift about in his chair, rubbing his forehead with his fingers, pursing his lips slightly.

"He's nervous about something now. I wonder what. Phonse is gone and you're still here, but no one blames *you* because funny things happen on the water. You can't blame anyone for what happens on the water. It must have been a man who made that up. What did the water want with Phonse? What did he ever do? It should have been him who came back without *you*."

"Nan," I said.

"Don't Nan me. Where did you go while I was lying down? Where did you creep out to?"

I looked at Reg. "I followed Reg to church."

"You look upset. Something happened. Don't make me worm it out of you."

I told Nan what had happened in the porch, glancing back and forth between her and Reg as I spoke. I was surprised when she merely nodded.

"His temper and his strength come back from time to time, but not for long. He grabbed hold of me once. When he let me go, I told him I'd tell the doctor and the priest if he tried it again. He never did. So much for him being deaf. He won't grab you again. I'll make sure of that." She drew her chair up close to Reg's. "You touch this boy one more time and I swear to God I'll tell the doctor and the priest I can't control you anymore. I'll say you should be put into a home before you kill someone. Ned here will back me up."

Reg's face bore no expression. His eyes had their usual glazed-over look. I suspected Nan was walking a finer line than she realized. I looked at those massive hands resting on his knees and imagined what one blow from him could do to her.

"You shouldn't goad him, Nan," I said. "You should keep your distance for a while."

"I'm not afraid of him," she said, her eyes locked with his. "Reg knows what's good for Reg. He's done for if he lays a hand on me. He knows. I don't know what he thinks he's living for, but he knows a lot of things. I hope I'm still around when he pipes up. And you, Ned, you'll be fine as long as you don't tell anyone else what happened. That priest of yours would pull you out of here in a second if he found out. Remember, you have nowhere else to go, either."

⚓

A couple of nights after the one on which I followed him to church, I finally heard Reg speak—in his sleep, I thought at first. But I soon realized that he was going on for longer and at a more measured and continuous pace than any dreamer would. The voice, coming from above, was so muffled I couldn't make out the words. I heard Reg, the floorboards squeaking as he paced about, heard him getting in and out of bed. His voice was conversational at times, as if he was talking to himself, at other times loud and toneless, as if he was caught up in some nightmare.

He made so much noise that he woke Nan, who paced about as if her sleeplessness and his proceeded from the same cause.

He went on for perhaps an hour, his tone rising and falling as if he thought he was addressing someone present in his room. Nan? Phonse? Perhaps he alleviated his guilt from time to time by speaking to his son aloud, recounting how he spent his day and what his modest plans were for the next.

But I was dissuaded from this notion when his voice rose to a shout and stayed that way for minutes as if he were denouncing or rebuking someone. I heard something slam against the wall, then fall to the floor, then slam and fall, slam and fall, again and again, as if he was smashing it to pieces.

3.

In its first eighteen months, the *Telegram*'s Ned Vatcher Fund raised $140. Duggan said it was probably the worst time in the history of Newfoundland to be raising funds for a cause like mine, one that involved not the fate of many indigent children, but that of the son of Edgar Vatcher, a boy that people could not stop thinking of as being rich.

Duggan had applied on my behalf to his alma mater, Boston College, for a track and field scholarship. He had spent seven years in the seminary at what he called BC, emerging as a Jesuit priest with a degree in education. He knew all the priests and professors there, had kept in touch with them since he'd been ordained and come back to Newfoundland. He assured me that he hadn't volunteered me for the priesthood, but he had described my situation to his former mentors and teachers. He'd sent them my officially certified athletic records, as well as a transcript of my grades, which, though they were not as high as many of my peers', were hopefully high enough. He'd also sent them copies of the stories and photographs of me that had appeared in the papers.

He said I was not a shoo-in. I was surprised when he said that if I was given a scholarship, it would be because of my high jumping, not my running. "They'll want you to do both if they take you. You're a fine runner, the best I've ever coached, but . . ." He shrugged. "You'll never win a big race up there unless you run a mile in better than 4:20, which you've never done so far."

I was as taken with the idea of going away to college as if he'd told me the scholarship was already mine. I knew nothing about Boston, nothing about Boston College, next to nothing about America. What appealed to me was the idea of escape, getting away, no longer being regarded as the boy who, though his parents had simply disappeared, had the pluck to carry on and become a local sports hero. A scholarship would be the answer to what I'd do after graduation. I could simply extricate myself from my current circumstances and assume a whole new set of circumstances. It was like being told I could simply enlist in someone else's life, become some other Ned Vatcher, a tabula rasa whose filling in would begin at Boston College.

I was too wrought up to wonder where things would go from there. We would hear in a few months, Duggan said. For now I should follow his example and put it out of my mind.

I continued to make occasional visits to the house on Circular Road, as if to prove to myself that it existed, that the three of us had lived there. I stared at it from across the street, watched its new owners moving about. I hadn't accepted that nothing could explain my parents having been missing for so many months but that they were dead. I didn't believe that, as some were saying, their remains and the car had been so expertly disposed of that they would never be found. I gave no credence to any theory but my own, which was that someday we'd be reunited. I knew it was absurd and I believed in it completely.

I made the rounds of the city, no longer with Duggan, walking about alone, often in such a daze of confusion and unaccountable guilt that I would return to the Flag House with little recollection of where I'd been or what I'd seen.

People stared as I passed them in the street. "Hello, Ned," strangers said, sounding concerned. I nodded to them but never stopped to talk.

I sometimes shouted out to my parents as I climbed the road up to the Heights, the one that, in his childhood, my father had so often climbed.

Fielding came by the Flag House often. We sat in Nan's kitchen after Nan and Reg had gone to bed. I tried to see past what she was, see what she might have been if not for her illness, her drinking and whatever else had made her what she was. I wasn't able to imagine any other Fielding but the one I knew. I couldn't summon up an unspoiled, unruined Fielding. I gave up trying. I was drawn to no Fielding but the one who, like me, had lost so much so early in life and had survived on her own terms, as I hoped to do on mine, whatever they might be.

I never saw the inside of what Duggan called his Spartan little room. Maybe he didn't want me or anyone but fellow Jesuits to see it. Maybe no one but fellow Jesuits were allowed to see it. I envied him his security. However abstemious it required him to be, he would have it for life, the certainty of a roof above his head, three square meals a day, a family of sorts, a place in society, in a part of the world that was beyond all earthly challenge.

He gave the impression of having been born to be exactly what he was. It had nothing to do with the success of his athletes, or with the moulding of character, or with physical conditioning or competition. He believed that you learned more from playing sports than you ever could by failing or succeeding in the classroom. I think he would have left the priesthood if staying had required him to teach indoors. He so rarely spoke of God that it would not have surprised me to find that he disbelieved in Him or was secretly uninterested in religion. We met him on the playing field or in the gym in winter, where we gathered for instruction before heading out to run, no matter what the weather, after which we came back to the gym and practised our respective sports as well as could be done between four walls.

No one can teach you how to run. The longer the race, the less they can teach you. I was a miler, like Edgar, but, as Duggan predicted,

I was faster. But I was an artless miler. My only strategy was to run as fast as I could for as long as I could. I led from start to finish. I couldn't help it, couldn't hold back and use the slower runners as pacers to improve my time. "The first time you finish a close second," Duggan said, "you'll run faster than you ever did." But I never lost. I felt as if I had little to do with making my body run. It went, I felt it go, and I loved it. I might as well have been a passenger whom my body was designed to please by gliding from one point to the next.

"You just broke your father's record," Duggan said one day at a track meet when he met me at the finish line. "I didn't think I should mention it before you ran." He hugged me. The record was announced to the crowd on the PA system. My teammates hoisted me onto their shoulders and carried me about the field.

Perhaps, if you've never high-jumped, you can't imagine how it feels at the moment you are certain you have cleared the bar. You are falling by then, though it feels like you are floating, drifting down in silence as you look up at the sky. Until then, you can dislodge the bar with a lagging leg that sends up that awful clatter that means failure—public failure, noisy, spectacular defeat. For the bar, even if you merely ease it off the hooks, falls loudly to the ground, makes the sound that all jumpers dread and hear in dreams on nights when it seems that healing sleep will never come.

You never see your body clear or hit the bar. You see and feel and hear nothing when you clear it. You are still in mid-air when the roar of the crowd confirms that you have made it. All tension leaves your body and your mind. You flop down onto the cushions as if onto a bed at the end of an exhausting day.

But when you hit the bar and bring it down with you, or on you, or tangled up between your legs, you fail so loudly as to attract everyone's attention. You startle spectators of other field events or races. You disappoint everyone who thought you would succeed, or had succeeded, or should have succeeded, had you not made that last-second gaffe born of complacency, born of prematurely thinking that you had made it and letting up too soon.

In jumping, you fail not only completely but inevitably because, in every competition, you must jump until you fail. You, your coach, the crowd, even after you have won, want to see how much higher you can go. Can you break the record? Having broken the record, can you, the new record holder, break it again and set a higher standard?—and so on, until you, the winner, lose your battle with the bar.

This must have been exactly how my father felt, elated, defeated. The crowd shared in your elation, but the embarrassment of your defeat was met with silence.

A runner who wins a race isn't asked to run again to see if he can do it faster, to better his own winning time, but all high jumpers, Duggan said, go home without the laurel wreath, which goes always to the "undefeated, ultimately dislodged, goddamned bar."

FIELDING

Ned was a jumper and a miler. Until Ned, neither had existed in my world.

Once, walking past the playing field at St. Bon's, I saw him jump over a bar higher than his head, except that he didn't so much jump as perform a gliding roll in a way so unlike anything I had ever seen that I couldn't isolate the movements that constituted the jump. He ran up to the bar at an angle, but after that I didn't really "see" anything until he landed on the cushions piled high on the other side. All I knew of what he did was that it was called the Western Roll, that Duggan taught it to him and that he was the first Newfoundlander to perform it in competition.

I waved to Duggan. He waved back and beckoned me to join him on the field.

He vigorously shook my hand.

"He's something to watch, isn't he?" Duggan said.

I nodded, but I felt like telling him that, though they had been occasioned by the disappearance of the Vatchers, I missed the nights the three of us had spent in the front room of the house on Circular Road. I felt like telling him that I missed seeing *him* so often, him, my only friend.

I wondered if he could tell that I'd stopped drinking. I was afraid to announce it, for I felt almost certain I would start again. I thought of Tolstoy, who began to condemn loose living the second he realized he was too old to enjoy it anymore.

Thanks to his mastery of the inscrutable Western Roll and his reed-like, gravity-defying physique, thanks to months of practice with Duggan, Ned became the Newfoundland high jump champion, though I didn't know whose record he had broken and didn't know of a single soul who was aware that to jump over a bar without landing on your feet was permissible in competition, or how it had come to be widely viewed as an accomplishment worthy of recording.

Ned was likewise the fastest of all the milers in Newfoundland track and field history, an accomplishment that surprised me almost as much as the existence of such a history.

Ned's name was everywhere. On the front page of every paper, on the radio, on the lips of people I passed in the street. He began to look healthier, almost happy.

In St. John's, it was the lowest point of the Great Depression. Starvation, malnutrition, diseases of indigence were commonplace. In parts of the city, people lived in shacks. Wood was stolen by those still strong enough to pillage it from their neighbours, who languished in torpor while the very walls of their houses were being made off with piece by piece.

I doubt that the spirits of the poor of St. John's were much lifted by the breaking of those long-standing, thought-to-be-unbreakable records for the high jump and the one-mile run, assuming that word of Ned's exploits even reached them.

NED

In the spring of '38, Duggan told me I'd been accepted to Boston College on condition that I upgrade my high school diploma until it was the equivalent of an American diploma—we had no grade twelve or grade thirteen—and that, by the time I had done that, my athletic skills remained unchanged or had improved. The schooling would take place in an annex at St. Bon's, the same one in which my father had upgraded his diploma so as to qualify to apply for the Rhodes Scholarship.

Duggan remained my coach after I finished grade eleven. He had coached star graduates before, though neither he nor the school were paid for it. We were together almost every moment of the weekends and every day in the summers. During off-school hours he had access to the gym and sports fields of other Catholic schools. I was never sure which gave us the most clout—his reputation, my success or the legacy of the missing Vatchers.

FIELDING

One night, having been told by Duggan that Ned had been accepted to college and was soon to leave for Boston, fearing that, with Ned gone, Duggan might think there was no reason for us to meet anymore, realizing how it would look if we went on meeting without the boy, I took my first drink in over two years.

I went to Crocker's Bridge below the Heights and stared down at the water. I saw exactly where the current of the ocean overrode that of the river, the two meeting in that chop and lop until the ocean won and pushed back upon itself the torrent that, ten thousand years ago, might have made it to the Narrows.

NED

Fielding stood at the midway point of Crocker's Bridge, between the lamps, facing the harbour just above the point at which the river narrowed and was channelled into rapids on its way into the sea.

She faced the breeze, her long grey hair trailing out behind her, rising and falling like a tattered, edge-frayed bolt of cloth that once had been a flag. Her clothes too, her brown dress, black scarf, black wrap, streamed out behind her.

Yes, it was Fielding, alone at night and unaware that she was being watched, as she had been the night I saw her put her hand on Duggan's shoulder to console him. I remembered hugging her as if I meant to crush her when she came by the house to console *me* after my parents disappeared.

She looked in my direction. I froze. She barely raised her free hand in a gesture of hello. I stayed put, ready to run the other way if I had to, yet having no clue as to why I might have to.

"What are you doing on my bridge, Ned Vatcher?" she called. I barely heard her over the roaring of the river.

"It's *Crocker's* Bridge," I said.

She smiled. "Well, I stop here at the same time every night, so that makes it my bridge. I own the river too."

I shook my head.

She smiled again as if in self-amusement. "What are you doing out so late?" she said.

"Nothing," I said.

"That's not true. You snuck out past Nan Finn," she said.

I nodded, walked to where she stood and stopped.

She turned away from me to stare again into the darkness of the harbour. "I'm sober for now," she said. "There's nothing in my flask but water." She removed the flask from inside her wrap, unscrewed the top and took a long pull. "Herder, my editor, says people like to think I write when I'm roaring drunk. I have to keep up my bad reputation so that he can sell more papers. Most of the city still thinks I drink as much as ever, but I've cut back a bit. The 'Stab does. Speaking of whom, it's late for someone your age to be out at night. If they see you, they'll probably arrest you for being an underage, oversized vagrant."

"I can't sleep, so I don't know what to do."

"You don't read books?"

I shook my head.

"You should. Radio, well—it's all right for some people, I suppose. I still don't have a radio. I think I'd feel strange listening to the radio all by myself. But you pretty much *have* to *read* by yourself."

I nodded yet again.

She was still smiling at me. Her eyes were large, her appraising stare impossible to meet. "How often can't you sleep?"

"Every night."

"Why?"

"I don't feel tired when it's dark. I don't mind it that much anymore. Except I might run faster if I got more sleep."

"You know, I used to stay awake for a *very* long time if I had to," she said. "But when I got older, well, I found ways to deal with it. I drank too much, which is something you should never do."

"All my aunts and uncles drink a lot. Megan said that Edgar drank too much."

"Megan must not have known many drinkers in her life. I'm afraid to quit completely in case I'd stop writing. The trick is to drink and not let on you're drunk. Then people think you're sober when you're drunk, and tipsy when you're very drunk, and merely drunk when you've been on a binge for days. But here I am mentoring you in the ways of dipsomania."

I thought about what it would be like to kiss her. I'd never kissed a girl, let alone a woman. "You're really nice," I said, wishing, the moment the words were out of my mouth, that I could take them back. My father, I was almost certain, had been in love with her.

I could see that she was so caught off guard by my declaration that she was at a loss for words. I moved a step away from her and turned to face the harbour.

"Edgar wished he wasn't married to my mother. I think he wished that he could marry you. I think he wondered if he'd be happier without my mother and me. He never even looked at my mother when you were in the house."

"That's not true, Ned."

"It is."

"We're going to write to each other while you're away," she said. "I promise that if you write to me, I'll write to you. You have to promise too."

FIELDING

"I promise," he said, as he turned away.

He broke into a run and I soon lost sight of him in the darkness. I took a long drink from my flask.

NED

I decided that I would write to her for as long as I could stand to.

I hugged Duggan goodbye on the playing field at St. Bon's.

"You'll do fine up there," he said, his voice quavering, his eyes blurred with tears as he looked up at me, his hands on my upper arms. "This is not the end of anything. You're stuck with me for life. My life, anyway. That's the most anyone can promise."

"Will you stay in touch with Fielding? I mean, please stay in touch with her."

"I will," he said.

I was tempted to explain, but turned away.

The night before I left St. John's by boat for Boston, I dreamed I found the Auburn Brougham. Its lights and its tires were intact, its windows unbroken but opaque, the same colour as the car, which looked as though it had been fashioned by an artist whose medium was rust, as if it would crumble into nothing if I touched it with one finger.

It was in a part of the woods to which no path or road had ever led. There was just enough room for the car to fit among the trees that must have begun to grow long before my parents disappeared, thick, tall spruce trees whose branches admitted barely enough light for me to see the car. It seemed as if it had been set down from above in a Brougham-shaped space reserved for it in a time that predated its creation.

I felt I'd been charged with a mission whose ultimate purpose I might never know.

VI

Dear Miss Fielding:

When we first met, you said that I could call you Sheilagh, but I still can't bring myself to do it. My parents called you Miss Fielding when speaking of you in front of me. But they are gone now, wherever the "gone" go, the wholly gone, the ones of whom no remains remain.

It feels strange to live so far away from where you live, while you are still so caught up in what for so long constituted my entire world—though I should say that Boston bears a strong resemblance to St. John's. The rows of attached, brightly painted clapboard houses, the smell of the Atlantic, the ceaseless, unimpeded wind, the hills on which, in spite of which, the city was built.

I've gone, with my team, to New York, which seems nothing like St. John's and therefore almost nothing like Boston. I think it's better to begin my American life in Boston than New York, though I feel as if, once I've found my legs here, I'll come to prefer New York and will likely wind up living there.

I know you know it well, having spent several years there. Perhaps you'll come back to visit once I know it well enough to show you how much it's changed since the Twenties. I like its pace and teeming streets but feel out of step with it, always out of rhythm and being left behind. Anyway, I'll be in Boston for a while yet.

I still can't sleep and go out running at night. I got lost once and had to ask directions from a police officer whose car I hailed as if it was a cab.

I am not the soloist I was in St. John's, but a member of a team of boys who, like me, never lost before they came to Boston College. We travel by train to compete against teams from universities in other states—New York, New Hampshire, Connecticut, Virginia.

It's become well known that I come from a country that is all but in receivership, that doesn't have a university, and that I was never on a train before I came here. The rest of the team tease me, calling me "Ned of the North," pointing to things they pretend I've never seen one of before and don't know the purpose of. They even point at trees.

Many of the boys think that Boston winters are severe, a delusion I do nothing to dispel, lest I inspire further teasing. There is the occasional snowstorm here that drops a lot of snow, but the wind doesn't come close to matching what we often have back home on a clear day, let alone during a storm.

It's at night that I most miss the wind. The sound of it somehow helped me get to sleep, even if only for a few hours—though it terrified me the night my parents disappeared.

I am the best high jumper on the team, but not really the best runner. But the other runners lack my willingness to push to the limits, including the ones who are, or could be, faster than me. Sometimes, near the end of a very close race, I picture you making the rounds of the city at night, no matter the weather, your cane and boots incessantly clacking as you maintain, going up a steep hill, the same pace you do on the flats.

I collapse after every race, often get sick, always lie on my back, my chest heaving with no help from me, my throat and gullet as raw as if there is more salt than anything else in the sea air. It always seems, as I lie there, that this mad panic of my lungs and heart will do me in.

When the other boys see me thus, it's Ned of the North no longer, but "Mad Ned" again. "Here comes Mad Ned," they say, because I told them it used to be my nickname in St. John's.

Only the truly great milers of other universities, the ones whose bodies seem to glide, can outrun me.

They linger at the finish line, their hands on their hips, slowly walking off the tension of the race, while I lie at their feet, gasping, my eyes wide open but focused inward on defeat, on having tried so hard to catch someone who merely drew farther away from me, propelled as if by nothing but his perfect form.

There is one who is much better than everyone else. I raced against him once. Nothing I did could keep the distance between us from increasing. He is of a different order of runner. I ran as unmindful as a racehorse of the harm I might do myself, and still that agonizing pull-away continued. At every turn, I thought of leaving the track, cutting the corner and throwing myself into his feet to bring him down. He might well have leapt over me and resumed his sprint without so much as breaking stride, his expression one of bland certainty that no force on the earth could slow him down. It didn't matter that I wanted to win more than him—I could not have narrowed the gap between us if a child of mine whom he meant to kill was waiting at the finish line.

His name is Greg Cunningham. He easily made the Olympic team and competed in Berlin. It was different for him there, they say. He had to *try* in order to win. I wonder how—should the day ever come before he quits—he'll respond when he's leading by so little he can see his rival on his shoulder, or when he's far enough behind to begin to doubt himself, or realize that a comeback is impossible, that his first defeat is certain.

I do better at the high jump, but there are better jumpers than me as well, and jumping is not the glamour sport that running is.

Sometimes I don't really know why I'm here or what I really want. In part I took the scholarship to get away.

I know I don't want to live the way my father lived, pretending allegiance to a man that he despised and knew to be a criminal and a hypocrite who himself answered to a country that was the robber-baron-in-chief of half the world.

I don't want the necessity of supporting a family to be my excuse for ignoring the promptings of my conscience or the flouting of my own ambitions. I don't want to wind up resenting my family as Edgar did.

I picture my father and me out there on the edge of North America, in the woods in a house made of moss, forced to overnight in it by a snowstorm, in darkness so absolute that I can only "see" when my eyes are closed, the two of us lying side by side, eyes locked, it might be, with those of whatever agency that, having fashioned our predicament, is looking down without concern, the storm roaring through the uppermost branches of the trees that, as we lie in that elemental cave, shield us from the wind. He says what he said one day when we were lying in a moss house that he'd built—that you can taint your entire life, spoil it, by doing one wrong thing. It's as if he can't help but speak the truth in the midst of a storm that is roaring in protest of deception. So

I fancy that he tells the whole truth instead of just hinting at it. But I don't know what the whole truth is, so it's there the fantasy ends.

I think often of what he did to my mother by inviting you to dinner, parading you before us, showing off to his wife the woman she could see he wished he had married.

I'm not blaming you for anything and I hope I haven't been too frank.

I miss you a lot.

Yours truly,
Ned

NED

My years at Boston College were a kind of track and field road show—the Boston College company of performers, travelling from venue to venue, city to city, state to state.

Summer semester, during which most other students went home, was our most important time of year. It was in the summer that we were expected to justify our scholarships or else have them revoked.

Some runners and jumpers who, in their home states, had been unbeatable failed to qualify in the opening rounds and, after several such failures, were dropped from the team or quit first to avoid humiliation.

It suited me fine that in track and field there was no off-season. I didn't have enough money for passage on a ship to St. John's and back once a year—not enough, at least, if I wanted to leave my trust fund untouched.

I might have become homesick if not for knowing what going home would mean: another sojourn at Nan Finn's, ubiquitous reminders of my parents, an upsurge in the welter of emotions that I lived with every day—grief, sadness, bitterness, vengefulness— some directed at my parents, some at the unknown agencies that so expertly disposed of them. I didn't want to spend a summer beset by feelings of abandonment, bewilderment, a summer of being gaped at and scrutinized in a place where my story was known to all.

As much of a tonic to my spirits as spending time with Duggan and with Fielding would have been, I doubted that I'd have been able to hold up under the strain of parting with them again, reliving at summer's end the first time I'd had to set off without them.

And I enjoyed being as frank and forthright as I could allow myself to be in correspondence. I'd have felt too inhibited to speak to them in person as I did to them in letters. I imagined Fielding appraising me with those kind but sceptical eyes of hers, wondering, perhaps, if I was brooding about that strange night on Crocker's Bridge. I thought often of that night, but not as often, I suspected, as I would have if I were living at Nan Finn's.

I imagined Duggan comparing the young man I had become with the one he thought I would have been by now if not that my parents had been so perfectly extracted from the world.

When Fielding wrote to tell me that Sir Richard had died, I remembered how he'd looked when Edgar told him he was going to resign—more amused than anything, as if Edgar had announced his resignation a thousand times.

My teammates knew that I had lost my parents, but not the details, or the lack of them, surrounding that loss. And they didn't ask.

It's not to their discredit or mine that I recall little more of them and my coaches than their names. Boston College was, for me, a way station on the path to the resumption of what I couldn't help thinking of as my life. I earned a degree by doing little more than run and jump, and travel, which we mostly did by train. Only occasionally did we go by plane from one stop to the next.

My first time on a plane was, for most of the team, their first time too. As it accelerated down the runway and, before takeoff, reached a speed far greater than any car could, I imagined what my parents' last moments had been like:

The two of them are in the Brougham as, somehow, for some reason, it reaches a speed it never has before, my father behind the wheel, looking straight ahead, my mother looking out her window, watching whatever she can see at night go by ever faster, and somehow faster still, until the Brougham gains altitude, launches into empty, unsupported space and then, unlike a plane, begins to fall, its engine at full throttle, my father's foot flooring the gas though he can see nothing through the windshield but the criss-cross beams of headlights in the snow; and my mother—my mother is unsurprised and silent as my father, releasing the wheel, leans his head back against the seat, closes his eyes and takes hold of her hand . . .

I turned away from the window, closing my eyes as gravity flattened me back against my seat, my body borne up by the climbing plane that, unlike the Brougham, roared on in defiance of catastrophe.

FIELDING

My son, David, still believing me to be his half-sister, died in the war not long after he joined it in 1941.

To the ten million dead, he made the measly contribution of one.

Drunker than I'd ever been, I tried to pick up men.

I enticed one man back to the Cochrane. The bed was there, very there. I told him I was the black sheep of my family and that I would forgo my tipple in favour of a tupping.

He told me I should put my mind to better use. I told him not to mind what I did with my body of knowledge and that I wouldn't mind if he put his knowledge of my body to better use.

He stared at me. I made a more direct proposal having to do with my bed, which was not that he sit in a chair beside it and wait for me to fall asleep so he could leave, but that is what he did.

I'd hoped that Ned would come home after graduation, but he wrote that he was going to New York. I'd stopped writing to him after I heard that David had died. Or rather, I wrote to him many times and never sent the letters. He didn't know that I had told him he should stay clear of the war. I was afraid to give him such advice lest he didn't take it and went off to war nursing doubts about himself that I'd provoked.

I hadn't seen Duggan in months, and I wondered if, for Ned's sake, he had written me off. I thought he would contact me if Ned told him about my protracted silence. He might, without my noticing, have seen me in the streets and, because of my appearance, taken me to be in the midst of some sort of decline wholly owing to my increased fondness for Scotch. I knew we couldn't openly associate, but I'd hoped we'd meet by accident and briefly chat.

Ned's letters kept coming. Was he wondering if I'd fallen ill again or had suffered some other misadventure? He didn't ask if there was anything wrong with me. Worst of all was the possibility that he thought I could no longer be bothered reading, let alone replying to, his letters.

I wondered if I should go to see Duggan. But what would I say and where would I say it? The sight of me up close, in my present state, would surely put him off. I looked as though I had reached the point where I should stay away from others who still cared for me, lest I drag them down. I wondered if he knew that, besides Ned and him, there were no such others, not really. If he did, he might consider me to be all the more desperate, and therefore all the more dangerous to his young protege and friend.

I decided I must write to Ned, now that I knew he wasn't coming home. I'd fancied, when I thought his homecoming was imminent, that I might cut back on the Scotch, spruce myself up, return to being something like the Sheilagh Fielding whom, as a child, as a boy, as a young man, he had been so taken with—the one he encountered by accident on Crocker's Bridge before he caught the boat for Boston, an engaging, intriguingly marred, dissolute, youngish woman whose worst years, it may have seemed to him, were behind her.

But now he was not coming home. He was not coming home and David was never coming home.

Ned was going to New York, where my daughter, Sarah, and her children lived. I didn't know why, but I hated to think that their paths might cross. I knew it was unlikely that they would. My New York, that of the Twenties, when idealists on the brink of disillusionment were everywhere and there was still some farmland on the north end of Manhattan, no longer existed.

The war would end as the other one had. Things never seem more promising, more fated for success than they do in the wake of war. Souls that almost flickered out burn more brightly than they ever did. There is something at the bottom of the pit of despair that, when brought up to the surface, ignites and gives off a greater light than people who have never known despair have ever seen.

I had seen it and felt its heat the day they told me I was cured, and the day I left the San. I didn't understand it. I would happily have forgone every stage of my first descent, and every stage of this one, for the light inside me now, like that of Lucifer himself, seemed to live nowhere but in perfect darkness.

In St. John's, during the war, men and women in uniform were everywhere—Brits, Yanks, Canadians. Most of them thought my being a Newfoundlander explained my every attribute, as if they had been posted to a country of eccentrics in which each native was regarded, even by his fellows, as an oddball.

In spite of the wartime curfew and blackout, I went out walking at night. Once, I was stopped on the street by carousing Canadians who asked me how I got my limp. I told them I was wounded in a war of words, a war of swords, a war of puns and guns and one of sons. I told them I hoped the word to end all wars would come before the war to end all words.

"Ask a stupid question," one of them said as they wandered off.

NED

Fielding stopped answering my letters, though I kept writing to her. I wrote to Duggan about her, too. He told me that, since my departure, they'd not had much reason to meet.

On my twenty-first birthday, Duggan wired me the money from

my trust fund: $1,181.62. He said he had told some well-heeled men of my success at Boston College and they had all chipped in. He suggested that I put it in a bank account and leave it untouched until I decided where and how to live, until I understood what a difference that much money could make in my life and perhaps the lives of others. "Tell no one but the people in the bank about that money," he wrote.

Tired of Boston, lacking friends because I was no longer a student, I decided to give New York a try. I deposited the money in a New York bank with the help of a wide-eyed teller who asked me if I was new in town and would I like it if she helped me find my way around. I told her that I had moved to the city with my parents. I saw her once a month when I went to check the balance of my bank account to assure myself that I still had a bank account and that my money was not somehow seeping from it.

I got a job as a busboy in an Irish pub on Cornelius Street, where the New York–born owner mistook my accent for an Irish one. I rented a room in a small, rundown hotel on Twenty-First Street, a room that I imagined was like the ones that Fielding and Duggan lived in. It was half the size of my room at Nan Finn's and a third the size of my dorm room at Boston College.

I worked at the pub for a month, watching the owner tend bar until I thought I could fake my way into such a job. I quit that Irish bar and got hired at another one as a bartender.

The owner of the new bar, Clancy, told me he knew I wasn't Irish, but said I should pretend I was. "I can also see you've never been a bartender," he said, "but any idiot can do it, and who wouldn't make allowances for someone who could pass for a movie star? My grand plan is that you'll bring in the women and they'll bring in the men.

You better hope it works, because if it doesn't, you're out the door. And have an answer ready when people ask you why you never signed up for the service. I don't care why you didn't, but there'll be some who will."

The patronage at the bar increased, but not dramatically. I was asked, time and again, why I hadn't joined the war instead of staying in New York to serve drinks to pretty young women and to young men on furlough who were risking everything while all I was risking was my virginity. I told people that I had tried to sign up but failed the physical. I said the doctor had me run on the spot, listened to my heart, shook his head and that was that. I said I didn't feel like there was anything wrong with me, but it wasn't up to me. The story was universally accepted, but received in a variety of ways. Sympathetically by many. When the enlisted men were sober, they seemed embarrassed for me and said nothing. But the drunker they got, the more scornful they became. "The faint-hearted need not apply," they said. "The Marines are looking for a few good men, not a few weak-hearted boys. It's just as well you didn't go overseas. No one's life depends on you here."

I knew they wouldn't believe the truth, which was that I would have enlisted if not for my parents. I'd come to realize that to find out what had become of them would be the main goal of my life.

I knew that no one arrived at the end of their life with all their issues and uncertainties resolved, but I felt I had to find my parents, felt as if doing so would save them, no matter how or why they'd disappeared, no matter if they were long dead or still alive by the time I found them. I felt I had to find them as if nothing but doing so would save *me*. I believed that even if I found out they had forsaken me, I could deal with it. I would, at last, *understand*.

I couldn't leave them as they had left me. I couldn't copy them or pay them back by vanishing as surely as if I had never been. If I went to war, I would put myself in harm's way, let mere chance determine if I lived or died, as if that decision would itself be the answer I was searching for.

My days of tending bar, of waiting out the war in the safety of New York, passed the way my days at Boston College had. I was biding my time, but for exactly what, I didn't know. I made friends, but not close ones, none I stayed in touch with or, after New York, ever saw again. I didn't try to pick up women and deflected those who tried to pick me up.

Most nights, after work, I joined the rest of the staff at the back of the bar, drinking the cheapest booze that Clancy could afford to give away, usually one of the low-end bourbons that were favoured by his worst-heeled customers. The war had stalled everything, but we rarely talked about it. The whole world had been diverted from its normal course, but the others believed that it would right itself and that some version of life as it was before the war would start up again.

But, as Nan Finn might have said, I did fall under the spell of America. The Americans I admired most acted as if, in spite of the war, they had never heard of death, as if all risks would be rewarded and all gambles would pay off. Even Clancy talked as if his bar was the first in a chain whose success was preordained.

Some nights, the buzz among the customers who stood along the bar was deafening, the place sounding like the floor of the New York Stock Exchange: *buy this, sell that, get in on this, don't be a chump, have you heard, have you heard, Pearl Harbor was a blessing in disguise, dollar bills blow like leaves on the sidewalks of New York.*

I kept my ear out for some venture or scheme that might be as foolproof in Newfoundland as it had been shown to be in New York, something that had already worked but had yet to be tried back home.

It was not what I heard but what I saw night after night that, ultimately, changed my life. Conversation at Clancy's often centred around stories that appeared in a kind of newspaper I had never read before—the tabloid. Hilariously lurid stories of sordid sex and gruesome crimes and aliens from outer space were received by many as the gospel truth. The *New York Daily News* was everywhere, read by everyone, even those who swore they didn't believe a word of it. I imagined how it would have depicted the disappearance of the Vatchers—a mob hit, or a sordid love triangle that ended in murder, an abduction by aliens doing research for the widely-known-to-be-imminent invasion of the earth from outer space.

What world-beating New Yorkers fell for and couldn't get enough of, Newfoundlanders who had never seen the outside world would not be able to resist—such was my far-fetched hope as I prepared to go back home.

VII

1. NED

December 1946. I had decided to travel first class, at least from Halifax to St. John's, though I had told no one but Duggan that I was coming home. The headlands of the island came into view as I stood at the rail of the ship, a gale in my face so cold it made my forehead ache the way it did when, as a child, I pressed snow against it.

"You look like you're thinking of jumping overboard, Mr. Vatcher," a voice beside me shouted above the wind and the screeching of seagulls. "Perhaps you'll feel better once your feet are on dry land."

I looked into the eyes of a well-dressed man. He smiled. "I knew your father," he said. "Not well, but I knew him." He clapped me on the back and moved away.

Looking up, I saw, straight ahead, through the Narrows, the hillside city of St. John's, the gull-shaped Basilica atop the hill. I couldn't help but think of the view of Manhattan from the Brooklyn Bridge. St. John's might have been a once-great city that, by some calamity, had been razed to its present state, a city whose citizens had despaired of reconstructing it.

As I debarked, I looked back at the ship, which would be making port in Southampton in two weeks. How easy it would have been to tell them to leave my things on board and to book passage to England.

"I'd hug you," Duggan said as we shook hands on the commons at St. Bon's, "but I'd feel foolish hugging someone a head taller than me." He stood back to appraise me. He told me that I had filled out and looked more like a sprinter than a miler. As for the high jump— he shook his head and grinned and said that I'd be lucky at my weight to clear six feet.

We went out for a walk. "There were some good American jumpers and runners here during the war," he said. "They thought pretty highly of themselves. I wished you were here to take them down a peg."

I laughed.

"Where are you staying?"

"In a rooming house, for now."

"You have a degree. You're Ned Vatcher, a sports hero. You could dip into that trust, spruce yourself up and get a job in no time."

"I don't want to work for someone else. I have an idea for a business. Don't ask. If I fall flat on my face, maybe then I'll find a job."

I asked after Fielding and he said she seemed to have declined in direct proportion to the increase in prosperity the war had brought. "She fell and broke her arm and hand pretty badly in '41. I decided not to write to you about it. I didn't want to worry you. With a bad leg and a bad arm, she was pretty much housebound for a year. I don't see her often. It's awkward, a priest keeping company with a woman, a non-Catholic at that. Anyway, you should see her as soon as you can. I'm sure it will give her a lift."

"Ned," she said as she opened the door of her room in the Cochrane, her wan face lighting up. She gave me a fierce hug, backing out of which she stumbled slightly. I reached out to steady her, but she turned away. "Forgot my cane," she said. "I was beginning to think I'd never see you again. But come in, come in. Have a drink with me. Duggan tells me you're a bourbon drinker now. But all I have is very bad Scotch."

The room, though reasonably clean, was all but unfurnished. There was an unmade bed in the far corner, the foot of it just beneath the window, whose drab green floor-length drapes were drawn. Opposite the bed, against the near wall, was an ancient rolltop desk, cratered by cigarette burns. I wondered if it was the same one I had seen at the *Telegram* more than twenty years ago. A high, narrow portable closet stood in the corner of the room to the right of the desk. A single light bulb hung from the ceiling by a string. There was a double-damper hot plate on the floor beside the desk; the desk, I guessed, served as her dining table. No cupboards or icebox were in evidence. An old cast iron Remington sat on the desk, its roller bearing a blank piece of paper. Beside the typewriter was the stub of a yellow pencil.

She took hold of her cane, which had been leaned against the wall. She sat at the desk and turned her chair to face the bed, to which she motioned with her cane.

"You should have told me you were coming, Ned," she said. "I could at least have made the bed. But sit down, sit down. Or I can sit on the bed if you'd rather have the chair."

"That's all right," I said. As I sat, the bedsprings loudly creaked.

"You look like you've become used to better," she said.

"It was good to live away for a while. You have to size this place up from a distance to see the lay of the land. I'd set you up in a nicer place than this if I could. Not that there's anything wrong with it, but—"

"Don't worry about me," she said. "And I'm neither offended by nor interested in your offer." She removed her silver flask from the pocket of the raglan that was hung on the chair, extending it to me after removing the cap. I took it from her, took a gulp and gave it back. "To my mind, even bad Scotch is better than good bourbon," she said, lighting up a cigarette and proffering the package. I shook my head. "Still don't smoke?" she said.

"No."

As if to herself, she said: "It's never good news when tall men come to visit me."

Duggan was right. The war years had taken more of a toll on her than on anyone I'd seen since I'd come back.

"Are you all right?" I didn't know what to call her. "Miss Fielding" seemed ridiculous now, and "Fielding" inappropriate.

"So what did you think of New York, Ned?" she said, ignoring my question.

"I liked it."

"I hated New York," she said. "I'll hate it just as much when I go back."

"When will that be?" I said.

She shrugged. "Oh, you never know. Next week, next year, ten years from now. The Sirens of Paris."

"What?"

"Something my father used to say. Never mind."

"But you're really going back to New York?" I said.

She looked at me as if my question was that of a simpleton. "Yes," she said. "Why is that so surprising? I won't be going for good, just to visit."

"I could go with you. I could show you my New York and you could show me yours."

"Mine is long gone. Just as well. You wouldn't have liked it."

"Why?"

"What do you plan to do now that you're back home?"

"Make money. Lots of it, I hope."

"Lots of it, you hope."

"I still think about that night on the bridge."

"You shouldn't. You should forget about it."

"I feel foolish about it, *still*. Look, I'm merely offering to help a friend. You won't be able to live like you do much longer."

"I'll be too old?"

"For the way you live, you already are. You drink too much, you don't eat right. You don't walk as much as you used to because you can't. This city is nothing but hills. You've accomplished so much. You deserve better than the Cochrane, better than living in one small, dim room. Surely you'd rather have a nicer place to live? Nicer clothes. What if something should happen to you?"

"Many things have."

"Don't you want to play it safe for once in your life?"

"Am I not respectable enough for you now? Why don't *you* change? Why don't you, in solidarity with me, your friend, take to wearing worn-out clothes? The two of us could walk around the city after dark, like sleepless hoboes."

"You're being absurd. You'll always live on your own terms."

"*These* are my terms. I came to these terms with life long ago."

"You could change. What if a day should come when you no longer want to write? What will you do with yourself?"

"That day will never come, though the day might come when I'm no longer *able* to write. I dread it. I'd be impossible to live with." She paused, then said, "I'm too tired to talk, Ned. I'm sorry. You've come at a bad time. I'll never get my column done unless I take a nap."

"Should I leave?"

"If I look half as bad as that expression on your face suggests," she said, "you might not get much sleep tonight."

"I'm sorry. I'm concerned about you. Duggan said you seemed—"

"You know you've come to a sorry state as a woman when even priests stop lusting after you."

"He's concerned about you too."

"Duggan wonders how fast I could run a mile with two legs of the same length. Otherwise, he never thinks of me."

"That's not true. He—"

"You see, Ned, I'm one of those rare people who is disheartened by a world war."

"What else are you disheartened by?"

She stood up and, thumping her cane on the floor, began to shuffle around the room. "What else?" she said. "What else? What else am I disheartened by? Let me see, what could there be? You, maybe. The sight of a money-grubbing young man makes me sick. Surely there are better ways a young man could occupy his time than by trying to get rich? But then, we might all be better occupied than we are. Not like France was occupied, or Poland. Young men gave their lives. Mothers lost their only sons, mothers whom the world wouldn't miss much either."

She stopped and looked at me. "You'd better leave," she said. "It's just that you remind me of—someone I barely knew who was lost in the war. He hardly knew me, yet I think of him more often than I think of you. I'm glad that you stayed away from it, though. I am. I'm not accusing you of anything, Ned, so go now. I have to save something of myself for my column. There's no telling what I'll say if you don't go. I might talk about some other woman's son who went away for good. His name was David. At the moment I can't think of his last name. I can't recall his face. I'm drunk, Ned, too drunk. You have to go."

I left, promising that I would come back soon, but it would be some time before I saw her again. I thought about New York and her nebulous plan to go back there though she hated it so much. I thought about David, the near stranger who died in the war whom she thought about more often than she did about me.

2.

It was from a man named Joey Smallwood that I first heard that Whitehall had decided to return Newfoundland to a kind of self-rule, to give us back the right to choose, in a referendum, what sort of nation we would be.

I knew Smallwood's story, the public part of it anyway. Failures led like a trail of breadcrumbs back to the house where he was born: Expelled from school. Signed on with the sinking cause of socialism in America long after the last of its skippers had abandoned ship. Became a skid row regular in New York because he couldn't stand to go back home and be taken in by the very people he had left home to escape. Walked the width of Newfoundland to secure a raise for railway workers that, one day after it was granted, was rescinded. Threw in his lot with my father's man—Sir Richard—who wound up running for his life from a mob who took exception to him lining his pockets with the pensions of wartime amputees. Compiled *The Book of Newfoundland*, the immolation of most of the copies of which was less time-consuming than selling them for next to nothing would have been. Started, and oversaw the closing of, a pig farm whose pigs refused to eat the parts of their forebears for which no other purpose could be found. Legend had it that he had invented eye shades for chickens to keep those on his farm from pecking each other to death, only to find, one morning, that an especially clever chicken had pried her shades off by hooking them in the wire mesh of the cage and had slaughtered all of the others who, able to see nothing but the ground, could not defend themselves.

It seemed to me that he was not so much dogged as unable to understand the concept of discouragement.

I conducted a business transaction with him, buying from him ten tons of newsprint for which he no longer had any use since his newspaper, the *Express*, had just gone under. I paid an absurdly low price, but when I gave him his money, he sniffed as if to say that I could have held out for much less.

I told him that an idea had occurred to me in New York. I was going to start up a tabloid similar to those that in the States were all the rage, leaving out that I had been emboldened to try this by the reading habits of the booze-crazed braggarts of a New York bar.

"Something like that won't last six weeks in Newfoundland," Smallwood said without rancour.

I wrote, without help of any kind, the first dozen issues of the *Herald*. I altered or rewrote copy from the wire—the Associated Press, UPI, Reuters —removing the bylines in favour of my own. I looked for the oddest, strangest, most far-fetched stories.

I hired, on a moonlighting basis, people from the *Telegram* to do things I couldn't do: design, layout and production. I paid for the off-hours use of a press from the same company that had printed Smallwood's short-lived *Express*. I made up, and passed off as true, stories about the sighting of ghosts and sea monsters, flying saucers, aliens from other planets, Hitler's just-captured son and heir-no-more to the Third Reich, the largest this, the smallest that, the excavation sites of hyper-sophisticated cities that supposedly preceded by ten million years those of Carthage, Athens and Rome, the five-legged boy from Atlanta, the bunker-born twins of Eva Braun who were the talk of Argentina.

I was as surprised as everyone by my tabloid's overnight popularity. Within two years, my *Sunday Herald* had the largest circulation of any publication in Newfoundland. But I see now that the time was right for a publication like it to catch on. The Americans who were lucky enough to be stationed in Newfoundland for some or all of the war had brought America to Newfoundland. And Newfoundlanders saw America as a fabled country where prosperity was commonplace, deprivation unheard of.

When the Americans left, Newfoundlanders were still ravenous for news about America. I fed that appetite. "American" was the word that subscribers, customers and advertisers wanted to hear. What worked in America worked in Newfoundland. All the old-fashioned markets had been cornered for a hundred years or more. It was time for something new. People knew me. I was Ned Vatcher whose parents had vanished. Ned Vatcher who owned the Newfoundland records for the high jump and the mile. Ned Vatcher whose father was second-in-command to Sir Richard Squires.

I made a lot of money very quickly, though I could just as easily have lost everything. I was young enough not to understand the risks, not to play it safe, to work without a net. I'd excelled in the only field I'd so far chosen. Sometimes you're better off not knowing that the odds are stacked against you. I can say that now because I *didn't* fall flat on my face. I could just as easily be the main player in a cautionary tale about the foolhardiness of youth as the man I am today.

The rich of St. John's didn't mind my success even when its permanence seemed certain. I wasn't picking their pockets or anyone else's. I was so new that I had no rivals, no enemies. Some of the families of St. John's whose fortunes were built on traditional industries—fishing, sealing, outport supply, shipbuilding, construction—dismissed me as a flash in the pan. I made no attempts to move in on their territory. There comes a point in money-making at which further risk is either minimal or absent altogether because you already have enough money to fall back on in case of a failure or two. Once you pass that point, however you come to pass it, money seems to multiply itself.

I wasn't a flash in the pan, but I succeeded as much by dumb luck as by hard work. Shoring up my swagger was my obsession with a mystery that, without money, would forever go unsolved.

Soon, I'd expanded Vatcher Enterprises to include a fish-processing plant and three radio stations. Then came Vatcher Foods, a small chain of five supermarkets that, in addition to offering mainland products, specialized in "Newfoundland-style" products—a seemingly endless variety of packaged moose cuts, ready-to-cook rabbits, pre-prepared versions of fish 'n brewis, seal flipper pie, Jiggs' dinner and shipwreck dinner. All of it was not as good as the real thing, but it was, I said, better than forgetting the real thing altogether as so many people who had grown up within a stone's throw of the sea and the land had done.

Then came Vatcher Factories, mass producers of what was known as cram—cheap confectionery goods that were popular among the poor majority of the city's parents who could not afford to fill their children's bellies with anything nutritious. Children loved cram and their parents availed themselves of my unending supply of it: apple flips, raisin squares, marshmallow squares, coconut squares, jam-jams and jelly balls.

I bought a large house that was not in one of the better neighbourhoods, planning to keep it until the house I was having built on the Heights was finished. I didn't want to live among the people who, when my father was down-and-out, did nothing to help him, lent him nothing, gave him nothing, refused to consider him for jobs for which no one in St. John's was better qualified.

※

Walking about with Duggan one day, I asked him what he thought of the coming referendum. He waved his hand dismissively. "I don't think anything about it," he said.

"I'll anonymously give some money to the Independents," I said, "but otherwise I won't get involved. I don't want to lose half my customers."

"That terrible tabloid of yours is doing very well," he said. "People think that whatever appears in print is true, you know. You're scaring some of them half to death."

I laughed, though I knew he wasn't joking. He stopped walking when I did. I looked him in the eye. "No one is ever going to fire me," I said. "I'll never be let go, like my father was."

"If you overextend yourself, you could lose everything," he said.

I smiled. "You're much better at coaching than you are at preaching."

"You don't have to be rich to be your own boss," Duggan said.

I shrugged. "Freedom is what I want, and unless you become a hermit, a dropout, you can't get freedom without money."

3.

I tried to hire the Pinkertons to look into the case of my missing parents, but they said it would be years before they could make time for me. I settled on another New York agency called Bellamy's.

Bellamy and his men arrived in early September '47. He was tall and thin with thick white hair, his complexion like that of someone who'd just come inside from a long deep-winter walk. Like the Pinkertons, Bellamy and his men dressed in black, wore homburg hats and sported gold-and-blue shields on the pockets of their overcoats. All of them stayed at the Bradley Hotel, where they took their meals together and were gaped at by the other guests. They might have been visiting conventioneers.

Fielding wrote in her column: "The Pale Imitations of the Pinkertons, who go by their acronym, the PIMPS, have washed up on our shores."

At Bellamy's request, we drove to Circular Road on a Sunday afternoon. I parked across the street from the house and we got out. It was about the time of day that I had come home to find the place dark and empty. This time, most of it was brightly lit. A couple and their two teenaged children, a boy and a girl, moved about from room to room on the first floor. "It looks almost exactly the same," I said. My voice broke and I pretended to clear my throat. "It's even been repainted the same dark green. The same white trim."

He pointed at the driveway. "So your father turned left and drove down to that next street. And then he turned left again. And—poof!"

I shrugged.

"Well, we've solved stranger cases. I don't think this one will be too tough. Leave it to us. I should warn you that our methods may make us unpopular."

"Do what you have to do," I said.

We agreed that he would update me each evening in the bar at the Bradley. There were no car rental outlets in those days, so I loaned him my Studebaker and paid some of the men who worked for me to let his men use their cars.

Each morning, they fanned out across the city, some in cars, some on foot and bearing clipboards. They kept at it well into the evening. They looked blandly certain that they would quickly solve a mystery that, if not for inept amateurs who had let the trail go cold, would have been solved already. They posted photos of the Brougham, and the most recent one of my parents, dated 1933, on telephone poles, shop windows and fence posts.

I drove around town in my Vauxhall just to catch a glimpse of them at work. Pairs of them stood stolidly on doorsteps, knocking, waiting, knocking again until the doors opened or they gave up and retreated down the steps in tandem, writing on their clipboards.

They retraced the Constabulary search of '36–'37. They dredged every body of fresh water that the Brougham could have been driven to, towed to or pushed to. They pored over the sea cliffs and the shore. They searched caves, abandoned mines and wells. At low tide, they searched the sea caves. They found nothing.

They interviewed those who had worked for Edgar, many of whom had lost their jobs the day he lost his. Some had found positions outside the civil service and some had had to leave the country to find work. A few were able to afford to save face by pretending to retire. "I'm sorry to say that they disliked your father as much as they disliked Sir Richard," Bellamy told me one night at the bar. "They aren't exactly tickled pink about how well you're doing for yourself. But I don't suspect them of anything more than sour grapes."

They conducted an audit of the finances of Sir Richard's government and, like the Commission before them, found no evidence of criminality. They conducted hundreds of interviews throughout the city, spoke to my father's colleagues, to politicians and businessmen he'd dealt with, to his friends and relatives, every last one of the Finns and Vatchers, including Reg, who merely stared at the ceiling when they tried to persuade him to read a list of questions and respond to them in writing. Nan told them not to feel special because Reg Vatcher had ignored them.

Kay phoned me. "They talked to Cyril and me like we were common criminals," she said. "They talked to all of your uncles and aunts. Even your nephews and nieces, and some of them were not even teenagers in 1936. A lot of people are upset, Ned. It's time to call off the dogs or you'll have more enemies than customers."

"My mother should have been there when I got home," I said. "She shouldn't have been in the car. Why was she in the car, Kay?" I realized how childish I sounded.

Her voice softened. "No one *knows* anything, Ned. We'll never know, whatever happened. It's hard, but that's how it is."

Letters of complaint poured in to the *Herald*, other papers and the Constabulary, who relayed them to me. The letters alleged that Bellamy and his men were telling people that, if they refused to be interviewed, they would be arrested, they would be suspects, they would be watched, as would their relatives and friends; that I had imported my own police force because I deemed the locals to be incompetent and to have bungled the original search.

An editorial in the *Telegram* read: "Mr. Vatcher and his goons are acting as if the entire city collaborated in the disappearance of his parents." The paper reported Gestapo tactics, strong-arming, late night knocks on doors.

"Everyone is a suspect, before, during or after the fact," Bellamy said to me when I suggested that he and his men should ease up a bit. "I guarantee you, if there was a double murder in a city the size of this one, someone knows something about it and they'll tell us what they know, but not if we play nice."

Weeks went by, but there were no developments. I saw beat-up, dented, rusting cars crammed with Bellamy's look-alikes, five men staring straight ahead, no longer looking complacent but grimly intent on solving the mystery of the Vatchers. I saw them huddled against the cold and rain in the backs of stake-body trucks.

"No one had a discoverable motive to harm your father, let alone your mother," Bellamy told me at the Bradley. "I'm ruling out a double murder. A murder-suicide seems more likely. It's easier to conceal a crime that you have no intention of surviving."

"It's too soon to rule anything out," I said. "My father may have borrowed from the kind of people who don't work for banks. Not locals, necessarily."

Bellamy shook his head. "Someone would know something. Only someone of means could have orchestrated such a murder. But why would the old money have had anything to do with it? Why would they risk it? What would they have to gain?"

"Revenge, maybe."

"For what?"

"Something personal."

"An affair?"

"Edgar wanted to have an affair with a woman named Sheilagh Fielding."

"How do you know?"

I told him, then assured him that Edgar got nowhere with her.

"But he may have confided in her about—well, who knows what, is that what you mean? Dissatisfaction with his marriage, unhappiness, despair?"

"Do you think she should be interviewed?"

"*You* think so, Mr. Vatcher. Or else you would not have mentioned her."

FIELDING

I headed home after hours of composing my column while walking through the city. The sun was just coming up. I took a shortcut through a park and, because the dew on the grass was still frozen, heard nothing but the crunching of my footsteps. The men came up behind me. One put a hand beneath my left elbow. The other put one on my lower back. Startled, I whirled about with my cane, under which one of them nimbly ducked, not even losing his hat. Two men in black coats bearing gold shields on their pockets. I faced them, both hands atop my cane, which I planted on the ground. "Pistols at dawn?" I said. "It's not in my appointment book."

"It's hard to make an appointment with someone who has no phone, sleeps all day and never goes out until after midnight," the red-faced one said. "I'm Bellamy. This is Fenner."

"So nice to meet you both. I'm cold and hungry and I'm going home."

"We'll drive you there."

I looked around, thinking I might get rid of them by making a scene, but I didn't see a single soul.

"We could get you a drink." He'd taken me to be what he'd been told I was. I felt my colour rise.

"I said I was hungry, not thirsty."

"Don't pretend that I offended you."

"What do you want?"

"To speak with you."

"So speak."

We stood on the field of Bannerman Park beneath the branches of the city's largest trees. We literally fumed at each other, one white puff of breath after another. While Fenner stood off to one side, Bellamy walked in a slow, tight circle around me, forcing me to shuffle about to keep eye contact with him. We were on a slight slope and the ground was uneven.

"You're a newspaper columnist. What do you write about?"

"People who get away with murder."

"Figuratively, maybe. Real murderers, well—I've known many. Irony would not discourage them. I was told you'd put up a better show, Miss Noelle Coward."

Fenner smirked.

"You're wasting my time," I said.

"You were a friend of the Vatchers."

"Yes, I was."

"Ned says his father wanted more from you than friendship."

"Edgar never said so to me."

"Did Megan ever say so?"

"Not to me."

"Your visits to his house stopped abruptly. Why was that?"

"I stopped visiting his house exactly as abruptly as he stopped inviting me."

"Why did he stop?"

"I have no idea."

Bellamy walked in an even tighter circle and stopped when we were face to face.

"For a time, you were a frequent dinner guest of the Vatchers, were you not?"

"I never had dinner with the Vatchers in my life."

"You're lying."

"Ned Vatcher himself will tell you that he witnessed me not having dinner with the Vatchers many times."

"What's that supposed to mean?"

"He'll explain."

"You were often at the Vatcher house?"

"I was."

"Did you often meet Edgar Vatcher elsewhere?"

"Yes, we often met outside a whorehouse. All on the up and up."

"Considering what you wrote about him in your column, why would Edgar Vatcher invite you to his home?"

"I don't know."

"Why did you accept?"

"I was curious. Look, Edgar said he saw me as a mere entertainer. He also said he would rather die laughing than be bored to death. His greatest fear was death by a dearth of mirth. It seemed not to occur to him that the person he was speaking to might feel the same."

Bellamy reached into the pocket of his coat and withdrew a bottle of Five Star rum, which he placed on the ground between us. "Yours if you co-operate."

"I told you—"

"You can take it home and drink it later. So he was bored. With her. With family life. How would you describe their marriage?"

"As having lasted longer than the only other one I've seen up close."

"Did Edgar ever confide in you?"

"Men tend not to see me as a confidante."

"Did you ever engage in inappropriate behaviour with Edgar Vatcher?"

"We bantered, but he wasn't very good at it, so I had to fake my euphemisms."

"You have a foul mouth. Mr. Vatcher is very certain that his father fancied you."

"No, he fancies that his father fancied me. He fancies that *he* fancies me. He fancies that he can make me fancy him."

"I could repeat that to him."

"It won't change his mind about anything."

"He says that you and Edgar were very close."

I put my face within an inch of his.

"What are you doing?" he said.

"I wanted you to know how it feels to be very close to a woman."

"Move away now. I'm warning you."

"Of course, of course, I understand. If I know what's good for you, I'll keep my distance."

"Move *away*."

I smashed the bottle into pieces with my cane. Shards of glass and drops of rum sprayed everywhere. Bellamy shielded his face with his arm. He was not hit but for his shoes and the cuffs of his slacks.

"You could have blinded me," he said, wiping the front of his coat. Fenner stepped between us, grabbed my cane away and tucked it beneath his arm. I almost toppled over. "You'll get it back if you co-operate. Otherwise Fenner will break it in half."

"I know nothing that Ned doesn't know."

"Look, I don't suspect you of anything criminal. I don't think Edgar was murdered, though Megan might have been, by him. But Edgar may have said something to you that, in hindsight, you realized was a threat, one too veiled to pick up on until it was too late. As much as the truth might upset Mr. Vatcher, he'd be better off knowing it."

"You're inviting me to lie."

"I'm inviting you to confirm what most people already think, including Mr. Vatcher, though he won't admit it, even to himself. You could simply say that Edgar confided in you, that you thought he was joking and realized too late that he was serious and felt too guilty or embarrassed to come forward until now. That little lie would cost you nothing, but it would set Mr. Vatcher's mind at rest."

"The truth doesn't matter?"

"The truth, the whole truth and nothing but the truth? There's no such thing. If we could trace cause and effect back to the dawn of time, we wouldn't find the truth."

Without the cane, I tottered and almost fell forward. As if he thought I had lunged at him, he retreated a step.

"A man named Prowse told us that you spend your life lamenting the loss of things you never had. He told us a lot. He was on the audit back in '32. Christ, what a mess. No wonder Edgar Vatcher packed it in. Drove off in a snowstorm with the wife. No sign since of them or their car. I think he shot her, tied her up and stuffed her in the boot. Her reward for driving him around the bend. She was quite far gone herself, they say. Gone further now."

"You spoke to Prowse?"

"You know him?"

"Not well."

"Prowse worked under Edgar Vatcher, more energetically than Edgar's wife did, if you get my drift. Prowse told us you went to New York with a man and came back with TB."

"New York. Another fatally alluring city."

"Strange that Vatcher didn't make a clean sweep of it. They usually do, you know. But Mommy and Daddy left Neddie behind. 'Vatcher is dead/He took his own life/One in the head/And one in the wife.' I made that up."

"A poet *and* a clairvoyant. How gifted you are. You should be rewarded by having a poem as fine as your own composed for you. Something like this perhaps: 'Bellamy comes not to libel the dead/He is a master of metre and rhyme/But should he be found with his head full of lead/Who but an arsehole would think it a crime?' Nothing to say, Bellamy? Fenner, I believe I have pulled the habit out of the rat."

Bellamy spat on the ground in front of me. "You're a drunk and a slut whose words are harmless." He pointed at my cane. "Throw that away," he said to Fenner, who took the cane from beneath his arm and, gripping it near the bottom, reared back and threw it with all his might. It spun end over end, landing unbroken on the ground a hundred feet away.

"Fetch," Fenner said. Bellamy turned and set off the way they had come, Fenner following close behind.

"Why did you sic Bellamy on me?" I asked Ned on the phone that night. We hadn't spoken since he'd come to visit me. "There was *nothing* between Edgar and me. And I haven't been withholding useful information all these years."

"I'm sorry," he stammered. "Bellamy and his men are getting nowhere. I was convinced, when I hired him, that they'd come up with *something*, some lead that would narrow the search, rule some things out, make a start that I could follow up on."

"No stone unturned, no bridge unburned, is that it, Ned?"

"No, no, absolutely not."

"Did you tell them to ply me with booze, Ned?"

"No, I—"

I hung up.

NED

"My parents and their car weren't assumed into Heaven like the Blessed Virgin Mary," I told Bellamy at what turned out to be our last meeting at the Bradley. "Maybe they dropped into a sinkhole or something."

"Sinkholes are very conspicuous. No matter how much it snows, they're still there when the snow is gone."

"What was my mother doing in the car? Why did she leave the house before I got home?"

"You think that's your trump card, don't you? It seems plausible to me that your mother might act abnormally under such circumstances as she found herself in. Impending homelessness. A boy she'd spoiled all his life who was about to find out the hard way what life was really like. A philandering husband. People say she was something of a recluse. Her doctor thinks she might have been suffering from some sort of mental illness that she was able to conceal from you. It seems highly coincidental that your parents just happened to disappear when their money ran out."

"I would like to have interviewed Sir Richard Squires," I said. "Back in '36, the Constabulary spoke to him for five minutes, by phone. He and my father may have had some enemies in common. The kind whose names don't turn up in the record."

Bellamy shook his head. "Sir Richard robbed from the poor and powerless. And even that was never proven in court. *I* would very much like to interview your parents, especially your father."

"Yes. So would I."

"People don't see what's there, Mr. Vatcher. They think they see what isn't there. They forget, misremember, change their minds, contradict themselves, make things up to get attention, tell you what they think you want to hear. Rich, poor, educated, illiterate, there's not much difference. Even the truth is of no use some of the time. But we generally get past all that. Bellamy's has always had *some* degree of success, something to show for what we've done. I can't believe that a case I thought would be so simple is the one that got away."

He let loose a sigh of frustration so loud that heads turned our way. "Christ," he said. "Every morning since you first brought me there, I've driven by the house that you grew up in. It's just a house, that's all. The car that we can't find is just a car. Your parents, you—I've met far stranger people. It seems that, if all the water on this planet dried up, if every ounce of soil was sifted through, many things would come to light, but your father's car would not be one of them. We've failed you, Mr. Vatcher."

"If you were just relying on gut instinct—"

"Sometimes, the best way to find something is to stop looking for it."

"I can't."

"So what will you do next?"

"I wish I knew."

VIII

1. NED

The outcome of the referendum, in July of 1948, was that New-foundland would become a province of Canada and that it would do so "immediately before the expiration of March 31, 1949."

Most Catholics in the city had voted against Canada. As what they called Newfoundland's last day drew near, there was much talk about the Last Newfoundlander, the last child to be born before midnight.

About midday on March 31, Nan Finn called to ask me if I wanted to go along with her, the Vatchers and the Finns, and some others from the Heights and other parts of the city to St. Clare's hospital, where the Last Newfoundlander might be born. "You could put something about it in the *Herald*," she said, "something true for a change."

I agreed to be part of this last token gesture of defiance even as I imagined the letdown if the child was born at a Protestant hospital.

At St. Clare's, the hours leading up to midnight were strange, chaotic ones. On the maternity ward, the doctors and nurses kept watch on their handful of patients, but they also kept watch on the clock. Word spread to those of us cramming the waiting room of a woman, an indigent named Lucy Drover, who had had a difficult pregnancy but seemed likely to have her baby near midnight, hopefully on the right side of it.

The only person in the waiting room who knew Lucy was her twin sister, Ruby, who sat apart from us and ignored anyone who tried to talk to her or offered her a drink from the many flasks and bottles that were making the rounds. Her back was all but turned to the door by which the doctors came and went, her arms folded, lips trembling, an occasional tear running down her cheek.

There were far more men than women gathered. Among the Vatchers and Finns who had turned out in what might have been the same dark, threadbare suits and the same frayed and mended dresses they had worn to Edgar's Boxing Day parties was Ambrose, back from the seminary after having changed his mind about the priesthood. The others, who I knew now referred to me as Mr. Big, kept their distance, eyeing me from time to time but looking away when I noticed. Except for Ruby, every man and woman in the waiting room was drunk or getting there, openly gulping from flasks and glasses and beer bottles, ignoring anyone who told them that no drinking was allowed. I drank bourbon but not enough to keep at bay the longing to be somewhere else.

It seemed to me that the Catholic defeat in the referendum did not augur well for Lucy and the child, whom the doctors said were fighting with each other for the right to live. Lucy was trying to rid herself of the boy for whom, after nine months, she could spare no more, and the boy, nothing but a mass of pure sensation and blind instinct, was fighting to stay in the only place that could sustain him.

As the clock turned toward midnight, word began going round that a woman in one of the Protestant hospitals was soon to give birth. If the doctors and nurses, and Nan and the men and women in the waiting room, could have exhorted the baby from Lucy's body, they would have.

When the boy came out of his mother in the delivery room, he was blue from head to toe, silent, lifeless, devoid of vital signs. After being given last rites by a priest, he was put aside and everyone attended to Lucy, who was said to have been too weak to notice the silence that greeted the boy's departure from her body.

In the waiting room, we looked at Ruby, with whom two nurses were sitting, trying to console her. Nan, after calling him on a pay phone, announced that Cyril, who was minding Reg in the Flag House, was going to pray for the boy and his mother.

The stillborn roused himself seconds later, just after some doctor drew a sheet over his head, his lungs accepting the first oxygen not delivered to him by his mother. At the very instant his mother drew her last breath, the boy drew his first, gasping as though surfacing from some great depth.

Seven minutes before midnight, March 31, 1949. Some said it was the sound of his mother in distress that brought him back, that he hoped the sound of his crying would bring *her* back. He must not have been in Limbo yet, they said, only on his way to it, able to do an about-face and make his way back to the world. Others said it was Nan Finn's quick thinking and Cyril's prayers that saved him.

He was placed in his mother's arms and held there by two sobbing nurses, who knew that Lucy, and the country, were gone. I don't know if his mother knew he had survived, but she died with her arms pressed around him, the tears of the two young nurses dripping onto both of them. That's what people said.

The boy came into the world at the price of his mother's life, dodging, by seven minutes, the infamy of having his birthday forever celebrated on the day the Old Flag fell, April Fool's Day, the day they put the final nail in the coffin of the Cause.

"He will be the Last Newfoundlander all his life," I told myself. I liked the sound of it, *the Last Newfoundlander*.

Ruby was led out of the waiting room by the two nurses, held up by them, her head bowed.

"Father unknown, mother dead, and one aunt without a cent to her name," Nan Finn said. "The Last Newfoundlander will wind up in an orphanage."

I thought of the boy, and of the grieving woman, Ruby, who was the spitting image of his mother. I thought of him as my fellow in abandonment and, on the spot, I decided to adopt him. He was a boy born out of wedlock, a boy whose penniless, orphaned mother died giving birth to him. A boy who came into the world devoid of prospects, as far behind the eight ball as it was possible to be. Who was less likely to be smiled upon by fortune? But what if an unmarried rich man chose him to be his son and heir? The Last Newfoundlander. Who better to be the Last Newfoundlander than a motherless bastard of unknown patrimony who was adopted by an unmarried orphan?

That, many would claim, was the reason I chose him—to seem as magnanimous as possible, to trump up the legend of Ned Vatcher. It was said by others that I adopted the boy I named Brendan because I regarded him as a souvenir of the lost country of Newfoundland, a souvenir I wanted no one else to have, accustomed as I was to seizing what I wanted.

I told no one my intentions that night. I consulted no one about it but Ruby. I knew that if Ruby, his only relative, was amenable, he was mine for the asking, for what government agency or court of law would deny an infant in his circumstances such an opportunity?

I contacted Ruby the next day by phone at the house of a nurse who had offered to put her up until something else could be arranged. I blurted out a proposal.

"You both could live with me," I said. "You could help me raise him. I wouldn't want you to think that I'm trying to take him from you. My house is big enough. If at any point it doesn't seem to be, I'll build onto it or buy a bigger one."

She was silent for a long time and then began to cry.

"There are no—strings attached, or anything like that," I said. "You would have your privacy and independence and I would have mine. It would mean a lot to him, I think, to be raised by his mother's sister. What I mean is, we'd both raise him. I would be his adoptive father. You would be—you are—his aunt. And nothing will change if I get married and have children, not really. Or if you do."

"You sound like a good man," she said, still crying. "I won't pretend that I'm not afraid. I don't know you. But you don't know me either. Lucy would want me to stay with her boy. But I don't think she'd want me to raise him by myself. I want to stay with him too. I had a hysterectomy a few years ago. I'll never have a husband because I can't have children. And I would find it hard living on my own. I never have lived on my own. I don't know what it's like. So, all right, yes. Thank you, yes. But I have nothing, you see, nothing at all. Will Lucy get a proper funeral?"

"She will," I said. "I promise you she will."

"All right, then," Ruby said.

I hung up, poured myself a glass of bourbon and downed it as Duggan had taught me to. Lucy would have a proper funeral. She would have one like my parents should have had. The one that, until now, I hadn't been able to bring myself to give them.

2.

Lucy and Ruby were identical twins, raised at Belvedere, a Catholic orphanage for girls in St. John's, where they were known, Ruby said, as the Drover Sisters, as if they were some sort of performing duet—much like the Vanishing Vatchers.

They were born in Ramea, a settlement on a remote island off Newfoundland's southwest coast. "Our parents died and no one else would take us in," Ruby said. They owed this bare-bones account of their origin to the nuns of Belvedere, who, when the Drover sisters asked for more information, told them they had none. Lucy and Ruby had no memory of their parents or Ramea, or of having come to Belvedere, so they considered themselves to have come *from* Belvedere.

They remained there until they were eighteen. After that, they worked at a succession of menial jobs and shared a single room at a boarding house. Ruby told me what she told newspaper and radio reporters—that her sister had been taken advantage of after having been forced to have too much to drink. Lucy was three months along before she told Ruby that she was pregnant, before she told her that she had been taken advantage of and had no memory of it or of having gone home afterward.

Lucy went out without Ruby because Ruby preferred to stay at home. But, Ruby said, Lucy was a good woman and only went out to spend time with her girlfriends, not in the hope of meeting men. Ruby had never met Lucy's girlfriends and she didn't know their names. Nor did Ruby know where Lucy went when she went out. She was surprised to learn from the reporters that *no one* could name even one of Lucy's girlfriends.

I placed notices in the papers asking those who considered the mother of the Last Newfoundlander to be a friend or even an acquaintance to come forward. No one did.

When Lucy's pregnancy began to show, the two sisters had had to live on Ruby's income because they knew that none of the people whose houses they cleaned would hire an unmarried, pregnant woman. And they couldn't keep Lucy's pregnancy a secret because she had to eat at the same table and use the same bathroom as the other tenants of the boarding house. The owner reluctantly allowed them to stay. They fretted constantly that they would be evicted, but they weren't.

By the time the baby was due, however, the two sisters were a month behind on their room and board and *were* about to be evicted.

Discreetly worded versions of this story appeared in all the papers. Ruby's story went unquestioned by the press. I supposed the papers reckoned it would be foolhardy to paint the mother of the Last Newfoundlander unsympathetically, to mock a story that was quickly becoming a legend that almost everyone wanted to be true. Why depict him as the bastard child of a woman who, through her own fault, didn't even know who his father was? Better, especially as she was deceased and could do or say nothing to tarnish the legend, to depict her as a grievously-sinned-against good woman whose historically notable son had been rescued from a childhood of deprivation by a man who seemed to be the opposite of the scoundrel who offended her and who himself was a child of legend—the mysteriously orphaned Ned Vatcher, who, in spite of his early circumstances, had risen to prominence and wealth.

I had been drifting along, making money in the hope that it would help me find my parents, yet unable to think of any kind of search that hadn't already been tried. At least now I had an immediate purpose—two people whose lives depended on my money and on me.

I'd moved into the new house I'd bought on the Heights. I readied it for Ruby, who was still staying with the nurse, and for Brendan, who was recovering in hospital. As I was clearing out one of the main-floor bedrooms, Cyril "happened" to be passing by when his craving for a drink was at its peak.

"You're a rich fish in a poor pond," Cyril said, looking about the spacious kitchen as if he'd never seen it before.

I didn't reply.

"If she knew Brendan was going to wake up, Lucy might have tried harder," he said. "She might be alive today."

"So my son is to blame for his mother's death. Is that what you're saying?" I demanded.

"Your adopted son," Cyril said, shrugging, as if Brendan's being adopted proved he was to blame.

"Lucy's death isn't anybody's fault no matter how you look at it. It isn't your fault, though Nan Finn called you when both Lucy and Brendan were near death and only one of them lived."

"So it's my fault?" Cyril said.

I said you couldn't blame a newborn for what happened to his mother, and you couldn't credit or blame the Seventh Son of a Seventh Son for his success rate.

Cyril sipped from his Scotch. "It's funny how things turn out, isn't it?" he said. "Belvedere is full of girls and Mount Cashel is full of boys who will never be adopted. But Brendan, well, it looks like he's the latest of the Vatcher golden boys. Life is all about luck, isn't it, Ned?"

"I suppose so."

"One brother goes to Oxford and gets rich. Another one goes nowhere and stays poor. Another one is lost at sea on a calm and sunny day. The first brother drives out into a snowstorm and disappears. There's no sense to it, really, is there? It's all up to God, don't you think?"

"No, I don't. Finish your drink."

"You don't believe in God? I wouldn't blame you after all He's put you through. But you landed on your feet, Ned. It's a credit to you, it really is."

"What do you want, Cyril?"

"I was wondering if you might want to follow in your father's footsteps and give me some spare cash for my household from time to time."

"For your household. If I hear from Kay that she never sees a cent of it, I'll cut you off."

Cyril nodded, his face expressionless.

When he was leaving, I tucked a ten-dollar bill in the pocket of his jacket.

"Much obliged," he said, and pressed his lips tightly together as if to stifle a protest about my meagre contribution.

FIELDING

Lucy. After Lucifer, the light bringer.

Brendan would always stand for something that never was but could have been. Poets and propagandists alike get more mileage on the road not taken than on the mundane one they travel every day.

Perhaps I shouldn't have gone to the wake, but I hadn't intended to cause such a commotion. I felt bad about having spoken so harshly to Ned after my encounter with Bellamy. It was also because of Brendan that I went to the wake, just as it used to be because of Ned that I went to the Vatchers'. And because of Lucy, who, like me, had lost a child.

Though managed by Caul's Funeral Home, the wake was held in the drawing room of Ned's new house, there being too many mourners for Caul's to accommodate. Another immense, unhappy house, though not unhappy because of its immensity.

Everyone turned to face the door when I walked in, craning their necks then looking in puzzlement at each other. Ned began to get up, but Nan Finn pulled him back down into his chair. Ned swatted away her hand and peered out over the sea of heads. He looked angry at first, but then his expression changed to concern. I lost sight of him and soon was face to face with an awful little man from Caul's.

"Please leave," he whispered.

"Is there some sort of not-to-be-admitted list?"

"This is a wake, not a party," he replied. He said something else, something about the way that I was dressed, but I couldn't quite make it out.

"I read the notice in the newspaper," I said coldly. "It said that those who wished to pay their respects could do so. I wish to pay mine. Do you think I go about the city crashing wakes?"

"I have no idea what you do, Madam," the man replied, "but I must insist, on behalf of Mr. Vatcher and Caul's Funeral Home—"

"She's drunk, as usual," a man hidden among the mourners shouted.

"But not *as* drunk as usual," I shouted back. "Some people, when that drunk, insist on making scenes."

"You've been asked to leave," the man from Caul's said. "If you don't, you'll be forcibly removed."

"By you?" I said.

But now a third man shouted, "Oh, for heaven's sake, leave her be." His defence of me was taken up by many others.

The man from Caul's scowled, did an about-face and disappeared among the crowd.

I again caught sight of Ned, who nodded and beckoned me with both hands. I made my way toward him.

"It's Miss Fielding," Ned said with a trace of a smile, along with a faint wince of trepidation. He pushed toward me through the throng, which parted hastily for him. The mourners resumed their conversations, though many glanced my way from time to time. I had probably written about half the people who were in that room. It was hard to think of another occasion that would have brought us all together.

Ned got to me at last and led me to the casket. Neither of us knelt. He must have known that I couldn't, owing to my leg. I glanced at Ruby, who was scrutinizing me, an expression on her face that I couldn't read. Her rosary was wound around her hand like a set of brass knuckles. Her lips barely moved, as if she was praying in a whisper lest she wake up Lucy, who lay beside her in the open casket. She glanced at Ned frequently, and at my arm that was linked with his. I would have looked otherwise if I could. Yellow-grey hair, gathered into a ponytail, hung down my back almost to my waist. My face was ashen and gaunt, my eyes sunken and deeply shadowed. Ruby shook her head slightly, or perhaps it quivered, as if she couldn't credit the look of me. I pretended to look at Lucy but stared only at her clasped hands.

Ned and I moved away from the casket—and suddenly Ned took me in his arms and began to weep in hiccupping sobs. People gasped and stared at the strange spectacle that was taking place beside the casket, and Ruby stood to confront me. "He was doing fine until you showed up," she said through clenched teeth.

Ned pulled away from me and wiped his eyes. "I'm sorry," he said. "That came out of left field, didn't it? You must be mystified."

"I'm not easily mystified."

To my great relief, he smiled.

Cigarette smoke, cologne, some sort of whiskey but not Scotch, which I would have recognized the smell of if he'd last had some a month ago—I detected all of these, and other scents.

"Ruby," he managed, "this is Miss Fielding. She and Edgar used to work together at the *Evening Telegram*, long ago. And Miss Fielding was a friend of my parents and often came to visit us."

Ruby merely scowled.

"I'm sorry about your sister," I said.

"You're only here because of Ned," she said. "There must be two hundred people here, but not a soul that Lucy knew except for me."

"Sit with us," Ned said. "Come, sit with us, please."

"Nan," I said, nodding to her.

"I'd hoped I'd seen the last of you," Nan Finn said, locking eyes with me.

"Many have come to grief on the reef of that hope."

"A strange thing to brag about."

"How's Reg doing?"

"The same. Cyril's minding him. Cyril spends more time at the Flag House than he does at home these days."

I sat among them, wondering how I'd once again wound up at the centre of Ned's life.

NED

I visited Brendan in the hospital many times during the three weeks it took him to recover from the trauma of his birth. Ruby was with me when they let us take him home. We must have looked like first-time parents as I carried Brendan down the hallway, Ruby beside me. As if to give us a send-off that in some small measure might help to sustain us through whatever lay ahead, the doctors and nurses applauded. *Goodbye Brendan, goodbye Mr. Vatcher, goodbye Ruby.*

I never felt such sudden joy as I did when the doors of St. Clare's shut behind us.

Brendan, after Saint Brendan, the monk who, in the fourth century, wrote of having sailed on a mere raft from Ireland to Newfoundland.

After we got him home, Nan Finn, whose house was near mine, came by to see him. She sniffed when I told her I'd hired a live-in nurse to help Ruby take care of the baby. "He looks strong," she whispered as she watched him sleeping in his crib.

We went to the front room and sat down.

"I suppose it wouldn't look right if the Last Newfoundlander went unclaimed. It's easier to take one in than to push one out. I've done both, so I should know," she said.

"I didn't take him in, Nan, I adopted him."

"You took him in," she said. "I took you in, don't forget, and I wasn't rich when I did it. I had Reg to take care of too. Still do. I suppose you have Ruby."

"Ruby can take care of herself."

"I don't know her, but I think a cat would use up its nine lives pretty fast if *she* was looking after it."

"It will be good for her and for Brendan to have each other."

"I don't know who's luckier, her or Brendan. It wouldn't look right if the aunt, the only living relative of the Last Newfound-lander, went unclaimed either, would it?"

"I didn't claim her, Nan," I said. "I didn't win them in a lottery."

"Well, no one's fighting with you over Ruby, that's for sure. There's no telling how a youngster who came from *her* sister might turn out. You'll know soon enough what's underneath the wrapping paper. There's not a drop of blood in him from a Vatcher or a Finn."

"The same is true of a host of non-criminals."

"An unmarried man adopting a dead woman's bastard baby boy whose father might be Santa Claus for all anybody knows. It's not how most people start a family. The closest thing to a mother this boy will ever have is me. Maybe the closest thing to a parent. You won't be walking the floor with him at three in the morning, will you? No, I'll be doing it when I'm twice as old as Ruby. I'd be willing to bet that neither one of you knows how to hold a child. I raised a brood of my own. I raised you when your parents ran off. You're in for some big surprises, nurse or no nurse."

3.

On my radio station, the broadcaster's voice said: "The Last Newfoundlander turned four last night. On this day four years ago, Brendan Vatcher made history just by being born."

By the time he was old enough to understand that his mother was dead and had died giving birth to him, I suppose he felt what, under the circumstances, he could and should have felt. He was four and as credulous as other four-year-olds. He believed that what grown-ups said was true. He believed, because we told him so, that Lucy was in a place that was far better than here, which, in spite of its many flaws, he seemed to think was pretty good. Lucy was with her parents, who died before she did. She had been reunited with them. She was waiting happily for him and Ruby and me. She didn't miss us, because no one missed anyone or otherwise suffered in Heaven. The four of us would be reunited someday. Those who had gone before us were merely far away and it would therefore take us a while to get to where they were.

The belief of the most devout of grown-ups was not as pure as Brendan's. He didn't fret about Hell and Purgatory as Ruby did, nor was he haunted by the idea of Limbo, as I had lately come to be.

I told him about my own parents, as much about them as I could bear to. I told him I thought they weren't in Heaven yet but would go there when they died. I bought back the Vatcher house on Circular Road, paying its owners more than twice what it was worth to get them to move. I pictured everything that was taken from it at the contents sale being moved back into it, everything somehow retrieved from homes and garbage heaps and thin air, everything put exactly where it was on my last night in the house.

NED VATCHER BUYS MISSING PARENTS' HOUSE.

Some such headline ran in all the papers.

My repurchase of the house from which my parents disappeared, my plan to leave it empty, my acquisition of a perfectly restored 1927 Auburn Brougham, just like the one in which my parents drove away on November 23, 1936, never to return, the full-page ad I ran in every issue of the *Herald* offering a reward of ten thousand dollars for information leading to the solving of the Vatcher case, my stable of cars that, in addition to the Brougham, included a Studebaker, a Jaguar and a Ferrari, earned me a reputation for eccentricity.

A political cartoon in the *Telegram* depicted me as Uncle Sam except that my hat was a fisherman's sou'wester. I had become, it seemed, an Americanized Newfoundlander, an entrepreneur whose self-reliance and seemingly effortless knack for making money had their origins in his troubled childhood and subsequent sojourn in America. At the same time as I dismissed such depictions of myself, I couldn't resist encouraging them, enhancing my ersatz reputation as some sort of oddball genius, a school-of-hard-knocks graduate. I appeared in public in a leather bomber jacket, sported cigars like some swaggering tycoon and sang the praises of Kentucky bourbon.

I found another job for Brendan's nurse, Rita, when it became apparent that, between the two of them, Ruby and Nan Finn could manage. Of that management I don't recall much, for I spent my days driving from one part of what Duggan called my empire to another. I'd come home in the evening exhausted, only to be met by Brendan, whose energy level far exceeded mine.

One evening, exhausted, sipping from a glass of bourbon, I watched from the doorway of Brendan's room as Ruby put him to bed. She stroked his cheek and smiled at him, cupped his face in both her hands and kissed him on the forehead. "You're not my little boy, you might not be *my* Brendan," she said. She brushed his hair back from his forehead. "You're sweet is what you are."

"So are you," Brendan said.

After reading him a bedtime story, she sat and talked with him for a while.

"You know that Ruby loves you, don't you?"

He nodded.

"Who loves Ruby?"

"I do. I love Ruby."

"So don't you worry about anything, all right? It'll all come out in the wash. Just like with Ned, who used to be too small to climb up on a chair and now he's taller than his father ever was."

Bedtime rituals were long because Brendan's insomnia was worse than mine, and he was forever coming down with colds, flus, earaches, sore throats.

"I don't know why you can't sleep," Ruby said. "There's no one knows, not even Dr. Vaughan, no more than he knows why you get so sick so often, though he says it's because you were sick when you were born. I tell him that I tell you not to think about it and he says you'll never get better if *someone* doesn't. But don't think about something if you don't like to think about it, is what I say. Think about nice things and maybe you'll go to sleep in no time flat and stay asleep all night, and wouldn't that be something?"

"Lights out," I said.

The two of us went to the kitchen and sat side by side at the table, where Ruby showed me photographs of "Baby Ruby," the name that was scrawled beneath each photo in the handwriting of one of the Belvedere nuns. Baby Ruby in Sister Muriel's arms, wearing a bonnet and a flouncy dress. In later photos, her hair was cropped short and straight—she said that Lucy used to cut her hair and she cut Lucy's. Ruby was Lucy replicated except for the tiniest little dollop of fat beneath her chin.

I dug out my photo albums and showed her a picture of Phonse, who looked like me, not quite as tall or broad but sparely muscular and with the same high forehead and square jaw. He and Edgar stood side by side, in the front yard of the Flag House, not touching, not smiling, but looking reconciled to mild contentment, Phonse unaware that he was eighteen months from the day that he would die, a man who, in spite of his profession, was too young to dwell on anyone's mortality, let alone his own.

There was a picture of Reg and Phonse, the two of them leaning, arms folded, feet crossed, against the back of a truck. Both were smirking as if they'd just shared a joke about the person behind the camera.

"I miss Lucy," Ruby said as she paused over a photograph of her and Lucy sitting on the steps of Belvedere. "It's strange that someone who looked just like me is gone. It's almost like *I'm* gone."

I looked at Ruby, the spitting image of Brendan's mother, who died, it seemed, from an illness of which Brendan was the major symptom and the only cause. I told myself that he should feel no guilt, because he'd never known her, because she existed only in the minds of other people, as did Phonse and the Vatchers, though I always attached the caveat of "unless" when it came to my parents.

Ruby took my hand as if to console me for the loss of my uncle Phonse, which she seemed to think I felt as keenly as she did the loss of Lucy. "Well, there's no sense getting caught up in all that, now, is there?" she said.

"Why don't you get married to Ruby?" Brendan asked me one night at bedtime. I suppressed a laugh, let it loose, suppressed it again, felt, and probably looked, guilty for having laughed, covered my mouth in a vain attempt to disguise a smile. He shook his head, biting his underlip.

"She needs a man more like herself than I am," I said. "Someone— She's not the one for me, is what I mean."

"Ambrose said she can't get a man, so she needs a man who can't get a woman."

"Well, Ambrose should mind how he talks to five-year-olds. Don't listen to what he says. Ruby is a good woman—"

"I know."

"I know you know. I'm just telling you what I think. I don't think she's lonely. She has the two of us."

"If she had youngsters, they'd be living with us."

"Yes, I suppose they would."

"Then she wouldn't be so nice to us."

"That's not true."

I invited Duggan to dinner, and Fielding too, but she declined my offer of a ride and insisted on walking up the hill with Duggan. "If you would let me drive you in my car," I told Duggan, "she wouldn't feel that she had to climb that hill." Duggan said Fielding could do what she liked, but he had no intention of becoming known as the Jesuit who was often chauffeured through the streets of St. John's by a millionaire.

"You'd rather walk conspicuously across town with Sheilagh Fielding?"

"I told her to let you drive her, but she insists on walking with me as if I'm the one with the bad leg, so what more can I do?"

I suspected that to be picked up by me at the Cochrane and driven to my house would remind Fielding too much of the evenings Edgar picked her up and drove her to the house on Circular Road, especially as I would most likely have used the Brougham, the spitting image of Edgar's car—I hadn't used one of the other cars in months.

FIELDING

It was April, sunny but windy and cold. A lot of snow had yet to melt, but none had fallen in weeks. The pavement bore long, snakelike streaks of salt and dust. I wished it was me who was lugging Duggan up the hill and not the other way around. Still, I could tell that he'd much rather climb it with me than by himself, though I was sure he'd go much faster without me.

It was as much his talking as his walking I couldn't keep up with. In either case, he never stopped, no matter how obviously out of breath I was, how unable to ask or answer a question, or otherwise hold up my end. He went on about Ned and Brendan and Ruby and about the missing Vatchers as if they'd gone missing yesterday.

He stopped on the hill just above me. "It's been a while since I last spent time with you," he said. "Too long."

I hoped he couldn't see that I was blushing.

"It's good to see you again, too," I said.

NED

Before dinner, Duggan sized up Brendan. "I think he'll be a sprinter," he said. Fielding looked at me and smiled and I remembered the night on Crocker's Bridge when I'd told her she was "really nice" and thought of kissing her.

"Are you a priest?" Brendan asked Duggan.

"Yes."

"You don't look like Father Clarke. He wears a big black hat. He never walks anywhere. He has a big black car. His house is called the rectory."

"Well, I'm a hatless, pedestrian, rooming-house kind of priest."

"Do you say Mass?"

"Sometimes. Mostly I teach boys how to run and jump."

"I know how to run and jump."

"I'm sure you think you do. Ned used to be able to jump this high." Duggan put his hand a foot above his head. Brendan rolled his eyes. "It's true," Duggan said. "You might do the same some-day. Or better. I might be your coach. A coach is a kind of teacher. I was Ned's coach. Your uncle Ambrose's too. And your grand-father Edgar's. I didn't get much mileage, yardage or footage out of Ambrose. You're the right shape, though I think you'll be more of a runner than a jumper. On the other hand, St. Bon's might decide that I'm too old to be your coach."

When we had a minute alone, Duggan said to me, "You're a long way from where you were the day you left your parents' house."

"I haven't changed all that much," I said.

"I'm not talking about money. You have Brendan and Ruby. That's good. Good for them and good for you."

FIELDING

At dinner, Ruby sat like some conscripted wife and mother, as if she was acquired to complete the family portrait, to make things look just right.

She looked up from her plate and caught my eye. "Ned *said* you wouldn't eat."

"It's a long-standing tradition," Ned said.

Duggan ate voraciously, accepting seconds and thirds of every-thing. It was a heartening sight and I couldn't help but smile. I glanced at Ned, at whose parents' house, I guessed, Duggan had last had his fill.

"Where does it all go, Duggan?" I said.

He playfully pointed his knife at me. "You should eat," he said. "It would make you feel much better. You'd eat more if you drank less."

It stung that he'd admonished me in front of the others.

"It's from being a coach," Ned said to me. "He can't help himself."

Feeling myself turn crimson, I said, "I'm not one of your St. Bon's boys. You should save your Jesuitical advice for the confessional."

Ruby gasped as if I'd mocked God Himself.

The meal continued in silence but for the clinking of knives and forks.

"I'm sorry," Duggan said later, when we were walking down the road. "Food is what makes *me* drunk. There's no telling what I'll say when my belly's full. I hope I didn't—"

"It's forgotten," I said.

He grabbed the upper part of the arm I held my cane with. I almost fell when I pulled free of him.

"Will you *wait* for a second?" he said.

I looked about at the rows of houses that flanked the road. Curtains moved. Some were hastily drawn shut.

"It's one thing for you to play the gentlemanly priest, Duggan, but you can't be seen having a spat with me on the side of the road."

He linked his arm in mine. "Then we'll stroll down the hill together and pretend that we're admiring the view. Make sure you smile while you tell me what a bastard I can be sometimes. Tell me how much half-pint, judgmental, stuffed-to-the-gills priests get on your nerves."

I laughed out loud.

I was well over what the women of the Cochrane thought of as the hill. In part because I couldn't give away what they were selling, even the new women were quite fond and quite protective of me.

My room was not known by its number but as Fielding's Room. I was the oldest institution of the city's oldest institution—the Empress of Skid Row.

I grow old, I grow old. In the rooms the women come and go, talking of Mike and Al and Joe.

4. NED

Brendan loved watching the weather, especially in the winter. He would often stay up all night to watch and listen to a storm. Alone in the enclosed verandah at three or four in the morning, he knelt on the sofa, looking out the large front window, his face and hands pressed to the glass, which in the morning bore the prints of his fingers and his forehead.

I too stayed awake all night when there were snowstorms, lying in bed, half expecting to hear the idling of a Constabulary car outside the house or Duggan downstairs stoking the fire, keeping what he thought to be a pointless vigil for my parents.

Brendan said he liked snowstorms because everything stopped. I knew what he meant. Everything *else* stopped. Worries, memories. Even nightmares, if he stayed awake, which I allowed him to do on weekends. Noises were drowned out by the wind and things were buried by the snow. It was as if the less of the world Brendan could see and hear, the more peaceful and safe he felt. A snowstorm kept *me* at home and visitors away. There were just the three of us, safe inside the storm.

But I hated the sudden ascent of the wind, the sifting sound that new snow made on top of the frozen crust. During storms, I missed Fielding and Duggan, who otherwise came by so often they seemed like members of the family. I extended an open invitation to them, telling them to feel free to drop in without warning, one or both of them. But it was never just one of them.

When I suggested that he become an official weather observer for the Meteorological Service, Brendan agreed. Soon, his most prized possessions were a funnel that caught snow and rain, a thermometer, a barometer, a chronometer, an anemometer, a hydrometer, and some others that I didn't know the names or functions of but which an official from the weather office installed and taught Brendan how to use.

Brendan had to keep a kind of weather journal that would have nothing in it but readings from his instruments and notes based on his observations. When he went out in snowstorms to check his instruments, which were each mounted on pedestal-like platforms in the backyard, he wore a heavy canvas coat with a hood that Ruby pulled so tightly closed I could barely see his face. He looked like a polar explorer.

"Do you know how you can tell that weather is coming?" Fielding said one evening when she and Duggan were over. "The sky is dark and the wind is howling."

"I help Brendan read his instruments and record his observations," Ruby said.

"Yes, she does," I said. "In fact, Ruby goes out by herself when Brendan's sick. She phones the Meteorological Service—"

"They record what we say," Ruby interrupted. "'This is weather station number 134,' we say, and then we read out the figures we wrote down, don't we, Brendan?"

He nodded and smiled at her.

"Ruby knows a lot of weather rhymes," Ned said.

Ruby all but closed her eyes and recited, "A robin means rain/a sparrow means sun/a raven means snow/a starling means none."

"I know one too," Fielding said. "Night follows day/day follows night/night is dark/and day is light."

"That's not about the weather," Ruby said. She threw down her dinner napkin, picked up her plate and carried it out to the kitchen, where she stayed, noisily puttering.

"I'm sorry," Fielding said to me.

One Saturday, when Brendan was confined to his room with an earache, I looked out my office window and saw Ruby measure the level of rain in the funnel perhaps a dozen times, each time jotting her findings in the log. Then she moved on to the anemometer, which she likewise consulted about a dozen times, again writing in the log. Having made the rounds of the instruments, she began again with the rain funnel and consulted it many times over before moving on.

"I think there's something wrong with Ruby," Brendan said, coming into my office in his pyjamas.

I went downstairs, put on my coat and shoes in the foyer and opened the back door. "Ruby," I said.

When she didn't acknowledge me, I hurried down the steps. She continued to consult the instruments, sometimes passing within a few feet of me. I was so taken aback, I only watched her.

After perhaps five minutes of this, I stepped in front of her and she stopped and hung her head like a child who was being chastised, her lips moving though I couldn't hear a word.

"I'm sorry," she said at last. "I do things like this. Usually when I'm by myself, but sometimes in front of other people. I don't know why. Lucy said it was because I was upset. I don't know what she meant. The nuns at Belvedere used to call it Ruby's Condition." She slowly looked up at me, closed the journal and extended it in a gesture of ceremonial surrender. I didn't take the journal, but instead placed my hands on Ruby's shoulders.

"It's all right," I said. "Come inside."

"Did Brendan see me?"

"That doesn't matter."

Ruby nodded over and over as if she were being told something for the umpteenth time, something she knew to be true but couldn't credit.

This happened several times over the weeks that followed, throughout all of which Brendan was more or less bedridden by a succession of earaches.

One night, it was Duggan who brought her inside. I saw them, Duggan and Ruby, out there in the middle of a blizzard late one night, Duggan holding up a lantern that swayed in the wind. Fielding was at the house, reconciled to having to sleep over because of the storm. She and I arrived in the downstairs hall just in time to witness Duggan and Ruby's entrance. Duggan's manner was that of a man returning home matter-of-factly after an absence of hours, though Ruby's face was red and her lips were trembling.

Duggan flashed Fielding a look of appeal, a plea to resist even the most casual allusion to what had taken place. Still, though Fielding nodded slightly at him, I couldn't help but stare at Ruby, who seemed preoccupied to the point of near dotage, her head nodding rapidly, her lips moving almost imperceptibly as they did when she was reading.

"Go up to your room and rest for a while, Ruby," I said as Duggan helped her off with her outer garments, including her wet boots in which, it seemed, Ruby would otherwise have tracked across the floor and up to her room. "Come down and join us later if you feel up to it."

Ruby stopped at the foot of the stairs and looked at Fielding. "You see," she said, her voice quavering, "we also measure, *I* measure, rates of what's called 'evaporation,'" as if this explained why a consultation of the instruments that should have taken five minutes had taken two hours and, if not for Duggan, would not be finished yet.

"Ruby, get some rest," I said. "Go upstairs and lie down. No more consultations for tonight."

"There's always weather, you know," Ruby said, looking to Fielding. "You'll hear people say that on such and such a night there was no weather, but there always is. 'Calm' and 'clear' are descriptions of the weather. A calm and clear night can be as memorable as a stormy one. Especially if something happened on that night. Do you understand? People remember what the weather was like on days and nights when something important happened. I do. Do you see? One night, when it was calm and clear, Lucy came home late. She started crying, but she went to bed when I asked her what was wrong. That was long before Brendan, though. Too long, you know what I mean?"

"Yes," Fielding said. "I think so, Ruby."

"Up to bed now," I said gently, and Ruby turned and slowly climbed the stairs.

Fielding said, "Are these attacks or spells or something? I've never seen anything like it."

Duggan said he had once known a man who suffered from what we all took to calling Ruby's Condition, as if that were its clinical term. "You might want to tell your doctor about her, Ned. Maybe he can find someone to help her."

"I don't think Ruby would—react well if I did that. She'd think it was the first step toward me having her committed."

Duggan shrugged. "There might be some kind of medication for her. That's all I meant."

5.

Cyril began to visit more frequently, pretending, as always, that he'd been out for a walk, had worked up an appetite and wondered if he might trouble me for a bite to eat. I told him he could forgo the pretence of being hungry and simply ask me for a drink, but he insisted that cold cuts like my mother used to make for him would hit the spot. So Ruby did as Megan had done, made up a cold plate that she knew Cyril wouldn't eat.

Ruby had once been deferential to Cyril, believing him to have saved Brendan with his prayers, but it had got to the point that she dreaded his visits as much as Megan had. "I can never wait for him to leave," she said after he was gone. "He's not the kind of man the Seventh Son of a Seventh Son should be, not that I'm an expert or anything. But a nicer man might have saved Brendan *and* Lucy both."

In the kitchen, I took from the cupboard the Scotch I kept there for him, a bottle I always kept one-quarter full, just as my father had done with the bottle of rye he set aside for Cyril.

On a Saturday afternoon when he must have had more luck cadging drinks than usual, he sat side on to the kitchen table, his thin legs crossed, pale shins showing above his socks.

"I'm retiring, Ned," he said. "No more prayers for anyone from me. I prayed for Brendan. He wasn't long out of Lucy. I prayed for Lucy too. It was yes for him and no for her. I don't know why, Ruby. It could have been the other way around. Or yes for him *and* her. Or no for him and her. There it is, you see, the inscrutable ways of God. Maybe what happened had nothing to do with me. I think it's fifty-fifty. Any prayer from *any*one could get you fifty-fifty."

"I'm glad you prayed for me," Brendan told him.

"Are ya? Got any spare cash on ya?"

Brendan shook his head.

"Just kidding, little fella. Well, I've had enough of it. I said a lot of prayers for a lot of people. I said some for myself, but I didn't have much luck, which is not a secret. I prayed to God to fix my back, but . . ." He threw up his hands. "Who knows? I might have helped some people. Nan says I helped Megan when she was having Ned. You'd think I'd get some reward for that, wouldn't you? Inscrutable. That's the word for the ways of the Lord.

"I charged people a fee, you know. I charged people, Brendan, for the prayers I said. Some paid and some didn't. If my prayers worked, most people paid. It's not the kind of thing you should charge for, I suppose. But the Church charges people, doesn't it? The collection plate. And church dues. They read your name out at Sunday Mass until you pay your dues. The priest must read my name out a lot, because I never paid church dues in my life. I haven't been inside a church for a long time. Reading out people's names like that, that's worse than anything I've done, Seventh Son—wise I mean, right? I suppose I'll find out soon enough.

"The Bosco priest has a nice big house and a nice big car. What odds. I've done worse than charge for prayers. A lot worse. If I go to Hell, it won't be for saying prayers for money. I never said no to anyone who asked. I never made anyone pay up front. I drank it all anyway. There wasn't much. Dribs and drabs. No one well off ever asked me for my help. Too bad."

"Did Nan pay you for me?" Brendan asked.

"A dollar, I think. I'm not sure. Two maybe. What was it, Ruby?"

"I don't remember," Ruby said. "Nan got it from Ned. I didn't have any money. I still don't."

"Two dollars. A lot for me. Not much for Ned, though."

"That's how much you asked for," Ruby said.

"Was it? A bargain for you, Ned, isn't it, even if Nan never pays you back? Even though Lucy died. I'm surprised Nan didn't ask me to give her a dollar back, Ned. No, no, just kidding. The customer is always half right. No one else ever asked me for something big like Nan did. She made me kind of nervous. She asked me to pray for Megan to have more babies. I did, but no luck. Too bad for you, Ned. You could have had brothers or sisters to keep you company after Edgar and Megan cut and ran." He looked at Brendan. "Nan Finn thinks God saved you because I asked Him to. She never blamed Him or me for Lucy. All the credit and none of the blame, that's how it works with God. What do you think?"

"I don't know."

"No one knows. Anyway, that's all over now. I'm not praying for anyone anymore."

"Why?" Ruby said.

Cyril shrugged. "So you had no money, Ruby. You landed on your feet, though. Look where you wound up. A house like this. You never know how things will turn out, do you?"

"I suppose not."

"Ruby's a part of the family," I said.

Cyril nodded and took a sip of Scotch. "She's Brendan's aunt."

"That's right."

"Family's important. Phonse and Edgar. Edgar and Megan. Family's important. And they're not forgotten, are they?"

"No, they're not."

"No, they're not. They never will be, will they, Ned? Ruby will never forget Lucy, will you, Ruby?"

"No."

"There it is, you see. Dead and gone, people say, but the dead are not gone. You never know when they might crop up, so to speak, do you, Ned? And not just in your mind."

"What are you getting at, Cyril?"

Cyril was silent for a minute, deliberating, it seemed, about how to answer me, faintly nodding, wagging his chin back and forth.

"They're in your heart as well, is what I meant," he said at last. "Megan and Edgar are in your heart. Phonse is in my heart and Nan's. Reg's, too." He drained his glass. "It's lovely stuff," he said, looking at Brendan, cocking his head and winking.

IX

By Sheilagh Fielding

FIELD DAY

HOW COULD PEOPLE not succeed in a place where no one had survived long enough to set a bad example? Ned Vatcher asked me during our interview. *He* had succeeded. He had shown the way. He said people could do better if they put their minds to it. Look at the Americans, the most resourceful, ambitious, self-reliant people the world has ever known. We have only to model ourselves after them, as he has been doing. They have get-up-and-go. If an American knows there is gold in the ground, he will, if he has to, dig a gold mine with nothing but a garden trowel.

He pointed out that berries ripened and rotted in our wilderness. He assured me that, no matter how remote the berry, an American would find a way to pick it. No American could sleep who knew that a berry that had grown at no cost to anyone was ripening on top of Mount McKinley.

"They'd find a way to get that berry, to make a profit from it."

"One berry?"

"Where we throw up our hands, they get down to business. Nothing motivates them more than being told that something is impossible."

I wondered if the lack of optimism in Newfoundland might be attributable to the centuries its people had spent slaving away in vain to eke out a decent existence in a place where to do so might cause even an American to break a sweat.

He made no reply.

1. NED

TV had all but remade America. It was only a matter of time before someone brought it to Newfoundland, but, as if I was the only Newfoundlander who had ever been altered by his American experience and come back home, no one tried to beat me to the punch.

By 1955, I had the means to act faster than anyone who might have thought of cornering the new, arcane, possibly short-lived, faddish market of TV. In that short time—1946 to 1955—I did my "best" work, but all it really amounted to was copying what had been done elsewhere. I invented nothing, discovered nothing, designed nothing new. All I did was spread the word.

When I started up the television station, it made money right away, for much the same reason that the *Herald* had made money right away. By 1955, St. John's was full of things made in America. Those who could afford it drove American cars. Many wore American clothes, read American magazines and books. But the Americans themselves had gone back to the country they had left just long enough to win the war as a favour to the rest of the floundering free world. My television stations brought back those Americans and many others, brought them right into the houses of Newfoundlanders.

To own a TV set, which almost everyone could afford to do, was like having one of those wartime Americans installed in your living room, waiting to be switched on, and switched off when you'd had enough of him. You could avail yourself of as much bravado, brazenness, fearlessness and unfettered self-reliance as you could stand, and then pull the plug on all of it, leaving your portable American in silence while you went back to your St. John's bed, your St. John's house, your St. John's job, your real, un-American, St. John's life.

Of course, television itself was part of the appeal—the ease and convenience of it, the non-stop stream of it. It was so different from the single movie you paid your money for and took a chance on if you went out.

Trying to erect a network of transmission towers, the men of my contracting company found themselves fifty feet and then some deep in bog that was too loose to support a fence post, and then they hit bedrock in which their diamond drill bits couldn't make the slightest dent. They tried different routes and brought in more advanced and more powerful machines. Everything took longer and cost more than they thought it would, but they ultimately joined all the dots that on the map stood for towns and settlements.

At home, we had a floor-model RCA Victor TV set in the living room, and three Westinghouse blue-panelled plastic portables, one for each bedroom.

"How does it work?" Brendan said, peering through the perforated panel on the back of the Victor.

"I wish I knew," I said, "but even though Ted at the station explained it to me, I still have no idea."

"Watch this," he said, pressing his bare forearm against the screen. There was a crackling sound, and when he slowly pulled his arm away, all the hairs on it were standing up.

"That's static electricity," I said. "That's what it's called, but I don't know what it is."

I took him to the TV station, which was on a street called Buckmaster's Circle, a few hundred feet away from St. Clare's hospital. It looked from the outside like a parish hall or school gymnasium, an impression confirmed inside by nothing but its high ceilings. It was windowless. There was a reception desk, behind which sat a young woman named Janet with brown hair and horn-rimmed glasses. She worked a small switchboard, speaking into the skinny mouthpiece of a set of headphones as she pulled out and inserted plugs of various colours. She flashed a wide smile at Brendan and twinkled the fingers of one hand as she likewise smiled at me.

We were led by my station manager through a winding hallway whose walls rose not far above my head, as if they had been hastily erected until permanent ones could be installed. He put his finger to his lips and tiptoed in what might have been a parody of stealth, which I assumed we were meant to mimic.

I heard the magnified, modulated voice of Don Jamieson; he was the host of my most popular programme, *News Cavalcade*. He looked, spoke and acted like a kind of avuncular vampire, his black hair slicked back so that it resembled a skullcap. His voice was flawless, mellifluous, unaccented. It flowed without the hint of a stumble or hesitation, pausing at exactly the right moment, for exactly the right amount of time. He and the small desk he sat behind and the clock on the floor-to-ceiling curtain behind him were the only things in the cavernous studio that were brightly lit. Only when he finished did less bright lights on the ceiling come on, as the banks of overhead lights went off with an eerie thud. Three tripod-mounted cameras that looked like anti-aircraft guns were pointed at him, the floor around them strewn with a mass of cables.

Out of a forest of TV set–like monitors emerged cigarette-smoking men all dressed in sweaters and sporting large head-phones. They wandered onto what I told Brendan was called "the set." They came from other sets not then being used, but lying empty in the darkness beyond the perimeter of this one.

"The picture on the TV in our living room back home comes from here," I said as I led Brendan onto the set, holding his hand.

Don Jamieson came toward us, hand out to me. "Hello, Ned," he said.

"Don, this is Brendan."

"Well, well now." His voice was as smooth and soothing as when he read the news. "If it isn't Brendan, the Last Newfoundlander, come to visit."

Others gathered round to meet Brendan, photographs of whom they had often seen in the *Herald*. When they left the studio, I waved around us at the set.

"I'm going to be on television," I said. "What do you think of that?"

He smiled and nodded his head.

Perhaps the most popular of all the non-news shows was the Friday night late movie known simply as the Monster Movie, for all the films centred on monsters of some sort—giant, Godzilla-like, world-menacing, inscrutably indestructible mutants.

Celluloid copies of these movies were sent in metal wheel cases to St. John's by plane from the mainland just in time to be broadcast, and then sent on to somewhere else, the discs continuously circulating. I had to pay a premium for these movies, as they were as likely to be stranded in St. John's because of bad weather as they were, because of bad weather, never to arrive in the first place. Fog, high winds, heavy rain, heavy and blowing snow, freezing rain—almost any combination of these closed the airport about once a week.

If they knew the Monster Movie had been cancelled, some viewers would not wait up watching shows they didn't like in the expectation that the Monster Movie would follow, so I didn't announce the cancellation until the last minute, when a printed message appeared on the screen: *Due to the non-arrival of tonight's Monster Movie at the airport because of severe weather conditions, VTV brings you an encore presentation.* The encore presentation was usually one of the few movies I owned a copy of, or else a stock TV show, a rerun of a TV show so often rerun the picture was all but obscured by snowlike static. The one person left to man the station would be bombarded by calls of complaint.

So I came up with the idea of filling the cancelled spot with a show that was at first called *Ned Vatcher Presents*—*my* show, produced and directed and written by me, starring no one but me. In truth, *Ned Vatcher Presents* was not produced, directed or written by anyone. It was a largely improvised two-hour segment of live TV in which I spoke to a single camera about whatever happened to be on my mind.

On the first episode, I announced that I was raising to twenty-five thousand dollars the reward that would go to anyone who could help answer the question of what happened to my parents. Tips poured in, none of them of any use, many proving, upon investigation by the police, to be fabrications. "Twenty-five thousand dollars is a lot of money," a detective told me in a chastising tone. "Enough to tempt honest people into wasting our time, never mind the ones who *never* tell the truth or the ones who aren't right in the head."

Because the makeup team had long since gone home, I used only what makeup I knew how to apply. The overhead bank of lights sometimes reflected off my forehead, my cheekbones and nose. There was a single cameraman, a single sound technician, a single light man, no introductory music, no fanfare and no fuss. There were no opening or closing credits except, in both cases, for the plainly written, modest-sized letters of the show's name, *Ned Vatcher Presents*, or, in the instance of an episode being repeated, *Ned Vatcher Presents an Encore Presentation of Ned Vatcher Presents*.

Ruby swore I hoped for bad weather so that I could fill in for the Monster Movie. Critics and viewers wrote letters to newspapers claiming that I was in violation of my broadcasting licence, to which I replied on the air, on my radio stations, in the *Herald* and in the other papers that the only licence I needed was the licence to freedom of speech, which is granted in the free world to every-one at birth. As for the audience, I said they were likewise free to turn off their television sets when they didn't like what was on the screen.

The longer I spoke in each segment, the more desultory became what Fielding called my "state of the universe address." I roamed wildly from one subject to the next, rambling from my youth as the son of a Rhodes Scholar to my days of running track at Boston College, where I was taught and coached by Jesuits. There were only two subjects I kept coming back to: my missing parents and what I called the American Way.

"I learned a lot during my sojourn in America. I learned the value of self-reliance. I lost my nerve when my parents died, but I got it back when I lived in New York. It's your fear of taking risks that's holding you back . . ."

Vatcher the Bachelor, I came to be called in columns in the local papers, though not in Fielding's. The most celebrated celibate in Newfoundland. Word spread of the eccentric Newfoundland tycoon, the orphan who had fashioned a fortune for himself from television, whose potential he had foreseen when others mocked it as a passing fad. The America-made free enterpriser whose countrymen thought him too brash, too flamboyant, too full of himself.

I was supposedly an individualist, a maverick, a renegade, a guru/practitioner of self-sufficient prosperity, an evangelist of capitalism. But I was merely someone who encouraged everyone to be the same. That's how I made money. I created a demand for something and then, for a price, satisfied that demand. I made money from my TV channel through advertising. My TV channel created a demand for television sets. My TV store satisfied that demand. I created a demand for Vatcher Foods by advertising Vatcher Foods on my television channel. Vatcher Foods satisfied the demand for Vatcher Foods, which wouldn't have existed if not for VTV. Round and round it went.

The trick was to avoid all middlemen and to make a want seem like a need. No one needed TV. But as soon as someone had what they didn't need, other people wanted it. How could you talk to people about what was on TV if you didn't have a television set? What was on TV didn't matter as long as I got enough people to watch it to make other people want to watch it. I published my TV guide in the *Herald*, which I also owned and which people were paying for and reading long before they had TV.

People from far away wrote to me, asking to meet me, asking me to grant them an audience, saying they admired me because of what I "stood for," which they never bothered to spell out. I declined them all. I granted only phone interviews, but, foreseeing the day when I would expand my empire to the mainland, I sent tapes of *Ned Vatcher Presents* to mainland radio and TV stations and newspapers and magazines, along with a portrait photograph of myself wearing my bomber jacket and sporting a cigar.

My fondness for bourbon increased, my need for it awakening in my blood as I neared the age which Edgar had been when he and Megan disappeared. I now drank bourbon as openly, unashamedly, matter-of-factly and near-constantly as heavy drinkers of tea drank tea, or heavy smokers smoked cigarettes. The way others were forever sipping tea or puffing on a cigarette, I was forever sipping bourbon. There were more snifters lying at the ready around the house than there were ashtrays. Every morning, Ruby cleaned and redistributed throughout the rooms the ones I had used the day before. Snifters sat on end tables, lamp tables, coffee tables, the kitchen counter, the kitchen table, the dining room table, the desk in my office.

I refilled them from what might have been a single self-replenishing bottle in my study. I never carried a bottle around the house or left one out where others could see it. Sometimes, Brendan glimpsed me topping up a snifter in my study as he happened to be passing by. He smiled at me and waved and I grinned as if he'd caught me in the midst of some harmless indulgence.

I sometimes sipped bourbon while I ate my breakfast, then walked to my car with a snifter in my hand. I kept a snifter and a fifth in the glove compartment of each of my cars.

I also sipped bourbon at work. It was one of the affectations of the eccentric Ned Vatcher, possibly one of the keys to his success, something exotic he had discovered while travelling in other countries where, for all they knew, it was customary for the rich to drink bourbon all day long.

I didn't slur, didn't stumble or stagger the least little bit. My mood never changed and my appetite for food went undiminished. "It greases my wheels," I said. "It's my measure of grog."

And for those times when, even for Ned Vatcher, drinking was prohibited, such as when I was in church, or walking about the city streets, I carried what amounted to a vial of bourbon with me, one that, entirely enclosed within my fist, I could sip from while pretending to stifle a yawn.

In the same way that others remembered the smell of their father's cologne or aftershave, I remembered the smell of Scotch on my father's breath in the year before he vanished.

2.

Unable to resist the fear that everything I had might somehow be taken away, I used TV to build upon it. How much did you have to be worth before you were invulnerable? History was filled with chastening examples of fortunes squandered, mismanaged, swindled away, of tycoons turned into chumps by those who thought that bringing people down was an entertaining game whose rules were known to all who played it. The economic depression that had brought my father and my country down had also brought down men far richer than me, men who, in mere days, lost everything and flung themselves from windows, preferring death to a return to the average lives they had clawed their way out of.

I advertised Vatcher Foods on VTV. I was "interviewed" by anchormen who worked for me, men who recited to me the questions I had written or approved. For these interviews, I dressed much as one would for a day in the woods, sporting a hunting/fishing vest, a watch cap, dungarees and rubber boots, colourful fishing lures, home-tied trout-and-salmon flies that hung off me everywhere—all of it brand new, never worn on the water or in the woods. I supposed I looked, to the undiscerning eye, like a man who was mainly an outdoorsman who occasionally stopped by his successful stores to make sure that things were as shipshape as he had led his customers to expect they would be.

I spouted what I assured Duggan was nonsense aimed at townies whose predecessors would have seen through me, tips about how the cod or trout were running or the likely availability of winter vegetables, or what kind of seal harvest there would be or how far from St. John's one would have to go in the fall to trap a rabbit, shoot a moose or see a whale. I convincingly portrayed an outdoorsman who just happened to have a flair for business, a free-market Daniel Boone, a hands-on entrepreneur of the water and the woods, a modest man whose calling, as he saw it, was to keep the old ways alive even in the city of St. John's, which, as he never failed to point out, was as modern, as urbanized, as removed from the wild as any city of North America—removed from the wild despite its close proximity to it, which made me all the more determined that the old ways not die out.

This was my TV persona, Ned Vatcher of the Woods, frontiersman-cum-businessman, hunter/fisherman-cum-capitalist, a man astride the past and present, the precious, indispensable traditions and the new, ground-breaking, future-shaping innovations.

"Butter wouldn't melt in your mouth," said Fielding, who often chastised me in her column.

THE BRAND NAME of the food division of Vatcher Enterprises is Verity Factories.

"We thought about *Purity*," Mr. Vatcher said, "but *Verity* has the Vatcher *V*."

"You think people know what *verity* means?"

"It sounds sincere. Verity, sincerity. You wouldn't drink something called 'Marginal Milk,' would you?"

I admitted that I wouldn't.

"Would you buy Fat Chance insurance?"

"I have no money and nothing insurable except my life."

I wondered about a slogan for the wild game sections of his supermarkets. I proposed one: "Moose from Verity Foods—shot, bled, gutted and dismembered with the utmost care and patience. And remember, if you find a hood ornament among the gizzards, your moose is on us."

"My Verity Variety packs in which, with their pennies, children get nut-balls, gum-balls, rum-balls, butter-balls, nut-gum, nut-knobs, nut-beans, rum-nuts and butter-barrels are doing very well, as are my biscuits, cookies, crackers, pastries and doughnuts. All very filling and vitamin-free."

"Hence the re-affordability of food."

"Precisely."

3.

On *Ned Vatcher Presents,* I took to wearing my leather bomber jacket, puffed on my cigar and squinted through the smoke at the camera. I sat in front of green curtains that on black-and-white TV looked grey. At times I abruptly excused myself, pushing my chair back from a desk that bore nothing but a glass ashtray and a coffee cup, standing and leaving the shot to make a trip to the bathroom or to refill the cup with bourbon, throughout which the broadcasting of the show continued. For minutes, viewers saw nothing but a stationary shot of an empty desk, sometimes the mug, sometimes the empty ashtray, sometimes a genie of smoke rising from the tip of my abandoned cigar.

Despite the initial complaints, the show gained a following, people who watched and listened because they didn't want to go to bed yet, regarding me, their letters seemed to indicate, with a mixture of scorn and fascination.

I talked about my athletic career, veered into speculation about my parents' fate, read aloud one of the columns Fielding had written about me as I did my best to seem amused. I often overshot the two hours, and went on speaking to the camera long past the conclusion of the broadcasting day, when the TV sets of viewers showed nothing but the test pattern with its Indian chief's profile against the propeller-like background. For a while, the cameramen were afraid not to indulge me, but eventually found the courage to tell me I was no longer on the air.

On those rare occasions when I watched a rerun of my show alone at home, I went round to the back of the set and looked inside, peering through the little grid of holes in the wooden panel in sheer Brendan-like bewilderment, sheer wonder that some version of me could be created in there. It seemed almost possible that, on the other side of that loudspeaker-shaped picture tube, an image of me exact in every way except for size was moving about.

I looked at the red light and wondered what it was for; and there was the smell of the dust that was warming on the tubes, and a faint hum from within when I put my ear against the side of the set. The wood of the cabinet was warm against my cheek. I knelt down at the front of the set and, putting my face so close that the hairs on my cheek stood up, I tried to look sideways through the glass to see how thick my image was, to see what it consisted of, only to have the whole thing dissolve into a mass of teeming dots as though I had light itself beneath a microscope. TV was a mystery.

Ruby, with Brendan sitting wide awake beside her on the sofa, almost always watched my show, in part to keep herself awake so that she could make me something to eat when I got home, which I sometimes didn't do for hours after the credits had rolled, preferring to first unwind in a bar among patrons astonished to see me in the flesh, in which case she went to bed and Brendan stayed up to greet me when I arrived.

I was often drunk but, I hoped, never really showing it, drunk because, when that red light on top of that camera came on and I stared into that dark lens as though into a telescope aimed at the void that prevailed before Creation, I always thought of my parents.

"Sometimes you're drunk, Ned," Ruby said. "I can tell and I can't stand it when you're drunk. Drunk on TV. You think you're fooling people by sipping bourbon from that coffee cup. The only one you're fooling is yourself. You never asked for my opinion, but you can have it anyway."

"I can't do the show sober," I said. "I can't talk for two hours straight unless I loosen up a bit."

"In that case, you must be always loosened up."

"Ruby, I'm as sober as I need to be when I have to be. In college I won races with bourbon oozing out of every pore. No one cared, not even the Jesuits, as long as I came first. Some of the boys used to call me Knob Creek Ned. They said I burnt bourbon like a car burns gasoline. I was popular. Ned Vatcher's Crowd, they called my friends—boys and girls. There were always lots of girls, Ruby." None of it was true.

"That's enough, Ned," Ruby said. "That you drink in front of Brendan is bad enough. You don't have to talk like that in front of him."

"The way I drink is better than sneaking a nip on the sly, like poor Reg has to do when his congregation takes him out for a drive around the bay. You're not Nan Finn, Ruby."

"I know who and what I am, Ned Vatcher. Not everyone can say the same."

You want to see a version of Brendan as strangely altered as the one of you. You want him to sit behind that desk at the station and be the locus, the focal point of everything, the camera and the man who aims it at him, the man who holds the boom, the lights, the various machines that no one ever adjusts, as if, though they work, no one knows how, the snaking strands of cable, the vaulting ceiling—you want Brendan at the centre of it with you.

When you ask him if he would like to join you, he instantly agrees.

You go through the motions of inviting Ruby to come too.

"There's enough said about me already in this city because of my Condition. What would happen if I turned up on TV and did the kind of thing I'm famous for?"

You tell her that her fame is all in her head, that no one is talking about her, but she merely folds her arms and looks away from you.

Brendan joins you at the desk, staring blankly at the camera as you speak to it. He wears his Bosco school uniform, the closest thing to a suit he owns. He is just a boy and not as strong as other boys his age. You can't come back from the other side without losing something.

He reads from a script you wrote. He introduces himself and apologizes for the cancellation of the Monster Movie. "Some of you may know me as the Last Newfoundlander. And I'd like to say that, if not for my mother's sacrifice of her life, I would not be here with you tonight."

"Well, Lucy was a great lady, as you say. She might be sitting at this desk with us if she was still alive. But there you go."

"Yes, there you go."

It occurs to you that this is by far the longest conversation about Lucy the two of you have ever had.

Holding a smoking cigar, you sip from your coffee mug, which contains bourbon. You ask Brendan questions and he answers them as you told him to.

"Where do you go to school, Brendan?"

"I go to St. John Bosco, Ned. It's a nice school and I like it a lot."

"I could have gone to Bosco too. It wasn't modern like it is now, so my father, Edgar Vatcher, sent me to St. Bon's." You turn away from Brendan to face the camera again.

Edgar and Megan, you fancy, are among the people out there, watching from some other world that cannot be accessed or even seen from yours.

If there is anyone who knows what happened to your parents, they too might be watching, listening. They might feel that you are looking at no one but them, that you are speaking and appealing to no one but them. They can see you, but you cannot see them. It's one thing to read a plea for help, another to look into the eyes of the person pleading with you.

You say you know that it was not because of an accident that your parents disappeared. An accident cannot erase itself.

"Write a letter. Make a phone call. You don't have to give your name. Tell me where the car is and that will be the end of it. There'll be no investigation." You drink deeply from the cup and set it down.

What did your father say or do to make your mother leave the house and drive away with him as if such an outing were part of their routine?

Why are you offering money to strangers as if to people more expert than you on your parents' private lives? *You* should know the answers. There must have been signs. How could you not have seen them? When your mother held you and looked at you the way she did that last morning, you didn't ask her what was wrong because you knew that everything was wrong. But off you went to school as if nothing was amiss, as if your parents, just for you, would find a way to fix the world by three o'clock.

You look into the dark lens of the camera that slowly moves toward you, a reverse telescope that allows others to examine you more closely than they have ever examined themselves. Drops of sweat trickle down your forehead, your neck, your back. You wonder if you might be sick, if the man behind the camera has noticed your distress.

The camera zooms in until there is nothing on the monitor but your head and shoulders. Without a word of explanation, you get up and leave the set, coffee cup in hand. You don't want Brendan or the crew to witness the spectacle of Ned Vatcher weeping for his parents. You try to say "Cut," but nothing comes out.

Standing in the darkness behind the flimsy walls of the set which you know will fall over if you lean on them, you knock back the last of the bourbon to stave off the tears and refill the cup from the bottle in your pocket. You peer out at the set. The red light atop the camera is still on and the camera is pointed at Brendan, whose image on the monitor transfixes you.

Brendan stares at the camera then looks down at the desk for over a minute, bites his lower lip, as you have often seen him do, to keep from crying. Trying to seem perfectly calm, to look, perhaps, as if he has momentarily forgotten that you were due to take a break, he too stands up and saunters out of the picture and off the set, turning right where you went left.

You can make out nothing off set but the red light above the nearest exit door. You know that, between you and wherever Brendan is, the floor is strewn with cables, sawhorses, stools, an assortment of breakable props and pieces of equipment. You stand just behind the back wall of the set, out of range of the cameraman who, for all you know, thinks that you and Brendan rehearsed this and doesn't dare stop rolling because the show is running live.

You look at the eerily empty, silent set, smoke coiling up from your cigar in the ashtray. People will want to know why you abandoned Brendan. Ruby will. You left him there, by himself, on the air, unable to meet the gaze of the camera, hands beneath the desk, shoulders slumped, eyes downcast lest the audience see them darting from side to side.

You go out and sit behind the desk, look around in mock bewilderment and shout his name. "Brendan? Brendan?"

He casually makes his way back onto the set, though his face is flushed and you can see that he's been crying. He sits beside you and you pose him a question as if neither of you has moved since the last word that was spoken.

"Who are you named after, Brendan?"

"Well, Ned, my namesake is Saint Brendan, the Irish monk who rafted the Atlantic, and made landfall in Newfoundland more than a thousand years ago."

He gets out of his seat as soon as you are off the air. The lights come up and you catch him as he runs for the exit, putting one hand on his shoulder. He turns around. He bites his lower lip again. You pull his head against your stomach.

"I'm sorry," you say. "I shouldn't have done that."

"Why did you?"

"I don't know. I thought it would be a joke, one that you'd find funny too."

He throws his arms around your waist and begins to cry. You run your fingers through his hair. He looks up at you, eyes leaking tears. "The boys at school say that Lucy died because of me."

"She didn't," you say.

You tell him he was not conceived or born of his volition. He'd had no more to do with his mother's death than he'd had to do with his own birth.

But you know there is nothing in the world easier to come down with than a dose of guilt. As if Brendan senses this, he asks, "Why did Edgar and Megan go away?"

You tell him you don't know.

"Because of you?" he says.

He is getting back at you for leaving him alone on live TV.

"What do you mean?"

He shrugs. "They didn't take you with them." It is almost an accusation, a demand that you explain yourself. *Why didn't they take you with them?*

"No, they didn't. They didn't really go away. Maybe they didn't. Some people think they had an accident in the car."

"The car is gone," he says, as if this proves that *they* are gone.

You don't want to tell him that most people think Edgar was

to blame and thus have to explain what, in this case, blame amounts to. You don't want him to know that you sometimes think it was because he didn't want to be your father anymore that Edgar went away.

You leave the studio, drive to Circular Road and park in a place from which you can see the house below.

"I grew up there," you say.

Brendan nods. "With Edgar and Megan," he says.

"That's right."

"Why did you buy the house back if you didn't want to live in it?"

You purse your lips and shrug. "I don't want someone else to own it. It feels as if it still belongs to them. I was going to leave it empty, but I have to rent it out or else the windows will get broken and the house will go to ruin. Maybe *you'll* live in it someday."

"You wouldn't want me if you still had your parents, would you?" he says. "I wouldn't be with you and Ruby. I'd be at the orphanage, not on TV."

"No, no," you say. "You'd be with us. There'd be five of us, counting Ruby."

Ruby was furious with me, but I had won Brendan over with renewed apologies by the time we got home, and this disarmed her somewhat.

From then on, we taped the show on Saturday afternoons. Brendan was my sidekick, my straight man, my jumping-off point, my sounding board, my preteen co-host, part of my audience, my partner in propaganda, my ingenuous, legitimizing premise. He was also "my son of whom I could not be more proud," words

I spoke only on *Vatcher Variety*, as the new show was called, and only to the camera and the audience at home, which on some nights may have been composed of little more than him and me and Ruby, and often only me, for he nodded off to the sound of his own voice sometimes after Ruby went to bed.

FIELDING

I didn't buy a TV set. I declined Ned's offer of a free one. The women of the Cochrane chipped in on one and I sometimes joined them, standing in the doorway when they gathered to watch it in one of the rooms on the lower floor.

The shows that depicted life as being the least like life in Newfoundland were the most popular. The women of the Cochrane couldn't get enough of those that seemed to be set on some nebulous planet that was divided into cattle ranches populated by gun-toting, white horse–riding families who had come by their ranches honestly but were forever having to fend off the depredations of gun-toting, horse-riding marauders who, though deservedly ranchless, were nonetheless ranch-covetous, and therefore equally as deserving of being shot and falling to the ground from black horses at full gallop, sometimes getting a foot caught in a stirrup and being dragged away through a haze of dust and a rolling volley of doom-portending tumbleweed, still covetous of the ranch that was receding from them.

Each house I passed on my walks in the night looked as if a lightning storm were taking place inside it. The blue light flared up, died down, flared up. The same silent storm took place in all the houses at the same time. When the light flared up, I saw the shadow-shapes of families and couples and solitary keepers of the television vigil. It seemed that an explosion should follow upon each upsurge of light, that the houses should blow up from within. In some houses, when it was very late, the blue light no longer came and went but stayed like some ever-glowing remnant of the storm.

It was past midnight. The sound of voices was being broadcast out into the street. The sound of a radio station, I thought, until I saw, in the window of Vatcher's TV and Appliances, a large television set, on the screen of which, sitting behind what might have been a teacher's desk, were Ned and Brendan.

It was the closest I had ever been to the screen of a television set. At Ned's house, there was a tacit rule that no one watched TV in my presence. "TV?" they must have thought. "She hasn't even got a radio." But now, on display in the window of Ned's store, was this enormous TV set on four short and sharply angled legs. Two panes of glass away from me in that otherworldly-looking place were Ned and Brendan talking to each other in the weirdly stilted way of people on the radio, an earnest, formal, confiding yet artificial way, as if they had never met before.

The store was closed, dark but for the television with its eerily blue screen, the street quiet but for the voices of Ned and Brendan. No one else on the sidewalk—and there were only a few—stopped to look, or even seemed to hear the voices. The effect of it all on me was doubly jarring when I heard the Ned facsimile say, "Fielding," and the Brendan one respond: "Yes she is, Ned." I felt as if I was discovering that word of my existence had crossed over into some dreamlike black-and-white dimension.

"She's very tall, Ned," Brendan said. "I believe she's six feet two inches tall, which is taller than most men. She also has a bad leg from when she had tuberculosis many years ago."

I stood there, wondering what else would come out of his mouth—a recounting, perhaps, of my most recent visit to their house. I would not have been surprised to see Ruby appear and start setting the desk as if it were a dinner table.

Ned turned away from Brendan and looked at the camera, which moved in until his face almost filled the screen, and began to talk about me. He described my appearance in greater detail, related the widely known facts of my life, the widely held misconceptions about me and about my writing. He spoke as if to an audience who had never heard of me, as if he were the host of a documentary about a little-known woman who ought to have been famous, who was no longer alive and whose accomplishments, if not soon celebrated, would be forgotten.

Still, I fancied that he was speaking directly to me.

"What did most young women from the so-called better families of St. John's do after World War One?"

"They got married, Ned. They had children."

"But what did Sheilagh Fielding do?"

"She went to New York."

"Yes, she did. And just like that, she became a writer for the *New York Times*. Joe Smallwood, who is now the premier of Newfoundland, was there. Others her age were there from all over, pretending to be socialists. By the time she got back to Newfoundland, she had TB and she almost died. They say that if TB gets into your bones, you're done for. But Sheilagh Fielding wasn't done for . . ."

Yes, I thought, she went to New York. And what would you think of me, Ned Vatcher, if you knew why I went?

"She was and is a woman ahead of her time."

Yes, I became a woman far ahead of my time.

But what would Ned have thought if he knew that I was once in love with not just one man but two, first Prowse and then Smallwood, if he knew that I had twins by Prowse when I was just a girl and was proposed to in New York by the other, whose proposal I would have accepted if it hadn't come too late? Prowse. And Smallwood who, had he known of my illegitimate children, would never have proposed. There could be no skeletons in the closet for a would-be, if low-born, politician whose peers already had him pegged as the man most likely to sink without a ripple into the sea of failure.

Prowse now had the job that Edgar Vatcher used to have. Smallwood was Prowse's puppeteer.

X

NED

I decided to throw a birthday party for Brendan when he was nine. Enough time had passed, it seemed to me, to justify celebrating the double-edged anniversary. The party would begin on the evening of March 31 and end early in the morning of April Fool's Day. It would commemorate Lucy's life, not the day of her death, mark the ninth anniversary of Ruby Drover's inclusion in our family and, of course, Brendan's birthday.

In the printed invitations, I stipulated that presents were unnecessary and suggested that guests contribute something to Belvedere

Orphanage in Brendan's name. As it turned out, he received one present each from Ruby and me, but also one from everyone who came to the party—Nan Finn, every one of my relatives and my many "flunkies," as Ambrose called the senior employees of Vatcher Enterprises, local luminaries, politicians, businessmen, anyone of local personality or celebrity status.

I was now minority owner of the *Telegram*, whose main rival was Smallwood's mouthpiece, the *Daily News*. Smallwood accepted my invitation but sent in his place someone whose plan, I suspected, was to arrive early, stay long enough to explain Smallwood's absence to me, wish Brendan a happy birthday, give him his present and leave before April Fool's Day. Prowse, in other words, the man who had been the other guest the night I first met Fielding, the man who was now in my father's old job.

FIELDING

"Dear Miss Fielding," Ned wrote. "Please do me the honour of joining me in celebrating the birthday of my adopted son, Brendan, the Last Newfoundlander. I will come and pick you up, or send a car for you, whichever you'd prefer. I've asked Father Duggan as well and he's accepted, though he has declined my offer of a ride. The party will begin at nine p.m., March 31, and it will end in the early morning of April Fool's Day, with a toast to Lucy, Brendan and Ruby."

I told myself I wouldn't go to the party, I wouldn't and shouldn't. Prowse would be there, as Ned would keep up appearances by inviting Smallwood. It was one thing to discreetly be a friend of the family. It was another to be in Ned's company when, surrounded by people who would rather read me than meet me, he'd be drinking even more than usual and I'd be drinking as I always did. I decided to answer the question of whether or not to go by simply not replying to his invitation.

Minutes before the party, I decided to go, then realized that I needed a present for Brendan and that all the stores were closed.

Inasmuch as there were enough things in it to do so, I ransacked my room. My single shelf of books included two copies of Judge Prowse's *History of Newfoundland*, one autographed by the Judge and inscribed to my father, the other a recent gift to me from my editor, Herder, on the occasion of *my* birthday, which Herder had guessed would otherwise have passed unobserved. As with Ned's invitation, Herder's gift had arrived by mail, accompanied by a typically laconic note that read, "Happy Birthday. Herder."

I decided I would pass on Herder's gift to Ned's son. I tried out an inscription: "To Brendan, on the occasion of your ninth birthday, March 31, 1958. Happy Birthday, love Sheilagh Fielding." Love—was that appropriate? Presumptuous? I changed my mind, and decided I would leave love out of it, even where Brendan was concerned.

I set out from the Cochrane for the Heights. The wind was blowing a gale, but the rain, which had all day gone slantwise past my window, had stopped. I tucked the massive book under my arm, knowing that I would have to drop it on the wet and muddy street if I slipped and needed to free my hand to keep from hitting the ground.

On Crocker's Bridge, I looked up and saw that Ned's house was strung with variously coloured lights and all the rooms were brightly lit but for the largest one, whose floor-to-ceiling windows overlooked the harbour. I was nevertheless able to make out the shapes of a large mass of people. I thought of turning back.

I rang the doorbell before I noticed the piece of paper plastered to the door that read: *Welcome. Please come in.* Putting my cane under the arm opposite the one in which the book was tucked, I tried to get a purchase on the door handle. After several attempts, I was able to grip it and depress the latch. It was a heavy door, and I thrust my shoulder hard against it at the very moment that someone inside pulled it open.

I lurched sideways into the vestibule, the inner French doors of which were open, or else my entrance would have been even more dramatic than it was. Still sideways, I stumbled into the kitchen, which, though many times the size of my room at the Cochrane, was so packed with guests that I sent some of them flying into the arms and backs of others, all the while managing to keep Judge Prowse's *History* tucked beneath one arm, and my cane, a treacherous hazard at such close quarters, beneath the other.

Just as I began to fall, I felt a hand on each of my shoulders, Ned's hands, as he was the one who had opened the door. And only then did I drop the book in order to put both hands on the knob of my cane and firmly right myself.

Guests whose drinks I'd overturned denounced my clumsiness, more good-naturedly than otherwise, until they realized who I was. "Jesus Christ, if it isn't Fielding of the *Telegram*," a short white-haired man said. "The woman who once crashed a wake to get an interview with Ned."

"I wish I could reciprocate," I said, "but I have no idea who you are."

"Well, well," a neckerchief-sporting young man said, "look who it is. Your hair, Madam, looks like a briar bush."

"No need to compliment me," I said. "The wind deserves most of the credit. Which of the elements should we congratulate for how you look?"

Ned, tuxedo-clad, intervened, Judge Prowse's *History* in his hands. "Miss Fielding, are you all right?"

"I'm fine, thank you, Mr. Vatcher," I said, mimicking his formality, resisting the urge to raise my hand to my hair to see just how much like a briar bush it felt.

"I'm so glad to see you," Ned said. "You didn't answer my invitation, so I assumed you weren't coming."

"I wasn't sure until tonight that I could make it."

"But you're here, and that's what's important," he said, thumping the spine of Judge Prowse's *History* with one hand.

"It's a present for Brendan," I said, nodding at the book. "I didn't think to wrap it." He gaped at the book as if he hadn't noticed until now that it *was* a book. "It's more talked-about than read," I said, "but perhaps when Brendan is older . . ."

"Oh no," Ned said, "he'll appreciate it now, and he'll read it when he can. Though I confess I've never been able to finish it. Tough slogging." He stared at the cover of the book. "Still, it's a wonderful, thoughtful gift. I have every edition of it ever published."

"Oh, I—"

"No, no, I didn't mean— I've started to collect Newfoundland books, just like my father did. Books about Newfoundland, or ones that merely mention it, and everything in between. I'm trying to restore his collection. I'm storing the books in the attic. When I've built a house for Nan and Reg and they move out of the Flag House, I'll move the books there. There are too many stairs in the Flag House for them to stay there much longer. Most of the books are godawful. But I have, to my knowledge, the largest collection of them in the world. I'll show it to you someday, if you would like to see it."

I felt uncomfortable as I remembered the pass Edgar had made at me among the stacks of *his* collection.

"I've never seen the largest collection of anything in the world," I said, "possibly excepting snow and"—I peeked into the next room—"well-wrapped birthday presents."

Ned laughed. "Well, come into the main room," he said, linking his arm in mine as he had at Lucy's wake.

Thus accompanied, I made my second entrance of the evening, this time into the dimly lit room I had spied from the bridge. I realized the lights were down so that the guests could see the harbour and the city—Ned Vatcher's harbour, Ned Vatcher's city, such was the panoramic view of them afforded by the windows. Heads turned in our direction.

"Well, look what Ned dragged in," said a man who bore the unmistakable features of the Vatchers, his face as angular as Ned's, though he was not as slender.

"Shut up, Ambrose," Ned said as offhandedly as one might shoo away a cat.

I looked out the window that faced the hill and the Flag House, which was dark but for the creases of light that shone through the shutters of Reg's window in the attic. I imagined him peering down the hill at Ned's house ablaze with light that brightened half the Heights.

I saw again the massive, neatly stacked barricade of birthday presents I had glimpsed from the kitchen, opposite the wall along which a table held scores of wine and liquor bottles, as well as what seemed like an acre of untouched food.

"Duggan sent his last-minute regrets," Ned said. "Or else there'd be a good dent in that food."

"Oh, he's not coming?" I said, disappointed.

"He thought *you* weren't coming," Ned said, which made me feel better. "The boys are tending bar. My boy, everyone's boy. I wouldn't be surprised if some of them are drunk."

He motioned to someone in the crowd, and Ruby, wearing a ruby-coloured dress and bearing a drink in either hand, presented herself. She looked even less pleased to see me than usual.

"You know Miss Fielding," Ned said, as if I had met Ruby only once or twice. He was drunker than I'd thought.

"Good evening, Miss Vatcher," I said, playfully mocking Ned's formality, the words no sooner out of my mouth than I remembered that she was not a Vatcher.

"I'm still a Drover," she said, "not that being left on the shelf is anything to be ashamed of." *She* was tipsy.

"It was a slip of the tongue for which I apologize," I said, trying to smile. "I too am on the shelf. I have more than once been taken down, only to be put back up."

Ruby looked askance at Ned, who merely smiled and put his hand on her shoulder. "Could you find Brendan and bring him to greet Miss Fielding?" Ned said. Ruby looked grateful to have a reason to leave us, which she did without a word.

As I scanned the crowd, waiting for her to reappear with Brendan, it occurred to me—not for the first time—what a catch Ned Vatcher would be for most of the single women of St. John's, or the mainland, for that matter, or even the States, where he was known to go on business trips. I doubted that his having a child would discourage most women who were looking. For all I knew, the room was full of women who were eyeing him, or who had already begun some sort of campaign to win him over.

I stood in silence beside Ned, who finally spoke.

"I have five uncles and two aunts, Miss Fielding," Ned said. "How many do you have?"

"I had a few. I have a half-sister. She lives in New York. We often write to each other. She always says you have to read a letter out loud to really understand it. I had a half-brother too. David. After he died in the war, I got into the habit of talking to him, even though he wasn't there."

"That's like praying," Ned said.

"Yes, I suppose it is."

I stood there, my heart hammering, wondering why I'd felt compelled to speak of Sarah and David.

Ruby returned, holding Brendan by the hand.

"Miss Fielding has a present for you, Brendan," Ned said, handing Judge Prowse's *History* back to me. "It's a very important present, because you'll have it forever."

"It will take him that long to read it," Ruby said, but Ned held up his hand and she fell quiet.

"You'll have it forever and you'll read it when you're older," he said.

I was at a loss as to how to present him with a book that both Ned and Ruby had all but dismissed as unreadable. Brendan looked at it with a face as downcast as I had ever seen and intoned a perfunctory thank you as he took the book from me, holding it on both of his out-held hands as if he was presenting it back to me.

Ned took it from him. Brendan looked up at me as if he was going to say something, but then looked at the floor.

"Sorry," Ned said, as if Brendan couldn't hear him, "he's received over a hundred presents tonight. He's a little overwhelmed."

A boy who Ned told me was Ambrose's son, Clar, came to gawk at me. "How come *you're* here?" he said.

"Ned and I are friends."

"You're some tall. How tall are you? What happened to your leg? Ambrose says that you have a special shoe to even out your legs. Did you have polio? I had a needle so I wouldn't get it. They didn't have needles before me, but now they do."

"He gets over his shyness very quickly," Ned said, "but he should work more on his manners."

I did my best to stay in step with Ned as we made our way among the crowd—a sea of tuxedos and evening gowns. Even the children were formally dressed. The boys, most of whom had that straight-from-the-barbershop look, wore suits or school uniforms, and the girls wore party dresses or school blazers and skirts. "A typical come-as-you-are party," I said. "It's nice to blend in for once."

Ned laughed.

We next encountered the man with the neckerchief. Seeing me on Ned's arm, he looked abashed and nervous. I winked at him. He pointed at me. "You're not much of a host, Ned. She should have a drink, unless she's reached her limit. The size of her, I'm surprised she has a limit."

"I don't," I said.

"I'm sure she's had her fill of you," Ned said. "I know I have." The fellow slunk away into the crowd.

"A few years ago," I said, "I realized that, except for death, I have no limit, so I tried to stop drinking. I started again, I stopped again. And so on and so on in its petty pace." I reached into the pocket of my cape and withdrew my silver flask. "Water, tonight," I lied, "but tomorrow night, who knows?"

"But would you like a drink?"

"I'm sure I *would* like one," I said. "I would like it all too much."

"Drinking may have done you less harm than you think."

"It is indescribably difficult to stop and all too easy to start again."

"I wouldn't put myself through that if I wasn't sure I had to," Ned said. "Do you disapprove of drinking now?"

"No, but even if I was inclined to join the temperance society and they were inclined to have me, it would be too soon. When I'm not drinking, I dream about drinking."

"I couldn't deny myself something I enjoy so much."

A tall man in a tuxedo, sporting a cummerbund, approached us. He wore silver-framed eyeglasses as he, whom I now recognized as Prowse, had not done when I saw him last, which was not at the Vatchers' house but in my room. I'd summoned him when David died, telling him that if he didn't come, the whole world would soon know of his illegitimate children. It was the first time he'd heard of David and Sarah, who he denied were his. He left without offering condolences. Now here he was again, as tall and blond and blandly handsome as when I fell in love with him at Bishop Feild.

The father of my twins, attending a birthday party for the city's most famous child. The inevitable Prowse, who I'd known would be there, yet the rush of blood to my head was such that I almost fainted. I swayed, planting my cane at an angle to the floor, praying that it didn't slip and I didn't fall in a heap in front of him.

"Good evening, Mr. Vatcher," Prowse said.

"Mr. Prowse," Ned said.

"Premier Smallwood sends his birthday wishes to your son. I put his present with the others."

"Tell Mr. Smallwood I said thanks."

"I will. He would have come himself if not for a prior commitment."

Ned nodded.

Prowse raised his glass and said: "Here's to your boy, the Last Newfoundlander."

Ned paused, raised his snifter and they both sipped from their drinks.

"How *is* young Brendan?" Prowse said. "He gave some people, me included, quite a scare when he was born. Barely pulled through, didn't he?"

"He's doing very well, thank you," Ned said. "Though he's not as robust, yet, as other boys his age."

Prowse. He knew that the son that no one knew he'd had by me had died in the war, and that David's twin sister was living in New York with children of her own, my grandchildren, mine and his. Yet he pretended, in front of me, to have been given quite a scare by the near death of the child of a woman he had never met. I pictured myself smashing his champagne glass with my cane.

"I believe you know Miss Fielding," Ned said.

"Miss Fielding." Prowse nodded to me, betraying not a hint of surprise at the sight of me linked arm in arm with Ned Vatcher, nor the least hint of concern that I might tell Ned or others about our children.

"As you know, Prowse and I have known each other since we were at school," I said.

Neither of the men said a word.

"We were quite a threesome in our day, weren't we, Prowse— you and I and Smallwood?"

"We were acquaintances," Prowse said.

"And who'd have thought that you would wind up working for Himself?"

"I quite enjoy my position," Prowse said. "I can't think of a man I would rather be second-in-command to than Premier Smallwood. Did you know that he has broken bread with Roosevelt?"

"And coughed himself blue in the face while sharing a cigar with Churchill," I said. "I have also heard that he corresponds with Castro."

"That is an unaccountably widespread misconception," Prowse countered.

"Smallwood used to be a socialist," Ned said. "No wonder Newfoundland is barely scraping by."

"We do not run our government as you do your business enterprises. We are not, as the saying goes, in it for the money."

"Well, I *am*," Ned said. "Money that bought the champagne you're drinking."

"Premier Smallwood drinks nothing but the finest wines."

"Not only that," I said, "but he costs the taxpayers nothing because he turns water *into* wine, and serves nothing but loaves and fishes that he multiplies whenever guests come over."

"Will we be reading that in the paper tomorrow?" Prowse said. "That's the kind of thing you pass off as journalism."

"It's actually a kind of irony," I said, "but one ironizes at one's peril in this country."

"Newfoundland or Canada?" Prowse said.

"I've never been to Canada," I said.

"You're in Canada right now, Fielding. Mr. Vatcher's house stands on Canadian soil, whether either of you like it or not. So, regrettably, does the Cochrane Street Hotel."

"This house," Ned said, "was bought with Newfoundland money. The ground this house was built on was here long before it had a name."

"Things change, Mr. Vatcher. You have to change with them."

"Said Hitler as his tanks rolled into Poland."

"Now, now," Prowse said, "you can't compare Premier Smallwood to Hitler."

"Then let's compare him to a summer's day," I said. "I think he is more lovely and more temperate."

"What?" Prowse said.

"Shakespeare," I replied. "He wrote many sonnets heralding the birth of Smallwood, whose eternal summer shall not fade."

Prowse, who looked flustered now, managed to say, "Mr. Vatcher, I have no argument with you."

"If you have one with Miss Fielding, you have one with me." Ned took a step closer to him. "I remember you from the night you came to dinner when I was just a child. You insulted Miss Fielding repeatedly. Just now you called her Fielding."

"I sometimes call her Fielding, as does almost everyone else. She said herself that we went to school together. She calls me Prowse."

"Do you call Smallwood 'Smallwood'?" Ned said.

"Certainly not. I call him Premier."

"Behind his back you call him Premier?"

"I do not speak of him behind his back."

"You go to parties for him. You convey his regrets for him. You promise people you'll relay their thanks to him. You deliver children's birthday presents for him. You do what he couldn't be bothered doing and you call yourself his second-in-command. My father didn't deliver birthday presents."

"The things your father did for Sir Richard may never come to light."

"You're a petty man, aren't you? Miss Fielding knows you better than you know yourself."

"Miss Fielding," Prowse said, his voice rising at last, "is someone about whom you know nothing, but I assure you that there are many men in this city who know *her* very well."

Ned smashed his brandy glass to pieces on the floor. All conversation stopped. I tried separating Ned and Prowse with my cane, pressing the cane against Ned's chest, but he grabbed it from my hand and threw it to the floor as well. He raised his fist to hit Prowse just as, pulled off balance, I fell between them. There were gasps and various exclamations of fright, astonishment and even amusement among the guests.

"Ned hit Fielding," I heard a man who was unmistakably Ambrose shout. "Knocked her out cold with one punch." His words were picked up by the others, as murmurs and stage whispers made their way around the room. Ned's fishermen uncles and cousins arrived en masse from some other room.

"Jesus, Ned," one said, "what did you hit her for?"

"I didn't," Ned said, bending to help me up. He took me under the armpits and managed to lift me partway, at which point Ruby joined him, supporting one of my elbows. Others pitched in, and I was soon on my feet.

Prowse had made a getaway while I was lying on the floor.

"I'm so sorry," Ned said, handing me back my cane. He turned around. I put my hand on his shoulder, but he shook it off. "Edgar," he muttered, then seemed to make an effort to stifle what else he'd thought of saying.

As if in pointless pursuit of the vanished Prowse, he headed toward the kitchen with an air of bravado that was so obviously affected that some men far enough away to do so without betraying their identity to him burst out laughing. "Little Neddie," I heard someone say.

I wanted to get out of there as fast as I could, but Ned soon returned from the kitchen and insisted that I stay. I had no idea why he'd said his father's name, but I didn't have the heart to leave him with Edgar so much on his mind.

Ned told one of his store managers to gather all the guests into the front room. Soon, the drab-looking Vatchers and Finns, all grinning, looking half mischievous, half sheepish, filed in through the doorways, forming a separate faction—they might have been the members of the opposition in some teeming parliament.

Everyone's eyes followed Ned and Brendan as, awkwardly holding hands, they walked to the window that overlooked the city whose gleaming lights reflected in the harbour. Ned stood Brendan in front of him and placed his hands on his shoulders. They remained like that throughout Ned's speech, as if Ned was putting Brendan forward as living proof of the truth of every word he said.

"This little guy is the Last Newfoundlander. He's the reason we're all here tonight. I think we should drink a toast to him on his birthday and to the country that he represents, and to his late mother, Lucy, and his aunt, Ruby. But first, I would like to say a few words.

"My father, Edgar, tried to teach me things about this place. He taught me a lot before my mother, Megan, interfered. I'm not blaming her. She didn't want me to become so attached to Newfoundland that it would break my heart to leave it. She had a dream, a pipe dream it turned out, that all three of us would go home to London. It's been almost twenty-two years since my parents disappeared. Vanished. Just like that." He snapped his fingers.

I saw Ambrose and Cyril elbow their way to the front of the crowd, both of them holding large glasses of what I guessed was rum and Coke.

"In my worst hours, the future looks very dark to me."

"You have everything a man could want," Cyril called out, but was shushed by those around him.

The whole room was silent. No one so much as sipped from a drink.

"Someone hand me my bourbon," Ned said. A man in an ill-fitting tuxedo hurried to him with a snifter. Ned let go of his son's shoulders to take it and stood beside Brendan. "Here's to our country. Here's to Lucy and Ruby Drover. Here's to my son, Brendan Vatcher, the Last Newfoundlander. To BRENDAN."

"To Brendan," everyone said, tossing back their drinks as both Ned and Brendan stared at the floor.

I, Ned, Brendan—each of us was an only child, though Ned lived in a world that teemed with aunts and uncles and first cousins. Five uncles, two aunts, and their spouses, and all of them had broods, as Nan Finn called them, fistfuls of children who were soon swarming about Brendan as he unwrapped his presents, in awe of a boy whose mother was dead beyond remembrance, the one whom the grown-ups called the Last Newfoundlander and who appeared on TV and had had his picture in the paper.

Even the grown-ups seemed awed by Brendan as they watched him rip the wrapping paper into pieces. There he was, the Last Newfoundlander who came out of his mother dead but then woke up the second *she* died as if her soul went into him because Cyril prayed to God to let him live, awed by the boy whom Ned and Ruby dressed to the nines and bought every toy he asked for, spending on him more money and time than some Vatcher parents spent on seven or eight children—a boy exempt from most childhood tribulations by the circumstances of his infancy, but also a strange-seeming, delicate, sickly boy who had no memory of the undiscovered country, though he had been there and returned from it, the tiny traveller who, because he had been where all of us would go one day, had surely come back trailing clouds of glory, glory by which he would forever be infused and which was but one more reason to believe that his future would lead to something great.

NED

I tried and failed with the toast to salvage something from the ashes of the evening. I threw a haymaker at Prowse just like the one Penny had thrown at Edgar at Black Point years before, an artless, clumsy swing whose only effect was to upend Fielding.

Though none appeared in the papers or on rival radio news shows, various versions of the incident were soon rampant throughout

St. John's: I had hit Fielding; Prowse had hit Fielding; Fielding had attempted to hit Prowse; Prowse had hit me; I had tried to hit Prowse who, in self-defence, had dropped me with one punch.

I thought of Edgar playing Sir Richard's mascot, the primitive serf-cum-learned gentleman. I thought of how outraged he had been by the pointless, frivolous slaughter of the seabirds. He had been required by his job, by the need to support Megan and me, to entertain just such men as I had no need of whatsoever, men I had nevertheless invited to my house to show it and the Last Newfoundlander off to them—the house, I wanted them to think, that I had built with no money but what I made through sheer smarts and force of will from the investment of my meagre trust fund, and the Last Newfoundlander, who would have been an orphan if not for me, obscure, uncelebrated, unwanted.

Edgar would have known the whole event to be a farce, a grand exercise in vanity, but would have had to attend it. But I had not been cornered into it by circumstances beyond my control. The birthday party had been my idea. I had made a drunken fool of myself, just as Penny had done.

Fielding. She might have been hurt, might have broken her already wounded leg, or might have broken the other so badly that she could no longer walk at all. As the party was winding down, I tried again to apologize, but she cut me off.

"It was Prowse's fault," she said, "his fault and mine. We have a history that, if and when I'm ready to, I'll let you in on. You were celebrating your son's birthday just as I, if I had a son, would do."

"I didn't have to celebrate it like *that*," I said. "We could have had a small party. Duggan would have come to a small party, but he had more sense than to come to one this size. Brendan would have appreciated a few small presents from people he knows more than he does the pile of presents thrust upon him tonight by strangers."

She looked at Brendan, who was sitting dazed among a wreck-age of wrapping paper and an absurd abundance of presents that he would likely ignore after tonight and that would one day be dispersed among his cousins.

FIELDING

After the disastrous birthday party for Brendan, I went back to New York, as I had told Ned I one day would.

Manhattan again. My third approach through the narrows of New York. The grey facade of the monumental city, the looming ramparts of America daring me to try to scale them one more time.

My father would have said that I had been lured back by the Sirens of Paris. He would have said that I was soon to come to grief on the reef of hope.

The Sirens of Plymouth Rock was more like it, as if it was America that had lured my mother away from him, as if the great might and magnet of America was his rival in love, not the man my mother left him for.

At Sarah's house, I saw that I could do no more than create an awk-ward scene, or worse, if I were to insist on the truth.

I was glad to see them, her and her husband, so united by their happiness. I was, in a way, relieved that they had more sense than to allow me to upset their lives. For what good would it have done Sarah to know I was her mother, her children to know I was their grandmother, her husband to know I was his mother-in-law? Though Sarah did know I was her mother. I saw it in her eyes. I saw too that she would never acknowledge it and didn't want to know my story in detail.

Long ago, you gave me up, as you did David. Keep your reasons to your-self. Lives you know nothing about have ended and begun since you left New York in 1924. I have no idea why you're here. Go home.

My grandchildren weren't there. I would have liked to meet them, or see them at least.

Sarah was taller than her husband, though not as tall as me. She had eyes like David's, blue, unlike mine, which are green. She was robust, curvaceous, big-bosomed and wide-hipped—a woman that the girl I was might have grown to be had I not fallen ill. She had eyes full of comedy and fight—ferocious fight. She would have protected her loved ones from me if she'd had to. "Just try me," they seemed to say even as she told me how glad she was to see her much-spoken-of half-sister at long last.

I saw Prowse in those eyes. I saw myself and David, and my parents. Her house was not far from the one in which, for six strange months, my body was a home for hers, had sustained and nourished hers in a locked and soundproofed room. She grew side by side with David, my body swelling as theirs were fed by the very blood that, after they were born, was wiped away to let them breathe.

I wished I could have crushed her with a hug, pressed her head against my shoulder, let loose long-stifled sobs into her hair. My baby girl. My child. My daughter grown to womanhood and motherhood. My Sarah, bereft of her brother, her twin, my David and hers who died in the war. My daughter, but thought to be my mother's, passed off as my mother's to preserve a host of reputations.

Had I been drinking—but I was sober, and I left her house that way, self-composed at a cost beyond reckoning. I left her there, my daughter, without having touched her and knowing that I never would, no more than I would touch David again, or touch my grandchildren, whose Nan they thought had gone to Heaven.

Minutes later, not far away in some forgettable hotel, I found the bottle of Scotch that I'd brought with me on the ship. I put it on the bedside table knowing that if, in the night to come, I woke, it would be there, a treacherous, obliterating antidote.

I didn't wake. I slept as deeply as if my soul dimmed down to a single spark. And then came the yellow sunrise and, by some upwards-tending impetus of what remained of me, I opened my eyes and saw, still full, unopened on the table, the bottle I would not have been surprised to find was empty.

XI

1. NED

I began to make forays into the city at night to see who was watching my television station; there were no other stations yet. I went out alone on random nights of the week at random times, cruised slowly through the streets in the car that anyone who saw it would have recognized as mine, for it was the only Ferrari in St. John's, the only car in the city of that gleaming, glowing, dying-ember tone of red.

I cruised across Crocker's Bridge and was soon on Water Street, from which I turned left and zoomed with a loud roar up a hill so

steep that all I saw through the windshield was the night sky lit
with stars.

People liked to turn out all their lights to watch TV. Most of the
city was dark but for the occasional flaring-up of blue light within
the houses, the windows all going blue at the same time, dying
down to dark at the same time, and then flaring up again. I sipped
bourbon from my brandy snifter and smoked cigarettes or puffed
on a cigar as I surveyed the houses, looking at the windows for that
telltale blue flicker of the television screen.

Sometimes I'd go home after an hour, sometimes after two or
three, and tell Brendan and Ruby that almost all of St. John's was
occupied in the same pastime. "They're all watching the same
thing at the same time," I said. "It's as if the same book, written
by me, is being read aloud in every home in St. John's on television
sets that they bought from me."

"Those people watching TV," Ruby said, "aren't you worried
they might recognize that car of yours?"

"So what if they do?"

"It seems odd," Ruby said, "prowling around, spying on people
like that."

"I don't spy on them," I said. "I just drive slowly past their
houses."

"You'll get a reputation if you're caught doing that," Ruby said.

But I said it was fine with me if I got a reputation because you
could not be exceptional without being thought of as odd by ordinary people.

"Peeping Toms are exceptional," Ruby said, and I laughed. "You
could use one of your other cars," she said. The Studebaker, she
meant, because it would be less conspicuous, as there were others

in the city. "I think you want people to know that you're out there watching them watch you on TV."

Cruising the streets one night, I noted how slowly the rain was dripping from the wires, a sure sign that it was almost freezing.

"The air is colder here than where the rain fell from. It's warm up there and cold down here." Edgar once said that to me. Soon, everything would be en-iced. All those wires would be ropes of ice. They'd get heavier and sag down to the ground. Every branch of the trees without leaves would look as if they were coated in glass, chandeliers hanging upside down.

Perhaps because I was thinking about Edgar, perhaps because I'd drunk quite a bit of bourbon and was still drinking, I didn't notice that, although I hadn't touched the brake, the car was gliding down the hill, the tires no longer turning because there was no traction, none at all.

The front of the Ferrari revolved slowly toward the left, edging counter-clockwise until it was smoothly, silently moving sideways down the hill. I feared it would tip over, but the front continued to turn until I was sliding backwards, facing the headlights of the car that had been behind me as if I were driving in reverse, as if this were my customary way of going downhill.

I was blinded by his headlights, as the other driver must have been by mine. He blew his horn repeatedly, though what he imagined I could do I had no idea. I wondered if, while gliding, I had crossed over into the other lane, the one occupied by cars trying to go *up* the hill.

The car swung further counter-clockwise until it was again

gliding sideways. It passed in this fashion straight through a four-way intersection and brought up with a sudden jolt against the curb. The bourbon in my glass sloshed out onto my jacket and slacks and doused my cigar. Someone rapped on the window, which I rolled down.

"Are you—" the man started, then stopped and walked away in silence, shoulders hunched, his hands in his pants pockets. I thought that, though he must have recognized my car, he had, when we were face to face, thought better of berating Ned Vatcher, even after seeing me with glass in hand, my slacks stained at the crotch as if I'd wet myself.

The other car was gone. Irate enough to rap on the window of my car and admonish me, the pedestrian had stopped in mid-sentence when he saw my face. I fancied it was the measure of how the very sight of me unnerved him. But then I realized he'd recognized the car and tapped on the window to see if I was all right, to see if I was hurt, and had been embarrassed for me when he saw me sitting there doused in bourbon, drunk behind the wheel of a car that could have killed him or someone else.

2.

In each of my supermarkets, there was a glass office raised about six feet off the floor from which my managers could keep watch on my employees and customers. Whenever I visited a store, the manager left the office to me. One day, one of the store managers rang me to say that a man who said his name was Mr. Lewis wanted to see me. "He said he doesn't have a complaint."

I turned to face the front of the store and saw a man coming my way whose head was absolutely bare and bald but for a pair of glasses.

He wore a beige raglan buttoned to the neck, grey slacks and brown corduroy slippers. He scuffed toward my office as if his feet were shackled, carrying a brown paper shopping bag with paper handles. My manager helped him up the stairs while I held the door.

"Remember me?" he said when he reached the top.

"I'm sorry, I don't."

He removed his glasses. "Remember these?" Small round ones with thick black rims.

"The guns," I said. "You took care of the guns for Sir Richard that day at Black Point. You're Lewis—Mr. Lewis."

He nodded. His complexion was sallow and there was a wattle beneath his chin. "After Sir Richard lost his seat in the House, he had to let me go. I got by on odd jobs and my pension from the war. It was rough. Rougher for you. That day—they shouldn't have said your father was almost in the war."

"Water under the bridge," I said.

Mr. Lewis shook his head. "I used to be good with a gun too. And with these." He raised his pale, liver-spotted fists and jabbed at the air a couple of times with his left. "Not as good as your father, of course. He would have made short work of me. But I was a bit wild when I was young. That's how I got old so fast. I'm sixty-one."

I would have said he was at least seventy-five.

"Things got out of hand that day. Shooting all those birds, I mean. Not what your father did. If I'd known what was in store for your parents . . . Mostly it's too late to learn from your mistakes. Too late for you, too late for other people. Those men at Black Point had been up all night drinking, but Sir Richard was almost sober. He should have called it off.

"That's the thing, you see. It never should have happened, none of it. Sometimes, once a thing gets started, there's no telling where it will go. Your dad was humiliated that day. Forced to apologize to a fool. Forced to apologize for giving Penny the comeuppance he deserved. He tried to save face when he threatened to resign, but that just made it worse. He knew we knew that he was bluffing. It was partly my fault. I was the only other person there who knew his way around a gun. I gave them the guns they asked for instead of the right ones, even though all those boys were watching. You were the youngest one, I think. I've often wondered what effect it had on you."

"I was in awe of my father that day. Any boy would have been."

"Were you? Well, that's something, then. And you've turned out very well. Your parents would be proud."

"I hope so."

"I've brought you something." He took out a box wrapped in ribbon and blue paper and put it on the table between us.

"You're giving me a present?"

"I'm giving something back to you. Open it."

I untied the ribbon and tore off the paper to reveal what might have been a cake box.

"Open it," he said again.

I raised the lid. Inside was a fedora just like the ones my father used to wear, but it looked brand new—a grey fedora with a black headband and a flattened black bow on one side, the top of it creased and dented just so. My father had had dozens of them over the years.

"It's your father's," he said. "He left it at Sir Richard's house one night and Sir Richard asked me to return it to him. I meant to, but I never did. Anyway, I found it recently and I took it to a hat blocker and had it all fixed up. I had him put your father's initials on the inside."

He removed the hat from the box, extending it to me across the desk as if it would shatter if he dropped it. I took it from him and, just as gingerly, turned it over. *E.V.*, it said on the dark green felt lining.

"Well, thank you, Mr. Lewis, but—"

"It was no trouble," he said. "A keepsake." He struggled to his feet. I stood and shook the hand that he held out to me. "Goodbye now."

"Goodbye."

I opened the door and motioned to the manager to help him down the steps.

A man I haven't seen in twenty-five years comes by my store to give me a gift-wrapped hat that he says once belonged to my father and was entrusted to him by Sir Richard. I didn't know what to make of it.

That night, I fixed a single coat peg to the wall on the long side of the kitchen table and hung my father's hat on it.

A couple of weeks later, the store manager phoned me at home to alert me to an obituary for Mr. Lewis in the *Telegram*. "Born in Harbour Grace . . . Worked for Sir Richard Squires . . . Unmarried . . . No known relatives."

"Cirrhosis of the liver, apparently," my manager said. "He was told he had two more years, maybe three."

When I told Nan about Mr. Lewis in the Flag House kitchen, she said that he must have been "making his soul." When I looked puzzled, she said, "He was tying up loose ends. Putting his affairs in order. Preparing himself to meet his maker." She nodded to Reg.

"There's one who will never make his soul. The Devil has his. What did you give him for it, Reg?"

"Making his soul," I said.

"It must have played on his mind," Nan said. "Little things like forgetting to return a hat play on people's minds. When something *very* bad happens to someone, people feel guilty for every little thing they ever did to them."

Cyril noticed the hat on the wall on his next stop by the house. I told him about Lewis.

"We used to go to some of the same bars," Cyril said.

"That's inevitable," I said. "You go to *all* the bars."

"He liked to pick fights. There's not too many crying for him." He pointed to the hat. "Imagine that. After all this time."

3.

The following Saturday afternoon, Cyril called me to ask if he could come by to discuss something. I thought this was another pointlessly euphemistic way of cadging a drink, but before I could reply, he said, almost whispering, "I have something that I think would be of interest to you, Ned. I'll say nothing more about it until I meet you face to face."

"Cyril—" I began, but he cut me off.

"It's in your best interest, so you just tell me where and when. I wouldn't want anyone else to know about this letter that I have."

"Cyril, you're drunk," I said, and was halfway to hanging up when he said, "Don't you hang up on *me*, Ned Vatcher." I would never have imagined that Cyril could cause the flash of fear I felt in my stomach, though I had no idea what I had to fear from him or from any letter.

"We'll talk in my car, Cyril," I said, speaking loudly lest my voice quaver and betray my fright. "I'll pick you up at the corner of Circular and King's Bridge at three tomorrow afternoon. Don't come to the house." I hung up quickly, my heart pounding.

There he was, standing at the corner with his hands in his pockets, dressed in what must have been his best clothes—dark jacket, smartly creased slacks, brightly polished black shoes. His thick grey hair glistening with lotion. From a distance, his resemblance to my father was striking and off-putting. This, I realized, was something close to what my father would have looked like by now. If he was still alive, it was how he *did* look.

I drew up beside Cyril in the Brougham. He opened the door and got in. By the time he had settled himself, the mingled smells of cologne, lotion and Scotch had filled the car. "Good choice of cars for this occasion."

"Why is that?"

"You know, Ned, I was never in your father's car," he said. "Not once. All that walking I did and not once did Edgar offer to drive me anywhere. I haven't been in many cars. You could have bought any car you liked, but you bought one just like his. It looks brand new. Cars have changed a lot, haven't they? This really sticks out, for lots of reasons. Even more than your Ferrari."

"I'm going to drive around for a while, Cyril," I said, "but I haven't got all day. You said something about a letter." I waited for a break in the traffic and pulled out into the street.

"'You said something about a letter,'" he muttered, staring straight ahead. "Yes, I did. I did say something about a letter."

I turned east, intending to go out around the bay to somewhere we could park and talk and be seen by as few people as possible.

"Wrong way," he said. "I think downtown is where we want to go. There's no telling how you might react, you see. I wouldn't want to be on some side road in the woods if you got so upset you couldn't resist the urge to murder me."

"Don't be absurd," I said.

"I won't be," he said. "I've had it up to here with being called absurd or worse. I've waited far too long. 'Don't let fear stop you,' Reg used to say when someone threatened to hit him. I've let fear stop me." He tapped one hand on the dashboard and spoke, as if to himself. "Not anymore, though. Time for things to change. Change is long overdue. Ned will know soon enough."

"You're drunk."

"So what? I shouldn't be afraid of you. There's nothing you can do to me that someone hasn't done already. I won't be afraid of you much longer. It's you who'll be afraid of me. Imagine that. A day you didn't know was coming will be dawning pretty soon."

I turned left at the next intersection, and left again. A lot of people were out for their Sunday afternoon drives, touring slowly through the streets.

"Neddie," he said. "That's what Megan used to call you. She doted on you."

"Do you know something about what happened to them, Cyril?"

"Your parents, that's all you ever think about. You adopted that youngster just for show. Took in his simple-minded aunt, just for show. Threw a big wake and funeral for his mother. Ned Vatcher—the generous, kind-hearted money man. But you never stop thinking about why Edgar and Megan left you to fend for yourself. You must be the only one who doesn't think Edgar did her in and then himself. That car will turn up one day, but what odds if it doesn't? No one would have bothered to do away with the two of them. The only thing that surprises me is that someone who thought as highly of himself as Edgar did left this world one second sooner than he had to."

If not for being surrounded by witnesses, I would have hit him.

"Myself and Edgar, we had an understanding," Cyril said. "It was more than just a few bucks per visit. I had six maw-mouthed youngsters. All he had was you. He helped me as much as he could. I didn't want to push him too hard because you never know. And there was only so much money I could flash around without making someone wonder where it came from.

"My youngsters are all out on their own now, but they don't have much, and *their* youngsters don't have much and I haven't got a pot to piss in, not since Edgar disappeared."

"He helped you out when he could."

"Not because he wanted to. Now here *you* are, helping out a youngster that's not even yours, a bastard boy straight off the streets. You're raising him like a prince. He'll be a credit to you, I'm sure. So, I want you to follow in your father's footsteps and pick up the slack for me. I wonder if you could help Ambrose find a better job. He went off to Nova Scotia and got himself some kind of a diploma, but he's nothing but a lab technician."

"Why should I do anything more than I've already done for you or Ambrose?"

"Well," Cyril said, "I'll give you my letter, and you'll understand when you read it. I have lots of copies. It's not really *my* letter, but it fell into my hands. It's a letter Reg wrote. One of his famous letters of confession to the priest, except he never showed it to the priest. They say 'what's done is done,' but that's not true."

"Does Ambrose know—"

"Ambrose doesn't know anything about anything yet. But I'll tell him when the time comes. He'll take over from me. He might louse it up, but I won't be around to see it." He rolled down his window. "You can let me out here," he said. "No need to pull over. I'll drop the letter on the seat after I get out and close the door. If I was you, I'd make sure I was somewhere private when I read it. It upset me a bit, I can tell you. I don't think you'll want anyone else to see it. It was the longest time before I could bring myself to let Edgar see it, and you should have seen how it affected *him*."

He got out, slammed the door, took an envelope from the inside pocket of his jacket and tossed it through the open window onto the seat. He poked his head partway in. "I'll be in touch," he said. "Lots of copies, don't forget. You wouldn't want this getting out."

I read the letter in my office, the door of which I locked for the first time since the house was built. Inside the envelope was a mimeographed copy of a letter that, judging by how much the ink had run, bleeding down in places from one line to the next, the many creases owing to the number of different ways the paper had been folded, the smudges whose causes I couldn't guess, was decades old. The original, I speculated, must now be in many pieces or consist of cracked, barely joined, barely adhering sections held together by Scotch tape, perhaps. The penmanship was primitive. The words, at least at first, were almost indiscernible.

My hands shook so badly that, in order to read, I had to weight the letter down, a book on each of the margins. I hunched over the desk, my arms enclosing the letter and the books. I squinted at the scrawled, erratic lines as if I hoped that, on second inspection, they might yield a different meaning. My head pounded as if my heart had switched places with my brain.

Edgar. Cyril's wife, Kay. Phonse. Reg. Megan. So many years ago it had been, but it seemed they had only now come to life. I grabbed the edge of the desk with one hand, realizing after the fact that I had almost blacked out. I poured a glass of bourbon and drank it in one gulp. I heard Ruby's voice and Brendan's from the kitchen. It seemed impossible that the doings of one group and those of the other were taking place in the same world. Drops of sweat pattered from my forehead onto the letter.

I looked at the single picture of my parents on the desk, my father smiling, my mother beside him, behind them the house, the Brougham. The Vatchers. Had the house beyond my office been empty, I would have thrown the picture against the wall and smashed it to pieces.

My father and Kay. Cyril smiling at me through the open window of the car as he tossed the envelope onto the front seat. I stifled the urge to be sick, my hand over my mouth, sweat pouring down my forehead onto my fingers, my vision blurred by tears. In one motion, I swept the books and the pages of the letter off the desk onto the floor.

I looked at the walls. How childish, vain, insipid, absurdly irrelevant my preening trophies seemed. My parents were long gone and I had never known them. I had been my father's dupe. Little Neddie. My mother—my mother I had regarded at best with a kind of indulgent scepticism, taking my cue from my father. It was infinitely less than she deserved. She had been infinitely more than he had made her out to be.

Cyril said he had shown him Reg's letter. I had seen in Edgar, the night before he disappeared, not weariness but the spiteful despair of a man who, though he had thought himself untouchable, had years before been bested by the least of the Vatchers. I pounded the desk with the heel of my fist and swallowed down the urge to scream.

REG'S CONFESSION

I saw Cyril's missus and some fella come out of that old fishing camp at the bottom of Nolan's Ridge one night in July . . . I was sure it was Phonse that was with her, I was sure. I couldn't speak up about it just anywhere. We had to be alone. On the boat was best. I took the boat down by Cape Bald. No other boats down there. I accused him. I hit him before he even knew that I was mad. There wasn't a fight. He wouldn't hit me. He said that it was Edgar that was with her, he said he had seen them too, sometimes. I didn't believe him. I hit him again. I grabbed him by the feet and hoisted him over the gunwale. It wasn't until he was goin' over the side that I saw in his eyes that he was tellin' the truth. It was Edgar I seen. I might've snagged him with the grapnel hook but he went under like a rock. I wish I never said a word to Phonse about it.

I made up that rogue wave. I had to. The boat was anchored and the sea was calm. The sides were too high to go over if all you did was trip. It was Edgar I should have been having it out with. Edgar, the big shot. But it was Phonse I threw over the side. I should've jumped in too and drowned meself. But I didn't. If Phonse had confessed, I would have told him to keep his hands off Kay from now on. That would have been the end of it. I never said a word to Edgar but I think he saw it in my eyes.

I read it through several times before I was able to grasp its entirety . . . My father and Cyril's wife, Kay. *My father and Kay.* Reg mistook my father for Phonse. Nan, who all along had disbelieved Reg's rogue wave tale, had been right, *was* right. She knew what hadn't happened, but would not in a thousand years have guessed that Reg was guilty of anything more than recklessness or negligence. My father and Kay, in whose mouths butter would not melt, for they had not—to my knowledge—betrayed themselves to anyone, had not raised the slightest suspicion about themselves, except to Phonse, and to Reg, who in the darkness of that summer night could not tell his sons apart.

Had my mother known about Kay? Possibly. I remembered the day I came home from school to find her crying uncontrollably. She would also have known that, if word of his affair with Kay got out, it would destroy us all.

I might never know the whole truth unless Cyril was holding in reserve a card that trumped the one he'd played today, the one he must have shown my father when I was but a toddler. It sickened me to know that Cyril had not only been the unctuous layabout he seemed to be, not only the innately passive, lazy, comical, innocuous fool whose absurd assumption of entitlement had won for him the status of mascot of the Vatchers—not only that, but also a wily, poker-faced, cool-headed blackmailer who, for my entire childhood, had slowly bled dry the man who'd cuckolded him, my father, his brother, the star of the family, Edgar "Rhodes Scholar" Vatcher.

Phonse had died because of my father—Phonse who was guilty of nothing. Reg had killed one of his sons because of the other. And Reg, because of my father, bore no resemblance to the man who confronted Phonse on the day of the rogue wave.

I wondered how Reg's letter to the priest had wound up in Cyril's hands. Nan said she had never found so much as one of Reg's confessions, and she was always looking. Who—if they happened on such a letter—would give it to Cyril? Had Kay had a child by Edgar? Ambrose? Given the uncertain duration of my father's affair with her, it was *possible* that Ambrose was my half-brother, not my cousin. It occurred to me that Ambrose and I might have some siblings in common. It occurred to me that, laughable as it seemed, all six of Cyril's children might be my father's. All of them might be my brothers and sisters.

I wondered if Cyril's ongoing blackmail of my father had had anything to do with my parents' disappearance. When my father was fired from his job, Cyril's supply of favours, monetary and otherwise, had been cut off, but even Cyril, as I now knew him to be, would not have had the means or nerve to commit or orchestrate the murder of any couple, let alone that of Edgar and Megan Vatcher. It was ridiculous to think he had had anything to do with it, and yet I couldn't get the thought out of my head.

Might the letter be a forgery? It seemed authentic. It was hard to say exactly why except that, physically, it appeared to be. The contents—especially the part concerning the manner of Phonse's death—seemed beyond Cyril's powers of invention.

Edgar had attributed my mother's unhappiness, her nervousness and accusatory manner to her being by nature high-strung and frail, but she might all the while have known the truth about him. Had there been other women besides Kay? I had seen that he was something like in love with Fielding, and that she was nothing like in love with him. But if she had been receptive, it now seemed clear, he would have had an affair with her.

Penny had said that my father got his hands dirty so that Sir Richard could keep *his* clean. How dirty? Affairs with women may have been his consolation prize.

The portrait painted of my father by the letter was not one I wanted Brendan or Ruby to see. I didn't want Brendan spending his life trying to live down the misdeeds of his step-grandfather. A child who didn't know who his father was, a child, possibly, of a rape, didn't need the added burden of a grandfather who had had an affair with his brother's wife, which had led to another brother's murder at the hands of their father, and his parents' and his wife's chronic misery.

And I didn't want to be regarded as the son of such a man.

Ambrose might be, or was and had always been, my half-brother. I doubted I'd be able to look him in the eye again—stare at him until he looked away, as he always did, sooner or later.

Cyril and I met again in my car at my request. At his insistence, we once again drove downtown in the broad daylight of a Sunday afternoon.

He stated his terms almost as if our first conversation in the car had never taken place. We would proceed as he and my father had. He said he wouldn't mind it if, whenever he came by the house for a drink, I tucked some money into his pocket as he was leaving, but not ten dollars as I'd once given him.

"No great amount, really," he said. "Whatever you can spare. I won't keep your generosity a secret. You'll be admired for it, just like your father was. Just a bit of cash to walk around with. A rich man helping out his uncle. Your father was good to me. We were brothers. I never hated him in spite of what he did. He helped out my children when he could. He might have done that anyway, who knows? His brother's family. The poorest family on the Heights if not for him. That's what people said. He used to say that not being able to help everyone is no excuse for helping no one. He got Ambrose into St. Bon's. He was a good man except when he wasn't.

"Kay was afraid of him. Afraid to say no, I think. A man as promising as that could have ruined anyone altogether if he wanted to. I'm not saying it wasn't her fault. I knew Ambrose wasn't mine before I saw Reg's confession. Kay and I, we weren't together until long after we were married, you see? Long after. It was still Edgar she wanted, not me.

"I remember the day she told me she was pregnant. That was a big surprise. A very big surprise, if you know what I mean. She told me she'd been with some guy from the mainland whose name she didn't even know. She doesn't know what happened to Phonse. She doesn't know Reg knows who Ambrose's father is. She doesn't know that you know now. I told Reg after he showed me his confession. We're closer than a lot of people know, Reg and me. Closer than Nan thinks we are. That's why I go along when that crowd of his take him for drives around the bay.

"Anyway, it's my children and grandchildren who need your help the most. I've done my best since your father, but there's only so much that one man can do. Six children, fourteen grandchildren.

Of course, one of those six children is Edgar's. I lie awake all night sometimes, worrying about them. So anything you can do, anything at all."

"Did Reg really give you the letter, Cyril?"

"Reg gave it to me all right, along with some advice about how to use it. I can't put into words how much he *hated* Edgar."

"Has it occurred to you that there might have been a second man in Kay's life and that he, and not Edgar, made her pregnant?"

"You'll do backflips to protect your father's reputation, won't you? Go ahead. Delude yourself all you like. Slander my wife and tell me she was worse than Edgar, just a slut who would sleep with any man who asked. You know there was no one else, but even if you won't admit it to yourself or me, it doesn't matter. That confession *proves* that Edgar was with her. It *proves* that Phonse died at the hands of Reg. That's what matters."

"Does this have anything to do with my parents' disappearance, Cyril?"

"I don't know anything about that, Ned. Nothing. Next thing you'll be asking if I helped Reg do away with them. I don't know where your parents went or why and I don't think about it anymore. I'll drop by soon to say hello. Some Scotch and some cold cuts might be nice, and then a nice chunk of change for dessert."

After that, Cyril came by about every two weeks. He stayed longer than he had before. I opened a new bottle of Scotch for him every time, much to Ruby's surprise, though she said nothing until after he was gone. He'd drink half and then stuff the bottle into the side pocket of his jacket. He'd ask Ruby if she would wrap up his cold cuts for him so that he could take them home. "I'll have them later on," he always said. "Or maybe Kay will, or one of Ambrose's youngsters, though Ambrose is doing much better now that he's managing one of Ned's grocery stores."

"Supermarkets," I said.

While Ruby was preparing what he called his doggie bag, Cyril and I conducted a swift transaction in the front vestibule.

"It's kind of strange, isn't it, Ned," he said once, "the two of us keeping alive this family tradition? I could hold out for more money if I had more to begin with. Ironic. That's the word, isn't it? But word would get out in a small place like this if I opened a bank account. I suppose I could hide money in the house somewhere, but it's not a very big house."

It wasn't the money that bothered me—a hundred bucks every two weeks, enough for him to "launder" by visiting a greater variety of bars and explaining to Kay that his coming home drunk more often was due to a windfall of generous new friends. What irked me was that he had much the same power over me as he had had over my father, his brother—my father whose reputation I was protecting to preserve my own and my mother's and Brendan's and Ruby's.

"Since when did Cyril become your best friend?" Ruby said after one lengthy visit.

"He's getting older," I said. "It's not as if I can't spare an old man a bottle of booze now and then."

Imagine that you're in the woods and, somewhere in the distance, you hear a stream. You set out to find it, but the sound of it grows fainter, or seems to be coming from a different direction. You change your course and head toward the sound again. For a while it gets louder, but soon you can barely hear it. You wonder if what you are hearing is just the wind in the treetops. But the sound comes back, and you go on searching for the source of it, the stream that somehow you can never find. You end up being as certain that it exists as you are that you will never see it, smell it, touch it or taste it.

My quest to discover my parents' fate felt like that.

I thought: *If all of time's lost lines of succession had been allowed to play out, how different things would be. I wouldn't be holding out hope for something as unlikely as the resurrection of the Vatchers. There'd be no such thing as the Last Newfoundlander.*

I'd never have heard of Brendan, my last-second son, the midnight child of Belvedere, the last child of March.

The Children of March, a term Fielding recently used to describe Newfoundlanders, would never have been born.

Lucy would have left St. Clare's with Brendan in her arms, Ruby beside her. They'd be raising Brendan now as best they could, their lives fused by his into a single life as if he had issued as much from Ruby's body as from Lucy's.

I felt as if I was regarding one of the early, wildly inaccurate maps of earth.

I visited Nan and Reg, though it was mostly Reg I wanted to see, Reg whom I now knew to be deserving of all the blame Nan had been heaping on him for decades, Reg who had put Cyril up to blackmailing my father, Reg who, with his worshippers, went to confession five times a week but withheld from the priest the truth about Phonse.

In the kitchen of the Flag House, I looked at him, wishing I could lend my voice to Nan's, take part in her never-ending interrogation of him, shove my face up close to his to see if *I* could make him blink, cringe or turn away.

"Ned is here to visit," Nan said. "Ned, Reg, Edgar's only child. He's gone a bit strange in the head from being rich, but he won't be as strange as you are any time soon."

Reg lay on the daybed or sat in his chair by the stove, seemingly oblivious to us. Perhaps he was, but he was still going to church, still writing confessions for the priest that no one else ever read, still going out for drives around the bay with his crowd.

"Reg never joined the search for Phonse—never. You'll never give up on your parents like Reg gave up on Phonse. Never. Maybe for your own sake and for Brendan's, maybe even for mine, you should, but you won't. Anyone can see that in your eyes.

"You need to know what happened to them like I need to know why two went out and one came back. But where should *I* search? What should I search for? Who'll help *me* search? Decades now since he went missing.

"It's not that I don't care what happened to Edgar. He was my son too. But many people think of Edgar and not so many think of Phonse, who was done away with by my husband, though I have no proof. Phonse died by his father's hand. Somehow. I'm not saying murder, but Reg won't even own up to carelessness or to making a mistake. Two went out and one came back. He was his father's favourite and his mother's too. A good man. There's not a soul who didn't think so. Strong and sweet. The sort of man that even fools are humbled by. I doubt that you've ever met such a man. No offence to your father, but Phonse was the best of my sons."

XII

NED

In the wake of Cyril's revelations, Brendan seemed more frail to me than ever. I fretted about him, wondering if he would ever throw off the effects of coming into the world the way he had. When he had one of the sore throats, earaches, stiff necks, colds or night-long bouts of insomnia that he had always been prone to, I would stand in the doorway of his room and watch him try to sleep. He would curl up on his bed all day, atop the blankets, his eyes wide open and darting about as if in search of something that might relieve his pain or somehow distract him from it. He was no worse than he'd ever been, but I couldn't stand the sight of him lying there, one or both ears plugged with cotton wadding, or his mouth swollen with an abscess, in spite of the ministrations of Dr. Vaughan, in spite of the antibiotics he prescribed, which seemed to have no effect on Brendan in spite of their success with the balance of the world's population. It was as if nothing less than the discovery of a Brendan Vatcher–specific antibiotic would help. Eventually, slowly, Brendan's ailments would fade away, for no other reason, it seemed, than that his germs had gone through their entire life cycle with him as their host.

At night, Brendan would often fall into a shallow, dream-ridden sleep in which, Ruby said, he twitched and whimpered, keeping her, three doors away, awake. Sometimes, when Brendan was sick, he slept in a room with Ruby, an empty-except-for-two-beds room that I nicknamed the infirmary. "Can I sleep in your bed?" he'd say. She'd say yes, but as soon as he fell asleep she'd get up and go to the other bed, knowing she'd have no peace once his misery-induced dreams began.

Brendan being ill worsened Ruby's Condition, which in turn made me less tolerant of it.

One evening, she went back and forth to the mailbox countless times even though I'd collected the mail when I'd come home. I opened the door and shouted, "Ruby, there is nothing in that bloody mailbox. *Nothing*. No matter how many times you look, there'll be nothing there."

She came in after a while, more anxious than chastised, rubbing her forehead and frowning as she listened to me tell her it was pointless to look in the mailbox hours after the mail had been delivered and brought inside.

Afterward, she sat in the living room, her hands on her tightly-drawn-together legs, her face partly averted from mine as if she was pondering a question I had posed to her that hinted at something about the proper care of my child that she had overlooked.

"You don't know, Ned Vatcher. You think you know everything, but you don't."

"What don't I know?"

"Never mind."

Brendan, as small a ten-year-old as I had ever seen, climbed onto her lap, put his arms about her neck and his head against her shoulder. She hugged him to her but stayed put, silently preoccupied, as if she was trying to commit my words to memory.

"I'm sorry, Ruby," I said. "I know you can't help it. It's just that I worry about you."

"Please don't," she said. "If you worry, I'll worry even more. I might get worse. I *will* get worse." She told me that Lucy had been the only one who could stave off an attack. "She'd tell me that we'd always be together, no matter what. We were a matching set," she said. "You can't break up a matching set."

Later that night, she sat for hours at the kitchen table, puzzling over columns of numbers she'd compiled with her pencil, looking, she said, for patterns, repetitions, anything that struck her as remarkable.

"Why?" I said.

"I don't know, Ned. I know you think I can just stop if I want to, but I can't, and I don't know why."

I told her to go to bed and she said she would when she got it all figured out. She stared at the piece of paper, rubbing her forehead with her fingers.

At my urging, Dr. Vaughan made more frequent house calls to examine Brendan, coming over when Ruby judged Brendan to be too ill to venture outdoors even long enough to make it to one of my cars. The sight of Brendan made Dr. Vaughan shake his head. Thin, pale, sunken-eyed Brendan was the very picture of many of the boys on the Heights. He looked as people on the north side thought a Vatcher boy should look.

He gave Brendan booster shots. Whatever treatment he received, Brendan thought Ruby and I, in solidarity with him, should receive as well, such as needles in the arm that made Ruby look away and sent Brendan into tears and Ruby to rubbing his shoulder and scowling at the doctor.

"It hurts because his arm is so thin," Dr. Vaughan said. "There's almost no muscle."

Perhaps because of the way I was now fussing over him, Brendan's own anxieties flared up more often and his sleep rhythms—erratic since he was born—became entirely opposed to most other people's. For him the onset of darkness and the onset of drowsiness were in no way connected.

Many nights, Ruby marched up to the Flag House taking Brendan by the hand and, in spite of her antipathy to Nan, left him with her so that she could get a few hours of sleep. Nan returned him to an abashed, worry-weary Ruby in the morning.

He went to bed, slept for a while, then woke up and stayed awake, at home or at Nan's, until Nan suddenly announced that, because he was keeping Reg awake, he couldn't come by at night anymore.

He'd go to bed when other children his age went to bed, but he'd always wake up, sometimes two hours later or sometimes in the middle of the night when the house was quiet and even the barking of the hunting dogs on the Heights had died down. He said he wasn't jolted awake by dreams or thirst or the need to pee. He simply felt that, for now, he had slept as long as he could.

"I don't care if you stay awake as long as you stay in bed," I told him. He tried. He turned on the little headboard lamp, read books, listened to the radio or watched himself on TV with the sound so low he could barely hear it with his face but a foot from the screen. This satisfied him for a while.

When Brendan was eight or so, Dr. Vaughan had said that some of his ailments would become less frequent and less severe if he had a tonsillectomy. He'd said the removal of his tonsils and adenoids was inevitable, as they aggravated everything relating to the ears, nose, throat and chest, especially in a boy who looked like a victim of the Dust Bowl. I'd broached the idea with Brendan, who became so terrified I told Dr. Vaughan to forget about it. The doctor had brought up the idea many times since, but I'd overruled him and told him not to mention it to Brendan. But now, Nan told me that Ambrose's son, Clar, had tonsillitis and would have to have his tonsils out. Anticipating his reaction, I repeated this to Dr. Vaughan, who said, "This is the perfect opportunity, Ned. The two boys can keep each other company. It will make it a whole lot easier on both of them. Even minor surgery loves company."

Two days later, Cyril and Ambrose and Dr. Vaughan came to the house with Clar, who, judging by his red-rimmed, puffy eyes, had been crying. "They need a ride to St. Clare's," I said to Brendan. "Clar is going there to have his tonsils out."

Brendan regarded Clar gloatingly, relishing this rare instance of having him at such a disadvantage, and Clar began to bawl.

"Myahhhhhhh," Clar went, his throat rasping. He looked at Ruby, who had yet to say a word, as if she had just sold him to a stranger, and accusingly at Brendan, who was still looking gloatingly at *him*. Here is your comeuppance for having such a father as Ambrose, Brendan's eyes were saying, the removal of your tonsils and the even more sinister-sounding adenoids, though I'm sure he had no more idea than Clar did what tonsils and adenoids were.

"I haven't got tossils, I have a sore throat," Clar protested.

"You have to get your adenoids out too," Brendan said. Clar ran to me and wrapped his arms and legs around my leg, pressing his face sideways against my hip. "Please, please, Ned, I don't want to go," he begged. "Don't let Dad make me go, Ned, I'll get better and I won't get sick again, I promise."

"Chin up, Clar," Cyril said.

"Dr. Vaughan's not punishing you for being sick," I said, running my hand through Clar's hair. "If you have your tonsils out, you'll get sick less often and you won't feel as sick as you do now." Clar banged his forehead woodpecker-fashion on my hip and hugged my leg as if to let go would mean his certain doom.

"Would you feel better if I arranged for Brendan to have his tonsils taken out too?" Dr. Vaughan asked.

"Nooo," Brendan said, as if hoping to discredit the notion before it took hold in my mind, but Dr. Vaughan nodded at me.

"You two boys can keep each other company," I said.

"No, no," Brendan said, trying to sound like a grown-up cajoling a child out of some unaccountably ridiculous belief, trying not to panic, as if he sensed that if he dismissed the idea out of hand as one too absurd to entertain, Ruby and I would be more likely to follow suit.

Clar, now silent, was wiping his nose, the usual signal that his crying jag was over.

"I think it might be a good idea, Brendan," I said.

"But there's nothing wrong with me," Brendan protested. "I haven't got a sore throat like him."

"He always has a sore throat," Clar said. "This is my first time."

"Shut up, Clar," Brendan said.

"Don't talk like that to him," Ambrose said.

Dr. Vaughan assured Brendan that the procedure was simple and that his tonsils would have to come out sooner or later anyway. He said that Clar and Brendan would be home in no time from the hospital, in a week or so, each of them having made easier for the other what for most children was a lonely ordeal.

"But there's nothing wrong with my tonsils," Brendan shouted. "I'm not going to the hospital just because *he's* sick."

"You do get sick a lot, sweetheart," Ruby said.

"Your tonsils are just small little things," Dr. Vaughan said, "easy to remove."

But Brendan shook his head. "You don't even know how to give someone a needle. You hurt my arm every time." He looked entreatingly at me.

"For Clar, Brendan?" I said, smiling at him. "He's not as tough as you."

"Clar is a SOOK," Brendan shouted, glaring at me through tear-blurred eyes. "And you're nothing but a liar, Ned."

"Take it back," Clar said. "I'm not a sook."

"Take it back, Brendan," I said.

He shook his head and turned his back to me.

"When are we going?" Clar said.

"Today, now, right away," Dr. Vaughan said. "I made arrangements for *you* a week ago, Clar. But I'm told that we can fit Brendan in as well. The procedure will take no time at all because they've agreed to do you one right after the other. By this time tomorrow, you'll be convalescing side by side."

Brendan turned and faced me. "You tricked me," he said, crying. "You knew all along, Ned. It was your idea. You don't care about Clar. You kept it a secret. You tricked me. I bet you're drunk, Ned."

"I haven't had a drink," I said. It was true. I hadn't had one that day, not yet. "And you're going to St. Clare's no matter what you say."

"I'm never going to speak to a single one of you again," Brendan said. "Not *ever*."

I drove them to the hospital. Ruby and Cyril sat up front with me, Ruby in the middle. Clar and Brendan sat in the back with Ambrose between them. Brendan pressed himself against the left door, turning as much of his back to Clar as he could without sliding off the seat, staring sullenly out the window as the squat little bungalows of the Heights went by.

Wet snow hit the Studebaker slantwise, gusts of wind slamming us on the crest of every hill. The snow had begun to gather in the ditches, but the road was covered with slush that splashed up on the windshield after each oncoming car.

"It's just having your tonsils out, boys," Cyril said. "I had my appendix out when I was your age. And my gallbladder a few years ago."

Ruby turned around and looked at Brendan. "When I was in hospital, I always wished that Lucy was there. When I had my hysterectomy, she came to visit me a lot."

"What's that?" Clar said.

"It's a different kind of 'ectomy," Ambrose said, laughing.

"Shut up, Ambrose," I said, glancing at Cyril, who smirked.

Brendan turned away at an even more oblique angle, then knelt up on the seat, his back fully to Clar and nearly so to Ruby.

The six of us walked across the parking lot of St. Clare's. I carried Brendan's overnight bag, Ambrose carried Clar's. Both bags were mine, plaid ones that I used for short trips away. Clar held on to Ambrose's free hand, but Brendan refused to take mine. Ruby lagged behind us, sniffling into a Kleenex. I tucked my chin against my shoulder, flinching from the snow, which was now mixed with sleet and coming straight at us.

"Merciful God, what a day," Ruby said.

I glanced up at the drab grey monolith of St. Clare's, the yellow brick smokestack behind it. I was sure that Brendan couldn't credit how the week that had stretched out unremarkably before him had been so suddenly transformed.

As we—Ruby, Clar, Brendan, Ambrose, Cyril, Dr. Vaughan and I, a second doctor and two nurses—proceeded through a maze of hallways to our room, other patients, all children or early teenagers, stared or smiled or waved at us. Clar smiled and waved back.

Ruby smiled and nodded and waved once at a girl with stringy black hair—she looked to be about twelve—who was walking gingerly with an IV drip attached to her arm, a nurse wheeling the coat-tree-like trolley beside her.

I hoped I didn't look as guilty as I felt. I considered calling the whole thing off, or Brendan's half of it anyway, but I pictured the upheaval and the scene that would cause. I glanced at Clar, whose lower lip was quivering as he gaped at the pale black-haired girl. It was hitting all of us now, the look of St. Clare's, the fact of our being in a hospital and our reasons for being there. "I hate this place," Ruby whispered to me.

They shared a hospital room that night, a private room with an extra bed—arranged and paid for by me, as Ruby made clear by telling Clar to say thank you to me.

"Thanks, Ned," Clar managed, looking around the room as if he wished he could bolt.

"This is the most Ned ever sprung for one of mine," Cyril said. "You could buy a lot of cold cuts and Scotch with what this room costs per day."

"We're having our tossils out at the same time," Clar said to a nurse. It sounded as if he thought they would lie side by side during their surgeries, holding hands and smiling at each other while one doctor did to him what another did to Brendan, the two of them cheerfully wide awake and chatting to each other as they did when they got haircuts.

Brendan managed not to speak throughout the hours between their installation in the room and lights out. Clar never stopped.

"Which bed would you like?" Shrug. "They gave me the one near the bathroom, so you have to take the one by the window. Would you like some of my apple juice? Ned, Brendan won't be much company for me if he never says a word."

"Clar's getting all the glory," Cyril said.

Brendan turned his head toward the window against which ice pellets clicked with every gust of wind.

"There's no TV," Clar said. "*Vatcher Variety* might be on tonight."

"You can't get reception in here," I said. "No matter what size rabbit ears you use."

Clar started crying again and told Brendan he could go home if he wanted to because he wouldn't mind staying there by himself, just like Brendan would have to do when his time came. "I'm not a sook," he said. "Make him take it back, Ned."

"I can't make him take it back. If I made him take it back, it wouldn't count."

"Yes, it would, because he knows I'm not a sook. *He's* a sook. They should put him in a room all by himself."

"The sook room," Cyril said.

"The sook room," Clar said, laughing and crying at the same time.

"Would you like to go to the sook room, Brendan?" Cyril said. "One room for the sick and one for the sook."

"That's enough," I said, cutting them both off.

Brendan let Ruby kiss him good night, but he didn't kiss or hug her back as he usually did.

"I'm staying here with the boys tonight," I said, in part to deprive Brendan of the chance of refusing me a hug.

Ambrose patted Clar on the shoulder again. "It's not much

different than going to the dentist," he said, adding that he would see us in the morning.

I stood there in my leather bomber jacket, my unlit half-smoked cigar in one hand. I felt like a fool. I felt like removing my vial of bourbon from the pocket of my jacket and downing it in one go.

"I love you, Brendan," Ruby said. "Does Brendan love Ruby?"

"*Clar* loves Ruby," Clar managed through hiccupping sobs.

"And what about Brendan?" Ruby said. "Does Brendan love me?"

He gave the slightest of nods and then sighed loudly.

"What about me, Brendan?" I said. I saw in his face the effort he was making not to cry.

"And you love your cousin too, don't you, Clar?" Ruby chimed in.

"Yes," Clar sobbed.

"And Brendan loves Clar, right?" I said. He gave no hint of assent and Clar let out a howl of desolation.

"Everybody loves everybody," Cyril said. "There. How's that? Does that cover it?"

"I'll drive Ambrose and Cyril and Ruby home and then come back," I said.

"Can Ambrose stay too?" Clar said.

"I have something called work to do in the morning," Ambrose said. "I have to work on Saturdays. Saturdays are the most important days of the week for a supermarket. I can't afford to take a day off whenever I want to, like Ned does."

"Kay will be here when you wake up," Cyril said to Clar. "Your mother has other children to take care of."

"But you're coming back, right, Ned?" Clar said.

"I'm coming back," I said, looking at Brendan, and thinking that I didn't want to see Kay, whom I hadn't encountered since Cyril showed me Reg's confession.

I knew Brendan would stay awake all night. If the storm got worse, he might, in spite of my affronting presence, stand at the windows and watch it. The wind howled and whistled and ice pellets the size of rock salt clicked against the glass of the big windows that rattled in their frames, as did the doors to all the rooms along the hallway.

Brendan rolled over on his side, his back to Clar and me.

"I WANT TO GO HOME." Clar howled it so loudly that a nurse came just as he got out of bed.

"Now, boys," she said, "other children are trying to get to sleep."

"I don't want to have my tossils out," Clar said. "I could have them out next year when I'm older. Brendan wants to go home too. He said we might not even have tossils. We might just have sore throats."

"Back into bed, NOW," the nurse said, and Clar obeyed. She tucked him in. "Not another word. Your uncle Ned will get mad with you."

"Ned is nice," Clar said. "He's my great-uncle, but Cyril says that doesn't mean he's great at anything."

The nurse left the room and soon returned with a little paper cup full of water and half a sleeping pill for Clar, telling him that it was candy.

Clar swallowed it down and soon drifted off, as did I in my chair by the window.

※

When I woke in the morning, Clar, whose procedure was to start first, was already gone. There was no sign of Kay. Brendan still had his back to me.

BRENDAN

I had expected the operating room to be the size of a dentist's office. But it didn't look like a place where anything minor or simple happened. There were large machines with flashing lights, and sonar-like screens everywhere, and what might have been small fridges.

There was a machine that beeped with every spike in the green line that moved from left to right. I wondered why the ceiling had to be so high. The room reminded me of church. All of this, all of these green-gowned, green cap–wearing, green-masked people, just to take out some things so small they could fit inside my nose and throat.

Two men hoisted me off the stretcher onto the operating table.

"Now, Brendan, we have to put you to sleep for a little while, okay?" Dr. Vaughan said to me, his voice partly muffled by his mask. He motioned to a man beside him who was also gowned and masked. "Dr. Hamlyn here will do the operation, and I'll be at his side all the while, okay?"

I nodded and tried to look unfazed by the prospect of being put to sleep.

In front of my face, held by the hand of a man behind me whom I couldn't see, appeared a triangular black leather mask with a spiral hose attached. As it closed over my nose and mouth, I grabbed the hand that held it and tried to pull it away.

As if the man holding the mask had expected me to do that very thing, the mask clamped down harder. The hand felt firm, calm, practised at quelling resistance while not betraying any effort.

A smell that was something like that of Scotch gushed into my nose and mouth. I held my breath. Dr. Hamlyn bent over and peered straight into my eyes, as if into the chamber that contained my tonsils.

Everything—me, the doctors, the hand-clamped mask, the bright lights high above me on the ceiling—began to spin, fast, faster, much faster, and to shrink in from the edges as if, while spinning, I was falling face up into a mine shaft, the entrance to which rapidly receded until there was only a tiny, giddily revolving, star-like speck of light.

When I woke, I swallowed. My throat felt as if I had been fed shards of glass. I tasted blood, then gagged as it bubbled up my throat and seemed certain to come spilling from my mouth.

Too hot to sleep, too cold to sleep. They smothered me with blankets when it was hot and took them away when it was cold. I wondered if I wet the bed. The sheets were drenched, and my pillow smelled like pee.

I dreamed of that unyielding hand that held the mask, that calmly confident mask-holding hand that resisted mine with such effortless perfection.

FIELDING

When the *Telegram* copy boy told me that Brendan Vatcher was dead, my soul sank. Eighteen years before, a man had stood in that same doorway and told me that *my* son was dead. This time I thought: How can a ten-year-old be dead?

I phoned Herder, who told me that the rumour wasn't true, at least not yet. The boy was gravely ill because of complications from a tonsillectomy, of all things, one he hadn't needed but had had only so that his second cousin, who *had* needed one, wouldn't have to go through it alone. The cousin had had one at the same time, in the same place, and had come through just fine. "The word is that the doctors botched it," Herder said.

I looked up Ned's number and called his house, but no one answered. I called the hospital and was told that, aside from a short statement Ned had released to the press, no information was available. I put on my coat and set out for St. Clare's without the slightest idea of why I was going or what I would do when I got there.

I found the Vatchers in the lobby. When Ned saw me, his face went blank, as if he doubted his own eyes. But then, in a kind of wistful way, he smiled and began to walk toward me. I half expected him to crush me in a hug the way he had at Lucy's wake. The little boy, Clar, followed him, but the others stayed put.

Ned extended his hand, took hold of mine and gently squeezed it. "Hello, Miss Fielding," he said.

"You can call me Sheilagh," I said, my voice going so suddenly hoarse that I began to cough. I cleared my throat—and I noticed, in that interval, that all the others, still clumped outside the cafeteria, were staring at us. Cyril was there, and his son Ambrose. And Ruby, who scowled at me.

"Clar," Ned said, "this is Sheilagh Fielding. Remember? You met her at Brendan's birthday party."

"You can call me Sheilagh, too," I said.

"What happened to your leg, Sheilagh?" he asked.

"Now Clar," Ned said.

I smiled at the boy and, my voice still hoarse and now quavering, I said, "A long time ago, I was sick. I had something called TB. It got into my bones. But then it went away. I got better, except for my leg." I patted my chest. "And my breathing's not what it used to be."

"Were you in the hospital?"

"Yes. For a very long time. I was in a hospital that looked like it was never new."

"I was only in here for a little while," Clar said. "Brendan's still here. He might meet up with Lucy, soon. He's here because of me. He wasn't sick. He's here because I'm such a sook. That's what he said." As if to prove the truth of Brendan's assessment of him, Clar began to cry and pressed his face into Ned's hip.

"I can tell that you're not a sook," I said. "Brendan was just upset, that's all."

And, as suddenly as Ned had embraced me at Lucy's wake, Clar released Ned and wrapped himself around my good leg. "He wouldn't take it back. He wouldn't even talk to me the night before we had our tossils out. If he goes to Heaven, he'll tell Lucy I'm nothing but a sook. She might not talk to me either. No one might talk to me in Heaven."

I smoothed Clar's back with the palm of my hand. "It wasn't your fault. It wasn't anyone's fault. No one knows why some things happen."

"Brendan wouldn't take it back."

I dropped my cane and picked him up. He put his arms around

my neck and rested his chin on my shoulder. He hugged me so fiercely that I almost broke down from the sorrow that was seeping into me from him.

"I'll take him," Ned said softly, and Clar was soon in his arms, desolation gushing out of him with every breath.

"I'm so sorry about Brendan," I said to Ned. Before he could answer, Ruby was at his side.

"You've made that boy worse," she said to me. "That's what you always do. You make people worse. Little Clar was doing fine. You're not family. You have no business being here now. Just because Ned invites you to dinner doesn't mean you're one of us."

I stooped as best I could, retrieved my cane and left just before tears started running down my cheeks, Ruby still talking at my back.

I had never held a child in my arms before. I was not the kind of woman other women asked to hold their children while they attended to this or that. The very look of me had always been enough to send a child-encumbered woman in search of someone else.

Clar had weighed next to nothing. He was all ribs right to the armpits. How fiercely he held on to me, his little face wet and warm against my neck.

"Brendan wouldn't take it back."

Take it back.

Children live in the certain belief that anything, everything can be taken back. It means more than to apologize or forgive. It literally means take back, turn back, start again, begin another draft from which the imperfections of the one before will be erased. They think the past can be endlessly revised. For as long as they are children, it will never be too late to start over, together, again.

No wonder, I thought, we have such need of Heaven, the place where *it*, no matter what *it* is, is taken back—a return to a childhood that will never end. The ultimate childhood where, after the first reconciliation, no others will be needed. History becomes pristine. No one is altered or bored by time. Innocence is wisdom, naïveté the only virtue.

Take it back. I wanted to. However well I learned to cope, to settle for less, to adapt, to accept the need for compromise, however convinced I was that I was forgiving and forgiven, I wanted to take it back. I wanted others to take it back. The second I saw Clar, I thought of Brendan lying elsewhere in the hospital, fighting for his life as, in the San, I so often fought for mine.

In hospitals, most deaths occur at night, in the early morning hours when the body is betrayed by its own routine, its innate rhythm. For most, nighttime is sleep time no matter what the circumstances. The body lets its guard down and mistakes death for sleep.

A tonsillectomy. His death would have been unbearably absurd even if he *had* needed the operation.

I grow old, I grow old, shall I wear the top of my stockings rolled? Should I dare to be a bitch, flirt with boys beside the pitch . . . In the wombs the children come and go, unclaimed by Mike and Al and Joe.

NED

Dr. Vaughan, after consulting with the surgeons, told me that, during the operation, there had been so much bleeding that Brendan couldn't breathe, so a doctor had performed a tracheotomy. A few hours afterward, Brendan contracted an infection.

Unable to identify the bacteria that were coursing through him, the doctors placed Brendan in quarantine, where he was as feverish and delirious as if he had malaria, spouting gibberish, thrashing from side to side, sweat oozing from him at such a rate that he went through a dozen IV bags a day. His temperature went so high that Dr. Vaughan predicted that, in the extreme unlikelihood he pulled through, he would have brain damage.

"Here we are again," I felt like saying when Duggan arrived at the hospital and we sat in a private waiting room.

Here we are again, the two of us, you keeping vigil with me, both of us pretending we don't know how it ends, or you pretending *I* don't know how it ends.

Edgar, Megan and Brendan. I had the feeling that my parents were among us, hoping pointlessly for Brendan, as Duggan, Fielding and I had hoped pointlessly for *them*.

"It's not your fault, Ned," Duggan said. Duggan and I drank Scotch as we had the night we sat up waiting for my parents.

The disappearance of my parents wasn't my fault and Duggan had never felt the need to tell me that it wasn't. That he felt the need this time to assure me I was not to blame I took as proof that his belief that I *was* to blame was as strong as mine.

I ran nothing on TV but a photograph of Brendan from the previous summer, Brendan in T-shirt and shorts and high-top sneakers, hands on hips, smiling at the camera. Brendan whom everyone thought would soon be buried beside his mother.

All of Newfoundland was asked by the archbishops of both Churches to pray for my son.

In my one statement to the press, I said that the final decision for the dual surgery had been mine, not Ruby's, not Dr. Vaughan's, not Ambrose's.

Nan Finn said, "Two went in and one came out. Just like the last time he was in St. Clare's."

Then, as inexplicably as it had arrived, and as swiftly as it had spread, the nameless germ in his blood died off, vanished as if his blood had done what the antibiotics couldn't—altered it, rendered it harmless and flushed it from him through his very pores.

When they moved him to intensive care, the doctors assured me that he'd survive, and likely be none or not much the worse—except that he would need another procedure because his voice box had been damaged during the frantic tracheotomy.

"It's a simple operation," Dr. Vaughan said.

"So is a tonsillectomy," I replied. "And they botched it."

"He bled far more than they expected. No one knows why."

"If he doesn't have this other procedure, will he lose his voice?"

"It's highly unlikely, but he'll sound very hoarse."

"I seem to be a lightning rod for the highly unlikely."

"He'll sound like he has laryngitis," Dr. Vaughan continued. "The procedure will take an hour, maybe less, and his voice will be back to normal in no time. It can be done in a few weeks, when he's got his strength back. The larynx won't heal by itself."

When Brendan opened his eyes, Ruby and I were sitting in chairs on either side of his bed and Clar was standing at the foot of it.

"He's awake," Clar shouted, his arm shooting out as he pointed at Brendan's face, as if he had been the first to spot something on the ocean that we had been scouring for days.

Ruby stamped Brendan's face with kisses, her tears dripping onto his forehead and cheeks. I buried my face beside Brendan's in the pillow and gripped his shoulders hard. When I pulled away, Clar was still at the foot of the bed, wide-eyed, terrified, waiting, I guessed, to see how much of a grudge Brendan still bore against him.

"Hi Clar," Brendan said, or tried to, looking startled by the strange hoarseness of his voice. There was an angry-looking scar on his throat beneath his Adam's apple—an X-shaped scar. X marks the spot.

"I'm not a sook, am I?" Clar said.

Brendan shook his head.

"Ned," Clar shouted, "he took it back." He jumped up and down on the floor in circles, his mouth open in a silent cry of joy.

"Hi Clar," were the last words Brendan would say to anyone for a very long time. Once, he tried to say my name, but only managed to croak it ingressively. He began to cry and held out his arms to me. I hugged him and told him he'd get better soon but that, for a while, his voice would sound like it did when his throat was sore.

"You said that Clar is not a sook," I said. "Am I forgiven too?"

He nodded his head slightly.

Brendan complied with every order he was given, except the one to exercise his larynx by trying to speak. He allowed himself to be examined by doctors. He co-operated with the nurses. He communicated with everyone, including me, by nodding or shaking his head, shrugging, rolling his eyes or writing in one of his school notebooks. In this manner he chattered away with Ruby as they sat side by side on the bed.

Dr. Vaughan agreed with a nurse who suggested that he not be given food or drink unless he asked for them out loud. "He'll talk when he's hungry or thirsty," the nurse said. I overruled both her and Dr. Vaughan, saying he would talk when he was ready.

When he came home, he continued to communicate with written notes. He would write me a note and smile at me in the uncertain, awkward way he had taken to smiling at me in the hospital. He consented to walk the halls of the house with me, the two of us holding hands as his legs were still unsteady. "Do you find the sound of your voice embarrassing?" I asked him. He shrugged. "Are you afraid people will make fun of it?" He stopped, nodded, removed his hand from mine and wrote: "Especially at school, so I'm not going."

I hired a tutor for him, a middle-aged retired teacher named Joan who came to the house every weekday for a couple of hours and did her best to teach him despite his refusal to speak.

Dr. Vaughan came by to check on him weekly. "Do you talk out loud when you're by yourself?" he asked Brendan on his second visit.

Brendan shook his head and wrote: "It hurts a lot."

"I know." Dr. Vaughan took me aside. "He'll be well enough soon for what we spoke about."

When I told Brendan what the doctor had said, he wrote: "I don't want another operation. I almost died. Lucy died. I'm never going into hospital again. I'm never having another operation."

When I relayed Brendan's answer, Dr. Vaughan said, "We need *your* permission to operate on him, not his."

"I'm not going to force him into it. He'd resent me forever, even if the operation worked. And what if it didn't and he lost his voice completely."

"Ned, I told you—"

"I know, I know."

Still, I imagined Brendan being rendered as mute as Reg when he was but a fraction of his age, mute and eternally aggrieved because of it. I looked at the X-shaped scar in the hollow of his throat, which Ruby insisted was shaped like a cross. He had almost choked, suffocated, drowned in his own blood because of me.

"I'm not going to make him do anything he doesn't want to do."

Another day, Brendan wrote: "I'm not going on *Vatcher Variety* again."

"Brendan," I said.

He wrote: "*You* do it. Go back to doing *Ned Vatcher Presents. Your* voice is still the same. No one tricked you. Why do you look out for Cyril? Cyril is not afraid of you like you're afraid of him."

"I'm not afraid of Cyril."

"Clar said you give Cyril money. He said Cyril said you're afraid of him. Why don't you put Clar on TV? His voice is still the same."

FIELDING

In spite of what Ruby said to me in the lobby at St. Clare's, Ned invited me to dinner again. He said that Duggan couldn't make it, so I accepted when he offered me a ride. I waited for him outside my hotel on Cochrane Street. Cars like his didn't often pull up there. Ruby was with him, in the front. I managed to hoist myself into the back. Nothing but pleasantries at first, between Ned and me, that is. Ruby said nothing.

"You should have a car," Ned said.

A woman your age, with a leg like that, is what he meant. Could I, with a leg like mine, drive a car? I wondered. It would have been something to see, me learning how.

"Let me buy you one," Ned said. Other men offered me a drink; Ned Vatcher offered me a car. Perhaps he offered cars to everyone he thought should have one. Half the city driving cars bought for them by Ned Vatcher.

I didn't want a car. I didn't use the streetcar or the bus, in part because of the cost, and in part because of the spectacle I'd have made getting on or off, forever being helped by well-meaning people whose names I wouldn't know, though they'd know mine.

I liked walking. I liked the independence of it. My body knew the city. My legs knew it, especially the weaker one, which hurt with every step. Even my inefficient, TB-shrivelled lungs liked walking, though I was always out of breath. What a city for a car-abhorring cripple, a city on the side of a hill that was covered in snow and ice six months of the year, and with mud and dust the other six.

Imagine a land so exacting and severe that it scared away the Vikings.

Still, it may have been the walking that kept me going. Uphill or downhill, I zigzagged to lessen the slope, which meant crossing the street so often that people thought me crazy.

"You should have a car. Please let me buy you one." Maybe he was so happy that his little boy was out of danger that he couldn't help wanting to reward the world. But the look that Ruby shot him, and then me, made him fall silent.

She is in love with you, I felt like shouting. He still didn't realize. Poor woman, it was practically expected in Newfoundland for a widower to marry an available sister-in-law. Though Ned wasn't really a widower, he behaved like one.

Ruby saw the way he looked at me, the way his voice changed when he spoke to me. I may have been done with love, but love wasn't done with me.

"Thank you," I said when he offered instead to buy me a year's supply of taxi vouchers, "but I like getting by without things like cars and television sets."

He sniffed in appreciation.

"The Cochrane," Ruby blurted. "We used to think it was haunted. We didn't understand what it was famous for. What *you* were famous for."

"Ruby," Ned said.

"Much of my reputation is deserved, Ruby," I said, "but not all of it."

"You haven't changed since the day we met. I bet you haven't changed since you learned to talk."

"Out of the cradle, endlessly mocking."

"You play the fool to get attention," Ruby said. "I do it because I can't help it, because of my Condition."

"No one thinks of you as a fool, Ruby," Ned said.

"*She* does," Ruby said. "Have you ever heard the way she talks to me?"

"I talk to everyone the same way," I said.

"Not everyone."

"Look at what she writes about me, Ruby."

"I don't understand a word of it. But I know she's making fun of you. You let her walk all over you, just like you let Cyril walk all over you. You're not the Ned you used to be."

NED

Brendan surprised me by asking, in his notebook, if Clar could sleep over. "Sure," I said.

I spied on them after they went to bed in the bunk room, hoping to hear Brendan speak. Brendan scribbled something in his notebook and handed it to Clar. Clar nodded, gave it back, lay back in his bunk and put his hands behind his head.

"You almost died. That makes twice you almost went where Lucy is. You almost went to Heaven twice. Nan Finn said you got close enough to see it, but it was far away, so you could barely make it out. She said Cyril came out of retirement and made God change his mind about you again, so you and Cyril must be connected. The germs went in when they took your tossils out and then those germs made more germs until your throat got too big to breathe. The germs were making germs as fast as you could spit them out, but you couldn't throw up enough germs because your throat was narrow, like a paper straw. The germs made you go to sleep and have bad dreams.

"They tied your hands and legs to the bed so you wouldn't knock the needles out. You got really hot, so they put you in a special tub. They said you might never wake up because your brain was broken. We had to wait and see. But you woke up. Your brain might still be broken, but not that bad. My brain is better than yours because I wasn't sick.

"Ambrose said that if you were dead, you'd still be the Last Newfoundlander. I said someone else would, whoever the second-last Newfoundlander is, but he said it didn't work like that. Ned said you'd still be the Last Newfoundlander except you'd be with Lucy and everyone who ever died, because Hell was just a made-up place and Purgatory too, and don't even mention Limbo that was full of babies and savages bouncing up and down because of gravity.

"One day, a boy told me you were dead. He said everybody knew except for me. He said Ned thought *I* might die if he told me you were dead. Ned put your picture on TV. He put it on for so long that people got fed up, but Ned said he didn't care, they could watch the other goddamn channel that just started up if they wanted to.

"I think most people watched the other channel. Ambrose said it's hard to look at a picture of the same boy you never met for very long, even if he's almost dead.

"Cyril said lots of babies almost die, but babies don't remember anything, so you really only did it once. I wouldn't mind almost dying if I knew for sure I wouldn't die. Cyril said Ned used to think you were famous but he doesn't anymore. Cyril said Ned thinks as highly of other people as he does of you. Higher, maybe, and no wonder. He said you didn't do anything, and what you almost did was no big deal. It's not like you need a special knack to almost die, even if you did it twice.

"Cyril said that Ambrose is going to be Ned's business partner soon, but Cyril will be calling all the shots. He said the three of them have talked about it. Ned has too much on his hands to do it all himself, so he needs his uncle's and his cousin's help.

"You're not part of Ned's family, not really. You're just staying with him until you're old enough to make it on your own. Then it's heave-ho, out you go, that's what Ambrose says. Cyril told him you're not in Ned's will or anything. My father is, and Cyril and his other children, and their youngsters, but you're not. Cyril says that's just the way it is. You might have no parents but so what? That might sound mean, he says, but he can't help how Ned feels and no one else can either, so that's the way it has to be. You're lucky that Ned took you in but he has to draw the line. You're his special guest until you're seventeen and then you have to go. I'm just saying what Cyril said, so don't blame me."

I went into the room and Clar jumped with fright. When I crouched down beside his bunk, he moved away from me, his back against the wall.

"Clar," I said, "was Cyril drunk when he said that, soon, he'd be calling all the shots?"

"Don't tell him or Ambrose what I said," Clar pleaded, on the verge of tears.

"I won't," I said, "I promise. But was Cyril drunk?"

"A bit," Clar said. "Not that much."

"Go to sleep now, the two of you," I said. "Not another word, Clar, all right?"

I considered telling Cyril to keep his mouth shut but reconsidered when I thought of the possible consequences.

I drank bourbon alone in my office late one night, flipping through the *Herald*, where I happened across an advertisement placed by a psychic who described herself as "renowned." I was in such a state,

I thought it might be worth a try to ask her to help me find my parents.

Her name was Miss Avery. She had the look of a hyper-vigilant librarian, ears perked as if for sounds of pages being torn from books. I invited her to my office, where I told her everything there was to know about the Vatchers.

Miss Avery said she thought she should spend a night alone in the house on Circular Road, which was empty, as I'd been unable to find tenants for almost a year. There was no furniture. Miss Avery said she was happy to sleep on the floor of what had been my parents' bedroom in a sleeping bag.

"It's best that I sleep on the floor anyway," she said, "instead of a bed that wasn't theirs. And it's a good thing that the house is empty or I might end up remembering things about people who've lived here since your parents disappeared."

"We wouldn't want that," I said.

When I went to the house the morning after her sleepover, Miss Avery said that, during the night, she several times woke among "presences" that she could feel, but not see or hear, whose pain and torment at being neither wholly in this world nor wholly in the next was pitiful and dreadful. She asked if she could stay a second night.

She came to my office the following day. To neither my surprise nor my amusement, she told me nothing at first that was not an oblique paraphrase of something I had told her. But then she said: "Early in the morning, the spirits of your parents returned to the house from the place of their deaths. They died by acts of dreadful violence. Your father betrayed someone and by that someone was himself betrayed."

I was startled and must have looked it.

"Edgar told Megan not to be afraid. He told her not to run, but she ran, poor thing."

"Afraid of what? What did she run away from? From him?"

"I'm sorry, Mr. Vatcher. I'd tell you if I knew."

I was feeling quite shaken as I escorted her to the door. I opened it just as Fielding and Duggan were coming up the steps. I introduced Miss Avery to them and told them what she had told me.

"Better to be vague than exposed as a fraud by giving details," Fielding said.

"The devil is in the details," Miss Avery said.

"Having someone locate the devil for you is a bargain at any price," Fielding said.

"You're a bitter, unhappy woman," Miss Avery said.

"My apologies," Fielding said. "Only an authentic psychic could see through this facade."

"Other women lost sons in the war," Miss Avery said, "and most of them are bearing up better than you."

Fielding blanched and turned away from us.

"Are you all right, Miss Fielding?" I said. She nodded but continued to face away from us. "You're shaking my confidence in you, Miss Avery," I said. "Miss Fielding's never had children. She *can't* have them."

Miss Avery nodded but didn't apologize. "Megan died first, then Edgar died," she said. "There was an accident—and then there wasn't one. There was an accident and—something else. I can't quite tell. They are not here, Mr. Vatcher, not in Newfoundland. They are somewhere far from here. But the car is still here. Underwater, I think."

Fielding faced us again and Duggan went to stand beside her.

"Very impressive," Fielding said. "A car that went missing on an island might be underwater. Whatever Ned is paying you is not enough."

"Can you be any more specific, Miss Avery?" I asked.

Miss Avery said, "These things don't come to me by words or sounds or images. I can't explain it. I really don't know how it works, but I've been proven right many times."

"Well," Fielding said, "you're bound to get something right when you predict that everything will happen."

"I don't predict the future," Miss Avery said. "I can only in a sense predict the past."

"Whereas I," Fielding said, "find it a lot easier to predict a hangover than to remember how I got it."

Miss Avery stared at her, unperturbed.

"Tell us more about the car," Fielding said. "Counting the spare, how many tires did it have? There's a number in my mind, something about four plus one—but no, I'm sorry, no, the number's fading now. It was so close, but I'm afraid it's gone."

"Two men you loved don't love you. But now you love another man."

"Hold up, Miss Avery," I said. "Miss Fielding is allowed to have her secrets, just like the rest of us."

"She has many," Miss Avery said.

"She's—" Fielding began, but stopped and seemed to swallow down the urge to cry.

XIII

NED

In spite of Fielding and Duggan, who urged me to ignore what Miss Avery had said, and Nan, who dismissed Miss Avery as her inferior in divination, my hope of finding my parents was revived.

I hired a pilot and his plane. No one had searched for my parents or their car by plane since 1947, when the technology of flight was far inferior to what it was now.

The pilot, whose name was Mark, was a perfect fit for his occupation—restless, adventurous, sceptical about the value of any job that was done indoors, any person who without ironic intent used the word *career*.

"Bush pilots burn out," he said, as if he believed he would be the exception. I felt like saying that they didn't so much burn out as give in to the pull of normalcy, that if you didn't die a renegade, you'd never been one in the first place. I fancied that he and I were literally in flight from a world by which we'd been betrayed as, sooner or later, everyone who put their trust in it would be. But he seemed to see me as a likeable poseur whose rebelliousness was just a hobby that my being rich forced other people to indulge.

He wore a khaki hat, a khaki shirt tucked into a pair of khaki pants. This outfit was not otherwise adorned except by a belt, as if he'd been stripped of everything that pointed to a past, heroic, unheroic, in any way eventful. I couldn't help but envy him.

Every Sunday afternoon for months, we flew along the shore, me scanning the coastline with binoculars, urging Mark closer to the cliffs despite his warnings that the closer we got, the more unpredictable the winds became. He spoke of updrafts, downdrafts, crosswinds and wind sheer, but I didn't heed a word of it.

I filmed from the plane using a hand-held camera that my station manager taught me how to operate, and reviewed the footage afterward.

When it was sunny, every shadow on the ocean floor looked like a car. Time after time, I had divers investigate, only to have them tell me, upon coming ashore, that what I'd seen from the plane was a plot of seaweed, a sunken reef or rowboat, a school of bottom-feeding fish.

The land was likewise rife with false alarms. The granite head-lands shone as if composed of steel and glass, which proved to be nothing more than rock faces glinting in the sun.

I urged Mark farther afield. Edgar, Megan, the car in which they drove away, could not possibly have been where we were searching, but we continued on.

"What's the point, Mr. Vatcher?" Mark said one day.

"You never know," I said, staring at the ground through the camera. I heard him sigh with exasperation. "Just fly, Mark," I said. "That's what I'm paying you for."

We kept flying, into the fall and then the winter. Mark flew, I filmed. We travelled low along the coast from St. John's to Bonavista, where Cabot landed in 1497. From there we went to the islands of Twillingate and Fogo, to Baie Verte and then St. Anthony, from which we headed south again along the coast of the Great Peninsula that almost stretched to Labrador.

We flew over massive herds of harp seals on the islands of the northeast coast, dark, squirming clusters that stood out against the ice like bacteria beneath a microscope. Small islands dotted the coastline as if Newfoundland had fallen to earth from some great height, casting off fragments in all directions.

We flew over Ramea, the home of the Drover sisters, Lucy and Ruby, in salute to whom Mark tipped his wings.

We followed the rampart-like headlands of the southwest coast, dipping into narrow fjords that snaked into the unknown core of Newfoundland. I saw brown herds of caribou that flowed to van-ishing points like slow-moving streams, a jigsaw of groves of dark green spruce and purple birch and intervening ice-caught lakes blown bare of snow by the ceaseless wind.

A few times we landed on those lakes, our plane weaving from side to side, our skis unable to gain any purchase on the grey, wind-polished ice. I filmed constantly, even after we set down on a lake, panning the camera along the shore in search of caribou. I wound up with hundreds of hours of footage of winter wilderness. Once, I sat the camera on the shore aimed at a stream that was frozen over but for a jagged opening that meandered down its middle, from which steam rose as if the water underneath was boiling. Such stationary shots made up whole episodes of *Ned Vatcher Presents.*

"This wouldn't be a good place or time to find out that the plane won't start," Mark said one day when, because of my need to record everything, we had lingered so long that the sun had almost set.

"It's no different in St. John's," I said, remembering the afternoon the snow began to fall as I stood on the steps of the dark and empty house. "If you're caught outside for an hour or two in cold like this, you'll perish. It's strange to think so, but it's true."

But it was somehow comforting to see places that my parents had never seen and to show them on TV.

"I'm done with this," Mark said one day in the hangar at the airport. "We fly back on nothing but fumes. You'll get us both killed if we keep this up."

I decided to go on flying anyway, having come to depend on the illusory search for my parents as much as I depended on my bourbon. I bought a twin-engine Cessna and kept it in a hangar at the airport and a reluctant Mark taught me how to fly. I hired him full-time to do nothing for a year but teach me how to operate my twin-engine Cessna. I was eventually licensed, though I had what Mark called "a lot of nerve and the bare minimum of skill." He nicknamed me the Ned Baron, so I called the plane the Baron.

"Things just *seem* to make sense up there," Mark said before my first solo flight. "Remember that. You're obsessed, Mr. Vatcher."

On weekday afternoons, I flew along the coastline, my route determined by maps that depicted every road, however primitive, however overgrown. I flew inland and scoured the shorelines of remote lakes and ponds to which nothing led but shallow streams. I knew there was no chance that the Brougham would turn up in such places, but, as it had done the impossible by disappearing, it seemed to me that the impossible was worth investigating.

What if someone had managed to do what no one else had even thought of trying? People found it intolerable that Amelia Earhart's plane might remain forever missing—how much more unlikely was it that an island-bound car should simply vanish?

The earth below resolved into shapes and lines you couldn't see on maps.

I preferred this bird's-eye view of earth, one from which you could trace the swerve and bend of every bay, the furthest reach of every inlet, the river-connected chains of ponds and lakes. I saw myself in better perspective as well. I was not so much a father as I was a man who had claimed a child who would otherwise have wound up on the rubbish heap of orphanhood. I had no wife. I thought I might be in love, all my life, with a woman whom everyone but Edgar and Duggan regarded as an embittered misfit.

The height and speed of the plane sped up my mind. There was the house on Circular Road and, seconds later, the Flag House—the house that I grew up in and the one I left it for. There was the school I walked home from the day my life was overthrown, and there was the harbour my mother walked across to complete our journey from London to Newfoundland. It seemed that my life was laid out below me in a code that I couldn't crack.

I was often near drunk when I flew. I drank from my vial of bourbon, raising it to my mouth as discreetly as I did in public, as one does with one's fist to cover a yawn or cough.

Brendan, who, after the passing of an entire year, was still not talking or going to school, still refusing the operation Dr. Vaughan said he needed, wanted to go up in the plane with me. Ruby asked me to tell him that I would take him up in the Baron when he was older.

"I couldn't stand it," she said, "knowing he was so high up. It's bad enough with you. I'd never sleep if I knew that sometime soon he'd be up there when the weather might turn bad or something. Lucy would never have let him go up in a *big* plane let alone that little one of yours."

"When you're a bit older?" I said to Brendan. "Because of Ruby?"

He wrote "OK" but looked resentfully at me as if he thought I was using Ruby as an excuse to shut him out.

I guessed that my father would have loved to fly a plane, given how he'd loved his car. Edgar Vatcher, car-loving adulterer. I now knew what he'd meant when he told me that you could taint your entire life by doing one thing wrong.

Looking down from the Baron one day, I tried in vain to find the site of the moss house Edgar had made for us. I imagined him caught in the snowstorm, forced to overnight in the moss house, lying on his back, talking to himself so as to quell what could be a fatal surge of panic, the rush of wind in the treetops drowning out his every word.

I flew especially low over the annual Government House garden party that I was always invited to but never attended, descending upon it several times, tipping my wings as if in the hope of provoking a protest, though I knew I would not be reported for flying lower across the city than the law allowed.

Rival papers said that, on these Sunday excursions, I flew about surveying my empire: VTV, VONP radio, Vatcher Enterprises, the seven Vatcher supermarkets, Vatcher Fisheries, the Vatcher cinemas, Vatcher Farms.

I flew low over the city at night, looking down at the dimming and brightening blue lights, the synchronous flickering of earthly constellations.

I was an explorer who had fashioned an obsession that was wholly mine. I had no rivals, no competitors. I was in quest of the heart of no one's darkness but my own.

It would not have been fine with me if, one day while I was in my office, someone who had found the answer to the question of the Vatchers with no help from me turned up in the doorway. It was of absolute importance to me that I be the one to rid the universe of this loose string which, I had begun to feel, might lead to the unravelling of everything.

I flew where Mark had flown when I first hired him. The sun-blasted headlands still sparkled all over as if glass and chrome were intermingled, as if the walls were fashioned, by eons of geology, from car wrecks and rock. As sunset neared, the cliffs took on a beautiful pinkish shade which might, in other circumstances, have been the reason I was out there.

I flew until the sun seemed to sink into the sea.

Go home. Go home while you still can. Someone who long ago turned on the lights is waiting for you at the house, wondering where you are and why you haven't heeded what you know to be the signs. Go home.

I felt always, as I headed home, that I was abandoning my parents, still undiscovered, still somehow hidden and alone. I flew back to the airport, always wishing there was something I could leave behind that would guide them home.

One afternoon, I passed out while flying the Baron but awoke just in time to pull out of what would have been a fatal stall. It felt as if a thing of irresistible strength that had been drawing me down had, its point proven, let me go. I thought I heard someone say, *Wake up*. Perhaps I said it, but the voice sounded like Megan's.

I veered away from a seagull-strewn face of rock. The gulls took flight and soon were far below me, assuming formations, as if they'd been thus disturbed to no effect a thousand times before.

Drenched in sweat that dripped from my forehead and onto my hands, tears streaming down my cheeks, I swore an oath I knew I wouldn't keep, swore that I would never act like such a fool again, never fly while I was drunk.

XIV

By Sheilagh Fielding   April 19, 1961

FIELD DAY

BECAUSE OF A countrywide recession, Mr. Vatcher has let go many of the people who worked for him. In the other papers, there is much hearkening back to the days when, charged with trimming the fat, Edgar Vatcher became known by the name I coined for him, the Grim Trimmer.

Many of the people Mr. Vatcher let go now work in Toronto for Inglis, a company that helped the Allies win the war by mass-producing Bren machine guns, after which they retooled their factory to make automatic washers, dryers and dishwashers, the very ones that Mr. Vatcher now sells in his stores.

"In a sense my people are still working for me," he said to me in a recent interview. "They would make it home for Christmas every year if the nearest job they could find was on the moon, but this is not to say that they are home-sick. They spend much time in a tavern where, by evening's end, conversation centres on what constitutes a home and how, after twenty drinks and without a cent in your pocket, you might convince a taxicab to take you there."

Mr. Vatcher's people assemble appliances bolt by bolt, screw by screw, wire by wire, wheel by wheel, latch by latch. They insert light bulbs in fridges and open fridge doors to make sure that the light bulbs work. Who, after doing that a thousand times a day, would be homesick, or wouldn't be tickled that his mother back home paid more for a fridge than he was paid to make it, the family being thereby left in a deficit which constituted the profit of Inglis and Ned Vatcher?

Mr. Vatcher made a revolving motion with his finger to indicate how, under what he liked to call his "system," money circulated endlessly.

Inspired by the new era of austerity which he is struggling through with the rest of us, Mr. Vatcher has compiled what he calls the Me-attitudes:

"Blessed are they who used to work for me for next to nothing; Blessed are the pacemakers, for they shall keep me alive until I own everything; Blessed are the poor in pocket, for their sons shall inherit their worth; Blessed are the fishermen, though they shall seek cod; Blessed are they who shop at Vatcher Enterprises, for they shall be honoured, though their warranties shall not; Blessed be me, for I say unto you that it is easier to pass gas through the eye of a needle than it is to get a job with Vatcher Enterprises."

NED

I started the building of a new house for Nan and Reg. I'd have done it sooner except that Reg had communicated to the priest that he didn't want to leave the Flag House, ever. But then he had a fall while climbing down from the attic, bruising his ribs so badly he could barely draw a breath.

Brendan, Ruby and I went to visit him and Nan. Reg was wearing some sort of truss beneath his shirt and, unable to sit up, was lying on the daybed. "Head over heels he went," Nan said. "Nearly killed himself. His days of sleeping in the attic are over. He'll be sleeping in what used to be Ned's room from now until you move us out."

She looked at Brendan. "Are you talking yet?" He shook his head. "You must be related to Reg in some way we haven't figured out. A distant relative. Dumb but not deaf. That's something at least.

"What about you, Ruby? How are you holding up now that Ned is in that plane of his most of the time and Brendan is clammed up like a cellar door? Is your Condition any better? I think I saw you—"

"Now, Nan," I said. "Don't pick on Ruby."

Nan shook her head and sighed. She went to stand beside Reg's daybed, her hands on her hips as she looked down at him. "Brendan won't say a word either, Reg. He's taken a vow of silence because Ned named him after a monk. The way things are going, we'll all be mute soon, the whole family passing notes back and forth. We'll need our own post office just to have a conversation."

Reg, his arm across his forehead, stared at the ceiling.

"We'll get you settled in the new house," I said. "It's all on one floor. Easier for both of you."

"We've lived here a long time," Nan Finn said, looking around the kitchen. "A long time."

"You won't be going far," I said.

"Remember, Ned," Nan Finn said. "You'll never tear this house down and it will always be Pink, White and Green. You make sure he keeps that promise after I'm dead and gone, Brendan."

He gave a solemn nod.

"It's a nice house, the new one," I said.

Nan said, "It looks like a motel."

"Not inside, it doesn't. The appliances are modern. A new stove and a fridge and a washer and dryer and a furnace that won't be always breaking down. Let me get you a TV."

"I don't want one. I've never gone to the movies in my life, so what do I want them in my house for? And you're in it or on it, whatever it is. I can see your face and hear your voice any time I want to just by going down the hill. I don't need you in a box inside my house. Will you come visit me even though I haven't got a television set, Brendan?"

He nodded.

"Brendan doesn't watch TV anymore," I said. "Not since he left St. Clare's."

"The priest blesses Reg's ears and throat once a year," Nan said. "I don't know what for. They still don't work. Or Reg is still pretending. Is that right, Reg? Still pretending? They pulled the gizzards right out of little Brendan. What's your excuse? A stroke? Nothing ever struck you without you striking back until that extra wave left us one son short. How come you never had another stroke when Edgar and Megan went away for good?"

I stared at him, hoping to see in his face some hint that he was unnerved by her suggestion that he harboured some grudge against them.

Nan and Reg moved from the Flag House to what Nan called the "Flat House" on a sunny but chilly Saturday in June, two months after Brendan turned twelve A great many Vatchers and Finns came out to witness their relocation. I decided that Reg, because of his ribs, shouldn't risk the walk, so he made the short journey in a wheelchair pushed by me, wrapped to his chin in a tartan blanket, Nan beside us in her church clothes, one hand on her hat because of the wind, dabbing tears from her eyes with a handkerchief.

The sight set a good many of the women to crying as well, and the men looked on as grimly as if Nan and Reg had been evicted by their grandson to some hovel in which they were unlikely to last very long. It was an era-ending event, the exodus of Nan and Reg from the house in which so many Vatchers had been born and grew up.

Later in the day, Father Clarke came by to bless the Flat House. It stood inside the fence that marked my property; Nan had asked me to enclose her new house with my fence, so that it would seem to anyone who had a mind to break into it that it was owned by Ned Vatcher, whom most knew better than to provoke.

On my television channel, late that night, I showed a still shot of the Flag House, a Pink, White and Green flag flying from the flagpole of the Pink, White and Green house.

Once the attic was emptied of Reg's possessions, I ransacked it, hoping in vain to find a hidden trove of his confessions. I intended to renovate the house, remove the old appliances, clear out the bedrooms and thus begin the transformation of the Flag House into a kind of book museum. It was my plan that, once the collection was big enough, bookshelves would be installed in every room but the kitchen, which I hoped would one day serve as the reception area for visitors.

I had found about half of Edgar's book collection, most of them sent to me from people in St. John's, only a few dozen sent from abroad. I felt certain that the missing half of the collection still existed and that most of those volumes were in the homes of people who, for some reason, were choosing to hold on to them. I supposed they might be conversation pieces, parts of other Newfoundland collections, or might be lying forgotten in attics and basements in never-opened cardboard boxes, but otherwise unprotected from the many things that could destroy or damage books.

They composed a kind of diaspora of books, a dispersal that I hoped would one day be reversed completely, all of Edgar's books reunited, as if it was the Edgar of my childhood that I was reassembling.

Brendan asked in a note if he could spend his nights at the Flag House, where, if he couldn't sleep, he'd be free to roam about as he wished without fear of waking anyone. I said he wasn't old enough to be left unattended all night long and asked him why he would prefer the Flag House to this one.

He wrote: "I don't. The only time I won't be here is when you and Ruby are asleep."

"But what if something happens?" Ruby said.

"Like what?" Brendan wrote.

"Anything could happen," Ruby said. "What if there's a fire or something?"

"There's no wood for the stove, Ruby," Brendan wrote. "And I won't start a fire in the fireplace."

Ruby shook her head worriedly. "I don't know if I'll be able to sleep, knowing you're not here," she said. "It's not natural for a little boy to be alone. What sense does it make? You by yourself in that drafty old house when you have this big one with the two of us in it just down the hill? What kind of family splits up like that at night? You seem to be in an awful hurry to move out, Brendan Vatcher."

"Not moving out," he wrote. "It would be like camping out."

"He's doing it to get back at me for the tonsillectomy," I told her after Brendan went to bed. "But a couple of nights in that creaky old Flag House and I bet you he'll be glad to be back in his own bed. I lived there for years and I was glad to get away from it. And it wasn't empty then."

"He's getting back at both of us," Ruby said. "Just like he's been doing writing in his notebook and staying home from school. You spend so much time up in your plane, you don't know what's happening in your house."

"I'll *handle* it," I said.

Arching her eyebrows, she shrugged and looked away from me.

"All right," I said to Brendan the next morning. "You can run away from home. You just can't go very far."

"I don't know what this family is coming to," Ruby said.

I ignored her and told him I didn't want him wandering around outdoors at night. He had to stay indoors until it was time to come down to the main house for breakfast in the morning.

"OK," he wrote.

Though that night he ate as much as usual at dinner, Ruby fixed him sandwiches and a hunk of chocolate cake, cramming what had once been his school lunch box until she could barely force it shut. "You might get hungry," she said, tears trickling freely down her cheeks.

"Don't be sad, Ruby," he wrote.

At nine o'clock, Ruby and I stood in the front hallway and watched him climb the hill to the Flag House.

He didn't get tired of the "creaky old Flag House," and word soon got round the Heights and, I had no doubt, the school he no longer attended that Brendan was living there. Soon, people were calling it "the House of the Last Newfoundlander."

Ruby's attacks grew more severe. She was afraid that, because of them, I would hire someone to take care of Brendan and send her away. But it seemed she only had her attacks when I was around to witness them, early in the morning or in the evening. Sometimes, she repeatedly rearranged the clothes on the clothesline, spacing them at different intervals, standing back to appraise them, then rearranging them again, and so on, over and over. Brendan and I would watch her for a while. I shook my head when Brendan wrote, "Nan said Ruby is off her rocker." Eventually I'd go out and bring her in, knowing that if I did so too soon, she'd only go out and start again.

"I'm sorry, Ned," Ruby said one evening before Brendan lit out for the Flag House. "It's just my way. That's what Lucy used to say—we all have our ways. I can't help it. I'd stop if I could, but my mind won't let me. The more I move the clothes around, the more I think they don't look right. And they have to look right or something bad will happen. It doesn't mean I'm crazy, does it? Please don't send me away."

"I would never do that, Ruby," I said, drawing her to me in a hug as she began to cry.

"Nan Finn thinks I'm crazy."

"Never mind Nan, Ruby," I said.

"I don't hurt anyone, do I?" Ruby said.

"No, you don't."

"I'd never harm a soul."

FIELDING

In the rooms, the men who come and go/Know ought of Michelangelo.

I walked past the darkened houses of people whose children had gone to school with Brendan at Bosco, families further from falling asleep than they were from waking up, past the halfway point of the time they spent in bed—normal, sleep-needing, sleep-relishing people who would wake replenished when the sun came up, dead-to-the-worlders for whom the night must have seemed to pass in an instant, though their bodies, erased of weariness, told them otherwise.

The moon shone like a sickly sun through the margin of the Narrows, its light deflected by the hills across the wind-planed water all the way to the river that ran beneath the bridge on which I stood, the water gushing noisily, unheard except by me, into the sea.

I roused from their ever-vigilant slumber hunting dogs whose barking inspired other dogs, as if a rumour of bad news was being relayed from house to house. The dogs settled down when they realized that nothing more was amiss than a woman who was out late and would soon be heading home.

I passed a house in which the kitchen light was on, an old man asleep, his head and chest resting on a table between his entreating, out-held arms. I caught the rot-like odour of cabbage from his garden and saw a beagle rise up lazily to assess me and, yawning and stretching, settle down again.

Moments later, I saw Brendan, sneaking about on the Heights. I knew he had permission to sleep in the Flag House but not to go out after dark. "Brendan," I shouted, but he ran off and hid somewhere.

Another night, when I went down the north hill to the harbour, I saw him standing on Crocker's Bridge, both hands on the rail, eyes closed as if he was relishing the feel of the wind against his face.

I scuffed my feet in the gravel. He opened his eyes and turned my way. "Brendan," I said, smiling, and motioned him toward me.

I placed my hand on his shoulder when he stood beside me. "I've seen you from a distance some nights," I said. "Have you seen me?"

He shook his head.

"I met Ned on this bridge one night, years ago. He's a night owl too, but he mostly stays indoors these days. We have a lot of things in common, Ned and I. At least one too many. Don't tell him I said so. You should stay clear of the north side of the city at this time of night. The bars are closing. I nearly get run over, and I'm easier to spot than you are. Or I would be if almost every driver on the road wasn't blind drunk. The sot calling the kettle black. The drivers were drunk when I was your age, but at least the horses were sober. Still not piping up?"

He shook his head.

"That's okay," I said. "Talking to you is much better than talking to myself, which I do a lot." I took out of my jacket pocket the little notebook and pencil stub I carried with me when I went out walking. I held them out to him. He took them from me, wrote something in the notebook and handed it back.

"Don't tell Ned," he'd printed.

"I won't," I said. "I promise."

He smiled, waved goodbye, turned and started up the hill.

There he went, up the Heights, a prodigy of empty streets. But for me, he had the night-silenced city to himself. He strolled as if there was nothing to fear from the houses in whose open windows curtains washed grey by the rain swayed slowly in the breeze.

There was no moon, but the sky was clear and smeared with stars.

He looked like a castaway from a world beyond recall.

Had another child come into my life?

NED

Someone told Nan, who told me, that they had seen Brendan standing on Crocker's Bridge late at night with Sheilagh Fielding. When I confronted him, he admitted that he'd been out walking.

"Wherever there's trouble, that woman is never very far away," Ruby said. "She should have told you he's been going out at night."

"It's not Miss Fielding's fault," I said.

"What kind of woman stands by herself on Crocker's Bridge after midnight?"

"One who is well able to take care of herself," I said. "One who's out after midnight a lot because she can't sleep. One who sometimes composes her newspaper columns while she walks around St. John's."

"So she says," Ruby sniffed. "Her real problem is she can't sleep when she's sober—"

"A better question," I said, "is what kind of twelve-year-old goes out after midnight when he knows he's not supposed to?"

Brendan wrote: "There's nothing on the radio and everyone's asleep."

"Well," I said, "you're the one who decided you wanted to spend your nights in the Flag House. You're the one who's boycotting TV and refusing to speak. Anyway, you're spending your nights in this house from now on. In your own room, awake, asleep, it doesn't matter."

He shook his head and wrote: "Not unless you lock me in my room."

"I won't do that," I said. "But we'll have to work out something soon."

He turned away, his expression blank.

A couple of days later, Fielding and Duggan dropped by and,

when I told them about Brendan, Fielding proposed a solution to the problem of how Brendan could occupy himself at night. She would come visit him at the Flag House from time to time for a couple of hours. She'd take him out walking with her. If he wanted to, he could ride his bike beside her. The sidewalks were always deserted, the streets nearly so until the bars closed. She would make sure that Brendan was back in the Flag House when their walk was done. She would accompany him to the gate and watch him go inside.

"Don't, Ned," Ruby interjected. "What makes her an expert on children?"

"My expertise in children is limited to my having been a child for many years—eventful ones," Fielding said.

"All she does is talk, Ned. Words, words and more words. Why should she have a say in what happens to Brendan?"

I looked at Brendan and froze with indecision. I shot Fielding a pleading look.

"I think we have all lost his trust," she said. "We need to earn it back."

Just before Brendan went up to the Flag House that night, I took him aside and said, "At some point, you'll have the operation. You can kick and scream and fight all you like, but you'll have the operation because you need to have it."

Brendan took out his little notebook, hurriedly wrote something, tore out the page, thrust it at me and strode away.

The note read: "When I'm old enough, I'm going to disappear just like the Vatchers did."

FIELDING

He climbed the hill from Ned's to the Flag House and waited for me. He depended on me showing up when I was supposed to, before it got dark.

This was just the barest glimpse of what it would be like to raise a child.

I'd stopped drinking again, for his sake, but I knew I wouldn't last.

He gave me a tour of the Flag House, a transparently disguised inspection of it for any hazards it might have acquired since the night before. Ned had yet to clear out the house, except for the attic, which now contained the book collection. Each of the several bedrooms had one bed with a metal headboard and loudly creaking springs. They were covered in identical pink quilts.

All of the Flag House had the smell of a place that had not been heated or aired out in some time, but this was especially so in the bedrooms. I opened the windows.

Brendan wrote: "Ned says we're not allowed to go up in the attic where the books are."

We sat in the kitchen of the Flag House and pretended at Nan Finn's table to play cards—Crazy Eights, Poker, Auction. He made up the rules, so I didn't have to let him win.

He opened his lunch box at ten. He loved cold bologna sandwiches with butter and mustard, but not date squares, which he gave to me to take home so I could eat them later.

We talked about things besides cards. We asked each other questions. He wrote his answers and questions in his notebook.

"Is my mother in Heaven?"

"Yes."

"Do you believe in Heaven?"

"Yes."

I could tell he wasn't sure if I did since I couldn't say yes with as much conviction as I knew I should.

"It depends on what you mean by Heaven," I said, and he rolled his eyes.

"Do you like Ned?" he wrote.

"Yes."

"How much?"

"Lots. How much do *you* like him?"

"He made me have my tonsils out for nothing. I almost died. Would you like him lots if he made you have your tonsils out and you almost died?"

"He thought he was doing what was best for you."

"He didn't have to trick me."

When he was done asking questions, I took my turn.

"Do you like living with Ned and Ruby?"

"Yes."

"But you like it up here better?"

"Just until I'm sleepy," he wrote.

"But even when you're sleepy, you can't sleep."

"Sometimes I can. Ned stays up late to watch *Ned Vatcher Presents* after he comes home from the airport."

"He watches himself. You used to watch yourself."

"Before my voice got spoiled. I might end up like Reg."

"You won't. And your voice is not spoiled. I bet it's nice."

"I'm not having another procedure. I'm not going on TV again. Even if my voice gets better, I'm not going on TV again."

Procedure. He spelled it right. He must have looked it up. He was quoting Dr. Vaughan and others whose words scared him more than his own—formal, grown-up, sombre, authoritative words.

He may as well have written: *I have to have another operation, but I'm not going to. You can't talk when you're dead.*

Dead men tell no tales. Another operation. Sick children have a solemn precociousness thrust upon them, a terrible maturity of language, tolerance, endurance, a stomach-sickening, quiet acceptance of what is possible, probable or certain.

What if he suffered a blow to the throat of the sort a boy might receive by accident while skylarking on the playground? He couldn't run like other boys, let alone like Ned had run at his age. When he ran, he wrote, it felt like his throat was on fire. A low but off-putting rasp came from him when he climbed a flight of stairs.

"Are you still mad at Ned?"

"I don't really belong to him," he wrote. "I belong to Lucy who's dead and some man who doesn't even know for sure that he's my father. A lot of men might be my father. Almost anyone. Except for Ned. He thought he wanted the Last Newfoundlander. Clar said I'm not what he bargained for. I'm just a dud and now he's stuck with me. He likes Clar more than he likes me. That's why he made me have my tonsils out with Clar. We're not related. But he's Clar's cousin once removed or something. Ruby told me that. She worked it all out at the kitchen table. She's my aunt and I'm her nephew but we're not related to anybody who's related to Ned. Not really. He'll get married someday and have youngsters that are really his. I'll be like a visitor who never leaves. So will Ruby. I told Ned I'd disappear like the Vatchers did if he makes me go to St. Clare's again."

He slowly rubbed the scar in the hollow of his throat with his index finger as if he was tracing its shape, then wrote again. "I'll probably lie all day on a daybed in a kitchen somewhere just like Reg. I'll have to write down what I want to eat and write my confessions for the priest. Ned is going to put Cyril and Clar and Ambrose in his will. They'll be rich when they grow up. I won't. When I'm seventeen it's heave-ho out you go. Cyril will soon be calling the shots, not Ned."

"Who told you this?"

"Cyril told Clar. He told Clar not to tell me but Clar told me anyway."

Cyril.

"Will you walk me down the hill to Ned's in the morning? Ruby and Ned said just walk in. The door won't be locked. But they might forget. You can write at the kitchen table while I'm asleep."

"Does the phone here still work?"

He nodded.

"Okay," I said, "I'll stay here. I'll tell the copy boy to come here to get my column. Someone else will have to type it. They won't put up with that for very long, though."

"You should bring your typewriter here."

"No, because I'm not moving in," I said. "This is just temporary for both of us."

The next night, he wrote: "I sound like I'm really old, about a hundred."

"I'm sure you don't—you don't hear your own voice the way other people hear it."

"Ned said you had an operation on your leg."

"I had three."

"Because you *had* to. I didn't have to. Ned made me."

"That's true."

"Can I come and stay with you for a while?"

"The Cochrane is just for grown-ups."

"You could sneak me in."

"If we got caught, they'd kick me out. I've been living there for thirty-something years."

"Clar said Ambrose said that Cyril said that when it comes right down to it Ned thinks that blood is thicker than water. Being a Vatcher trumps being a Drover. Ned wanted me to keep Clar company in the hospital, not the other way around. A doctor put this black rubber cup over my face. He kept it there. I pulled on his wrist with both my hands. I pulled as hard as I could but he wouldn't take the cup away. It smelled like when Ruby scrubs the floor. I saw black spots. My throat felt really sore when I woke up. I woke up about a hundred times. A woman put bits of ice in my mouth. Ned said I was dreaming but I wasn't. I was awake sometimes when I couldn't open my eyes, when I couldn't move. But it wasn't like a dream."

XV

1. NED

The police chief, a man named Browne, calls you at home to pass on some information that he thinks might be important to you. You have never met him. He has never called before. You feel as if you know what he's going to say before he says it.

He tells you that this morning, out near Black Point Cliff, an eight-year-old boy who was camping in the woods with his friends fell into what his rescuers took to be a sinkhole, the ground having given way, they thought, because of subsurface erosion. The boy slid about fifty feet before he brought up on a narrow ledge of rock that saved his life. He was conscious, uninjured but for cuts and bruises.

Firemen kept him calm until the hole was illuminated by a search-light and one of the firemen was lowered into the hole in a basket. To the cheers of those who watched from nearby, the fireman soon re-emerged with the boy in his arms.

The fireman, however, said the boy had not fallen into a sinkhole, but had broken through a layer of thick moss into some sort of cave as narrow as an elevator shaft. It was very deep. The fireman said it looked as if it went all the way down to the level of the sea.

"He *saw* something down there," Browne says. "He's certain it's a car. He couldn't tell what kind of car, or how old it was, or how long it's been down there.

"There used to be a timber road near there. It's mostly grown over now. But, as far as we can tell, no one's ever heard of there being a cave or a sea cave of that size at Black Point, so I don't think someone used it as a place to dump a car. I don't know of other cars that have been missing long enough for that thatch of moss to have grown over the opening. I'm not saying that this is your parents' car, but there's a good chance that it is."

You can hear in his voice that he knows it is the Brougham. *You* know that it is.

"Some men from the fire department are going to try to get all the way down there and check it out."

"I'm going with them," you say.

"They won't let you do that. I'll *tell* them not to let you. I called you so that you'd know what was going on, not to invite you to risk your life for what might turn out to be nothing. They'll find out whatever's down there, if anybody can."

"I'll make it worth your while," you hear yourself say. "And theirs. I don't mean money. But everyone has problems they could do without. Your children, your family, your friends—I could get rid of things that may have been holding them back."

"You could wind up dead down there. You can wait with the rest of us up top. You'll be the only civilian allowed that close."

Black Point Cliff. On the day of the bird-hunting party, how close had you been to this cave, you wonder, how close to the patch of moss the little boy fell through?

You drive to the site in your Studebaker, thinking it would seem odd to drive there in a car identical in every way to the one that might be brought up from the cave. As you near the place, you see that the landscape is like that of the area where your father built the moss house in which the two of you lay side by side. The trees are near dead because of the sodden ground, as thick in the trunk as they are at the top, a few green but ragged leaves on some of the branches, the bare spruce trees looking in the summer light like birch does in November.

You drive up the old timber road, passing walkers along the way who must be headed to the site. Some of them turn to look at you, then turn away likely having recognized your car.

There is a clearing up ahead, but it doesn't remind you of the one the hunting party gathered in before moving on to the path that took you to the cliffs where Lewis waited with his armoury of weapons. Why should it remind you of anything? It's been thirty years since you were here.

The entrance to the clearing is blocked by a police car. You wave to the driver, who nods and moves his car to let you through.

You remember that, on the morning of the hunting party, fog and drizzle obscured the far side of the bay. You were doused by water from every branch of every tree you brushed against. Today it is sunny, the bay barely disturbed by an offshore breeze, the ice that would have turned the wind about having long since drifted past Black Point and melted in the warm Gulf Stream.

The entire clearing has been roped off, curiosity-seekers standing behind the ropes, craning their necks to see over the police cars, fire trucks and emergency personnel that stand between them and the grove of deadwood, in the midst of which a group of men in yellow safety helmets stand in a wide circle, staring at the ground.

The onlookers gape at you, never having seen you in the flesh before. You're used to being gaped at in silence, but not silence of this kind. Today, you're the Ned Vatcher whose parents may have been found at last, whose remains may even now lie beneath your feet. It seems that this is the kind of ending called for by the case of the Vanishing Vatchers, the accidental discovery of their car in a dark and secret place.

You hear someone say that a car could not have been better hidden by the hand of God Himself. You think of the moss house that Edgar built, the sod-thick strips of moss you peeled from the ground, the drowned trees you pulled up by their roots. You remember the conversation you had at the moss house, Edgar hinting at a crime he seemed to think had ruined his past, present and future life.

A man in a yellow hat whom, because of his uniform, you take to be Browne raises his hand in a kind of salute. He stands with the others, who, hands on their knees, crouch to stare down into the hole. You walk to him. When you reach the edge of the dead-wood grove, your feet sink into the moss.

"Well, there it is," Browne says.

There it is, a well-like opening in the earth, its perimeter covered with tarp, in it a metal ladder that looks as if it might extend to the centre of the earth. It's as if a patient has been protectively and discreetly covered but for the site of his surgery.

"It doesn't look like much, does it?" Browne says.

You shake your head.

There is no telling, Browne says, how many people tromped safely over the sagging moss, oblivious to the odds they defied. Browne motions to the man nearest the ladder. "He can't see the bottom from there," he says. "It drops as straight as a chimney, but it's a long way down. There's a lot of dust in the air, more than there was when Walsh went down to get the boy."

You feel certain you are about to find them after all this time, and with them the Answer.

"It might not be their car," Browne says. "Who knows? It might not even be a car."

You know.

You will soon see them again, something you never gave up hoping you would do. You try to prepare yourself, even as you try not to imagine what you'll see.

Two climbers, one after the other, go down the ladder. They take with them a copy of the photo of the car that you have shown many times on VTV. They carry cameras, notebooks and clipboards. There is no basket this time, only harnesses, a pair of winches, and ropes that are tied to the bumper of a fire truck.

The winches creak loudly with every inch of the firemen's descent.

You hear their voices from below the ground, hollow-sounding, echoing. The winches stop turning and the ropes go slack. Now there is not a sound from below. Some of the firemen crouch on their heels to wait. Others lean against the truck, talking in low tones, looking your way from time to time.

Half an hour. The ropes pull tight again, a signal from the climbers that they wish to come back up. Firemen crank the winches, which creak louder than before.

"What did you find?" you shout the second the first climber's helmet appears above the ground. "Are they down there?"

When he reaches solid ground, he averts his eyes from you and motions to Browne, who takes him to one side. No one speaks or moves as the two of them confer, Browne nodding his head and glancing at you. The second climber reaches the top and joins them.

"Let's talk in my car," Browne says to you.

He tells you that the car at the bottom of the cave is the Brougham, no doubt about it, the Auburn Brougham in which, in November of 1936, your parents drove away for good.

It is their car, but there is no sign of them, none whatsoever, not the slightest trace. No sign of them in the car, in the trunk, no sign of them outside it. No clothes or shoes.

"There's nothing down there but the car. No way in but down. No way out but up. This hole is not man-made, but it's perfectly circular. The walls are white and green and yellow, a blend of gypsum and limestone. No granite. Here it is, late July, and there's still some ice down there, on the walls, on the car, on the ground. Maybe it never melts. It must ice up pretty good down there in the winter. The only scavengers in Newfoundland that could get down there and back up again are rats. But rats are not big enough to make off with everything."

Browne tells you the upholstery has turned to mould that crumbles at the slightest touch. Any bloodstains or fingerprints there might have been are long gone, washed away by the water that drips constantly from overhead, erased by the passage of time, by rust.

You ask Browne how the car wound up in a cave whose only entrance would have been as overgrown by moss in 1936 as it was when the boy fell through. Who could have dumped it there if no one even knew there was a cave?

"I don't know," he says. "Maybe your father knew about it. He knew these parts as well as anyone. Maybe it went in by accident."

"But he's not down there," you say. "Neither is she. How did the car make its way over those rocks? It would have left a path between those trees."

"It's the oddest thing I've ever seen," Browne says. "It makes no sense. But a lot of things make no sense, Mr. Vatcher."

"Someone else must have been involved."

"Maybe. Maybe not. All we know now that we didn't know yesterday is where the car wound up."

It seemed that the Brougham had fallen several hundred feet through space as dark as pitch, unseen, unheard by anyone. The rug of moss that covered the cave sprang back into place and, over the years, repaired itself, its torn roots reweaving the moss around the hole.

It was likely that, on the night of the storm, as you and Duggan waited in vain for a knock on the door, your parents' car was down there, though they were somewhere else.

Why would anyone who could have ended it all by driving off a cliff drive instead into a grove of deadwood a mile away from the sea?

❧

A few days later, you receive a visit from a federal geologist, a man named Kendler whose field job keeps him tanned and fit though he is nearly sixty. He wears a denim shirt and jeans and brown work-boots and has a neatly trimmed white beard. He tells you that he and his colleagues have been to the site and discovered that the bottom and the walls of the cave are, as Browne said, made not of granite but of carbonate rock. He sounds very excited and seems to think you should be too.

He tells you that your parents' car is in the pit of what, tens of thousands of years ago, was a deep, vertical, brackish water–filled cave that was open to the surface, what is now known as a blue hole. Such holes are called blue holes, he says, because their small width and great depth make them intensely blue. He says he thinks that this dormant blue hole survived the ice age because it was hemmed in by granite.

He says the cave should be thought of as the fossil of a blue hole. It is mostly made of calcified limestone, which is something like petrified limestone. There is evidence that it was once filled with brackish water in which swam fish and other marine life whose fossils have been found in the rock at the bottom and along the walls. It is likely that, for a very long time, most of the cave was below sea level. There must once have been an opening at the bottom that allowed sea water in and perhaps linked it to other, larger subsurface caves, while fresh water fed into it from surface streams and the runoff from rain and melting snow. But that opening has long since been sealed by limestone and calcium.

It is possible, Kendler tells you, that this blue hole first formed in southwest Europe or the northwest horn of Africa and was never active in what is now called North America. Contained, hemmed in by granite, it may have held its form as the continent of which it was a mote of cargo drifted westward after the breakup of the single supercontinent known as Pangaea that made up most of the land mass of the world ten million years ago.

"I'm getting ahead of myself," Kendler says. "But continental drift is a scientific fact. If we find fossils down there of life forms not native to North America, we'll have our proof. This is very exciting. Intact, dormant blue holes this old, that migrate this far, are almost unheard of.

"If this *is* one, the government will probably appropriate the site and the surrounding land. They'll bring the car up and you can take possession of it if you like. It will be a while before they can do that without damaging the cave. They will have to bring in some experts and machinery from the mainland. Until then, the site will be off limits to the public, though I expect you will be allowed supervised visits."

You have never heard of blue holes, but it turns out that they occur worldwide, usually on small islands, where they are the main attractions of spas, parks, villages and towns.

This now-dry, dormant blue hole, which owes its existence to a convergence of innumerable flukes, has, by the convergence of many more, wound up as the resting place of your parents' car, undiscoverable if not for the final fluke of a little boy stepping where countless others almost stepped before.

In a sense, Miss Avery was almost right when she said the car was underwater, as Bellamy had been almost right when he expressed his belief that the atoms of your parents and their car had been dispersed beyond detection.

A dormant blue hole, perfectly camouflaged by nature.

A wave where no wave should be. A cave where no cave should be. A car where no car should be.

You know that it will take months to raise the car from the cave once the police have finished what will be a fruitless investigation undertaken out of courtesy. The car, however expert the salvage company they bring in from the mainland, might fall to pieces the second it rises from the cave floor.

You'd thought that all your questions would be answered, but only one of them has been.

Where are they?

You know that Browne is right. The discovery of an empty car in a cave that no one knew was there makes none of the possibilities more or less likely than they have always been.

In 1936, people said it was as if the Brougham had disappeared by magic, meaning by Divine, or Evil, intervention. Now it seems as if the likeliest culprit is absurdity, a series of acts that, being random, cannot be pieced together. The Brougham interrupted the darkness and the silence of at least a hundred thousand years, perhaps ten million, just as the boy did the darkness and the silence of twenty-five.

Unknown to almost everyone, surely known to someone, the Brougham had been rusting, gathering dust, dripped on by melting snow during winter thaws and in the spring when the moss, soggy, sagging with water and slush, somehow stayed in place.

You tell Browne again that you want to go down into the hole to see the car. You say you understand why he refused before, but the site has been secured since then, the walls are more solid than the firemen expected, the crowds are gone, the police and the scientists have had their turns. There's no telling when, if ever, the

Brougham will be brought up to the surface. The recovery effort might fail. It was in this car that your parents, whose remains might never be discovered, were last seen. It is, for you, a kind of shrine.

Browne relents but tells you not to touch the car. You promise him you won't. He says the car is the only evidence they have and you promise him again, and he reminds you that his job is on the line if you get hurt or break your word, so you promise him a third time.

One fireman above you, one below, each of you wearing a helmet with a miner's lamp attached, you begin the strange descent, the creaking of the winch becoming fainter as the light begins to fade. Sitting astride a safety harness, both hands on the rope, you spin slowly, clockwise, counter-clockwise, until you feel you might be sick. The cave entrance above you narrows to a starlike speck of light.

Soon you can see nothing but what the lamps reveal, eerily green limestone stained yellow by water that, for eons, has been running down the walls, which are dry today. It seems that time itself unwinds as the rope plays out and lowers you into the past until you reach the bottom where the Brougham is lying where it landed the day the house was dark when you came home from school. It looks as if the cave was fashioned to accommodate the Brougham.

It is so cold you can see your breath. Down here it is always cold. It was cold before the Brougham, has been since the Brougham, and will be when the Brougham is gone.

The firemen don't say a word as they free you from your harness, but the scuffing of their feet and the clicking of buckles funnel up between the walls.

At first, you see nothing but the light from their headlamps. They move away from you and stand with their backs to the rock, hands clasped in front of them, heads bowed like a pair of under-takers attending a client's first viewing of the dead.

The cave doesn't smell of the salt air that, on the surface, turns your cars to rust before their time.

As the afterimage of the headlamps fades, the Brougham comes into better view.

It dropped straight down, landing on its four tires, colliding with nothing along the way, so straight, so undeviating is the chimney-like chute of the cave.

It bulges from the centre on both sides, the doors and the window frames bent almost in half from the impact. It looks as though the hood popped when the car hit bottom, but you can tell by the freshly scratched paint that the trunk was recently pried open. The spare tire on the right side of the rear compartment is deflated but otherwise undamaged. The shattered headlights still project like the eyes of an insect from the grille. In places, the black interior shows through the mould that coats the seats. The steering wheel is bent, but the gearshift is intact, as is the engine. The can of Altoid mints in the glove compartment is the only thing that points to the car ever having done anything but occupy the cave.

It has been here, exactly here, all along, empty but for a can of mints. There is an explanation for this that, should it come to light, will make perfect sense.

There is barely enough room to sidle around the car without brushing up against the walls. Your guides comply when you ask them to switch off their lamps. When the light dims, it seems there is no one in the cave, no one looking at the car, but you. It's hard to believe that your parents were never here, that it wasn't to here they came the day they disappeared. They didn't die here, but their having been separated from their car, which wound up here, makes it certain that they died *some*where—but you suspect you will change your mind about this when you go back up.

There is the rear compartment in which you sat, looking out the window, when the Vatchers went for drives around the bay.

Spotlit by the lamp in the darkness of the cave, it looks as if it's on display, the floor model for the wrecks of 1936.

It is a vision from November 1936, a moment of time almost perfectly preserved.

You walk around the Brougham like someone shopping for a car. You appraise it from every angle, get down on your hands and knees and scrutinize the tangle of tire spokes, every one of which your father scrubbed on Sunday afternoons until they gleamed. You're not sure what you're looking for—some clue Browne's men might have missed, something whose importance would be lost on others and has meaning for no one but you.

The car hugs the ground, folded in upon itself like an animal about to pounce.

It seems absurd that the weaving of the Vatchers' fate began so long ago.

You think of Edgar, drunk perhaps, driving crazily about in the storm until they wind up at Black Point, where the Brougham falls into a trap fashioned for it by the earth itself ten million years ago. But where *are* they? If their absence absolves Edgar—if it's not his fault that the Brougham wound up in a place it has no business being—there is no one left to blame.

Though it makes their disappearance seem even more sinister, you're glad the car is empty, glad they haven't been down here in the darkness for decades.

Whenever your mother was in the car, you were in it too, so you never saw them as someone surely must have the day they disappeared, the two of them in front, the rear compartment empty. But you picture them that way, side by side in the front seat of the Brougham, expressionless, intent on something they thought it best to shield you from, some purpose, some destination they may have shared with others who have not come forward and may not be alive.

Who were Edgar and Megan when they had yet to meet on the path that led to you? There would have been no you if not for them, no *them* if not for you.

Wherever they are, they may not be together. Worse than neither of them being found would be Edgar turning up without your mother, Megan forever lost, forever alone. You think of how fiercely she hugged you and looked into your eyes the last day she saw you off to school, the last time you saw her.

You tilt your head back. Your lamp lights up what appears to be a solid ceiling of rock to which a length of rope has been attached—an illusion, you tell yourself, a trick of the vanishing point that only makes it *seem* that there is no way out. But you feel dizzy and, despite the cold, drops of sweat fall from your forehead. You look at the Brougham, the other dead end.

You start to cry and cannot catch your breath. The air that was cold and clear has turned to dust. The walls are caving in, but your two guides are unfazed. You drop to your knees, fall forward onto your hands, your miner's lamp pointed at the ground . . .

You come to on your back up top, men standing around you in a circle, their hands on their hips, Browne kneeling at your side, sitting on his heels.

"You blacked out," Browne says. "Panic. Claustrophobia. Something. The boys had to bring you up by the arms and legs. You could have been a goner. You'll have some rope burns and some bruises for a while. I should have known better."

2.

"I'm so sorry, Ned," Fielding said the next time she and Duggan came to the house. "But they found the car. That's something."

"An eight-year-old boy found it," I said. "I gave his parents some money to hold in trust for him. The reward still stands."

Duggan gave me a hug. "I'm as mystified as everyone," he said. "I can't imagine how you must be feeling."

"I can't help thinking of that car. I see it when I try to sleep. A wall of rock in front of it. A wall of rock behind it. Walls of rock on either side."

"Now you'll never give up," Ruby said. "The police say they're no closer to an answer than they were before, but you think you are. I can see it in your eyes."

"You're right, Ruby. I feel as if *something* has been put back into play. That cave wasn't meant to be their final resting place."

After Fielding and Duggan left, Ruby sat at the kitchen table with a pen and a notepad and calculated the number of days it had been since my parents went missing, the number of days between their disappearance and Lucy's death, the number of days since Lucy died, the number since Brendan's tonsillectomy.

"What's the point, Ruby?" I said.

"There's no *point*, Ned," she said, beginning to cry. "I just have to know what the numbers are. I have to. I have to memorize them or I'll never get to sleep."

"You won't find any patterns, Ruby. And even if you found some, what would they tell you?"

"I don't know."

The discovery of the Brougham inspired no new speculation, just a reconsideration of the rumours of 1936: accident, suicide, murder, it had to be one of them, even though now they seemed to make even less sense than they had before.

As word of the discovery made its way across Canada and the United States, tips poured in. The *Herald* reprinted wire service stories that a couple resembling my parents had years ago been spotted at a gas station in Maine, at a restaurant in Maryland, dancing at a nightclub in Montreal, arguing while having breakfast in a deli in New York.

I thought of the car down there in the darkness, decaying year by year. Someone knew, or had known, about it. If the remains of my parents had been found in the car, picked clean but for their clothes, I'd have been no closer to the truth.

Murder? How could Edgar have been enticed to drive out to Black Point with Megan, in a snowstorm? How obliging to their unknown and motiveless killers.

An accident? What were they doing out at Black Point in the first place?

Double suicide or murder-suicide: Edgar, alone of all the people in St. John's, knows about this cave and keeps that knowledge to himself; you never know when a cave might come in handy. He warns none of the boys, not even me, about it at the hunting party at Black Point. He somehow drives the car over the impassably rough ground into the cave without winding up at the bottom of it himself. He does all this so as to protect me and/or his reputation, to disguise murder and/or suicide, thereby causing me and everyone else to *consider* murder and suicide.

Every possibility required the acceptance of an *impossibility*.

Nan Finn walked down from the Flat House to visit. Sitting at the kitchen table with a glass of blueberry wine, she said, "Strange place to park a car. If you have a grain of sense, you'll leave it where it is. No one went in. No one came out. Leave it that way."

"I can't just leave the car down there. It's not a grave. Besides, it's not up to me when or if the car comes up."

"It's just a car. That's all it ever was. They should cover that hole with something. Close it up for good. Out of sight, out of mind."

"The scientists won't let them. And you haven't given up on Phonse, so why are you nagging me?"

"A rogue wave. A rogue cave. You're wasting your time. God knows what your parents were up to back in 1936. I'm not surprised they turned up at the bottom of a hole."

"Their *car*, not them."

"I'm still not surprised. Like father, like son. Here, have some blueberry wine with me. Lay off that American whiskey before it kills you. Remember the Christmas Eve we sat at *my* table, drinking blueberry wine?"

I nodded.

"You were fourteen. You didn't have a pot to piss in. You had no one in the world but me. I told you about spells, remember?"

I nodded.

"I left one out that night. Spite. Spite is the spell of the Vatchers. Every one of you is full of it. I didn't want to tell you until you were old enough to understand. I'm still not sure you're old enough." She filled my glass. "You're right, though. I should give up on Phonse. I should give up on Reg." She touched my cheek with her hand. "I'm as big a fool as you are."

I wondered what she'd say if I told her what I knew about Edgar and Kay, Phonse and Reg, Cyril and Edgar. I knew she wouldn't keep it to herself. Everyone would know what Edgar had done, would know that Megan had been betrayed and made a fool of and might think she had put up with it for my sake. Kay's life would change for the worse, as would her children's, as would others', including Brendan's and mine. I couldn't ever tell her.

XVI

1. FIELDING

I was so startled when, at last, he *spoke* that I jumped with fright.

"Want some sandwich?"

His voice was a rasping whisper that, though he managed it without so much as wincing, sounded as though it had to be causing him some pain. I hoped I didn't look as disconcerted as I felt.

"He speaks!" I said. I took his face between my hands and kissed him on the forehead.

"Don't tell Ned," he said, smiling. "Don't tell anyone, promise."

Promise. Not a question—a demand, an ultimatum: *Or else I'll go back to not speaking to you.*

"Do you talk to anyone else?" I said.

He shook his head and said "Promise" again, the word seeming to come from deep inside his chest.

"I promise," I said.

If he spoke for any length of time without pausing to rest, his voice failed and he seemed to swallow with difficulty.

I wondered what he would do if I tried to persuade him to have the operation, wondered if what he wanted was a guarantee that he'd survive it and that it would succeed. His mother had died for no reason that anyone could name. He had almost died.

For all I knew, a person could be constitutionally predisposed to react badly to anaesthetic and surgery. As gravely ill with TB as I had been, I had survived three operations on my leg. Ruby, Lucy's twin sister, was far from robust and it may have been that her psychological frailty had its origin in some physical frailty to which, under the stress of surgery and anaesthetic, Lucy had succumbed, and which would surface with such virulence if Brendan had surgery again that not even the best of doctors could stop it.

"It's nice of you to talk to me," I said, making it sound like a question: *Why me? Why only me?* He smiled slightly and glanced at my leg. Was that it? I was his fellow in permanent affliction? Three operations had left me still unfixed, still broken. But I carried on in my way as, he probably thought, he would in his.

I couldn't help feeling disappointed that it might only be because of my leg that he had made an exception of me.

But then he said, "Can I sit on your lap?"

My eyes filled so suddenly I didn't dare blink. "Sure you can," I said, and he climbed aboard my lap.

"Can I hold your cane?" It was leaned against the wall beside my chair. I took hold of it and gave it to him.

"Careful, it's heavy."

He grasped it in both hands. "It *is* heavy," he said, turning it around slowly. "It looks pretty old."

"Yes, my mother gave it to me when I was half your age."

"She's gone, and your father is gone."

"That's right."

"Lucy is gone, but my father is not. Maybe. He's in St. John's. He doesn't want me. I'm the last thing he needs, whoever he is. He wouldn't want me to find out who he is."

"I guess Clar told you that."

He nodded. He settled his head against my shoulder and closed his eyes. Soon, he was asleep, breathing deeply, peacefully. I rested my cheek on his head.

A woman is commemorated by her children as no man can be by his. If Prowse had died a second after their conception, it would have made no difference to my children. It seemed cruel to think such a thing, to think it even of Prowse, who, when he was on his deathbed, might still be trying to convince himself of my children's non-existence.

But then, David was neither mine nor Prowse's anymore. He was commemorated only by a cross in Arlington Cemetery.

Prowse. He would forever be the schoolboy who I fancied loved me as much as I loved him. I only swelled the number of the many who had been fooled by Prowse.

David. The sinking, leaden weight of grief for a son who died before his time would never lighten, let alone be lifted from me. Grief, unmodified, lies in the guts of the living like a stone, in the mind like dark unending. But for now, there was Brendan.

And after I brought Brendan back to Ned's every night, I thought about Duggan.

I'd have said I was smitten with him, but *smitten* is a forward-looking, hopeful word and Duggan was a priest. Who, smitten by love, could give up? But one can as easily be smitten by love as by an illness. He well understood love who first used the word that way. *Smitten*. Smite down. A word previously reserved for the wrath of God.

I had been twice smitten, though some women never are and are none the worse off for it, perhaps.

So: once more unto the breach? Or should I make a lock of my heart and throw away the key? *He is a priest*. But my heart had no better sense. By its revolt, my mind and soul were overthrown.

All Ned represented was wealth, youth, security, stability, family and home, the prospect of not dying unloved, unremembered and alone. Was it better to live hand to mouth, a single woman in a room in a hotel otherwise occupied by prostitutes, wishing that Duggan was not a priest, than accept the closest thing to love that I could find?

I had never wanted Ned, but I knew that, in some sense, he wanted me. Maybe because I would never leave him. Nothing but death could take me from him, which it would most likely do when he was much younger than me. He would lose me to nothing but nature. If he ever again suffered a betrayal, abandonment, it wouldn't be at my hands.

"Never give all the heart," Yeats said. Hold something back, just in case. Reserve an uncommitted space, however small, because the person will never be born who might not change. Leave something untainted by love, something that, in time, might redeem the rest.

I was so young when I fell in love with Prowse. It might be that, once broken, the heart can never wholly heal.

Ned still sometimes looked at me as doe-eyed as he had the night on the bridge when he blurted out that he really liked me.

I was as alone, and lonely, as people had warned me I would be when I was fifty.

I was past the point on the vine of my life where I could have ripened into anything, a sub-spinster who propped up neither man nor child.

Never give all the heart.

"Cyril's the only one that Ned's afraid of," Brendan told me in the Flag House when we got back from a walk. He put his hand against his throat as he spoke as if he was now, in front of me at least, more embarrassed by his tracheotomy scar than by the sound of his voice. "He does whatever Cyril says. He never gets mad with Cyril, but he gets mad when Cyril is gone. He goes to his office and locks the door. He's still mad when he comes out."

"Maybe he just doesn't like Cyril."

"He doesn't. But he's not afraid of everyone he doesn't like."

I laboured up the Heights, past Ned's and the Flag House, until the slope grew so steep I had to stop to rest from time to time. Cyril's house, propped up on stilt-like posts, seemed to hang suspended in mid-air. It was so hemmed in by spruce trees I could barely make it out.

"Most people use the back door."

It was Kay, standing, hands on hips, on the stoop that lay at the top of a long set of grey, never-painted wooden steps.

"You've never walked this far up the hill before. It's not as nice here as it is at Ned's. What do you want?"

"I want to talk to Cyril. He puts ideas into Clar's head that wind up in Brendan's."

"You should go back to where you think you belong."

"I haven't said a word about this to Ned, but I will if I have to."

"He's in the tool shed," she said, pointing to her right at a structure so small it might have been a smokehouse. "CYRIL," she shouted. "CYRIL the SQUIRREL. Miss Fielding is here. She requests an audience with you."

There was no answer from the shed, though cigarette smoke was wafting out of it.

"You'd better go to him," Kay said. "He'll never come to you." She turned around and went inside.

I found Cyril surrounded by shelves of beer bottles and others heaped with a rusting assortment of nails, bolts, hinges, doorknobs. He was sitting on a chair at the back of the shed, drinking a beer and smoking a cigarette.

"Taking a break," he said, obviously trying not to find the sight of me surprising. "I'm a collector *too*," he said, motioning to the shelves.

"Taking a break from what?" I said.

He grinned. "Family life. I had a nice view of the city from this chair until you blocked the doorway. So here it is—this is where I live. This is my spread. Cyril's Eyrie. The highest on the Heights. The house, the outhouse and the shed. Eight people used to live in that little house. Four girls and two boys in one room. Two pairs of bunk beds and a mattress on the floor. You don't look too impressed."

"I've seen worse."

"I'd say pull up a chair if there *was* another one. I'd offer you a beer if I could spare it."

"Brendan says that Ned's afraid of you."

"He is?" Cyril laughed and raised his eyebrows. "I don't think so. Why would anyone, let alone Ned Vatcher, be afraid of me?"

"I don't know, but that's what Brendan thinks. Ruby thinks it too."
Cyril shook his head and grinned sheepishly.

"You and Ambrose talk to Clar about Brendan a lot," I said.

"Well, I don't know about Ambrose, but I don't."

"Brendan says you do. Clar tells Brendan what you tell him not to tell him."

"So Brendan is making things up. That's not my fault. God bless him, but there might be something wrong with him up here." He tapped his temple. "Just look at his aunt. Who knows what Lucy was like? Worse than Ruby maybe."

"Do you know, Cyril, what the boys on the Heights are saying? 'When I grow up, I want to be just like Cyril Vatcher.'"

"I don't think I like you very much."

"I come to query Cyril, not to please him. I'm about your age and I don't remember a time when, among boys, to grow up to be like you was the fondest wish. You are *sui generis*. Self-invented.

Lacking in antecedents. But that the boys admire you should come as no surprise to anyone, given what you've made of yourself. If you were a man, you'd be ahead of your time."

I watched him as I spoke, waiting for him to object or laugh or lose his temper, but all he did was nod, his eyes averted from mine, his expression almost reflective, as if he were a doctor and I a patient enumerating a long list of grave-sounding symptoms.

"What do you want?" he said at last.

"Why is Ned afraid of you?"

"He's *not* afraid of me."

"Brendan said that you tell Clar that you'll soon be calling the shots. What's that supposed to mean?"

"It's just a joke. A joke at my own expense."

"Why does Ned act like he's afraid of you?"

"Reg asked him to take care of me. That's all I know."

"Reg also asked Edgar to take care of you."

"So? What do you *want*?"

Lifting my cane, I pressed the point of it to the hollow of his throat beneath his Adam's apple. "Don't move. Under the circumstances, a primitive tracheotomy is the most that I can promise."

"You'll go to prison, or worse," Cyril said, wide-eyed, the beer bottle stalled halfway to his mouth.

"Why would I go to prison?"

"You're threatening me."

"No," I said, "you jumped to that conclusion just because I'm poking you in the throat with a lethal weapon."

"Stop."

"You never know, Cyril. On this bad leg, I could easily fall forward by accident. That's what I'd say. *I began to fall forward, tried to press my cane against the wall to keep my balance, in the process of which I impaled poor Cyril through the throat.* In the absence of any motive, why wouldn't they believe me?"

"I prayed to God for Ned, for Brendan and for Lucy. I prayed for Brendan twice. He might not be alive if not for me. God works in mysterious ways."

"His blunders to behold."

"Whatever you might think of me, whatever I might think of myself, I don't think you should mock people who see me as an instrument of God."

"I hope you're an instrument of something, Cyril, or else you'll have to bear all the blame for being you. And if I were you, I wouldn't make analogies right now between myself and someone who was crucified."

"I didn't make up the Seventh Son of a Seventh Son. I can say more prayers for Brendan if he wants me to. Tell him that, when he has his operation, I'll pray for him. Tell Ned."

"You don't stop in on the other Vatchers very much, do you?"

"Not as much. Ned has more to spare."

"And more to fear?"

"From me? Not even Ruby is afraid of me. I don't even scare Brendan. He's more afraid of Ned than he is of me."

"You're hiding something, Cyril, but it's not your loathsomeness."

"We're all hiding something."

"You can't help reminding people that there's more to you than meets the eye."

"Nothing wrong with a little joke now and then. Or a little drink for that matter. Or something else. I don't suppose—"

"You shouldn't suppose."

"You'd be surprised what you might do if that fancy flask of yours was mine and you had nothing to your name. And you were parched like me."

"What would I do, Cyril?"

"What you've done before. How else do you keep yourself in so much Scotch? They say that some men like odd-looking women. Old and odd. Cripples. Short ones. Tall ones. Freaks. I hear they get top dollar."

I pushed the point of my cane harder against his throat. "You never know what might happen, Cyril. I've been drinking. I'm so upset my hands are shaking. You insulted me. Offended me."

"I doubt it."

"What are you up to, Cyril?"

"Minding my own business until you came by."

"We often chat about you, your wife, Kay, and I. 'I can't say enough about Cyril,' she often says. I tell her she's right. Just the other day, I said, 'No matter how much I say about Cyril, there's always more to say in his defence.'"

"You're a—"

I pushed the cane harder still.

"You've never spoken to Kay," he managed to whisper, but he was sweating now.

"Just imagine, Cyril," I said, "how close you are to finding out what the next world is like. How curious are you?"

"Not curious."

"The car at the bottom of the cave. You know something about it, don't you, Cyril?"

"How should I know anything about that?" he said, his eyes widening. "No one does. It's a mystery."

"A mystery. An act of God."

"I don't know anything about that cave or that car."

I lowered the cane. There was a red spot just below his Adam's apple.

"You'll get yours," he said, standing up and moving away along the wall, still holding the beer bottle in one hand, his cigarette in the other.

"Are you threatening *me*?" I said.

He raised the bottle as if to throw it at me. "Go on, now," he said. "Go, if you know what's good for you."

"Goodbye for now, Cyril," I said.

A week later, as I walked up the hill to Ned's with Duggan, I told him about visiting Cyril. He laughed. "A good thing you *didn't* lose your balance. A good thing for him, anyway. That name Kay called him, Cyril the Squirrel—they used to call him that when he was a boy."

We also talked about Ned, who, for the past few weeks on *Ned Vatcher Presents*, had been holding forth about nothing but his parents.

"Do you think he remembers what he says on TV from one night to the next?" Duggan asked. "Other people do. Ruby does."

"I don't know," I said.

Duggan brought it up at dinner. "Ned, has it ever occurred to you that some nights there might be no one watching, no one listening, because they've had enough?"

"It occurs to me all the time," Ned said. "You have your soapbox, I have mine. I talk to people just like you do. I like looking at that dark camera lens. I like talking just to see what I will say. It helps me think things through. It's not like talking to a friend or to myself. I don't know what it is about TV, but some nights I feel like I'm talking to my parents."

I looked at him, but he avoided looking at me.

The Vatchers left, like my mother, without warning, without a word of explanation. But my father stayed and told me where she went and why. I'd had that much and still did.

Ned sat in front of the TV camera and told his parents about Duggan, the man if not for whom he would have been destroyed, and about me. He wanted them to know, he wished he could say, that, unlike his father, he was free to love me, for he did not, by loving me, betray another or himself.

He told them about Brendan, his adoption of whom redressed his parents' abandonment of him. The Last Newfoundlander, a title Edgar would have worn with pride, or have been proud to confer upon his son.

He had never said so on TV, but he wanted to be forgiven by them for his worst mistake, his sin against his son, which was all too similar to the one that Edgar and Megan committed against him—abandonment to the hands of strangers.

He didn't admit his mistakes and shortcomings, because they had their origins in traits that he inherited from them or acquired because of what they did to him. It was as if he was saying: see what you made me do? He would not ask for it, but he wanted their forgiveness, because where, in the absence of God, can absolution come from but your parents?

2.

Two weeks later, Ned called me and asked me to dinner—not at his house but at Stirling's restaurant. I was flummoxed.

"It's hard to sneak around with a woman my size in a city the size of St. John's," I said.

"We wouldn't be sneaking around. We'd be having dinner in full view of other people having dinner. I've been stared at since I was fourteen."

"So have I, which means that I've been stared at for twice as long as you and for different reasons. The sight of one of us causes a commotion, the two of us together—"

"So what? Dinner at Stirling's. I insist."

"Ned, I'd be sitting among people who think about as highly of me as they know I think of them. People I've written about."

"They're afraid of you. And me."

"They're not afraid of me."

"Dinner at Stirling's," he said, and hung up.

NED

She is waiting on the steps of the Cochrane when you pull up in the Brougham. No one else is in the car. She turns round as if she means to climb the steps and go back inside, but she stands there for a while, then faces the street again. You jump out, come around and open the passenger door. She comes down the steps and hands you her cane, which you tuck beneath your arm as she climbs into the car.

"Thank you," she says as she gets in, but she grabs her cane from you.

You wonder how you look to her. You wear a brown jacket with black slacks, a white shirt, a dark blue tie and newly shined brown loafers. "It's just Stirling's. Nothing too fancy."

She sighs and looks away from you. "Ned, as you can see, I am underdressed for nothing too *drab*, and these are my best clothes." She tugs at the throat of her dress. "This is all I have." She taps her shoes with her cane. "*These* are all I have." She looks you up and down. "Think of how self-conscious you'll feel when everyone stares at you like I'm something you don't know is stuck to the sole of your shoe."

"I won't be self-conscious if you're not."

"I'm thirty years and a flask of Scotch beyond self-consciousness. Why don't we just go to your house?"

You grin and shake your head.

"God," she says, "*Stirling's*. Well, I know some different sorts of places. Why don't we go to one of them?"

"All right."

She rolls her eyes as if picturing how you'd be received in one of *her* establishments. She points straight ahead. "Drive somewhere *now*," she says. "Or else my fellow roomers will be on the steps and you and I will be an item in the gossip pages of the *Herald* in the morning."

You start up the Brougham, wishing you had chosen the Ferrari and could playfully embarrass her by revving the engine so loud that it would draw a crowd.

You drive to Stirling's, a restaurant that Megan liked, not located in London though it was. There are better, more expensive restaurants in the city, but you have never been to them. You get out of the car and hurry round to the other side to open her door.

She looks up at you from under her eyebrows, which are arched as if to say you must be kidding. You step back and look away as she struggles from the car. When you're sure that she is clear of it, you close the door.

"I'm not going in there," she says, her arm fully extended as she points her cane at Stirling's, from the window of which a middle-aged couple seated opposite each other at a table stare at you, mouths agape.

Leaning her cane against your car, she lights up a cigarette, her hands shaking so badly you almost have the nerve to ask if she needs help. She gets it lit, inhales deeply and erupts into a fit of coughing that leaves her so red in the face you think she might be ill. She cocks her head at Stirling's, where there are now four people staring at you from the window.

"We've caused a scene without even going inside," she says, inclining her head so that the wind blows her hair away from the cigarette.

"I'm famous," you say. "You're famous. This car is famous. People will gawk for a while, but then they'll stop. The last thing that people who think they're stars ever want to seem is star-struck."

She raises and drops her arms and looks about as if in search of someone who will help her plead her case, her cigarette tucked into one corner of her mouth. "Fine, Ned," she says, each word a puff of smoke. "In we go. You first." She makes an exaggerated sweeping motion with her hand.

You reach for the door handle, but the door seems to open by itself. A young man wearing a gleaming white shirt, black slacks and a slightly askew bow tie emerges from the gloom, hand outstretched. He smiles as you take his hand as if it's been a long-standing practice of yours to dine at Stirling's and your usual table is waiting for you. You stand aside to allow Fielding to precede you, which, to your great relief, she does without a word.

The two of you follow him among the tables, Fielding, it seems to you, limping more than usual and stabbing the floor more loudly than necessary with her cane. Stirling's is as dimly lit as you remember it, a candlelit lamp at the centre of each table. The young man seats you by the window that overlooks the harbour. Every person in the place is staring at you, even those who have to crane their necks or turn around to do it.

Fielding sits before the young man can help her with her chair. He nods, tells you that your waiter won't be long and, bowing slightly, strides away, hands clasped behind his back. You clip the end of your cigar and light it from the flame inside the lamp, hoping to impress her.

"I used to come here on Sundays with my father," Fielding says as she lays her cane on the floor and looks out the window. "The doctor dining with his daughter who stood in for his wife, the two of us brave-facing it among his colleagues and my schoolmates. People stared then like they're staring now."

"Let them stare. They'll soon be acting as if they didn't notice we came in."

The waiter comes and hands you the wine list.

"Come to think of it," Fielding says, still looking out the window, "we won't be having dinner, just drinks. Perhaps you should move us to the bar."

The waiter looks at you. "We'll stay here," you say. "We may change our minds about the menu."

"I'll have a double Scotch, neat," Fielding says.

"Your best Scotch," you say. "And the same for me."

The waiter plucks the wine list from your hands and hurries off.

"I should have remembered," you say. "You never eat."

"I eat when I'm alone," she says.

The waiter brings your drinks, removing his hands from them with an ironic flourish as he sets them down.

Fielding picks up her glass and, her little finger extended, sips from it and puts it down. "This will be my only drink," she says.

"I've never seen you nurse a drink."

"You've never seen me drink from a glass."

You nod. "You drank from your flask that night on the bridge all those years ago. Water, you said, but I wasn't fooled."

"Ned, why are we here? I'm sixty years old. You're thirty-eight. I don't think it's cynical of me to think that you could have your pick of the single women of St. John's and a good number of the married ones. The long shot of true love or the certainty of money—which do you think most women would choose?"

"That *is* cynical."

"You're as naive and vulnerable in matters of love as I was at fourteen, as I still was in my twenties. You think you love me, but you've never said you do. I don't know what you see when you look at me. You and me and Brendan perhaps. The closest thing to a restoration of the Vatchers as there can ever be. I was part of your childhood. I sat at your parents' dinner table when, like them, I was in my early thirties. You associate me with a time when the three of you were still together."

You panic, reach into the pocket of your jacket and remove the green velvet box that holds the engagement ring you bought a month ago.

"Don't—" Fielding manages to say before you place the box on the table in front of her, in the middle of the light cast by the lamp, intending to open it so she can see the ring.

"Sheilagh, will you—"

She snatches the box and deftly slips it into the pocket that you know contains her flask. She picks up her barely touched Scotch, downs it in one go.

"Listen to me," she says, her voice low but insistent. "Listen and don't interrupt me." She looks around the restaurant and sighs. "All right, here goes:

"You know I went to Bishop Spencer when Prowse went to Bishop Feild. We met. By the time I turned fourteen, I was six feet tall and five months pregnant.

"Wanting to have nothing more to do with Prowse and knowing that my father would want to have nothing to do with a family as poor as the Smallwoods, I told my father that the baby was Joe Smallwood's.

"My father framed Smallwood, making it seem that he had written a libellous letter about Bishop Feild to a newspaper. In an attempt to clear Smallwood and keep my father from being justly accused, I falsely confessed that it was I who slandered Bishop Feild, for which I was nearly put to the paddle by Prowse. Smallwood intervened, leaving Prowse without a paddle and himself up a certain kind of creek.

"My father sent me to New York, to visit my mother, he told everyone. I had twins, a boy and a girl.

"So it was that Prowse's babies, which my mother pretended were hers, allowed me to pretend to be a virgin, my mother to pretend that she was a mother for the second time, my stepfather that he was not sterile after all, and my father that he was not a grand-father at the age of thirty-eight.

"Because of my height and haggard look, I was able, back in St. John's, to pass myself off as a grown woman and get a library card. But the women who ran the library would not allow me to borrow books deemed by men to be unsuitable for women. So I con-vinced my father, who believed he knew what I would do if I had nothing else to do, to borrow and return for me the books whose titles I found in the guide to world literature that I stole from a local bookstore.

"I read at a rate that caused people to wonder how someone as busy as a doctor and a single father could find so much time for books. He was soon seen as a man who consoled himself for the loss of his wife and the delinquency of his daughter by immersing himself in the classics.

"The consumption and procurement of books and booze were my main pastimes for three years. Sometimes I ventured outdoors at night to walk and think. I decided to write a book but got no further than the title: *Fielding's Guide to Womanly Pursuits.*

"By day I went out walking and noticed nothing but women pushing prams. It seemed that women who had made off with my twins were everywhere. It seemed that my mother was *everywhere*, disguised, pushing pram after pram, each one of which contained my children.

"At night, when my father was asleep, I went out to revel in the silence and the solitude. I stopped in places where I was sheltered from the cold and couldn't be seen and looked up at the stars. I remember the wind roaring in the trees whose branches creaked with frost.

"For as long as I could stand it, I put off going home.

"In New York in 1920, I had a steamy affair with Smallwood that almost boiled over into holding hands. He proposed. I said nothing. He stormed out. Back in St. John's, he proposed again. I was no longer indecisive. Nor was the woman he proposed to, whose name was Clara."

She leans back in her chair. "That's it. The whole story."

You stab out your cigar in the ashtray. "Prowse and Smallwood?" you say, incredulous. "All this time you've kept it to yourself?"

"You're not the only one I've hidden the truth from."

"For your *own* sake."

"At first, yes. But since then? For the sake of my children and grandchildren."

"Prowse knows about the children?"

"He denies that they exist."

"Why are you telling me now?"

"I should have told you sooner."

"Did my father know?"

"No."

"No. Of course not. Edgar would not have been so enamoured of Miss Fielding if he had. He might not have just up and disappeared if he had known."

"You know that makes no sense."

"I have no idea what makes sense where he's concerned. Look where their car was found. Does that make sense? Maybe it was *his* hidden life that got him and my mother killed."

"What are you talking about?"

You grab her by the wrist. "Do you know anything about it? Is there more that you've been hiding all this time?"

She shakes free of you and almost falls off her chair. "That's ridiculous," she says.

You stare at the table, shaking your head in disbelief. "Prowse," you say with disgust.

"That's right."

"Did Prowse force you?"

"I was bedded, willing and able."

"He seduced you."

"No, we spoke for hours, each of us countering the other with cogent logic. We swooned in tandem. He had his way with me. I had mine with him. After which we parted ways."

"You make a joke of it. Children out of wedlock. Jilted by the likes of Prowse, that sycophant. You ridicule yourself."

"Not just myself. Tit-for-tat."

"You ridicule everyone."

"No."

"You were in love with him?"

"Yes. I was. Remember, I was fourteen."

"Are you still in love with him?"

"No."

"What about Smallwood?"

She shakes her head.

"That psychic, Miss Avery, she was right about you."

"She made some lucky guesses. But she said she thought the Brougham was underwater."

"She said my mother was afraid, so afraid that she ran, even though my father told her not to be afraid. She said there was an accident and then there wasn't one."

"Which makes no sense."

"She said that you were in love for the third time."

She turns her head and looks out the window.

"Well, *are* you?"

"My son, David, died in the war," she says, ignoring your question. "He died not knowing that I was his mother."

"Your daughter—"

"Is happily married in New York. She's never openly acknowledged that I'm her mother. Her family thinks that we're half-sisters."

"I'm sorry, but aren't such things all the more reason to change your life while you still can?"

She stoops to pick up her cane, but before she can take hold of it, you grab her by the arm again and again she pulls away.

"Wait, you didn't give me a chance," you say, looking around the restaurant to see if anyone has noticed. No one looks your way or appears to be making an effort not to. Blood pounds in your temples. You would knock *your* drink back if you felt certain you could raise it to your mouth.

You have missed the signs. You have missed them all your life.

You feel yourself turning crimson. You haven't been drinking enough for this. She has. No one has ever spoken so openly to you before.

"I am not in love with you, Ned. Is that plain enough for you? I am in love with someone else."

You can tell by how she looks that you look dumbstruck. "Who is it?" you say.

"I'm going home," she says. "I'm walking home. Don't get up until I'm gone."

You feel like shouting at her, but you won't stoop to drowning out her voice with yours.

She picks up her cane, stands, and takes the ring box from her pocket, her fist entirely enclosing it. She extends her fist and you do likewise with your hand palm upwards, discreetly accepting the box and returning it to your jacket as she makes her way toward the door.

3. FIELDING

I met Prowse on Water Street that night. He had always been able to tell at a glance if I'd been drinking. I had had quite a lot more since leaving Stirling's.

"Fielding," he said. "Tut, tut, tut, tut. What a sorry sight."

"Don't you have an errand to run for someone, Prowse?"

"You like to be scandalous, don't you? You bring it upon yourself. Everyone knows that just because not everything went your way, you renounced your upbringing to play at being poor. No one is fooled, Fielding. No one is as shocked as you think they are and would like them to be. Isn't it about time you got on with it? That life is unfair comes as no surprise to anyone but you."

"You're right, Prowse. It was very affected of me to come down with TB just to acquire a limp and justify my sporting this cane and wearing this corrective boot. I do my best to seem more sinned against than sinning. I court pity, but scorn it when it comes. Poverty is just a hobby that any time I want to I can drop in favour of extravagant wealth. I drink too much because it gives me the nerve to say and do outrageous things. Who but a poseur would go so far as to will infertility upon herself just to get attention?"

"You're proving my point. It does all come down to self-pity, doesn't it, Fielding?"

I tried to seem unfazed. "*Two children*, Prowse," I said, my voice quavering. "One dead before you set eyes on him. Another alive and oblivious to your existence. Does no thought of them ever cross your mind?"

He looked about to see if anyone had heard, but we had the sidewalk to ourselves. "Shut up," he said. "I have no proof that these children even exist, let alone that they're mine. You've borne me a grudge all your life because I broke up with you when we were in school. In *school*, Fielding."

"That's right, Prowse. It's the loss of you that torments me still, not the loss of my children."

I turned around and walked away from him. I went back to my room at the Cochrane, lay down, closed my eyes and hoped for sleep that I knew would never come.

In the rooms, the same men come and go / Their names are Mike and Al and Joe / They like to think their wives don't know.

4.

Only days later, Duggan and I went to see Ned, who had surprised me by extending an invitation through Duggan. I wondered if Ned meant to tell me that I couldn't spend time in the Flag House with Brendan anymore.

It was a cold night, but there was no wind as we climbed the hill. Looking up at the sky, I saw the distant lights of a small plane and wondered if it was Ned's.

Duggan took my arm on the steep part of the slope and I told him about Ned's proposal. He seemed perturbed.

"I hope you said no," he said. "I mean, I didn't know—" He trailed off into a brooding silence.

"I did say no."

〰

Ruby met us in the vestibule. "Ned is in a foul mood," she said. "I don't know why." She glared at me. "Don't make him worse."

Ned came out of the kitchen into the hall, a snifter of bourbon in his hand. "Just in time for dinner," he said, waving us toward the dining room. "Mustn't let it get cold, Duggan. Today, I'm going to do as my friend Miss Fielding does and watch while the rest of you chow down. It must be fun or else she wouldn't do it."

We sat at the table. I smiled at Brendan, who smiled back.

"Ruby always says grace," Ned said. "Why don't you do it this time, Miss Fielding?"

"I can say it," Duggan offered.

"I'll say it," Ruby said.

When she was finished, Ned looked at me. "There. Not so hard, is it, Miss—"

Ruby, cutting him off, said that Reg had taken a turn for the worse. Nan had told her and Ned that, according to the priest, Reg's written confessions had become impossible to understand, a gibberish of words. He had to be led to bed, the daybed, the dinner table and the bathroom. She said it would soon be time to put him in a home because Nan wouldn't be able to deal with him much longer.

"I offered to hire someone to live with them to help her, but she said no," Ned said.

Nan had said that Reg had gone to church for the last time. From now on, the priest would come to the house to give him Holy Communion. "Poor soul," Ruby said.

"Yes," Ned said, "poor soul indeed."

I looked at Duggan, who was moving food about on his plate as if in search of something that he liked.

"You know," Ned said, "I've been keeping Brendan's weather log for him. Ruby doesn't have the time to do it anymore. I report his findings to the Meteorological Service. He wrote me a note saying he'll never use a phone again until his voice gets better. But he still insists on not going for the operation. He won't go near the weather garden anymore, won't go to school, won't go anywhere. All he does is look forward to the evening when he can go up the hill and meet Miss Fielding at the Flag House. Miss Fielding, you might as well do us the honour of moving in with us."

Ruby looked aghast at him and then at me.

"Ned—" Duggan began.

"Never mind—it was just a joke. To record the weather is to record history in its most basic and objective form. There is so much deception in the world. So much treachery. Backstabbing. It seems there's no one you can trust. But empirical facts and sensory observations are pure forms of truth."

"Brendan," I said, "let's go up to the Flag House now."

"Ned decides when Brendan goes up there," Ruby said, but Ned turned his face toward the window.

Brendan got up from his chair and ran off to his room, followed quickly by Ruby.

"Why do you only want what you can't have?" Ned said to me.

"That's not fair, Ned," Duggan said.

"I knew you'd tell Duggan," Ned said.

"He's my friend."

"Ned," Duggan said, "this is not like you. Miss Fielding can't help it that a man she doesn't love fell in love with her."

Ned stood up and came around to put his arm on Duggan's shoulder, which he shook slightly. "Quite right, my friend," he said. "My one true friend."

Duggan wasn't finished. "How much money do you need to make up for what you think your parents did? You've come to believe that you must have everything or else be robbed of what you have and wind up with nothing, which is what you once had for so long you're never sure that anything is yours to keep—that it might not all be taken away from you and given back to those who, by the arbitrary precedence of blood and tradition, are entitled to it.

"No trace of you is detectable anymore, Ned. I wonder where you have gone. The brave young man I knew—"

Ned swept the dishes off the table and against the wall, where they shattered into pieces.

"Stop it," Duggan said.

Ned left the room, and seconds later we heard the slamming of the back door.

"He'll go up in the Baron now because of you," Ruby said. She had come back to stand in the doorway. "You'll both be to blame if something happens."

NED

I flew out over the Brow, climbing slowly, sipping from my vial of bourbon. The sky was clear, starlit, the ocean dark below but for the lights of ships.

Edgar had said of his job: "Of all the things a man could be remembered for. Of all the ways to make one's mark." I'd had no idea what he was talking about.

I knew now, knew in the wake of Fielding's rejection and Duggan's chastisement of me. My core was not only empty but had been since my parents disappeared.

There simply was nothing at the innermost of me, nor, it suddenly seemed, at the innermost of others. The notion that, though finite, the universe was enlivened by something that could never be extinguished seemed absurd.

I'd thought I was writing a masterpiece, but in a flash of panic and despair I suddenly saw that every word was gibberish.

I was the origin of nothing. Grocery stores. Fish processing plants. Coastal supply companies. A tabloid newspaper. Radio stations. Ever-proliferating television stations. Supermarkets. Candy on which children spent the few pennies their parents could spare.

Nothing began when I was born and the world would in no way be diminished by my death.

I flew back to the airport and drove home. As I pulled in, I looked up at the Flag House. The kitchen light was on and I could make out Fielding and Brendan sitting at the table.

I went to my office and locked the door. I felt a great weariness for which I could think of no better word than boredom.

Over the next few days, I didn't eat or sleep. I didn't even drink much. I hid behind the locked door of my study and didn't answer when Ruby or Duggan knocked. I suppose I had what's called a breakdown.

I thought of Duggan, who, when I'd found myself suddenly alone, acquired me, much as I'd acquired Brendan.

I tried to drink myself to sleep but couldn't.

Then I tried not to drink so as to stay clear-headed. I puzzled over my parents' disappearance until I couldn't stop. How could the discovery of their car not have led to *something*? What was it that I should have been able to see but couldn't? What was it that, for years, had been staring me straight in the face?

"Come out, Ned," Nan shouted on the morning of the third day of my self-confinement. "Even Reg never hid his face after Phonse and Edgar died. Little Brendan comes out of his room every morning even if he never says a word."

I ignored her too. I was pouting, sulking, which should have seemed ridiculous but didn't to me. I couldn't have felt ridiculous any more than I could have felt ecstatic. I was deaf to the tones of my own life.

At last, I allowed Dr. Vaughan into the study to examine me.

"There is nothing wrong with you," he said when he was done.

I told him he was fired, rehired him on the spot and apologized.

"You're not getting any pills," he said as he was leaving. "Not from me at least."

On the phone, I played the same "you're fired/you're hired" game with many of my employees, whose voices quavered with fear and dread. "You're fired," I said. I hung up, then phoned them back and said, "I changed my mind. You're hired again," and hung up once more.

I began to receive calls from other employees who said they'd heard that I was firing everyone who worked for me. I said it was true, then said that it wasn't. I felt no shame, no guilt.

Television. It's from two Greek words. *Tele. Palai.* One means long ago, the other far away. The first words of a story. Long ago and far away, there lived—

There's no better way than death to wash your hands of something. I considered it. I considered little else.

There was no point in building the tallest this or the biggest that, because eventually it would either be outdone by someone else or fall into ruins.

All records would be broken; scientific discoveries were beyond my scope.

Each worker repeated ad infinitum one of the many tasks that together composed the making of a television set but knew nothing of the other tasks. The foremen, though adept at none of the tasks, understood how and in what sequence they should be performed. Each day, thousands of TV sets were made, though there was not a single soul who by himself could make a TV set.

In this way, over billions of years, the world that was once thought to have been the doing of a solitary Agency was assembled. Six days and nights. Billions of years. It was hard to say which idea seemed the more absurd.

It seemed my ultimate goal was nothing more profound than self-amusement.

My parents. They existed nowhere now but in the minds of those who would themselves cease to be someday.

I thought of Brendan. He was the greatest of the wonders of Ned Vatcher, my adopted son who, only twelve had twice dodged death and now preferred to mine the company of a woman I realized I had never really loved.

It was dark outside. I fell asleep momentarily and dreamed that I was looking out the window of my childhood home at the snow that was falling, at the mound of white in the driveway, within which was the Auburn Brougham. In the dream, I knew that my parents were inside the car. I went outside and wiped the snow from one of the windows. It was like letting light into a tomb.

They might have died while I was sleeping, their deaths taking place unknown to me. It hardly seemed possible that I could wake from sleep and not know they were gone. There were no links of love, or else how could two souls slip away and others not even notice?

I put my hands and face against the window, a boy again looking out from the house on Circular Road. Out in the city, word was spreading, but there were some who didn't know that my parents were gone. People were going from house to house, putting them out as one might put out candles. Something surged up in me, a feeling like waking from an unremembered dream.

When I came to, I was on the floor beside the desk.

XVII

FIELDING

The breakwater of the New World. The European's first impression of America. The Far East of the West. I'd taken the train to my section shack many times since my first stint there ended in 1926. Thirty-five years ago and almost everything still looked the same, even the station stops. Innumerable rock-surrounded ponds, endless acres of cratered peat bogs never trod upon, lavender-coloured fireweed bending in the wind. It may have been a trick of memory, but I thought I even recognized certain trees, their size and shape unaltered.

Everything, even the shacks and telegraph poles, was bent eastward by the wind. Shallow soil and shallow ponds, and, underneath, nothing but unyielding stone. Skin so thin on this massive rock you could peel it off by hand.

What is the opposite of a settlement? An abandonment. The coast was strewn with abandonments. It traced out the broken histories, the starts and stops, the first arrivals and final departures. Old maps showed sea routes that ran from one abandonment to the next, linked abandonments of which nothing but the names remained. I thought of the seemingly featureless interior of the island that no one had ever set foot or eyes upon, the blank and silent core.

I was still sick when I first went by train to the section shack from St. John's, still unsure that I was cured, though every doctor but my father said I was. "You're better off out in the country for a while," he said. "You'll never learn the knack of that leg on the hills of St. John's." What he meant was that he didn't want me to learn the knack of my leg where those who were scandalized by my contracting a poor person's disease could see me.

I went there to convalesce and wound up with a job. The railway was maintained by men and I became their assistant along ten miles of track.

I had changed since then as much as Sectionville had. The men I worked with, their wives, their families, were gone. Many of the shacks lay empty. The art of railway maintenance had been refined, rendering some occupations and vocations obsolete. I'd heard that there were plans to let the railway fall into disuse and replace it with a fleet of buses.

I had started drinking heavily again the night after Ned swept the dishes off the table, too heavily to spend time with Brendan.

Now, a many-times-assayed task had to be assayed again. Here, alone. I felt as though this was my last chance. My body thought it was. I was going too far from help to send for it, to ask for it. Too far to change my mind. Too far from anywhere to even allow me to beg for what, unless I forswore it, would cause me to cease to be.

I telegraphed Duggan ten days later: "Worst is not yet past. You were right. Nothing left. Won't come back like this. Twelve Mile shack. Don't reply. F."

Before leaving St. John's, I had told Duggan of my plan to go to my section shack to quit drinking. He'd warned me against it, insisting that to be out of range of a doctor or a hospital or, at the very least, someone experienced in minding people along the way to where I meant to go was madness. He told me he would come with me. I told him I would think about it, but I had quit before, among doctors, nurses, clergymen, nuns and all manner of ex-drinkers. I'd put myself in their hands and they had helped me through it, yet I was convinced that my having had help was the reason I had relapsed every time. I believed sobriety wouldn't take until I went through the whole thing on my own.

I promised Duggan I wouldn't go to my section shack without first telling him exactly where it was. But I did. I eventually discovered that, two days after I left, he phoned the Cochrane and was told that I'd gone and hadn't said when I intended to come back. Next, Duggan contacted Ned, who had no idea how to find my section shack. There were such shacks at one-mile intervals along the fifty-mile stretch of the Bonavista. No one who worked at the train station in St. John's knew which shack was mine. Of the fifty shacks, only ten were officially still lived in.

The telegraph operator at the station sent telegrams to all ten section men, who telegraphed back that they had never heard of me. There was nothing Duggan could do but hope for my return. Ten long days and ten nights of fitful sleep later, he received my wire. Duggan told his superiors that a childhood friend who was a section man on the Bonavista branch of the railway was ill and had asked that he come and visit him to hear his confession, give him Communion and administer last rites. Duggan told me later that he convinced himself the lie was justifiable because the friend who had sent for him, me, was in need of something more important than the sacraments.

At Riverhead, Duggan was told he'd have to hitch a ride on a maintenance car to Twelve Mile Shack from the train's nearest station stop. But he'd dressed in his habit and collar and word of his "mission" soon made its way to the conductor, who made a rare, special stop at Twelve Mile Post to let him off. Duggan departed his car to a chorus of "God bless you, Father."

I had been asleep but was woken by the unmistakable grinding of the train's brakes and its blasts of steam. I peeked out through the curtains and was startled by the size of it, a behemoth of metal, a man-wrought mass of purpose and technology stalled where it had never stalled before, alien in the midst of so much unarranged, untended wilderness.

So as not to be spotted from the train, I waited until Duggan approached the door, and then stood behind it as I opened it to let him in. He looked as though he wanted to hug me, but he didn't. Nor did I hug him, even though the curtains were drawn and the shack was lantern-lit at noon. We stood apart, perhaps because of the inhibiting proximity of the train and its passengers, the sound of it just yards away as, with another blast of steam, its wheels screeching and rumbling, it resumed the journey it had interrupted just for Duggan and the poor "man" who had sent for him.

"How are you?" he said, removing his hat.

"It's good to see you, Duggan," I said, and started coughing, my upper body convulsing time after time. I pressed my fist to my mouth and leaned my free hand against the door. Duggan put a hand on my back, but I shook my head. When I was through coughing, I patted my chest. "My lungs have never been the same since the San," I said.

"You walk a lot," Duggan said. "I bet all that walking is good for them."

I nodded and moved away from the door. "No electricity," I said. "Only the active shacks have it, so you won't be able to watch Ned on TV."

"I never have."

"I get my water from a pump out back. It's very cold. I boil it to take a bath. Some potatoes, carrots and turnips grow by themselves in the garden every year. Otherwise, I'm afraid it's trout or rabbits, which you'll have to catch and trap, because I haven't been able to, lately—no energy for it. I did set some rabbit slips before I ran out of Scotch. You can check them. But if I caught any, they might have gone off by now, so you'll have to set the slips again."

"Immaculate decrepitude," Duggan said, looking around the shack. What little there was by way of furniture had a battered, weathered look as if I had scrounged it from what others threw away: a rightward-tilting bookshelf that bore a dozen books; a table that had been someone's storm door, held up by two sawhorses; two rickety chairs with peeling, blistered patches of white paint. The raftered ceiling sagged in the middle, and the floor, which was covered in overlapping strips of tattered cardboard and linoleum, was warped in mimicry of the land the shack was built on.

"Outhouse as well," I said.

"Just like old times."

"I can't help feeling a bit like Kurtz. That makes you Marlow. A few more days alone and I might well have lost my mind." I told him I feared I would wind up in a hospital if I went back to St. John's. "Ned would insist on putting me in one."

"Yes. He has a history of doing that."

"Or I'd fall down or pass out or something and wake up in one. I swore long ago that I'd never be a patient again. It's very Brendan-like, isn't it?"

"Ned seems to be doing better."

"Really?"

"Well, maybe he just seems better because he's started going up in that plane of his again."

"I may be wrong, but it seems to me that, if I let others do this for me, I'll lose my nerve, or I'll lose my strength and never recover, or I'll recover too soon and go back to the Scotch. There's plenty of it in St. John's, but it's harder to get out here. There is moonshine out on the end of the Bonavista and I've even heard there's rye whisky, but I haven't tried to get any. So the shack is dry. Unless you brought something special for me in *that*." I pointed to his little suitcase, which he'd left just inside the door.

"No," he said, "just some clothes. No Scotch. Not even a secret supply for myself. No chalice, in spite of what I told the Bishop. No wine, no Eucharist, no sacred vessels."

"They wouldn't tell the agent at Riverhead, but the section men know I'm here. They protect my privacy. But once they hear that a priest is staying with me, I might fall a notch in their estimation. Word will get back to St. John's that you're out here with me. People will draw assumptions and start rumours."

Duggan shrugged. "No priest was ever defrocked who didn't want to be," he said. "Besides, my superiors will see that I'm telling the truth when I account for myself, however upset they'll be about what their congregation believes or suspects. And it may be me who turns out to be Kurtz. They may send a young Jesuit in search of me. I wouldn't be surprised if he turned up at the door tonight."

"Duggan, I haven't felt this tired and sick since I was admitted to the San. I wouldn't have asked you to come if I thought I had TB. This feels—well, it feels like nothing else I've ever had. I wouldn't entrust myself to anyone I know but you."

"You go lie down," he said. "Your eyes are more often closed than open. I feel like I'm boring you to sleep. Are you able to get yourself ready for bed?"

I told him that I was and that, if he was going to light the stove, there were some wood junks out back that needed to be split. After closing the door of my little room, I took my boots off and all of my clothes but for my slip and lay down on the bunk on top of the blankets, and drifted off to the sound of Duggan moving about one wall away, getting settled in the bedroom that was even smaller than mine.

It was dark when I woke. I heard the sizzle of what I guessed were trout frying in the pan in the kitchen. Trying not to be disconcerted by the black spots that appeared in front of my eyes when I sat up, I eased my legs off the bed, put my clothes and boots on, tapped the door open with my cane and joined Duggan.

"I caught these on that," he said, pointing to a short bamboo fishing rod and reel that stood in the corner to the left of the back door. "I haven't been fishing in decades. They swarmed my hook as soon as it hit the water." He looked me up and down the way he did prospective athletes, wondering, I'm sure, if he should insist that I let him take me to the nearest hospital.

"Don't worry," I said, "it comes and goes. I should have cleared my throat before I opened the door for you earlier. I hadn't spoken in a while. Bad first impression."

He was no longer dressed in his habit but in a green denim shirt and black overalls and black and red tartan slippers.

"I haven't been out in the woods in a long time," he said. "I forgot how nice the spruce trees smell, the turpentine, the juniper needles when the ground is warm, the sound of the wind in a stand of alders. It brings back a lot of memories—good ones. Mom and Dad, my two sisters. They're in Boston. I haven't seen them in over thirty years, but we keep in touch. I'm a bay man born and raised. That's why I could never work indoors. I have to work outside."

A wave of dizziness washed over me. "You eat," I said. "I got up too soon. I'll go back to bed. Don't worry, I'll be fine."

I closed my door and lay down. No magic potions, no cure-alls, nothing to stifle the urge. Nothing to relieve it either.

I never remembered the worst of drying out. I only knew as much about it as I could feel once it was behind me. Its legacy. Though I felt less afraid now that Duggan was there.

The first few days there'd been a steady stream of visitors who came to make sure I was all right. The remaining section men and/or their wives. If I hadn't answered the door, they would have kicked it in. They were very sweet. They came with food from their gardens and rabbit and trout and cans of this and that. It took some doing, but I convinced them that I would send for help if I needed it.

They knew from my previous sojourns that I liked to keep to myself. I told them I came for the privacy and solitude that I needed to write and couldn't always find in St. John's. It was partly true, but I'd come down here for all kinds of reasons over the years, not just to get a respite from the city.

They also knew how I was regarded in St. John's. They'd never put much stock in that, or in St. John's, for that matter. They more or less expected a lame, unmarried woman of my size and age to drink too much. They'd never known me to carry on with men, so those rumours were discounted, except by some of the women.

Once they knew a priest was staying here, they'd be sure to keep their distance.

I'd sent for Duggan only after I managed to fall out of bed and woke up on the floor. I stayed there for two days, sometimes awake, sometimes not, too weak to feel distressed or fearful, exhausted to my very core, with what felt like a searing ball of ice in my gullet.

I had a fever that came on late at night. I woke with my hair and my pillow drenched in sweat. When I walked, I felt as though I were towing a ton of lead. A thousand other things I can't describe.

I was bogged down in something that might not be the legacy of drying out.

I got up again a few hours later. Duggan was standing in the open doorway of the shack, looking up at the night sky. When he saw me, he closed the door.

"I'm bogged down in something, Duggan," I said. "It's not just giving up the booze." I tapped my head and then my heart. He nodded, not just to indicate that he understood, it seemed, but as if to say he had once been overtaken by the very sort of torpor I described. "I often touch my jacket pocket to make sure that my flask is there. Even though I know it's empty, my hand doesn't know. Sometimes, I put the flask under my bed and leave it there all day, and still I reach inside my pocket and feel about for that phantom flask."

He nodded again.

Dinner every night was fried trout and fried potatoes and carrots. Fish hash, Duggan called it, followed by squares of the bittersweet chocolate he had brought with him, and strong tea.

"Whisky and moonshine just ten miles away," I couldn't help telling him again one evening.

He shrugged. "Did you sleep?" he said. "It didn't sound like it."

"Restless," I said. "Unremembered dreams."

"They must have been bad ones."

Some of the trout he caught were small enough for him to eat without removing the bones. He didn't use a fork and knife, just picked one up by the tail, raised it above his head and either bit off one piece after another, saving the salty, crunchy tail for last, or ate the trout in a single mouthful. "That's how my father used to do it," he said.

I tried to smile through my queasiness. For days I hadn't been able to eat what little food he'd managed to prepare. "I can't eat yet," I said. "It's better not to try."

"You have to try sometime," he said.

I nodded, but lit up a cigarette. "Eat mine," I said. I pushed my plate across the table. It was soon as empty as his. "I have never known anyone," I said, "who relishes food as much as you do."

"I always have," he said, grinning.

He cleared the table, leaving the dirty dishes in the rack beneath the window. "Something to pass the time with later," he said.

The kitchen was lit by a single lantern on the windowsill. It cast our shadows on the opposite wall and on the ceiling.

"Let's sit closer to the stove," I said.

On the Bonavista, most clear summer nights were so cool that mist rose from the barrens and the ponds, and condensation fogged up all three windows. He moved his chair to within a few feet of the stove, pulled open the door and helped me up from my chair, which he put slantwise to his. I sat down again and stared at the flames.

He went to his room, took the patchwork quilt from his bed, came back, folded it in half and draped it across my shoulders. "There now," he said, "you should be toasty front and back." He poured more tea for the two of us, sat down and lit himself a cigarette.

I decided it was time I told him what I'd told Ned. The long love life of Sheilagh Fielding, the short love life of Sheilagh Fielding. The short-lived loves of Sheilagh Fielding. Prowse, my children, Smallwood and New York, my parents, my father, David who died not knowing he was my son, or Prowse's. David who died. Sarah, who still believed, or pretended to, that I was her half-sister. Edgar, Megan and me.

I held forth, staring into the fire, which he fed with wood from time to time. I looked at him as he listened. His face bore as little expression as if he'd heard before everything that I was saying.

"I thought of asking my mother why loving me did not trump loathing my father. Did she think herself well rid of both of us? What kind of child so disenchants her mother by the age of four as to seem deserving of abandonment? Any life without him seemed preferable to any life with me . . .

"I contracted TB in New York, became feverish and decided to come home. My father admitted me to a sanitarium. I read a book there about a man who reads books while fighting TB in the San. *The Magic Mountain* by Thomas Mann. Its hero was Hans Castorp."

"Haven't read it."

"Hans's sanatorium wasn't like mine. It was an Alpine mountain retreat where bracingly fresh air and the most nutritious of fresh food were in abundance, and the medical staff was composed entirely of robust, optimistic citizens of Switzerland.

"Hans's tuberculosis was not like mine. *He* caught TB while visiting a patient.

"His fellow patients were not like mine. He talked to them for seven years without getting bored. He was regaled by the unaccountably tubercular aristocrats of western Europe, as well as rich businessmen, and esteemed professors, some of whom, though asymptomatic, unaccountably died. Hans's only symptom was a sort of vague enfeeblement complicated by an occasional cough.

"He left his sanitarium fully cured of everything except an unaccountable urge to enlist in the war in which, it was implied to my great delight, he perished.

"As I do with all introductions, I saved until last the introduction to *The Magic Mountain*, which informed me that the book was heavily symbolic. I decided that Thomas Mann should be tied to a heavily non-symbolic anchor and thrown into the sea . . ."

Duggan laughed.

Not until perhaps ten minutes after I fell silent did he finally say: "Sheilagh Fielding, you are . . . Well, you should go to bed now. I'll wash the dishes and stay up until this flame dies down."

"No," I said. "I won't sleep if I go to bed. *Let* the flames die down. I'm not that cold."

The two of us sat there in silence until the blue gloom of dawn showed at the window.

Using dishtowels and water from the crank pump, he made cold compresses that he laid across my forehead while I slept.

He sat on the floor beside my bed and wiped away the drops of sweat that trickled down my face. He reversed my pillow from time to time, or replaced it with another.

He washed the pillow slips and, depending on the time of day, dried them on the stove or on the clothesline.

Sometimes he was lying on the floor when I woke up, eyes closed, breathing more easefully than I suspected I had since my mother went away when I was four.

"Have you seen that little path out back?" I said.

He shook his head.

"You'll find it," I said. It was very narrow and canopied by tree branches and bushes. "It's a rabbit path," I said. "That's where I set my slips. Could you check them? Remember I mentioned the rabbits? If there are any rabbits, throw them away. It could be as much as ten days since they were snared. Do you know how to reset the slips?"

He gave me a playful look of scorn.

"Sorry," I said. "But I think I might soon be able to manage some rabbit. I like it cold. I always ate it cold. I used to fish it out of the leftover stew that my father put in the icebox."

Duggan came back hours later with a brace of rabbits. "New ones," he said. "I threw away a few, but I found these on the way back, just caught. I don't like cold rabbit. I'll skin these, make a stew and take out some pieces for you. When yours are cold, I'll reheat mine."

We passed the evenings sitting in front of the fire. I fell asleep and woke, fell asleep and woke, trusting Duggan to keep me from spilling my tea, or toppling off my chair.

"In that pond that you've been fishing in," I said one night, "there's a little cove that you can't see the tracks from, and vice versa, I hope. When it's warm enough outside, and when I'm not in something like my present state, I go there with a bar of soap and take a bath, and sometimes a bit of a swim if I have the energy. Anyway, I don't care how cold the water is, I'm having a proper bath one of these days when I feel up to it."

We heard and felt the train go by, the shack shaking for minutes, the windows rattling, the rumble so loud we could only sit there, staring in mute wonder at the door or the fire. Even in the summer there were delays due to problems with the train or the tracks, so there was no telling when the Bullet would go by in either direction. Once it had passed, Duggan went outside to see if any sparks were smouldering on top of the shack or in the grass.

One night, Duggan helped me up a short ladder that he propped against the side of the shack and went back down for our chairs. We sat on the roof for as long as I was able to stay warm beneath the blankets that Duggan draped around me. We looked up at the stars.

Around nine-thirty, a three-quarter moon reached its highest point and lit up the ponds and shallow pools for miles around, as it did every night the wind dropped off to nothing. The pond beside the shack was calm, except for the occasional ripples made by the trout that, after sunset, came close to shore.

"I was up here just like this on referendum night," I said. "It was the same kind of night. I used to have a radio. I came up here after they announced the final count. I didn't vote. Did you?"

"I spoiled my ballot on purpose," Duggan said. "All the priests went as a group to the polling station. It was meant to be a show of force. Vote for Independence, or else. It was all so ugly. It brought out the worst in everyone. But it must have been a quiet night out here."

"It was."

His right hand was near my left, resting on his knee. I reached out and took it in mine. He didn't pull away. He didn't look at me. He rubbed my fingers with his thumb.

We sat there like that.

We were still holding hands when I fell asleep.

When I woke, the hand I'd held was on my shoulder.

"You'll catch cold, Sheilagh Fielding," he said. "Time for you to turn in."

✳

"You must have found it very lonely out here by yourself when you were younger," he said.

I slumped back against my chair and swallowed some tea, feeling on the verge of tears and not knowing why. "I did go mad, for a while, I think, mad from grief, after David's death. I spent the balance of the war setting down in words an alternative version of my life, which I called *The Custodian of Paradise* and which I fancy I might someday publish. Such was the measure of my despair that I devised a fictional existence that was far stranger, far more fantastic than my real one."

"The custodian of paradise. I'd like to have a word with Him."

"Do you still read my columns?"

"Yes. I always assume that what's written in the papers isn't true, but I read them anyway."

I laughed.

"I'm leaving the priesthood," he said after a short silence.

"Why?"

"I'm not renouncing anything. I'm not leaving the Faith. I'm just leaving the priesthood."

"All right, but why?"

He shrugged and shook his head. "I'll tell you when I'm sure."

I felt hopeful, guilty.

"I would like to have met your father," he said.

"No one who met him ever said that they were glad."

"Still."

✳

I began to feel better.

I started to wear my outdoor clothes, even though I stayed inside most of the time. I looked at myself in the little mirror in my room. I wore loose-fitting dungarees, and a grey, fisherman's knit sweater. The sweater was much too big for me—it was given to me by a section man—so that a good deal of my upper chest showed, my skin so pale and unblemished it was hard to believe it was that of someone with hands like mine. My collarbone was so prominent and fragile-looking that I fancied that, if I were able to press my shoulders together, it would fold perfectly in half.

I preferred oversized clothes because they hid my shapelessness. In the mirror, there was no evidence of breasts beneath my sweater.

Two weeks at the shack and the backs of Duggan's hands were nicked with dozens of cuts in various stages of healing, and his palms were blistered and calloused. There was dark dirt in the moats of his fingernails and beneath the nails, and the cuticles bore cracks like those of near-shattered glass. His bottom lip was likewise dry and cracked. He was ruddy-faced from having spent so much time outdoors.

"What have I done to you, Duggan?" I asked.

He grinned.

Duggan was outside. I couldn't calm the shaking of my hands as I struggled to light a cigarette. One match guttered into a wisp of smoke and I hastily threw another one aside as it burnt down to my thumb and forefinger. At last, with the third match, I succeeded, inhaling deeply and closing my eyes, as if I'd been deprived of cigarettes for weeks. I leaned back in my chair and, eyes still closed, rested my head against it. I sighed deeply, smoke issuing upwards from my mouth and nose.

"We all know that we'll die," I said to Duggan. "But no matter what our age or circumstances, we think of death as something that will happen not just yet."

"I try not to think of it at all."

"I sometimes dream that I am guilty of murder," I said. "I have crossed over into guilt and will never know innocence or light-heartedness again. What a relief it is to wake from those dreams, to realize that after all I am not damned or lost."

There was an untouched cup of tea on the table in front of me. My teeth chattered though I wasn't cold.

"Could you help me drink my tea?" I said. "I can't seem to—"

"Of course," he said. He picked up the cup of tea and held it to my lips as if it was water. I gulped deeply from the cup. I might have emptied it if he had not lowered it and replaced it on the table. "You'll make yourself sick."

"I'm so afraid," I said. "Not of what might happen. But of what might not."

I knew that, if he left the priesthood for the reason that I hoped he was leaving it, I'd be blamed. Weeks in that shack with that woman. Sheilagh Fielding, boozy, floozy, seducer of a Jesuit priest, the final flourish on her career of debauchery and scandal. Duggan the

Jesuit priest who, on the very brink of Heaven, forsook it for an old woman of inglorious renown.

"I've been thinking about it for a lot more than a few weeks," Duggan said. "I've already told them I'm leaving the priesthood. I've told the Archbishop. He's shocked. It's something they expect to hear from younger priests. For three years now, they've been advising further reflection. If they have their way, I'll be reflecting on my deathbed. I want to have been something in my life besides a priest."

"You have. You've been a coach, a friend."

"Yes, but within the priesthood. Maybe not in my case defined by it, but contained by it. You are always contained by it, no matter what kind of priest you choose to be. I'm not sorry I became a priest. I won't be sorry when I cease to be one."

"So what will you be when you are uncontained?"

"It depends. A man. Jesuits are carpenters, you know, like Jesus and his father, Joseph. But I could still be a coach if another school would have me."

"A carpenter, a coach."

He took a breath. "And, my dear Sheilagh, I would be your husband if you'd have me."

"Duggan." I clung to the table with both hands, my heart pounding.

"My leaving the priesthood is not contingent on you saying yes."

"No—I mean, I know."

"You've never thought about it?"

I have, I almost said. I've been in love with you for years. But I've never let myself think about it because you're a priest, and because you're so much like me.

He reached out and took my hand. I pulled it away as if his had burnt it. He was not deterred, but reached out and brushed my hair back from my forehead.

"What a woman you are."

"Do you really think of me as one?"

"I do. I think of you."

"You've never said so."

"You're more forthright than I'm accustomed to. In a woman or a man. And I'm a priest. I'm not extending to you the sort of lewd proposition that the people of St. John's like to believe you extend to men. And others. So far in your life you have put off making big decisions."

"Well. I seem now to be faced with a lifetime of decisions."

"Yes. I believe you are." He moved closer, intending to kiss me, I thought and hoped, but he only leaned his forehead against mine.

"I will," I said. "I will have you."

We heard single maintenance cars and trolley carts go past by day and early in the evenings. As they neared the shack, we heard the voices of the section men become subdued or fall silent. Not until they were well past us did they start up again or return to normal pitch. "We must be the talk of the Bonavista," I said.

My cane in my right hand, Duggan holding my left arm, one of his hands above my wrist, the other above my elbow, we made our way down to the cove through a break in the bushes and the trees behind the shack.

It was sunny and warm and windy, but the cove was sheltered. The warmer the day, the stronger was the southwest wind that bore on it the smell of spruce and juniper. There were no ripe berries yet. Blueberries were part white, part red, like tiny apples.

The cove was closely flanked on both sides by juniper trees. A clear, cold-looking brook ran into it, making a current in the pond at the end of which trout often breeched. Duggan carried my towels over his shoulder and my bar of soap in the pocket of his overalls. The sun shone so brightly on the water, I had to shade my eyes to see. Duggan put my towels down and placed my soap on top of them.

"I can't swim very well," I said. "I never go out over my head. But the water here isn't very deep, so I'll be fine on my own."

It crossed my mind to tell him that, just in case of a rare passerby, I sometimes left my slip on, so he, leaving his own underwear on, could join me if he liked, but I didn't. I didn't say a word as he knelt in front of me, untied my boots and slipped them off, along with my socks.

He stood up quickly, pretending, I think, not to notice my lopsidedness, now that I was standing in my bare feet. I was still taller than him, but not by much.

"Half an hour?" he said.

I nodded and smiled. He nodded back, then turned and slowly made his way over the rocky shore to the end of the path. He stopped momentarily, as if he meant to look back and wave, or say something, remind me of something. But he moved on and I soon lost sight of him amongst the trees.

I stripped down to my slip, folding my clothes on a flat rock and weighting them down with stones, and then hobbled out until the water was up to my knees. I knew that the water in the cove was warmer than that of the rest of the pond, but still it felt as if my lower legs were enclosed by ice.

At first I bathed standing up. The bottom of the cove consisted of small stones on which I was easily able to keep my balance. Intending to discard it just before I went swimming, I did my best to keep my slip from getting wet above the hem, bunching it around my knees.

I scrubbed as much of my upper body as I could. The water had the faintly gamey smell of mint-weed and lily pads. My slip got wet nonetheless, so I decided I'd better take it off and afterward climb back into my clothes without it before Duggan came back. I removed it and my underclothes, which were almost as wet. I waded partway to shore and, balling them up, threw them as hard as I could. They landed on the shore within two feet of the water.

I soaped myself all over. I decided that the fastest way to wash the soap off would be to lie down where it was shallow.

I stared at the jagged red scar that ran almost the length of my leg. It was as if someone had depicted a railway, using my leg as a map. I had rarely looked at it for this long. I ran my hand along it. I wondered what Duggan would make of the scar the first time he saw it. Every time he saw it.

I slowly eased myself into the water, leaning back on my forearms until nothing but my head remained above the surface.

Duggan wanted me to be his wife. He wanted me. Our friendship had been a courtship of glacial pace. The sight of the two of us together, the fact that we sometimes slept under the same roof when snowstorms detained us at Ned's, these were made to seem innocent by the presence, the common cause and common ground, of Ned, on whom we had focused so intensely we had even fooled each other. Was that possible? He had legitimized us, as Brendan and Ruby had Ned and me, as Ned had Edgar and me.

Of all the men I knew, the one I had most in common with was a priest.

"I'm an agnostic priest, Sheilagh," he'd said to me that morning. "Not the first and not the last. I decided long ago that the domestic life was not for me. But now it seems that the monastic one doesn't suit me either. I think I was meant for something in between."

The perversely appealing solitude of priests, the allure of forbidden fruit, the affront of chastity and other kinds of self denial. For these reasons, some women were drawn to priests, and for similar ones, some men were drawn to me. Duggan's life, being so much like mine, had not intrigued me at first, or so I thought. He may, at first, have regarded me as I did him.

Duggan was sleeping through the sound of me typing just outside his door. Twice now he had called me Sheilagh and I hadn't thought to ask *his* name. He knew I needed to write, knew that, if not drinking came at the price of not writing, my relapse was a certainty.

How nice it felt to hold his hand. How nice it felt to be wanted and to want.

I wondered if I could safely walk the track with my flashlight and my cane. The tarred railway ties, the crushed stone in between them, the slick iron rails—a fall could mean the end of me, but then, that had been the case for decades. How pleasant it would be to stretch my legs the way I would if I were in St. John's.

One mile up to the next post. One mile up, one mile back.

Two miles would have been nothing for me a month ago at this time of year, but my legs were weak from lying in bed and sitting by the stove and from not eating. The scar had been flaring up.

If I woke Duggan, he'd insist on coming with me, or try to talk me out of going. I didn't want company. It seemed like forever since I'd been outdoors alone at night. There was no chance of me losing my way.

I eased the door shut behind me, waited a few moments and, satisfied that Duggan was asleep, slowly made my way up the narrow path from the shack to the railway bed, leaning more heavily on my cane than usual, my bad leg quivering.

I tried not to disturb the gravel or breathe too loudly. I made it to the tracks and, one hand beneath my leg, hoisted my larger boot over the rail and stepped onto the ties. I hadn't used the flashlight for fear of waking Duggan.

My chest heaved and drops of sweat trickled through my hair and down my forehead.

I looked up. It was clear, but the moon had long since set. The sky was so thick with stars I had trouble making out the constellations. They cast sufficient light for me to see the dim shapes of distant hills, the tops of trees, the faint sheen of nearby ponds and the condensation on the curving iron rails.

I saw my breath and heard it, puff after puff. I swallowed down the itch to cough. It was colder than the last few nights, but just as calm.

I turned left and began to walk, picking my way gingerly between the ties so as not to stub a boot on one and sprawl face first in the gravel. A dozen yards from the shack, I pointed my flashlight straight at the ground, heading east, barely moving seaward on the Bonavista.

There was almost no chance of a train, or even a two-man trolley car of the sort I used to crank alone, coasting on the downgrades, when I worked mile twelve in '25. The next shack, at which I planned to turn around, had been abandoned since just after '49. I doubted that anyone else went out on the tracks at night. I had them to myself. I was the sole disturber of the silence. I stared for so long at the circle of light on the ground that, when I looked up, I couldn't see a single star.

It had been summer when Smallwood began his country-spanning walk, warm enough for him to go on walking after dark to make up for the days when his feet were so bad he couldn't walk at all. He must sometimes have woken the residents of section shacks, asking for a place to sleep. They would have welcomed him at any hour, their peripatetic unionizer.

Smallwood was, in every sense, far from the Bonavista now, and I was, in almost every sense, exactly where I'd been back then, except for Duggan, except that I was sober, for now, and I was older. Still writing in public disagreement with those few whom few others dared to challenge, though to little practical effect. Still convinced that the truth was of uppermost importance, regardless of the context, no matter the circumstances. Still a reckless, idealistic nuisance. A woman to whom someone who was trying to be helpful had once said: "Do you have to be so truthful?" Still unable to forget, still mourning my lost son and the daughter I gave up to my mother as keenly as if they had left my body only yesterday.

When I made it to the next, abandoned shack, I shone my

flashlight through its broken windows and the doorway in which the door hung by a single hinge, askew, aslant, dangling, looking as if it had swung so in the wind since the world began.

I turned round and rested again, facing west now, up the Bonavista as the section men said, toward the continent of Newfoundland, the intersection of the main line and the branch, the never-glimpsed wilderness from which the question we had failed to answer had been borne to us, the country that would never be discovered or forgotten, the colony of unrequited dreams that would never be acknowledged as a nation except by those of us who made it one.

A hurt I'd never felt before rose up in my throat. I couldn't swallow or breathe. The flashlight fell from my hand. I stabbed the gravel with my cane to keep myself upright. I closed my eyes, wondering if this was death or yet another one of its imposters.

"It's all right," a voice I knew was Duggan's said. "I've got you, Sheilagh. I've got you. Don't be afraid. If I can help it, no harm will ever come to you again."

XVIII

FIELDING

I walked to Ned's house, hoping to tell him our news in private. If he heard it first from someone else, it would hurt him even more.

He wasn't at home. Brendan was in his room and Ruby was in the kitchen, sitting at the head of the table, when, as I was accustomed to doing, I walked in without knocking. She jumped when she saw me.

"Merciful God, you nearly scared the life out of me," she said. On the table in front of her was a blank piece of paper, a pen beside it.

"Writing a letter?" I said.

She scowled and pushed the piece of paper away from her. "I haven't written a word," she said, as if I'd accused her of something. "I don't like it when Ned is away. He's up in that airplane of his. Drunk probably."

"Do you mind if I wait?" I said. She shook her head slightly. I sat at the end of the table so that I could extend my leg.

Ruby crumpled up the piece of paper and threw it in the wastebasket beside her. "I'm trying to write a letter to Ned, but I don't know what to say. I don't know how to say it."

"A letter? Why don't you just talk to him?"

"Most of the time he's holed up in his room. Sick, he says. He's been there a lot since you went away."

"Maybe I could help you write it."

"It's none of your business. All I did this morning was say your name and Ned got upset. All you have in common is that you drink too much. It's not a competition, Miss Fielding. He doesn't have to drink as much as you to drink too much."

"That's true."

"It's a curse, not a gift, to be able to seem sober when you're drunk."

"Not always. And it's sometimes better to seem drunk when you're sober—at least it's sometimes better for me."

"Just don't encourage him to—to keep up with you."

She saw that I could tell what she really meant.

"He has a *child*," she said.

"And he has you. *They* have you. They'd never get by without you."

"They could if Lucy was alive."

"Perhaps she needed you as much as they do."

"No, I needed her. I've always needed looking after. The story I told everyone about her isn't true. Not all of it. I never worked. Never cleaned anyone's house. I couldn't. Lucy had to make enough for both of us. She made extra money sometimes. From men. She knew who Brendan's father was, but she never told me. I never worked, you understand? Never.

"I'd spend hours every day trying to figure out some little thing that was impossible to figure out. Or I'd read the same sentence over and over, trying to get it just right in my head. It stopped when Lucy was with me. She worked. I didn't. I waited for her to come home."

It was a brave admission, one I doubted she had ever made before, and one I would not have thought she'd make to me.

"Why does everything have to come at such a price, Miss Fielding?"

"I don't know, Ruby. That's a good question."

"Don't talk to me like I'm a child. Brendan is my sister's son. I'm his aunt. You're nothing to him. He used to like spending time with me and with Ned. Now he never talks to anyone but you. Yes, he told me in a note that he *talks* to you. He's been in the Flag House every night, alone, since you went away. Every morning he asks when you're coming back. I knew we couldn't count on you. You can't just go away without a word when there's a youngster depending on you. A little boy all night in that deserted house.

"You've got him fooled. He thinks you're as smart as you think you are. So does Ned. *They find you so fascinating.* Every day, your picture and your name are in the *Telegram*. You're so—I don't know what. You smoke and drink. What good are you to anyone? Who, if they were in trouble, would ever come to you for help? You've wasted everything God gave you. If He had given me what He gave

424

you—but what did He give me? I'm Crazy Ruby. Lucy sacrificed everything for me. Everything. She loved me and she didn't want me to end up in some awful place.

"I might be dead by now if not for her. Instead, she's dead because of me. She had Brendan because of me. Do you understand? She cleaned other people's houses and went with men for money while I stayed at home because I couldn't focus my mind long enough to scrub a goddamn floor. I stayed at home talking to myself about things I didn't even care about. I couldn't stop. I still can't. My mind won't let me stop.

"Lucy couldn't find enough work to support the two of us, so— There were only a few men. But they always asked her to come back. I don't know who they were. I don't know where she went with them. Each one of them knows he might be Brendan's father. I don't know if each of them knows who the other men who might be Brendan's father are."

Ruby thinks it's her fault that Lucy died. Ruby couldn't keep a job, so Lucy had to find a way to support them both. She found it. And so it was that Brendan came to be. I grow old, I grow old . . . In the wombs the children come and go, the works of Mike and Al and Joe.

"I'm sorry, Ruby."

"You don't think much of me, do you?"

"I know of no one like you. I mean that as a compliment."

"Really?"

"I had two children, Ruby, twins that almost no one knows about. One of them is dead and the other lives in New York with her family. David and Sarah. Sarah has children of her own. She and David were raised by my mother. They thought *she* was their mother. It all sounds like a Sophoclean riddle."

"I have no idea what you're talking about. I never do."

"I'm sorry."

"Don't tell anyone what I told you. I shouldn't have told you. I don't know why I did."

"I won't tell a soul," I said.

"Don't say a word to me about it either."

"All right."

I stood. I was about to call out to Brendan to tell him that I was back and that we could meet in the Flag House after dinner when Ruby said, "Don't go, yet." She covered her face in her hands and began to cry. "I have to write to Ned," she said. "I have to get this letter written or I'll lose my mind."

I sat down again. "Of course I'll stay."

"I don't want Ned to know that Lucy was a prostitute. Especially that she was one because of me."

"Don't tell him. I've already told you *I* won't."

She shook her head as she lowered her hands to the table. "It was nothing, you see. At first we thought—but it turned out to be nothing. But his parents, they're all he ever thinks about. So—I feel so guilty, I don't know what to do."

"Calm down, Ruby," I said. "Tell me what's wrong."

She looked away from me at the kitchen window. "Lucy came home one night. She said she was with a man who said he knew what happened to the Vatchers. He said he was in on it."

My heart pounded in my chest. "Ruby, are you saying that *you* know what happened to the Vatchers?"

"I don't know anything about it. Let me tell you what happened. Once my mind starts, it never stops. There was another woman there. There were two men. Lucy didn't know their names, but she knew what they looked like and the street the house was on. I don't remember much of what she said about the men. She said they didn't own the house. They were renting it, for the night maybe, or one of them was, or something. It doesn't matter now.

"Lucy went into a room with one of the men. The other woman went into another room with the other man.

"They all came out after a while. There was music on the radio. They drank a lot and everybody danced with everybody else.

"And then one of the men said he knew what happened to the Vatchers. He said he was in on it. The other man told him to shut up. He told Lucy and the other woman that his friend was always talking big when he was drunk, so they should pay no attention to what he said.

"That was all that happened, Lucy said, though I think she knew a bit more than she told me. Maybe that's why she was scared. Or maybe not. I don't know. Once I start thinking about something, I can't stop. Everything gets all mixed up. I can't keep track. I can't remember where I started."

"What else happened, Ruby? *Something* must have."

"Lucy used to tell me everything that happened to her. I told her everything too, but I didn't have as much to tell as her.

"She said we mustn't tell a soul about those men. She said that, most likely, the man that she was with was just talking nonsense anyway. But word might get out if she tried to turn them in, or something. Others might have been involved. And if they *did* have something to do with the Vatchers, *anything* might happen.

"She said there was nothing she could do to bring the Vatchers back, but she might get herself into a lot of trouble if she went to the police. Even if she didn't, she might already be in a lot of trouble. Those men might think they had to shut her up, or put a scare into her. Even if that man was just talking big, he wouldn't appreciate her going to the police about him. He wouldn't want the whole world knowing that he was with a prostitute. And she wouldn't want the whole world knowing that she *was* a prostitute. She said she would never have anything to do with those men again."

"How long before Brendan was born did this happen, Ruby?" I asked, dreading the answer.

"A few years," she said.

"You're sure?"

"Yes."

I couldn't help but sigh with relief. It had crossed my mind that Brendan might be the son of a man involved in the disappearance of the Vatchers.

"So nothing else happened?"

"She made me promise not to say a word. I promised, and I made her promise too. We just waited to see what would happen, but nothing did. Lucy never heard from the men again. We sort of forgot about it after a while. Not really, I mean, but we never talked about it. I thought about it a bit when Ned got in touch with me about adopting Brendan.

"But that was three years later. What could I have told him? One night a man whose name and face I didn't know told my dead sister he knew what happened to the Vatchers? I would have had to tell him that Brendan's mother was a prostitute. He might have changed his mind about Brendan and me. All because of nothing. So I never said a word.

"But every time I see Ned's face, I think about what Lucy told me. It's been like that since we first met. My Condition got worse. When I saw Ned on TV talking about his parents with Brendan right beside him—and now Ned is in some kind of decline. That's what Dr. Vaughan called it. He'll put me in a home if he finds out what I did. But if I *don't* tell him—" She slumped onto the table, crying, her head sideways on her folded arms.

"Nothing will happen, Ruby," I said. I moved my chair next to hers and put one arm around her shoulders. "*Nothing* will happen. And Ned would never put you in a home. The best thing you can do for him is go on keeping this a secret. Lucy was right. It was just a drunk man talking big. There's no reason to make Ned more upset about his parents than he is already. Imagine him going on TV and repeating what you told me. This can be our secret, Ruby, yours and mine. I'm not your sister, but I'd like to be your friend."

Ruby nodded faintly. "I do remember one more thing that Lucy said. After that one man told her that he knew what happened to the Vatchers and that he was in on it, the other man said, 'Shut up, Squirrel. Shut your squirrel mouth.'"

Duggan and I made our way up the hill. I had told him what Ruby told me. I hadn't said a word to Ruby about Cyril.

I warned Duggan that, if Cyril saw the two of us approaching in such haste, he would make a run for it no matter what he thought we wanted.

"He won't run," Duggan said. "He's too smart for that."

As we drew near to the house, Kay came out onto the landing as before. "A writer *and* a priest," she said. "There must be something *very* wrong."

We stopped and looked up at her. I was too winded to speak.

"We need to see Cyril," Duggan said.

"He's not here," Kay said. Her voice quavered and she swallowed before she spoke again. "I don't know where he is." She spread her arms wide and looked out across the city. "He's somewhere down there."

"We know about the Vatchers," I managed to say. "We know everything."

She sighed. "Jesus," she said. "Prowse, that spineless—he's the only one you could have heard it from."

Prowse? I tried not to look startled.

"That's right," Duggan said, putting his hand lightly on my arm.

"I knew that sooner or later he'd tell someone." Tears ran down her cheeks.

"But he hasn't told anyone else and he says that he's not going to," Duggan said. "He said he had to get it off his chest. We know it wasn't just Cyril. We know that Cyril wasn't in charge."

"We know everything," I said again.

"I very much doubt that you know everything," Kay said. "But it sounds like you know a lot. So it's better that you *do* know everything. It might convince you not to repeat it to anyone."

She let us into the house, where we spoke with her for more than two hours.

"Cyril will panic if you confront him," she said as we were about to leave. "He'll ruin us all. And Ned—well, he won't want this becoming common knowledge. I'll speak with Cyril. And then I'll speak with Ned."

NED

I didn't solve the riddle of the Vatchers. No one who knew only what I knew could have solved it. The solution came to me by way of the confession of someone I'd had no reason to suspect.

On August 22, 1961, still hiding out in my office, I wrote, "All that I can think of now is finding them. Whichever way it is resolved."

The next day, Kay appeared as if I had sent her the note, as if she had felt herself summoned to my house.

It was early in the morning. She'd stood by the locked gate in the late summer coolness until Ruby had noticed her and gone out to ask her what she wanted.

"I have to speak to Ned," she said.

"He's sick," Ruby said.

"I know," Kay said. "I know how sick he is."

I was lying on a cot in my office when Kay knocked. The floor was strewn with empty bourbon bottles and unwashed dishes. I told her to go away. She slipped a sheet of paper under the door that read: "Edgar and Megan."

I sat with Kay outside on the wrought iron bench to the right of the front door. It was still cool; morning mist hung over the city and the harbour.

She folded her hands in her lap and looked up at the sky. She was still slender, still carried herself with the same effortless grace, was still able to wear anything and make it work. Looking at her, it was easy to imagine the young woman Edgar had been drawn to, the one he brought down at no cost to himself until the day that Cyril, emboldened by Reg, had intervened.

"What do you know about Edgar and Megan?" I said.

"Your friend, that Fielding woman, paid Cyril a visit a couple of months ago. She put the point of her cane to his throat and asked him why you're afraid of him. She asked him how the car got where it did. He's hardly slept a wink since. He told mc he's tired of keeping secrets. He said he thought he should tell someone everything he knew. The police, maybe. I told him there was no point ruining so many lives and reputations after all this time. I told him to keep his mouth shut. But just yesterday, your friend, Fielding, came to visit *me*. I didn't tell Cyril what she said, but he's in a panic.

"So. I'll tell you what happened, Ned, before Cyril tells God knows who and brings us all down.

"There's no one left that I'm afraid of. Harmless young men they were, most of them. They're harmless old men now, the ones who are still alive. Remember that. I don't have to ask you to keep it to yourself. I know you won't tell another soul. You'll want revenge, but not at any price.

"You've been through a lot. So have I. All this time. Some things you can't confess to priests. I'm not as pure as the driven snow, but I'm not to blame for everything. I think you might destroy yourself if I don't tell you, and I don't want to be to blame for that. You're coming apart, bit by bit. What will happen to Brendan if something happens to you?

"So. I'll tell you what I know, which isn't as much as *they* know, so you'll want to talk to them.

"You know about me and your father. I should have said no to Edgar. He wasn't in love with me, but I loved him. I wasn't in love with Cyril. It was your father I wanted, but he never paid the slightest bit of attention to me. So I settled for a man I was young enough to think was second best—your father's brother who, when he was young, looked a lot like Edgar. But, for a long time, I couldn't bring myself to let Cyril touch me.

"And then, when he couldn't have me, Edgar noticed me. It was as if I'd been invisible until I married Cyril. Now, nothing but having me would do. Not that I'm putting all the blame on him. I could have said no. At least, I think I could have. But I was in love with him and he had yet to be in love.

"Edgar was with Megan then. He was unhappy. I was unhappy. We were so young, we had no better sense. I didn't tell Edgar that he made me pregnant. I told Cyril I was pregnant, but we hadn't been together yet, if you know what I mean, so I had to make up something. I said the father was someone I met on the north side of the harbour, someone who was just passing through St. John's. Someone who was so long gone I couldn't remember his name.

"Cyril was upset for a while. I think he would have walked away except he thought no one would believe that the baby wasn't his and he'd be blamed for abandoning his wife *and* child. It's a sin for me to say that, but it might be true. Anyway, he didn't walk away. He stayed with me. He told me not to tell anyone else that the baby wasn't his.

"If it wasn't for Reg, nothing more might have happened. But Reg saw Edgar with me and thought he was Phonse. I know Cyril told you he never told me that part, but he did. Eventually. But there's a lot I know that you need to know.

"When you mocked Ambrose, it was your father and me that you were mocking. The blending of my nature with your father's did not produce a child like you. Perhaps the fault is mine. I'm not Megan. But Ambrose wasn't raised with your advantages. Nor were you raised with Cyril as your father, so who knows what might have been?

"I've been on the verge of telling you many times over the past twenty-five years. I've thought about telling many people. But there were always my children to think about, one especially. The destruction of my family wouldn't make up for the destruction of yours. It wouldn't bring your parents back.

"I might have wound up in jail for withholding evidence, but I took the chance. My children are older now and it's clear that Cyril's ways will never change. When you come right down to it, there's no longer any risk involved for me or mine. That's because of Brendan. You won't say a word to anyone because of Brendan and because of how loath you are to sully your parents' reputation. I look at you and I imagine Brendan thirty years from now. And then I remember the little boy and the sweet young man you used to be. I don't want Brendan to end up like you.

"I wish Cyril had told me what Edgar was up to in time for me to think of something. But he didn't and it doesn't matter now. When it was all over, I hid Cyril in the house, kept him in his room for weeks, told the youngsters he was sick. You'll soon know why. I know how your parents ended up. And I know how close you are now to losing everything or throwing it away.

"That Depression, back in the thirties, brought some of the high and mighty down to next to nothing. And people like Cyril and me down to less than nothing. Remember that when you speak with Cyril."

Ruby was watching TV and Brendan was up in the Flag House.

"What do you want with Cyril?" Ruby said when I told her he

was coming to the house and might be here for some time. "I'm not making him cold cuts at this hour of the night. I'll never sleep knowing I'm under the same roof as that man."

I told her there'd be no cold cuts and no Scotch tonight. "I need to talk to Cyril about something."

"What?"

"I might write a book about Edgar and Megan. I don't know much about Edgar's childhood. Cyril does. I'm going to talk to a lot of people. My other uncles. Nan, Duggan."

"Now it's a book," Ruby said. "Brendan's in the Flag House by himself and you're down here with Cyril, writing books."

She shook her head, then went down the hall to the stairs.

It seems, as you write, that you are about to lose your parents for the second time.

You find your father in the front room, his back to the window. Once you touch him, you will not see him again. You will only, through the years, from time to time, almost remember the way he was before he became a part of you. You will not, but almost, remember how to step back and see him, strange and real. Perhaps you should wait. You could walk about him now for as long as it takes to memorize everything. And yet you know that, no matter what you do, the world, when you touch him, will come between you and you will never see him again. So neither will you remember that, slow as sorrow, you put your arms about his neck. You hug him hard and kiss his cheek; and, as you do, he says your name.

You find your mother in her room, at her desk, writing a letter to someone who years ago stopped writing back—writing, looking like a woman on the cover of a handwriting primer: feet on the floor and slightly apart; posture perfect; pen hand, free hand and paper each in its right relation of angle and space. She has stopped, pen poised, above the paper. You have caught her in the middle of a sentence already written. There are words on either side, but those to come she cannot see. If you could tell her now, before you touch her, you would tell her that she need not write. You'd say, "Put your pen down, please. Stop. Stay here." But you can't. So neither will you remember that, slow as sorrow, you cross the room and, stretching forth your hand, touch her cheek. There is a fine tinkling sound like that of sleep falling from her eyes.

XIX

NED

"I was hoping you brought me here to give me some money," Cyril said.

I grabbed him by the front of his shirt with both hands. "If I have to beat it out of you, I will," I said. "Ruby's a sound sleeper. Not that she'd mind. If I let you go home, you aren't going to lay a hand on Kay."

"I never have. Never in my life, Ned, I swear."

I let go of him. "Talk," I said.

Cyril sat in my chair in the study, his back to the desk, watching me as I strode back and forth in front of him. He told me what happened.

When he was finished, when I was able to speak, I said, "I want you to write it all down for me, Cyril—everything that you told me. Don't leave anything out. Don't invent anything. Write down what you said."

"A confession? You said you would leave the police out of it."

"No police. Just write it down. It might be of some use someday. And I want to have a record of everything."

CYRIL'S CONFESSION

You've never lost a child. You've never had one of your own and I bet you never will. I'm not criticizing you. One of Reg's children died at his father's hands and the hands of Edgar. On a calm and sunny day at sea, because of your fool of a father, and because of Reg, *my* fool of a father. The other died in the woods in the twilight of November. Because of me. But not just me. Not by a long shot. You lost your parents. Most people do. Your mother and father died in the same twilight of that same November day at the scene of the same crime. Because of one death, one murder, other people died.

I wish I'd never seen Reg's confession. He burned most of them. He threw them in the fire whenever Nan went out. He had to hold on to some of them for days, waiting for his chance. She never figured it out. She still thinks they must be somewhere in the attic or some other part of the Flag House or even the Flat House. Reg gave me the confession I showed to you, but he never showed it to the priest. He thought about it, but he didn't trust the priest to keep his mouth shut.

He wrote me a note, telling me how I could make use of the confession. He told me I could bleed my brother dry. He hated Edgar. I did too, after I read Reg's confession. Reg said that what happened to Phonse was Edgar's fault. Because of Edgar, Reg killed Phonse, murdered his own son, his favourite, the only person in his life he ever loved. Oh yes, he hated Edgar.

I went by Edgar's house one afternoon while you were still in school. Megan was surprised to see me, but she let me in because I wouldn't stop knocking on the door. She must have been afraid of what the neighbours would think. She always was. She knew I wasn't there for cold cuts, but she did give me a drink. I told her about Edgar and Kay and Ambrose. She never said a word. It shut her up good, let me tell you. I was fed up with that voice of hers, that fancy English accent. You should have seen the way she looked when she realized what Edgar really was. Her husband, Edgar. I never said a word to her about Phonse and Reg. I knew Edgar wouldn't either.

She was pretty pale by the time I left, and I could see that she knew I was telling the truth. I don't think she ever told Edgar that she knew about him and Kay and Ambrose—but who knows? The next time I saw them, they seemed the same, only now she knew why he put up with me the way he did and she was afraid of me— not like before.

Edgar got it all started. It was years after he was fired. He was flat broke, up to his ears in debt. He said he had a lot of documents from when he was Sir Richard's man that he was willing to part with for a fee. Papers, he said. Information that the right sort of person could make a fortune from.

"Why don't you make a fortune from it and give some of it to me?" I said.

"I'm not the right sort of person," he said. "Sometimes you need a lot of money to make a lot of money."

I nodded because I knew that, by then, he was not much closer to being rich than I was. The teachers said that I was as smart as Edgar. I should have made something of myself.

He told me that someone would meet me in a bar. Who'd be surprised to see *me* in a bar, or going into Edgar's house? *He* couldn't be seen talking to a stranger in a bar. But who'd be surprised to see me chatting up some stranger for a drink?

I was the go-between, the legman. Edgar said he didn't want to write to the people he was dealing with, or vice versa. He didn't want Prowse writing to them or vice versa. He said you could never tell in whose hands letters might wind up and he didn't trust telephones because you never knew for certain who you were talking to or who else might be listening.

He said he knew I wouldn't want the truth about him and Kay and me and Reg and Phonse coming out, so he could trust me. It was like it was him blackmailing me this time—except that I'd still be getting paid. Not as much as him, but a lot. I told him that I could never launder an amount of money that was otherwise worth the risks involved. It would do Kay and my children no good if, instead of making money for the future, I wound up in prison. He said he would show me how money could be hidden. I told him I might call his bluff. He said go ahead, because he had nothing to lose, and he looked and sounded like it.

I didn't know what to do. If this scheme of his failed, he was done for and so were you and Megan. I could just picture him dragging me and mine down with him. And Nan and Reg and who knows how many more. So I went along with it. I was almost certain it would come to nothing. What men with real money would have anything to do with me? Hard times were the only kind I'd ever known. I didn't know how desperate men who had lost a lot of money might be to get it back.

I told Edgar what they told me to and vice versa. Edgar said they had no way of knowing if everyone was on the same page. They only had my word for it.

You see, Ned, I also told Reg everything. Ever since I was a boy, I'd told him everything. He used to be able to tell, just by looking at me, that I was up to something, so sooner or later I told him everything. Back when I told him what Edgar was up to, his mind wasn't as bad as it is now. He wasn't what you would call normal, but what he wrote made sense and he could read a bit.

When I came by to see him, Nan would go for a nap. "I could do with a few hours without him on my hands," she'd say. So I wrote things down for him and sometimes he wrote an answer. I'd take the notes back to my house and burn them in the stove. So I told him I was Edgar's go-between. I told him every name I knew. I wrote it all down for him, bit by bit, as the days went by.

I was scared, you see. I had to talk to somebody. I told him I wanted his advice, but he never gave me any. He didn't tell me to back out of it. He didn't look like he thought I was in trouble. All he did was nod.

A few days before the meeting with Edgar and the other men, he wrote, "I want to go along." I told him the men I was dealing with would never agree to that. He nodded. But then he wrote, "I'll tell Nan what you're up to."

I had to come up with some excuse for bringing Reg along. I had to come up with it fast or the whole thing would be wrecked.

So I did think of something. I told Lewis, Sir Richard's bodyguard—you knew him, I'm sure—that Nan's was a good place to pick me up because there were no other houses close by.

Just before Lewis came, I told Nan that Reg's crowd were dropping by to take him out for a drive. "Another nap for me," Nan said. So far, so good.

She was asleep when Lewis arrived. He was the only one in the car. "Nan is gone to help out at her sister's," I told him. "Their father's very sick."

"So what?" Lewis said.

"So I have to stay with Reg," I said. "Even if there was time to get someone else, it wouldn't matter. He gets all upset unless one of us is with him, Nan or me. The last time he was left with someone else, he tore the house apart, broke out all the windows. He nearly killed himself."

"Jesus *Christ*," Lewis said. "I knew you'd arse this up, Cyril. Edgar said it had to be today. And you're the only one who knows the way to where he wants to meet with us. You're the only one who knows the way *back*. *Jesus*. We'll have to call it off if there's still time. I don't know what Edgar will do, or who he'll talk to, if he goes to that clearing and we're not there. He's a desperate man."

"Reg could come with us," I said.

"*What*?"

"He could. Listen, people take him for drives sometimes and I go with them. I have to or, like I said, he gets upset. He's a shut-in and people feel sorry for him. They take him for drives, a bite to eat, maybe a few drinks. He doesn't know what's going on around him, Lewis. As long as he's with me, he won't make a peep."

"Go get him, and be quick about it," Lewis said, shaking his head. "If he ruins this, Cyril, I'll wring your scrawny neck."

You see, Ned, my job that day was to lead them to the meeting in the woods. Edgar had picked a place he told no one but me about, just to be safe, he said. And he wanted someone there who was on his side, because he knew there'd be more than one of them.

What happened was just bad luck, an accident mostly. None of us were any good at any of it. Not really. We weren't professionals or anything. How we got away with it, I'll never know.

There were five of us. Me. Reg. Prowse. You know him. Prowse was there to examine what Edgar was selling, to make sure it was worth something. There was a big fellow named Morry. Gerry Morry. The brother of the guy who beat you up downtown. That was Len Morry. Gerry got drunk later and told Len everything and then warned him not to turn him in. Len went around town shooting his mouth off for weeks about how he knew what happened to the Vatchers. But he never said *how* he knew, thank God. Gerry Morry was there in case things got out of hand. A muscleman. He and Len have been dead for years.

Lewis put it all together on their side. He said he was working for someone else. "Someone big," he said, "someone on the mainland." He might have been lying. I don't know, and I'm glad I don't.

We were waiting in a little clearing for him. Edgar drove his car up that timber road—not the one near to where they found the car in the cave, another one. We heard it from a long way off. He parked beside the car we came in. We heard a door open and close. He came into sight, carrying a suitcase.

He raised his hand to us as he was coming up the path. None of us did anything. We could tell that the suitcase was heavy. He was having a hard time with it. He stopped and put it down and looked at all of us. I'm sure he was scared. I was. His eyes went wide when he saw Reg.

"Dad?" he said. He looked at me and then at Lewis. "What's he here for?" I think he thought it was some sort of double-cross. *Give us the suitcase or we'll hurt your father*, something like that. He'd have to renounce the money for Reg's sake.

"There's no problem, Edgar," I said. "We had to bring Reg along. Nan went out, you see, and left me with Reg. He can't be left alone. So—"

"You're an *idiot*," he said, and looked at Lewis.

Lewis said, "Believe me, it wasn't my idea to bring your father along. He's not in any danger."

Edgar had no sooner picked up the suitcase again than we heard another car door opening and closing.

"Who's that?" Prowse said.

"I've no idea," Edgar said.

"Did someone follow you?" Lewis said.

Edgar shook his head.

Now everyone was scared. If it was the police, there'd be no getting away from them because they would already have spotted the cars.

"EDGAR," a voice I recognized as Megan's called. It sounded like she was coming up the path toward us.

"That's his wife," I said.

"Christ," Prowse said. "What did you bring *her* for?"

"She wouldn't let me go without her," Edgar said. It was almost as if he was begging Lewis to believe him. He was so flustered I could barely make out what he was saying. "I had to come back to the house, you see, Lewis, because I forgot some things, important things, papers that should have been in here." He tapped the suitcase. "I'd put this in the boot of the car the night before when I'd been drinking. It was stupid of me to forget those things, but I had to go back home to get them.

"She was fine in the morning when I left, but when I got back to the house—well, the slightest change in routine makes her upset. I was gathering up the papers in my study and she followed me around, saying she knew I planned to leave her and Ned. I denied it and tried to calm her down, but—I've never seen her in such a state.

"She asked me about the papers. I told her they were for Sir Richard, whom I'd be meeting with this afternoon about a job. She said I was lying—she'd read in the paper that Sir Richard was travelling abroad. She said she would go from door to door, Lewis, telling the neighbours I wouldn't take her with me because I was having an affair with someone. She was at the breaking point. Who knows what she would have done? I had no choice—there was nothing I could do but take her with me or else not leave the house. I didn't know what you lot would think when I didn't show. I didn't want to ruin what might be my one and only chance.

"She doesn't know anything. I told her to stay in the car until I got back and we were on the main road again."

"Mr. Vatcher," Lewis said, "you sound as close to a breakdown as you say your wife is."

"No, no," Edgar said, trying to collect himself. "I'm not, really—"

"Let's get out of here," Prowse said.

"This won't do," Lewis said. "Another time perhaps, but not today. Go stop her before she gets here and sees us. Christ, Mr. Vatcher, you called *Cyril* an idiot?"

"She won't tell anyone. She doesn't know anything about this. She's sick. Cyril?"

"It's true," I said. "No one will listen to anything she says. It's been years since she said anything to anyone besides her family."

"I told you, Mr. Vatcher," Lewis said, "stop her before she gets here."

"And leave this suitcase with *you*?" Edgar said.

"We're leaving," Lewis said. "Maybe we'll do this some other time. Maybe not. Let's go before *another* one of the goddamn Vatchers turns up."

You see, Ned. That's what it was like. Amateurs we were. It might all have gone as smooth as silk if Edgar hadn't had to go back to his house. It probably would have.

But, before we knew it, Megan came running up the path, her shoes in her hand. It must have been easier to run without them. She had nothing but stockings on her feet. She didn't have a hat, either. I'd never seen her outdoors without a hat.

"We have to go, Edgar," Megan said. "You said you wouldn't be long. Ned will soon be home from school."

Edgar shouted, "You're ruining everything. This is our last chance."

Megan said, "Ruining what? Where is she? I saw that other car. You've come to meet her here before, haven't you? Did you think I would just stay put in the car while you met up with her again? Why did you ever take up with that woman? Nothing since has been the same. That suitcase. There must be a house somewhere. A cottage with a cozy fireplace, no doubt."

It wasn't until she stopped beside Edgar that she saw us.

"Who—" she said. She couldn't catch her breath. "Who are these *men*?"

"It doesn't matter who they are," Edgar said.

"Cyril?" Megan said. "What are you doing out here? Is Kay here?"

"Don't say anything, Cyril," Prowse said. "Not a word."

"We're conducting important business, Megan," Edgar said. "I'm doing this for you and Ned. Go back to the car and wait for me. You're not dressed for the cold. You'll freeze to death."

"Reg?" Megan said.

Reg stared at her as he always did at anyone who came to visit him.

"We're leaving," Lewis said.

To get to the path, he and I and Prowse and Reg and Morry had to walk toward Edgar and Megan. Maybe that's what spooked her. I don't know.

She dropped her shoes and ran. She ran off into the woods.

"Go get her," Lewis said to Edgar, but Edgar shook his head.

"I'm not leaving this suitcase with you. She won't go far. She'll stop and she'll call out to me and I'll guide her back with my voice. I'm not leaving this suitcase until I have what I want. Just hand it over and you can have the suitcase."

"Prowse has to examine the contents first. You know that. It will take—for Christ's sake, Cyril, go get that woman and bring her back here. God knows what Edgar will say or who he'll say it to if she gets lost. God knows what she'll say if she makes her way back to the road and flags down a car. She ran off like she saw a ghost."

I called her name, but Morry told me to shut up. He took an axe handle out from under his coat and shook it at me. "Just go find her and bring her back," he said.

That was all I was going to do, Ned, bring her back, I swear. By the hand maybe. I thought it might be that easy.

I was wearing the closest thing I had to a winter coat, a jacket that was way too small for me. I took it off and dropped it on the ground. I figured I could run faster and move better without it. All I had on now was a long-sleeved undershirt. I knew that, in the woods, there'd be no wind.

I ran off in pursuit of her. Edgar was right—she didn't go far. She'd never been in the woods in her life. She had nothing on her feet. But she went far enough.

There were no paths and the woods were thick. That's what people might not understand, you see, Ned.

"EDGAR. EDGAR, I CAN'T FIND THE PATH. I CAN'T SEE ANYTHING, IT'S TOO DARK. COME AND GET ME." A minute later she called out again, "EDGAR."

"OVER HERE," I shouted.

Just as I was about to shout again, I heard her call, "WHO IS IT?"

I knew that the last answer she would want to hear was "Cyril."

"IT'S EDGAR," I shouted. "JUST WALK TOWARD MY VOICE."

"All right," she said. She sounded relieved.

I guided her toward me by shouting her name every few seconds.

"These woods are so thick, Edgar," she said. "I can't . . . My feet are so cold. I wish we were home with Ned in front of the fire."

"We will be, soon," I said.

Every other word that came out of her was *Ned*. I'm not just saying that. She thought the world of you, right up to the end.

I heard her crashing through the woods. She wasn't coming straight for me, but she was getting closer.

"YOU'RE NEARLY THERE," I said, which was true—I could hear the rasping of her breath.

I was waiting beneath a stand of trees to the west of the clearing. Finally, Megan showed, picking spruce needles from her hair and trying to wipe them from her dress.

"My hands are all full of turpentine," she said. "Now my dress is covered with it. Let's go *home*, Edgar. Ned will wonder where we are."

"We will," I said.

"We have to *hurry*," she said. "Ned will soon be home and the house is locked."

"You'll be home, soon," I said.

Her face. It was scratched and bloodied from the branches. I knew she would make quite a sight when we got back to the clearing. I worried what Edgar might do.

"You're not Edgar," she said when she got close. "I knew it didn't sound like him. Who are you?"

"I can easily take you to him from here."

She stared at me as if she'd never seen me before.

"You know me," I said. "I'm Cyril. You saw me just a few minutes ago. Cyril. You know me. Edgar's brother. Cold cuts and Scotch."

There was just enough light to see the look of terror in her eyes, the disarray of her hair and clothes.

"Cyril," she said, backing up a few steps and looking at the ground around her as if she was searching for something she could use as a weapon.

Her hair had come loose from its pins. Thick tangled strands of it hung down across her cheeks and some of it was wet and matted to her forehead. Her face was pale and dotted all over with droplets of blood.

"There's no need to worry," I said. "I know the way back."

"I'm not going anywhere with *you*," she said.

"Then just *follow* me."

She bolted back into the woods.

I knew it wouldn't be long before she was lost again. If she strayed too far, she might reach the western crest of the ridge and head down the other side, where I'd never find her.

"No, Megan," I shouted, and went after her.

"YOU STAY AWAY FROM ME," she screamed.

If I didn't catch her in the first few seconds, I never would. A spruce branch lashed me across the face. I swore out loud and she screamed again, and I got a fix on where she was—just a few feet in front of me. I ran right into her and grabbed her to keep from falling. I didn't mean to, but I grabbed her hair. I yanked her back.

I don't know if you've ever been in the woods in the dark, the real woods, Ned, but when the sky is overcast, you can't see a thing, *nothing*. And there was snow coming down now. I felt her in my arms and pulled her to me so that she wouldn't run away.

"Please," she said, as if she was begging God to help her.

She scratched my face with one hand and tore at my throat with the other. I'm sure she thought she was fighting for her life. Twice our heads knocked together. Her forehead struck me just below the eye and then the back of her head caught me underneath the jaw. I would never have thought there could be such fury in a woman her size. I tried to put my hand over her mouth, just to quiet her long enough so she could hear me, but she thought I was trying to smother her.

My God, Ned, she was certain she was being murdered. I realize that now. But at the time I couldn't understand why she wouldn't give me a chance to explain that I only meant to help her.

She called out to Edgar. It's hard to describe the tone of her voice. It was like she was accusing him of handing her over to me. I wish I could forget the way she sounded when I held her in my arms. She truly thought I was trying to kill her. It is an awful thing to think that she thought *that* just before she died, that that was her last thought.

I still wake up thinking that I hear Megan calling out to Edgar in the woods. She bit me on the lower left arm, bit me right through my undershirt. Even while she was kicking and scratching and punching me, I felt that bite.

She managed to turn around. I felt her fists against my face, her heels against my shins, her fingers clawing at my eyes and hair.

I had to control her, I had to. I tried to get hold of her arms and turn her around so I could pin her against me. I kept shouting her name. She should have known that no one who would call her Megan meant to harm her. But it only seemed to make her struggle all the more.

Finally, I grabbed her head in both my hands to make her listen. I heard a kind of snap and I felt it in my hands. She fell and landed on her back on the ground.

I didn't mean to hurt her. I didn't.

I could barely see her, but I knew that she was dead. One arm lay across her face.

I put my hand to my face. What I'd thought was sweat was blood. Blood was running from my nose, seeping into my mouth. That's how hard she struggled, Ned.

It took me several tries before I managed to hoist her onto my shoulder. I somehow made it back to the clearing.

When I came out of the woods, Prowse was holding a flashlight. I saw the falling snow, the faces of the others.

"I didn't hurt her," I said, "she hurt herself." Just as I said, "She's dead," Edgar saw her and said, "Megan," as if he was asking a question.

That's all he said.

That was his last word. Reg came up behind him and struck him over the head with the axe handle. How Reg got the axe handle from Morry I don't know.

Edgar dropped to his knees, then onto his face in the dirt.

Reg raised the axe handle to hit him again and Prowse said, "No," but he didn't try to stop him. Reg hit him a few more times. I didn't look, but I heard it. Prowse threw up. I thought I was done for too, but I figured my best bet was not to make a run for it.

"I won't say a word, I swear," I said.

"No, you won't," Morry said. "You'd get yourself into just as much trouble as the rest of us. The five of us would hang for *her*, let alone for him. You should see the way you look. It would take some explaining if you had to face the police."

"We should get out of here," Lewis said.

"I swear to God I didn't mean to hurt her," I said.

"I want nothing more to do with this," Prowse said. "I wash my hands of this. I don't want a cent from this. The rest of you can have what's in that suitcase."

"I'm out too," Morry said. "From now on, you can all act like you never met me."

Lewis looked at me. "You're out too," he said. "*I'll* take the suitcase. Maybe it's worthless, maybe it's not. But it never cost me a cent."

That was fine with me. Then Lewis looked at Reg, who was still standing over Edgar, the axe handle in one hand.

"He can't talk," I said. "His mind—he's been crazy since he lost his son."

"He's not crazy," Lewis said. "He's got more nerve than *any* of us, and more reason to keep this to himself than all of us put together."

There was snow on Reg's cap and the shoulders of his coat. His chest was heaving as if he was the one who had chased Megan into the woods and carried her out.

He stared down at Edgar's body. I wonder what was going through his mind. Maybe he killed his son without thinking. Maybe he did it because he knew it had to be done. He couldn't have planned it. I think he saw his chance for revenge and took it. I don't know.

I was shivering, but it wasn't because of the cold.

I forgot to pick up my jacket. Everyone forgot about it until it was too late to go back and get it. Lewis said it didn't matter. Even if someone found it and traced it back to me, he said, what would that prove? But I thought about that jacket, Ned. I thought about it a lot for a while.

We had to do *something* with their bodies. If we buried them, you see, dogs or other animals would have dug them up. We had to do something else and we had to do it fast . . .

There was only one lantern burning in my house when I got back. Everyone but Kay was out. I went inside and shone the lantern on the bite on my left arm. It was big and hurt so much I forgot about my face. "Jesus," Kay said when she saw me. She put a bandage on my arm. I told her I was in a bar fight and she never asked a single question, though she asked a lot the next day when she heard the Vatchers were missing. I told her the truth and she kept it to herself, until yesterday.

I didn't show my face for ages, never left the house. That was not unusual for me. I knew it would take weeks for the scratches on my face and hands to heal. And that bite on my arm. The marks of your mother's teeth are still there, Ned. Two scars on my arm.

It festered for months. I thought it would never get better. At one point, my arm was so swollen I thought I might lose it.

The mark of Megan Vatcher. A doctor told me it would never go away, and he was right. I unbutton my sleeve ten times a day and look at that scar. I can't help it. Even without it I'd never forget that night, but the bite mark makes it worse. It's hard to imagine a stranger way to remember someone, isn't it? If I live to be eighty, that mark will still be there. The last moment of her life will still be there.

Sometimes, when I can't sleep, I run my hand over the scar. I lie there in the dark and run my hand over it. I hate having to carry it around with me. Having to hide it. Keep it covered. Looking at it every time I wash my hands or take a bath.

I have never known a silence like the silence in the woods that night after Reg hit Edgar. How many men who have ever lived have known such silence?

I think about it a lot. The woods she never left alive are like the ones outside my window, the one the branches brush against when the wind is on the rise.

I should have known how much the sight of me would scare her. I blame myself for not being strong enough to control her and carry her to safety. My stupidity, my weakness—these and a hundred other things I think about.

How different everything would have been for everyone if Edgar hadn't gone back to his house that afternoon to get those papers.

What should I have done, Ned? What would I do if I could do it all again? Would Megan be alive today if someone else had been sent to bring her back? If *anyone* else had been? I feel as though I failed her. I do. And Edgar. Reg was there because of me. He murdered another son because of me.

How I lived, how others treated me, spoke to me, how I was regarded in St. John's—none of it mattered, because I was more often drunk than sober. When Edgar gave me money, when *you* did, I went to bars and bought rounds for the house, bragging about having turned over a new leaf. My so-called friends egged me on each time until the money was gone.

If I had died in those woods instead of Megan and Edgar, if I had simply disappeared, who would have cared? Who would even have been surprised, given how I'd lived? It would have seemed to everyone who knew me like a fitting end for Cyril Vatcher.

I've set aside nothing for a funeral or a headstone. I can't afford to be buried in a proper cemetery. I'll be buried with the poor. They mark their graves with wooden crosses. They write nothing but their names and numbers. And the weather makes short work of them.

I'm afraid of old age, Ned. What happens when I can't make my way around, when I'm housebound with no one to look after me but Kay? What then?

Like father, like son. I've seen Reg pretend to pray. Reg and his confessions. The patron saint of hypocrites. At least I confessed for real, even if you're not a priest. I owned up to what I did.

Maybe God punishes the wicked. A hundred times, I thought about leaving a letter of confession and doing away with myself. I did, Ned. I swear to God.

NED

"Shut up, Cyril," I said. "I don't know what I'll do if you don't shut up."

I asked him to take me to the clearing in which he and the other four men met my parents. He said he had recently gone in search of it but couldn't find it.

"It's been twenty-five years," he said. "Everything's grown over. Nothing looks the same."

2.

I phoned Prowse and told him I wanted to meet with him privately about a venture—it was time, I said, that Vatcher Enterprises started doing business with the government.

"Come right over," he said. "We'll have the house to ourselves."

On the way there, the fog was as thick and close as the overcast I often had to fly above.

Upon arrival, I shook hands with him but declined his offer of a drink. "On the wagon," I said.

"Yes," he said, "I heard you were ill or something. I even heard rumours of a breakdown."

"Bronchitis," I said. "But I'm better now."

His study was furnished as I imagined the cabin of a ship's captain would be. There was a table heaped with large navigational charts, though it was clear from how tidily arranged and tightly scrolled they were that he rarely, if ever, looked at them. Scattered haphazardly about were navigational instruments—sextants, chronometers, barometers, small telescopes. Mariner's instruments mounted on small pedestals like statuettes.

On the walls were hung the heads of caribou, black bear, lynx, even the head of a polar bear. The floor was covered in grey sealskin rugs. There were stacks of snowshoes, and sealing gaffs bound in twine. Hanging from the ceiling on clothes hangers as if they were for sale were overcoats and hats that flanked photographs of sealing ships under sail or steaming through the Narrows of St. John's. Framed maps of Newfoundland drawn by early, best-guess cartographers, or, as Edgar had called them, "Here Be Monsters" map-makers.

"It all belonged to my grandfather, the Judge," Prowse said. "The so-called great historian. It impresses visitors, ostentatious though it is. The rest of the house is more tastefully decorated, as you saw.

"I'm sorry about that misunderstanding at your boy's birthday party. That woman, Fielding—I don't know why she's still employed, or how she got that way in the first place."

"She's one of a kind," I said.

"I certainly hope so," Prowse said.

He wore a heavy black woollen sweater from the neck of which protruded the starched collar of a white shirt.

I tried to imagine him as he was when they had met, when he was school captain of Bishop Feild and she was the scourge of Bishop Spencer. The young Prowse whom she had so adored. The same age as her, though he looked much younger. There was no sign in his eyes of a tortured conscience. There was no sign in them of anything.

I imagined him staying up late at night, alone, watching me on TV as I appealed for help in finding out what happened to my parents. Cyril, Morry, Prowse and Lewis, they might all have tuned in to *Ned Vatcher Presents*, Cyril watching me on the set I'd given him.

He waved to a chair on one side of a gleaming oak desk that bore nothing but our blurred reflections. He tapped the surface with two fingers after we sat down.

"So—" he began.

I leaned forward and rested my forearms on the desk, clasping my hands.

He leaned back in his leather chair.

"Do you keep a gun nearby?" I said.

He seemed about to speak but paused, eyes fixed on mine. He smiled. "As nearby as my hunting rifles are," he said. "In a locked box in the basement."

"My father and I went hunting a few times. I never liked it much. But he was good with a gun. Some people said he was the best shot they'd ever seen. Sir Richard said that."

"Hmm, did he? Well, I'm a decent shot at best."

"He was good with his fists too. A boxer at Oxford."

"Yes. A boxer."

"I have a gun in my jacket pocket," I lied.

"For self-protection, no doubt," Prowse said, though now he looked scared.

"I could kill you, Prowse. I'm not sure I'd care what it cost me. Or maybe I'll just break your neck and say that you attacked me first. Who'd be sad to see *you* gone? Who'd think of me as a killer?"

"What are you talking about, Vatcher? You *did* have a breakdown. Maybe you're still having it."

"You were involved in the murder of my parents," I said. "You and four other men. No shots fired. I'm not looking for revenge or justice, only the truth. I have the signed confession of my uncle, Cyril Vatcher. I don't foresee the two of you conspiring to have me done away with or doing it yourselves. But it's a small city. Our paths may cross from time to time, which I predict will bother me less than it will you.

"You're going to tell me what happened, Prowse, and then you're going to write it down. After that, I'll be on my way. And then you're going to resign from your job."

Red blotches had broken out on his neck and throat and even on his hands. He looked as if he might not survive the task I'd assigned him.

PROWSE'S CONFESSION

Edgar said he was in possession of papers that, if used the right way, could make someone a lot of money.

I was as desperate as he was. I had no job. It seemed there would never again be jobs, not for those of us the British blamed for the state that Newfoundland was in. I was close to losing everything.

"Used the right way." He said I'd know how to make use of the documents when I saw them. I never did see them, as it turned out. I don't know if he meant blackmail, embezzlement, crooked invest-ments. I knew it might be a ruse, but I felt I had to take the chance.

I had asked Edgar why, if the documents were so valuable, he wanted to sell them. Why didn't he want to use them to make a lot of money for himself—more than he was asking for? He said he didn't have near enough money to fund the kind of thing he had in mind. He didn't have the time to wait for it to pay off. He needed money right away. He had this notion that, if everything worked out, he and Megan and you could go to London and make a new start.

I'm the one who brought Lewis into it.

"I have to be the boss," Lewis said. I told him that was fine with me. I told him I *wanted* him to be the boss. He would soon have some bosses of his own, he said. Men who, in spite of the Depression, were still rich and would know how to use the documents the right way. I only wanted some money up front and then I was going to wash my hands of it. Nothing bad was meant to happen, I swear . . .

Then Cyril came out of the woods with Megan slung over his shoulder. We couldn't just walk away from it now. We couldn't just let Edgar go off with her. If you had seen her, you'd understand.

Reg killed his son with the handle of an axe that he grabbed from Morry. If Reg hadn't killed him, someone else would have had to. Lewis or Morry. I couldn't have done it. I don't think Cyril could have.

"Never say a word about what happened here tonight," Lewis said. "All of us could hang for this."

"I *won't*," Cyril said, as if Lewis had been talking only to him.

Lewis opened the trunk of his car and dragged out a rug-sized roll of khaki tarpaulin. "I brought it along just in case," he said. "I wasn't about to take any chances with a boxer who's good with guns and might be half out of his mind." He tapped the breast of his coat. "Brought along a pistol too."

So as not to get any blood on the car, we rolled them in the tarp.

"They're not bleeding much, anymore, anyway," Lewis said.

I shook as though I was convulsing, as indeed I may have been. No number of hands, no amount of weight, could have kept me from shaking.

My shirt was wet through with sweat. It was still cooling on my skin by the time we reached the road . . .

NED

Here, cast in my words, is the balance of what Prowse and Cyril told me:

When my parents left the house, the snow had yet to start.

Hours later, with darkness and the storm coming on at once, it must have seemed to those five men that the elements themselves were in concert with their souls. The evidence of what they'd done seeped into the ground, which, by the time the snow melted, would bear no trace of it. I've seen snow newly stained with the blood of wounded animals. Bright red drops among footprints that trail off into the woods.

After the men who killed my parents left, the snow fell unseen on the clearing, as it had earlier on the hats and shoulders of these same men whose footprints it filled in, erasing the trail that they made as, holding them by either end, four of the men carried my parents to the Brougham and put them in the back.

In the car that no one but he had ever driven, Edgar was ferried with Megan to what, if not for the strangest of flukes, might have been their final resting place.

A small procession of two cars made its slow way through the storm on roads otherwise abandoned for the night. Lewis drove the Brougham that contained my parents. The other car, driven by Morry, with Reg riding shotgun and Prowse and Cyril in the back seat, followed close behind. No one said a word. There were no other cars on the roads, which, though snow-covered, were pass-able as the wind had yet to come up.

The two cars, the five men, were in a race against the wind, which would soon have piled up snow in drifts across the road, stranding the cars and the men and the bodies of my parents until the storm was done and the road was ploughed.

They made their way to the cliffs at Black Point. They were going to push the Brougham off the cliff, make it seem like a suicide, or a murder and a suicide—they couldn't make it look like an accident because the cliffs were too far from the road.

Because of the weather, they were all wearing gloves, so they didn't have to worry about leaving fingerprints.

They parked the cars where the meadow began to slope down to the cliff. They got out and Lewis walked along the edge of the cliff. He came back to the cars.

"This is not how I remembered Black Point. There's a wall of rock along the edge. No way to push or drive a car over it."

"What now?" Prowse said.

"We throw them over," Lewis said. "We'll leave the car where it is. It will still look like suicide, or murder and suicide."

They took my parents from the trunk, laid them on the ground, unrolled the tarp, removed them from it and put the tarp in the trunk of Lewis's car.

Cyril and Prowse held my mother by the hands and feet, and Lewis and Morry did likewise with my father, and they carried them to the edge. Someone threw them over, but it wasn't Cyril and it wasn't Prowse. They couldn't do it. They couldn't watch. They turned their backs.

"That's that," Lewis said.

They headed upslope toward the cars.

Cyril was the first to notice that the Brougham was moving, slowly but surely, away from them.

"Jesus Christ," Lewis said. "I didn't put the hand brake on."

They ran after it, or tried to. It was hard, because of the snow and the slick grass beneath it, to get much traction. Under other circumstances, it might have been a comical sight, four men in hopeless pursuit of an out-of-control car that was headed for a cliff while, behind them, a fifth man walked along as if nothing was amiss, the handle of an axe over his shoulder.

The Brougham skidded sideways on the snow, righted itself and continued downslope, though it was now parallel to the cliff and picking up speed. "It's headed for that deadwood," Lewis said. "It's all bog and swamp. We'll never get it out of there."

He stopped running and the rest of them did likewise.

"Who cares where it ends up?" he said, gasping for breath. "It'll look like Edgar lost control of the car. With all this snow, there won't be any footprints or tire tracks."

The rear of the Brougham bucked like a horse as the car cleared one obstacle after another. It manoeuvred between the deadwood trees as expertly as if someone was driving it.

And then it seemed to simply evaporate.

"What in God's name?" Lewis said.

There was no sound but that of the wind and the sifting of snow along the ground.

They ran toward the trees, Lewis in front. He paused at the edge of the deadwood, then crept along as if he was sneaking up on something.

"Stop," he said when Cyril, Morry and Prowse caught up with him.

"Where did it go?" Prowse said.

"Give me the flashlight, Prowse," Lewis said. Prowse handed it to him and Lewis shone it on the ground. "It dropped clean through the moss," he said.

"Is there an abandoned well there?" Prowse said.

"The nearest house is miles away. No one's ever lived out here. No reason for a well or a cellar to be here. Besides, that hole's a lot wider and deeper than it looks."

"There's no hole," Prowse said.

"There is," Lewis said. He pointed. "Right there. It was covered by moss. Grown over by it."

"It still is."

"Not quite. It's like when you poke your finger through a piece of paper."

"Is it a trap or something?" Prowse said.

Lewis sniffed. "I guess it is now. It goes a long way down. The moss grew over the hole at least once. It might grow over it again."

Reg walked up behind them and looked down at the ragged, snow-covered flaps of moss, his expression blank.

"What if someone finds it?" Prowse said.

"Even if they do, they won't have a reason to come looking for any of us," Lewis said.

They walked back to the car and the men piled in and drove away, unseen, unheard, into the storm.

Lewis dropped Prowse off at his house, Morry at his and Reg at the Flag House, then drove away lest Nan come out and see the car. He went partway up the hill and told Cyril he would have to walk the rest. It would not be until two hours later that Duggan phoned Nan to ask if she knew where the Vatchers were.

Prowse wanted to keep talking when he was done writing his confession. He looked at me from time to time as if inviting me to make of his soliloquy a conversation. But I couldn't bring myself to speak.

"I once went to Lewis's house," he said. "Lewis came out before I could knock. I was going to suggest to him that one of us, anonymously, write to you and tell you, without supplying incriminating details, what had happened to your parents and where you could find their car.

"He struck me in the face and threw me down the steps into a bank of snow, onto which a large amount of blood spilled from my broken nose. It was the first time in my life that I had been struck in the face. I got into my car and drove off, one hand on the wheel, blood pooling in my free hand.

"Punched and thrown down those steps as if I was the drunken patron of some tavern. I doubted, I still doubt, that I would be sated by any measure of revenge. I don't think he made any money from the contents of the suitcase. And now he's dead.

"Megan and Edgar. They have for years appeared to me in dreams. But I will say no more about them, for to do so will not bring them back.

"I once had something like a conscience, but I know what I am and long ago stopped caring about what others think of me. I have no idea what will become of me, or to what further depths I might yet be reduced. I simply don't care, Mr. Vatcher.

"You must believe that our encounter with your mother was entirely unexpected. But you must not think that I feel any guilt or shame. I don't wish to be forgiven for what happened. A man should pay no heed to any judgment of himself except his own. By the terms of that judgment, however, he must abide or else become a fool.

"I have spent years terrified that, someday, perhaps in a fit of repentance, someone would go to the police or do away with me because they feared that I would go to them. I couldn't find the courage to go to the police myself, to be tried and accept what some- one no better than me pretended to believe was justice.

"A jury of my peers? *My* peers have done worse things than me.

"For a while I found it hard to accept that we merely went back to our houses that night. I tried to fool myself into believing that we would not have been there in the clearing if not for Edgar and that therefore whatever followed from our being there was not our fault but his. And hers for having no better sense than to get lost in the woods at night.

"I decided that the easefulness of my life was more important to me, of greater value to me, than the life of someone else. I admitted as much to myself one night while sitting in this very chair, and nothing since has been the same. Because of guilt, you may be thinking, or because of remorse or shame or fear of retribution in this world or the next.

"I feel small measures of them all from time to time, but they quickly pass.

"When virtue is tested, as ours was in those woods that night, it will not stand.

"I have no doubt that, under the same circumstances, I would make that choice again. You may object that there are many who would have spared your father or fought to save him from the others even at the cost of their own lives. I have no doubt that this is true. But we are only speaking of a quantitative difference. For even the most noble of souls, there is a set of circumstances under which the animal, or evil, will prevail. We are all such stuff as murder is made of.

"There was a brief time when to admit this made me ill. I couldn't stand to see my own likeness in a mirror or a window or a pool of water. Now, when I stare into my own eyes, I cannot keep from laughing.

"Prowse. I scoff at Prowse. As I do at you. Though I understand you. There was a time when, if my parents had disappeared like that, I'd have never known a moment's peace. I'd have lain awake at night wondering why God had let them die. I'd have wondered whether those who killed my parents were not only still alive but prospering.

"I could have become more bitter and self-ashamed, more convinced of my cowardice and insignificance. I could have wished that things were different, daydreamed about it. The empty, pointless fantasy of things that might have been."

I'd had enough by then and stood up to leave.

"Fielding told me that you are the father of her children," I said.

He nodded. "Perhaps I am. But I owe her nothing. I never have."

I drove away from Prowse's house, the rear tires of my Ferrari spinning in the gravel, my mind in chaos, each of the revelations of November contending for my concentration.

Lewis and Morry were dead.

Cyril. Prowse who, in spite of his wife and children and his many acquaintances, would live out his life alone.

Reg. I wasn't sure what I would have done if Reg had been fully alive—Reg who had brought down the handle of the axe on his own son's head and killed him.

Five men. Each had crossed over to a state of soul from which they could never cross back.

Of all of them, even Lewis, Reg was the most lacking in remorse—entirely lacking in it, it seemed, calmly, blandly, bitterly adamant that Edgar died as he deserved to die, and Megan as dictated by circumstances for which Reg was blameless. As Nan had said, Reg's spell was spite.

Revenge was his vocation. He believed he had done right by his son, that he had made of his vocation an absolute success, and he saw no reason he should not be regarded and treated as he was by the people of the Heights.

Reg unsettled my soul more profoundly than Prowse and Lewis did.

It was hard to resist the notion that he had wilfully withdrawn from the world, willed his own deafness, renounced his voice, communicated with no one but Cyril and the priest, read nothing but what few words the priest wrote to him when he assigned his penance—hard to resist the notion that he was relentless in his disdain for a universe in which so many events could conspire to bring about the deaths of his two sons.

I drove out of town and parked on the headland where, when I was a boy, Edgar, Megan and I had often gone for picnics on Sunday afternoons, Megan facing into the ceaseless wind so that her hair wouldn't blow about her face.

By the dome light of my car, I read the confessions again.

I had stumbled onto Morry's brother just a few weeks after my parents died. Len Morry had told me he knew what happened to them. I'd been that close, when I was fourteen, to finding out everything that I knew now.

Each of the men had gone home and waited for a knock on the door that never came.

Blessedly, horribly, unthinkably, thankfully, dreadfully, for days and weeks and months and years, their lives went on just as they always had—a time of seeming blamelessness and innocence, with no world-upending interventions such as suspicion, rumours or arrest.

None of the men confessed or evened the score by taking from themselves what they had taken from the Vatchers, or suffered a decline from fretting over how God might be regarding them.

I had known four of them and had had a violent encounter with Morry's brother. One of them had worked under my father, another for the man to whom my father had been second-in-command. I had lived with one of them, whose son had many times been a guest in my parents' house and mine. One of them was the father of the children of the only woman I had ever thought I loved. I had lived with them, among them, crossed paths with them. I had been their host, their patron and their dupe.

Lewis, at the end of his life, had come to my store to seek forgiveness for what, compared with my parents' murder, amounted to nothing. Had he thought that the return to me of my father's hat was, in God's eyes, a sufficient gesture of contrition? Had he been bargaining with God, bargaining just in case there *was* a God?

The other four had squared it with the universe as Prowse had: the first death was an accident, the second a justifiable necessity, if not for which the five of them might have hung. Edgar Vatcher was just as much or more at fault than Cyril was, or than Megan was, for Megan's death. Edgar shared with them the purpose for being, at that moment, in that place. He was complicit, as was Megan in her bumbling, interfering foolishness.

The five of them had defiantly persisted. They too had wives and children or reputations to look out for, families who didn't deserve to suffer just because the men lacked the gumption to keep a secret.

Average, ordinary people, they pretended to be mystified about the fate of the famously vanished Vatchers whom they had killed and disposed of as only those with blind luck on their side could have got away with doing.

Lewis, Prowse and Morry. And my grandfather and my uncle, Reg and Cyril.

Who is the fifth man who, like some sort of escort, walks beside the other four as they carry the bodies from the clearing to the car?

Who stares straight ahead as they carry the bodies through the snow to the still-bare path that winds through the woods to where the cars are parked beside the road?

Who is it that, at the start of the path, falls in behind the others, the axe handle still resting on his shoulder as if he thinks he needs to keep an eye on them lest they make a run for it?

Who is it that, with both hands, with feet spread wide, stands behind my father like a lumberjack addressing a chopping block as he prepares to split a chunk of wood, and brings the axe handle down on my father's head?

Whose footsteps run parallel to those of the others and the trail of bloodstains in the newly trodden snow?

Whose?

My grandfather's.

Two went out.

Edgar and Megan.

No.

Seven went out and five came back.

How had it come about that Megan Chidley, London-born in

1898, had wound up, her life just ended, being carried from the woods by Cyril Vatcher on a cold November night in Newfoundland? She'd survived the war, the Spanish flu. Pregnant with me, she left the *Bruce* and made her way across the ice, miles of polar wreckage that rose and fell like some great raft that had no chance against the sea. She survived fifteen years of homesickness and fifteen years of marriage to my father. But she did not survive a struggle in the dark with Cyril Vatcher.

How had it come about that her husband, Edgar Vatcher, the pride of his country, born in 1897, had been at the same place at the same time and had been murdered by his father moments after his brother emerged from the woods with the body of his wife slung over his shoulder like someone he had rescued from a fire?

They were not newly dead, but it seemed so to me, because they'd been stalled in time for decades, waiting for the truth to nudge them forward through the final moments of their lives.

Prowse and Cyril and Morry and Lewis and Reg, the small-minded, small-souled men by whom my parents were brought down, would play no part in anyone's story of the Vatchers, the truth about whose deaths I would keep to myself.

I took my vial of bourbon from the glove compartment and drank it dry.

I went back to the city, driving the Ferrari at random through the streets that Edgar loved and Megan hated. I made the rounds of every neighbourhood, noting the number of flickering TV sets in the houses of St. John's, the number of homes in which people who would otherwise have been asleep were sitting in the dark, watching images of me, a man they mocked but dared not say a word against, lest it be overheard by a "friend" of mine.

Tears streamed down my face, but I felt nothing, not rage, hatred, bitterness or sorrow.

My body was running well ahead of my heart.

I gunned up every hill in the Ferrari, slammed back by gravity against the seat, the engine rising to a screeching pitch on the steepest slopes. It must have seemed to the people of St. John's that all control had been lost for good to those who owned expensive cars.

I idled the Ferrari at the top of Barter's Hill, the summit of the city. How tempting it was.

How easy it would have been to simply disengage the brake and plummet down the hill into the harbour. There'd be no need to hit the gas. The harbour lights beyond the city centre seemed so close. The streets were clear. It would be as if my car had fallen from the sky into the water, as the Brougham had done into the earth.

I looked above the harbour at the Heights and saw my house, the compound lit though the house was dark. The Flag House too was dark, for Brendan was in his own bed because of an earache.

Ruby might be waiting up for me. I knew that, in spite of his earache, Brendan was waiting up for *something*.

They would be destroyed, or as nearly so as I had been when the Vatchers disappeared. They would be, as I had been, left to wonder *why*. Kay would not come forward a second time, so they would *never* know.

XX

Sometimes my mind is clear and sometimes it's not. It won't be long before I can't tell the difference.

I can't read lips. I've never tried to learn. I don't like things that remind me that I'm deaf, like a man's lips moving but making no sound.

I think of Edgar's wife out there in the woods, alone, afraid, lost as it was getting dark and colder, rubbing her arms to keep warm as the snow came down around her. But I think more often of Phonse as I last saw him. And of Edgar.

Some think I believe that all things will be righted in the next life and that therefore men like Edgar should be allowed to pass unpunished through this one. The truth, despite my being regarded in St. John's as a kind of saint, is that I ceased to believe in God when Phonse died. Or, should I say, I gradually ceased to believe in God during the days and nights that my son was missing, the days and nights during which, against all reason, I held out hope that he'd be found alive.

But he was not even found dead. He is still out there. He never did come home except in dreams. Cruelly joyous dreams, which I struggle not to wake from, in which he simply shows up at our door as if no time had passed since we had seen him last.

Nan stays awake all night for fear of encountering his ghost in dreams, for fear of dreaming that her boy is still alive or that his body has been found.

I am guilty, but only of every breath I could have prevented Edgar from drawing, every moment I let him live since I realized that it was him, not Phonse, who I saw with Kay.

For many years now, I have been silent in a silent world, often spoken to but never speaking. Things that once made sounds have for years made none, though I have never stopped expecting this to change, never stopped anticipating sounds that never come, sounds of collisions, voices, vehicles, the striking of hammers and the blowing of whistles, the sounds of footsteps and the galloping of horses, the shrill pitch of the wind.

It has long seemed that the world is buried deep in snow or lies submerged beneath the fathoms of a sea that muffles every sound.

Perhaps because I have been for so long not quite fully alive, I have no fear of death, no feelings at all about it in fact. I will do nothing to hurry the day of my death, but will merely wait for it.

Edgar Vatcher, who, when he killed Phonse, ceased to be my son, has ceased to be.

REG. AUGUST 1961

He isn't gone. She isn't gone. Nor is their son. What Cyril said isn't true. Edgar has his son. I see Edgar and Megan and Ned every day. Little Neddie.

The man who took my son still has his only child. The boy goes up the hill every night to sleep in the house I built with my bare hands.

Ned says Edgar threw us out to make room for his books, that someday there will be nothing in my house but Edgar's books. The Flag House. The flag of the country he didn't lift a finger for.

He put us in this house—the Flat House. It's nowhere near the size of his garage. He took us from the Flag House and put us in the doghouse.

He comes to visit Nan and me with Megan and the boy. He got rich somehow. Sir Richard's right-hand man.

He should have stayed clear of his brother's wife. Married to Cyril but Edgar knocked her up. How's that for a bargain? Mr. Fancy Pants. Went away to school in a place Kay knew she'd never see if she lived to be a hundred.

Phonse and Edgar. Look-alikes. Twins they might have been. That's what people said. I should have known it wasn't Phonse I saw her with, but I never thought that Edgar would have anything to do with a woman who grew up on the Heights. Edgar, a man who was going places, getting out, shaking the dust of this place off his feet—what did he want with Kay?

He was always Nan's, never mine. I think he was ashamed of me. He was my son, but even Cyril was more of a son to me than Edgar ever was.

I don't know why he bothered to come back. He should have stayed over there with his own kind. With her, Megan. He knocked up Miss Fancy Pants too. Plenty of his own kind over there. He tried to let on like this place was in his blood, even though he worked indoors. He lived indoors. He came back and she wasn't far behind.

I couldn't stand the sight of him. He reminded me so much of Phonse. What Phonse would have looked like, maybe. He reminded me of what I did because of him. I couldn't stand the way he looked at me. Like he thought I was as good as gone because I couldn't talk or make out what he said.

I couldn't stand it when he took my side when Nan went aboard of me about her son. *Her* son. As if he wasn't my son too.

Now he's got it all. Big house. Four cars. A wife and son.

Phonse—he had no wife, no children. He hasn't even got a grave. He hasn't even got six feet by four. Nothing but a headstone with his name and numbers on it.

NED

When I got home, I took my father's fedora off the kitchen wall and burned it in the front room fireplace.

I sat at my desk in my office and kept drinking, my plan being to pass the night that way until I fell asleep.

I did fall asleep, but woke about three. There was the faint but unmistakable smell of smoke, of burning wood.

I left my office and went from room to room. Nothing was amiss.

I looked in on Brendan. He was awake but in bed, his hands behind his head on the pillow. He smiled at me.

The smell of smoke came and went.

I looked out the window at the Flat House. The porch light was on.

I wondered if there might be a fire in the woods above the Heights.

I decided I'd better check on Nan. I opened the front door of my house and was met by what I thought was fog but it was smoke, slowly billowing about the yard as there was not much wind. Smoke from where? I looked up the hill. I couldn't see the Flag House.

REG

The stairs to the second floor were just inside the door, and those to the third floor led upwards from them. I had to feel along the walls in the darkness to find the doors to the book rooms, which, like the front door, were unlocked. I opened one, stepped inside.

I have never known darkness so absolute. I carried two lanterns in one hand, both of them brimful with seal oil. I removed the glass globes, lit the wick of one lantern with a match and replaced the globe. The room came into view as the stage does when the lights come up.

Shelves of books. Books that by day and night stood there in the darkness as if they were being aged until they were ready to be read.

I stood the lit lantern on the floor on the opposite side of the door from the other lantern. I went to the far corner of the room and, walking backwards, splashed the shelves with oil, swinging the lantern the way the priest swings the thurible in church, as if I were anointing the books with chrism.

I went from room to room until the lantern was empty.

I smashed the lit lantern in the hallway.

I smelled the oil and the sickening smoke. I felt the heat of the fire on my face, through my shirt and slacks. But I heard nothing, no crackle of flame.

After some time, burning books fell from the shelves and landed soundlessly on the floor. Only in my mind was I able to hear the fire. I stayed put as long as I could, then ran from the doorway and was on the top step of the stairs when I felt in my feet the vibrations of what turned out to be his footsteps.

FIELDING

By the time Duggan and I got there, a crowd had gathered round the Flag House. I saw people pointing up at one of the top windows, from which the glass was gone and in the frame of which stood Reg, his hands on the ledge as he silently mouthed something at the firemen below. Reg, whom the doctor had declared too feeble to go to Church or even to care for himself, was in the house.

His face was smeared with soot, and tears and sweat ran through it down his cheeks. He coughed and "shouted" almost at the same time, his mouth agape.

Smoke that got thicker and darker funnelled out of every window and from underneath the eaves and through every gap and fissure in the wood, from which there came a sound like nails being pried loose, as if the walls would soon give way. It seemed that the inside of the house was more boiling than burning, the smoke confined like steam that, at a certain pressure point, would pop the roof clean off. But the smoke let up when fire started shooting from the windows.

"Save yourself, sir," men yelled just as Reg left the window, in which flames soon took his place.

"He can't hear you," someone shouted. "That's Reg Vatcher. He's deaf."

I saw Nan, Ruby and Brendan in the crowd and went to them. "What's Reg doing in there?" I asked Nan, who seemed not to hear me. She stared wide-eyed as if one of her predictions of catastrophe had at last come true.

Ruby, in tears, shook her head. "Ned is in there too," she said. "He might have gone inside to save Reg. Reg, the poor soul—who knows why he took it into his head? Ned's trying to save his precious books too. He might not even know Reg is in there."

Windows burst as if struck by projectiles travelling too fast to see. The fire moved through the tops of the trees behind the house like a great red flag unfurled by the wind. "It's spreading," someone yelled just as the blaze reversed itself and spared the house next door.

People all but canopied by fire stood transfixed, looking up as if at something they had heard was possible but had disbelieved in until now. The air was filled with what might have been strange forms of precipitation, embers, flankers, sparks and ash that, with the smoke, blocked out the flame so that an eerie cast of light like that of an eclipse lay over everything.

NED

I tried to save as much of the Vatcher collection as I could. I threw armloads of books out the second-storey windows. The books were on the third floor, the top floor, Reg's attic, which I'd renovated so that it now consisted of several rooms. The fire was confined to there but wouldn't be much longer.

I ran up and down the stairs, going again and again to the second-storey windows to release armloads of books. I didn't pause at the windows, didn't look down. I heard nothing but the fire.

FIELDING

People followed Ned and Reg from window to window. It seemed absurd, as if all of us, those in the house and those outside it, were caught up in some kind of frenzied game.

"No one can help them now," Nan said, tears streaming down her cheeks. "They've lost their minds, the two of them."

She began to make for the Flag House, but two men held her back.

NED

Such was my state and so thick was the smoke that, when I saw Reg, it took me a moment to recognize him.

"The books," I said. "Help me save the books."

He stared at me, then smirked as if to say that it was no surprise to him that I had come to this.

FIELDING

"You can't let the child *watch* this," a woman said to me. I held tight to Brendan's hand and Duggan put an arm around his shoulders. Brendan's eyes darted about as if he was searching the upper windows to see which one, Ned or Reg, would appear next.

Reg thrust his head out of the window directly above us, appearing from the smoke with his mouth wide open, gulping air like someone emerging from the ocean just short of having drowned. Some of the crowd drew back, the women covering their heads with shawls and sweaters as sparks and embers shot like bullets from the house.

Two firemen raised a ladder, propping it beside Reg's window. Reg pushed it away and watched as it fell over to one side.

REG

He wanted me to help him with the books. "Help, Reg," I think he said. He held out a pile of burning books to me like a dying man entrusting his children to a friend. It wasn't fair to Phonse that Edgar was alive. I shouldn't have waited so long. This was bound to happen. How could both of us be Vatchers yet be so unalike? Risking his life for books he never wrote or read.

I stepped back until I hit the wall of the landing. Smoke poured through the open doorway of the nearest room. For that reason— and, I suppose, because he was in such a panic to save his books—he didn't see me. He ran straight into the room and seconds later emerged with an armload of books, some of them on fire.

While he was in the room, I thought of running down the stairs but decided against it, though not because I was worried that onlookers who would recognize me might have begun to gather. I had resigned myself to being caught for having lit the fire. I was resigned to dying in the fire if I had to.

The shelves of books burst into blue and orange and the fire rippled outward from the centre of the ceiling. Seeing the look in his eyes as, in the smoke, he made to run past me convinced me that nothing short of his death would satisfy me even if it meant my own. I stepped in front of him.

He said my name. And something else: "Help me?" It seemed it hadn't occurred to him that I had set the fire, though it must have been clear that someone had. "Reg, help me?"

How many times had my other son cried out to God for help because of him? Phonse. I hated it that he was Phonse's brother more than I hated that he was my son. My son killed my son.

I'm sure that no thought of Phonse or Nan went through his mind. I think, when I took hold of him, he thought I was trying to drag him from the burning house and thereby save his life.

NED

The sight of Reg jarred me, brought me to my senses. That's how it seemed—that I had woken from a dream in which I was trying to save from a fire all that was left to me of my father, my mother, my life before they went away. What was Reg doing there? How had he made it there from the Flat House without help?

Just as it occurred to me that he must have been faking his disability as he had, for so long, faked the effects of a stroke, Reg smirked at me. Edgar's and Megan's deaths, it seemed, were not enough for him. He nodded to me. A nod, it might have been, to the only man on earth who knew, or would ever know, who and what he really was. He wanted the Vatchers' son to die, wanted Edgar, though he knew him to be dead, to atone for Phonse's death by losing me.

REG

I grabbed him by the arms, but he shook me off. I quickly saw that I could not subdue him. There was a time when I could have. But he was a powerfully built man with shoulders that made mine look like a child's. I cast about for something to strike him with.

At that moment I caught a glimpse of myself in a standing mirror. I was on fire, my hair, my shirt sleeves, the cuffs of my slacks.

NED

It was the first time I noticed his resemblance to my father. He might have been Edgar come back from the dead to help me save his books, or to save me from the fire, Edgar hoping the mere sight of him would jar me from the state of mind I was in.

"Reg," I shouted.

He stared at me as he had when he confronted me in the porch the night I followed him to church. His face was smeared with soot that was streaked by what might have been black tears that dripped slowly from his chin.

He opened his mouth wide in a prolonged, silent scream and then charged toward me, arms outspread, head lowered, as if he meant to take me with him through the wall behind me. I tried to dodge him, but his head hit my chin and slammed *my* head against the wall.

The two of us slid to the floor, Reg on top, as limp and heavy as if he was dead.

Still reeling from our collision, staring into a swarm of shifting shapes and colours that seemed to be resolving into darkness, I thought of trying to get out from under Reg. I tried, but nothing happened. My body paid no heed to my mind. It seemed that Reg had separated them for good. I wondered if my neck was broken. I thought of being found like this, Reg pinning me down, my grandfather's body melded to mine by the fire, our flesh mixed past the point of extrication. It might be thought that he had been trying to shield me from the flames, trying what he knew to be impossible, or would have known if he were not himself as good as gone.

I tried again to throw Reg off me and he rolled to one side, face down on the floor. I didn't know if he was dead, but I knew that I'd die for sure if I tried to remove him from the house.

The smoke was thinnest near the floor. Lying on my stomach, I closed my eyes so as not to be led the wrong way by things I thought I saw. I slithered along like a soldier crawling under barbed wire.

I knew where the stairs were. I knew where the doors were. I felt the heat of the fire on my back. I wondered if my shirt and slacks might be ablaze, or if anything was left of them.

I heard, as if from a great distance, a muffled, slowly escalating roar, the swelling protest of a house that knew its end was near, the final bellow of a peaking conflagration.

I reached the stairs and ran down them to the first floor and followed the path of the smoke, which was pouring like a river through the open door of the house.

Men began slapping at me with their hands as I was falling to the ground outside.

"Don't touch him, Brendan," someone said.

Brendan.

FIELDING

Flames shot out the doors and windows of the first storey, as if the fire had somehow skipped the second. It seemed clear that the only way Reg and Ned could escape was by jumping from one of the windows above, which the crowd urged Reg to do.

"Where's Ned?" Brendan said. He started coughing.

"His throat. The smoke," Duggan said. "We should take him down to the house."

Brendan grabbed my arm with both hands. His expression seemed to say that he would lose all trust in me if I made him leave, that he didn't want to abandon Ned, who would never get out of the house if we simply turned our backs on him and walked away.

A ladder was raised to another one of the windows, but before anyone could begin to climb it, Reg shoved it away and withdrew as flames shot out on either side of him. He never appeared at the window again.

Some people began tending to a man in the front yard who, they said, had tried to save Reg. The man was on his hands and knees, black with smoke from head to foot.

"That's Ned," I said. "Ned Vatcher," I added, as if to convince myself that I was right.

Brendan broke away from us and ran to Ned, who rolled onto his back on the ground, his forearms held away from his body. Ribbons of skin hung from his arms like tattered bandages.

"NED," Brendan said.

The whole of the Flag House was enclosed in a single, giant globe of flame. The flame reached its greatest height, illuminating everything, warming everything within a mile.

Then the Flag House collapsed inward and the flames shrank to within a few feet of the ground.

They found Reg's body, buried in burnt books, clutching to his chest a number of volumes to which the skin of his arms had been fused by the heat of the fire.

I was among the few still at the site when the sun came up. Smoke rose from a mound of ash from which black beams of wood stuck out in all directions.

Some of the books scattered about were completely charred, others burnt along the spines or at the corners. The upper halves of some consisted of black ash while the bottom halves, though smudged, were perfectly preserved. Partly burnt ones lay open as if some reader were in mid-perusal of them. Some looked as they might have when they stood side by side on the shelves in the Flag House. Otherwise wholly preserved books bore black scorch holes, embers or cinders having fallen on them and burned through the covers and deep into the pages, as if they had been used for target practice.

Scattered here and there were tiny scraps of paper bearing legible words, randomly preserved fragments of sentences or paragraphs.

I thought of Reg spending the last minutes of his life in what used to be the attic, surrounded and buried by burning books, on his hands and knees perhaps, or prostrate or supine between the stacks, while outside, half the people of St. John's stood, solemn, speechless, incredulous that, after such a troubled life, he would die *like that*.

NED

Fielding and Duggan told me that Brendan said my name when he saw me on the ground, but I didn't hear him. The first word he had spoken for months to anyone but Fielding.

"He said it over and over," Duggan said, but I didn't remember feeling or hearing or seeing anything after I went running through the doorway as if borne outside on the smoke that was gushing from the house.

Duggan said that, as I lay on my back on the ground, I held my burnt arms up like a just-scrubbed surgeon and rolled slightly from side to side as if I thought my back was still on fire. I remembered none of it.

I woke up in hospital, by which time it was almost two days since

I'd arrived there. It was night and no one sat beside my bed but Ruby, who was sound asleep in a chair, arms folded, head slumped on her chest.

Reg was not suspected of having set the fire. No one was. The papers said the police described the fire as being "of uncertain origin." That the ruins of the house smelled of seal oil surprised no one since it was known among the Vatchers and Finns that I preferred it to kerosene.

XXI

NED

On the eleventh day after Cyril and Prowse confessed, the tenth since the Flag House fire, the first since I was released from hospital, my hands free but my arms still wrapped in bandages, I flew the Baron back and forth along the headlands of Black Point, closer to the cliffs than ever, and closer to the water into which Megan and Edgar had been thrown.

Vatchers' Cliff, as it was afterward called, became one of the most gazed-upon and photographed sites on the island, a place that for many was the focal point for a day of leisure on the water, or a hike, something that an afternoon's outing could be built around.

The flattened wreck of the Vatchers' car was found there, you see, there, right there, two hundred feet below the ground. Nothing more is known of their mysterious erasure from the world.

I paid for the wreck of the Brougham to be extracted from the cave. It was loaded onto a flatbed truck, draped in a tarp and driven to my house on the Heights, while hundreds lined the roads to watch. The crumpled, jagged-edged, rust-eaten Brougham now sits under lock and key in a garage on my property.

They were gone, twenty-five years gone, as if it had taken the day of their deaths that long to pass. They had been on the other side of time, waiting to be discovered, to be touched so that, for me, the present could continue and the illusion of the future could seem real.

I know they're gone. I know they are. But I can't help hoping for their return, or the discovery of something in the sea that will "prove" that Prowse and Cyril told the truth.

At Black Point, I walk along the shore in late November, the beach rocks sliding out beneath my feet. I don't look up the cliff but out to sea.

But now I spend much of my time in America, in Wickenburg, Arizona, a place more unlike the one where I grew up than any I have seen. Every morning, I go out to watch the sun come up like thunder on the hills above my house.

When I come back home, Fielding regards me as if I've been lured to my doom by the Sirens of Paris. I feel like telling her that Edgar was lured to his by the Sirens of Cabot's Rock.

She still writes her inscrutable, oracular columns, still to no practical effect.

I still live in what I now call Prospect House for part of the year.

I call my house in Wickenburg the House of Light. That's from the Latin, *Aula Lucus*, the name of an eighteenth-century alchemical text by Sir Thomas Vaughan.

Alchemy. There's another alchemical book I have, called *Fragments of a Faith Forgotten*.

It reminds me of the Vatchers and much else besides.

FIELDING

I think of Ned, who, with Ruby and with Brendan, spends his winters far away in Arizona. He has a ranch there. He and Brendan ride horses and take turns flying his plane. He comes home in the summer when there are fewer things afoot to remind him of the past. The top storey of his Arizona house is a television studio from which he runs the station in St. John's and broadcasts *Ned Vatcher Presents* to all of Newfoundland and other parts of North America.

Brendan agreed to the operation, during which I thought about his account of his first, the hand that held the rubber mask in place, the immovable hand that in the end resisted everything.

But nothing went amiss this time.

While he was a teenager, he spent almost as much time with Duggan and me in the house on Circular Road, which Ned gave us as a wedding present, as he did with Ned and Ruby in the House of Light in Arizona. He spent much of his school years living with us, attending St. Bon's. He's come to regard us as being two of his five parents.

We have a TV set, but Duggan never watches it.

I am one of those who tune in to *Ned Vatcher Presents* late at night, or on Sunday mornings, as he holds forth from Arizona or, in summer, from his studio on the hill above St. Clare's. It's easy to fancy that his words are meant for me, that he's asking me if I believe in what is called the larger scheme of things. If so, do I think that his parents were excluded from it? Is he? Would it trouble me to know that I have played no part in it and never will? What if I knew that, even in the almanac of stolen countries, even in the register of things that might have been, Newfoundland would not be named?

I think of Reg who, for the last months of his life, pretended to be bedridden while he waited for his chance to get revenge. There are only a handful of us who disbelieve in the myth of Reg, the man who lost his son to the sea and, if not for his faith in God, would have lost his soul to it as well.

I often think of Phonse, who is all but overlooked in the story of the Vatchers; Phonse, whose memory was kept alive by Nan Finn's unflagging scorn of Reg. He was never old enough to understand that even a good man might be the engine of a tragedy.

It's tempting to believe that someone lost at sea might still come home. It's hard to give up hope when two go out and none come back.

I think of Lucy, who brought home to Ruby what would prove to be the key to solving the conundrum of the Vatchers.

I think of Brendan, whose voice sounds nothing like the one he would have had by now, though he likes it and has come to think of it as his own.

I think of Ruby. Ned will never love her, never leave her or marry someone else, not even if Brendan leaves them both with no one but each other.

I think of Lucy and Ruby making their way to St. Clare's in the last light of March, 1949.

I can't help but think of Prowse, though our paths haven't crossed in twenty years.

The sight of Duggan when I walk into a room still startles me.

I'm older now than I thought I'd ever be, more than twice as old as the Vatchers ever were, though these feel like the early years of my umpteenth life.

I write as much as ever, in spite of Duggan, who says I've been going like mad from day one.

I stand at the windows of this house, as I know the Vatchers must have done. I see what they must have seen. I occupy their space, their rooms. I slowly spin the globe in the front room where we kept vigil with Ned, where Edgar sat alone beside the fire after I left, as Megan lay alone in bed upstairs and tried to sleep.

Every night, at sunset, Duggan turns the light on in the porch. He says the house must never be as dark as it was the day Ned came home to it from school in 1936.

I think of the Vatchers whenever it begins to snow, whenever the light begins to fail, whenever I see Ned behind the wheel of "Edgar's" car.

Whenever snow that moves like dust begins to gather on the pavement and makes a cold white desert of St. John's, I think of the Vatchers, and of the snow falling unseen on the clearing that no one knows the way to anymore.

ACKNOWLEDGEMENTS

I would like to thank my publisher and editor, Anne Collins; Kristin Cochrane, president and publisher of Penguin Random House Canada; Brad Martin, the chief executive officer of Penguin Random House Canada; my siblings and their spouses; my many nephews and nieces; and my wife, Rose, this book's first reader—red Rose, proud Rose, Rose of all my days.

WAYNE JOHNSTON was born and raised in the St. John's area of Newfoundland. His nationally bestselling novels include *The Son of a Certain Woman*, *The Custodian of Paradise*, *The Navigator of New York* and *The Colony of Unrequited Dreams*, which was an international bestseller and has been adapted for the stage and optioned for film and television. Johnston is also the author of an award-winning and bestselling memoir, *Baltimore's Mansion*. He lives in Toronto.

A NOTE ABOUT THE TYPE

First Snow, Last Light is set in Monotype Van Dijck, a face originally designed by Christoffel van Dijck, a Dutch typefounder (and sometime goldsmith) of the seventeenth century. While the roman font may not have been cut by van Dijck himself; the italic, for which original punches survive, is almost certainly his work. The face first made its appearance circa 1606. It was re-cut for modern use in 1937.